Copanatec

A Timecrack Adventure

by

William Long

 New Generation **Publishing**

By the same author

Timecrack

An Unexpected Diagnosis

A collection of Irish short stories

www.williamlongbooks.com

Acknowledgements

Many thanks are due to the following:

To my daughter and son, Alex and Ryan, as always, for their ongoing encouragement. My very good friend, Linda McConnell, who kept me on track by asking on numerous occasions when the book would be ready. The latest member of our extended family, Paloma Fraile, for her work on my website. Andrew Haire at www.andrewhaire.com a young artist with exciting potential, for his very welcome contribution on the creation of the map and glyph. Tamian Wood at www.BeyondDesignInternational.com for her work on the map. Berne Williams for the cover design. Rachel Malone at Author Press for editing and advice. Sam Rennie at New Generation Publishing for his support and exceptionally fast responses to the many emails I sent him. And to everyone along the way who expressed an interest in Archie and Richard and their latest timecrack adventure.

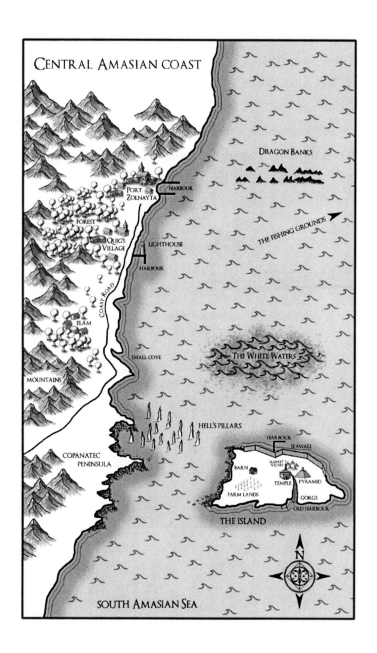

Contents

Part One

Malcolm and Lucy 1

1	Captured	3
2	The Cell	9

Part Two

The Yucatan 13

3	Grimshaws	15
4	Ed Hanks	21
5	The Yucatan Plan	29
6	The Unlucky Guide	32
7	The Mark	40
8	Haçienda Paz	46
9	Lords of the Cloud	53
10	The Mexican	62
11	The Burial Trail	68
12	The Site	76
13	Under Attack	81
14	The Mudslide	89
15	The Notebooks	100

Part Three

Port Zolnayta 113

16	The *Serpent*	115
17	The Amasian Sea	119
18	Approaching Port	129
19	The Auction Shed	132

20	Kristin	137
21	The Bombers	142
22	Portview Terrace	149
23	Sunstone	155
24	A Narrow Escape	169
25	The Kitchen	178
26	Father Jamarko	184
27	Elmo's Journal	193
28	The Emergency	199
29	Archie's Plan	203
30	Marcie	211
31	The Pendant	219
32	The Body	226
33	The Man of Dust	232
34	The Hidden Valley	242
35	Copanatec	252

Part Four

The Tunnels   257

36	Return to Mount Tengi	259
37	The Quayside	267
38	On Board the *Serpent*	276
39	Richard and the Pendant	281
40	Harimon	289
41	The Pyramid	303
42	The Seawall	311
43	The Builder	319
44	Lieutenant Han-Sin	325
45	In the Tunnels	333
46	The Uprising	337

Part Five

The Immortal Wand   349

47	The Gorge	351
48	Lord Pakal	359
49	The Temple Gardens	370
50	Inside the Temple	382
51	The Battle in Temple Square	394
52	Malcolm and the Boys	403
53	Hell's Pillars	413
54	The Temple Steps	424
55	Cosimo's Plan	431
56	The Ossuary	437
57	Richard's Choice	447
58	In the Antechamber	453
59	The Corridor	457
60	The Chase	463
61	The Man in the Tunnel	470
62	The Adits	476
63	The Boatshed	482
64	Escape from Copanatec	488
65	The White Waters	499
66	Cosimo's Revenge	506
67	Aristo's News	516
68	The Legacy	525

This one is for Vi
For always being there

Part One

Malcolm and Lucy

Chapter One

Captured

Malcolm thought they had landed in the middle of a nightmare – but he was wrong.

This was for real.

He was standing beside Lucy in the middle of a village compound, the air thick with burning smoke from burning huts on every side. Dark-skinned men and women, dragging children behind them, were running in every direction, screaming and yelling in fear for their lives. One of the men fell near them. Trying to save himself, he reached out a hand towards Lucy for support. Instead, he grabbed at her shirt, ripping it away from the shoulder, exposing part of her arm and back.

Lucy screamed. The man lay at her feet, the bolt from a crossbow protruding from his back.

'What's happening?' she cried. 'Where are we?'

'God only knows, Lucy, but by the look of things around here we'd better make ourselves scarce!'

Malcolm grabbed Lucy by the arm, pulling her close to his side as he looked for a way to escape. It seemed only a short time ago that they had been trapped by the sudden storm floods on the flat of a large stone, near the edge of the dig they had been excavating. The mysterious blue cloud close to the pyramid they had been watching had descended rapidly, sucking them into its core, a tunnel of intense yellow light that must have transported them, somehow, to this strange place. A place with people he didn't recognise, and seemingly under attack.

His best guess, as far-fetched as it sounded, was that they had been caught up in some sort of freak tornado and then dumped somewhere else in the Yucatan. But the blue cloud that had swept over them was unlike any tornado he had seen before. Nothing like the tornado he and Lucy had witnessed a couple of years earlier off the coast of Playa del Carmen when they had been waiting for a ferry to the island of Cozumel.

It had all happened so quickly. He remembered little of what it was like in the cloud, except the feeling of weightlessness and tumbling through space. And none of the madness going on around them made any sense – but it was obvious they were in danger and had to find somewhere safe.

Ignoring the pain in his knee, Malcolm tried to move quickly, but it was no good. He had lost his walking stick in the blue cloud and now he found it difficult to take more than a few steps at a time without it. As they made their way past one of the burning huts towards a rocky ridge and a clump of trees on a height behind the village, Malcolm winced with pain, coming to a sudden halt.

'Please, Malcolm, don't stop,' pleaded Lucy. Her eyes were red-rimmed with tears as the thick, acrid smoke choked the air around them. 'We have to get out of here.'

'I'm sorry – it's this damned knee. I need to find a stick or something to support it.'

The fear in her voice unsettled him. He was beginning to dread what might happen to them, but before he could utter another word they were confronted by a group of men – and a more, ugly, dangerous lot, Malcolm couldn't imagine.

Four guards, swarthy and squat, with heavy brows over slit eyes, pug noses and broad yellowish features, were driving some of the village men towards them. They cracked vicious-looking, metal-tipped whips above the heads of the men while two more guards marched in front, armed with short bronze and silver coloured crossbows held across their chests.

'Haggh! Haggh!' The men with the crossbows called out, or so it sounded to Malcolm.

The strange words of the language were unknown to Malcolm; unlike Spanish, or any Mayan words that he knew, and certainly not English. But the meaning was very clear: a warning to stay where they were, which in the face of the weapons they carried, seemed to be their only option. He put his arm around Lucy's shoulders, drawing her close to his side.

'Stay calm, Lucy,' he whispered. 'Let's see what they want.'

One of the men; Malcolm assumed they were some sort of guard, stepped forward and flicked his whip, threateningly, near Malcolm's face, the metal tips almost touching his skin.

His heart thumping wildly, Malcolm shouted at him, first in Spanish, and then in the few words of Yucatec Maya he knew, and finally in English, hoping the ugly devil would understand.

'What do you want with us? We have done you no harm!'

The guard lowered his whip and looked curiously at Malcolm. Like the other guards, he was dressed in brown leather leggings and calf-length boots. A belted, dark-red tunic open from neck to waist exposed a thick, hairy chest. He stared for a moment, and then turned his gaze to Lucy, inspecting her a little too closely for Malcolm's liking. He seemed to make up his mind about something, and without saying a word he strode across the compound towards another group of villagers and guards.

Malcolm watched as the group parted to allow the guard to approach a man clutching a long black rod, about four feet in length, who was herding several

5

terrified male villagers into a long, narrow mesh cage at the rear of what appeared to be some sort of tracked vehicle. He was much taller than the guards or the villagers and his face was decorated with little tattooed feathers. With long black hair reaching to his shoulders he had the appearance of a fierce-looking bird ready to descend on its prey. He wore a close fitting yellow robe, tied at the waist with a black sash, and like the guards, he wore leather calf boots.

'What are they doing with those people?' whispered Lucy.

Malcolm felt Lucy shiver, through cold or fear, he wasn't sure. He gave her a reassuring hug, but as he did so, he tried to shake the terrible thought that was beginning to form in his mind.

Were these men slave traffickers? God, surely not!

He looked around at what was left of the village. All the huts had been destroyed, the smouldering remains a pathetic reminder of what had apparently been a small village community in the middle of the jungle. Several bodies lay on the ground, including women and children, alongside several dogs and goats, all of them showing evidence of indiscriminate butchery. Only the men had been taken and were now being driven towards the cage.

The guard pointed with his whip towards the prisoners when speaking to the tall man. But when the guard returned with him to the group, it was clear that the tall man's eyes were fixed on Malcolm and Lucy.

Malcolm experienced an icy chill course through his blood as he wondered if their fate was about to be decided.

The tall man stopped in front of Lucy, his piercing grey eyes examining her from head to toe, like a horse breeder considering the merits of a new pony. He walked slowly around her, taking in the contours of her body, while Malcolm seethed with anger at the indignity of their treatment. Despite the condition of her muddy clothes as a result of the flood at the pyramid, the tall man nodded approvingly. Suddenly, he stopped to look more closely at Lucy's shoulder where her shirt had been torn. His fingers reached out to trace a pattern on her skin.

Lucy screamed and tried to pull away from him. Malcolm swung her round to place his body between Lucy and the tall man, but as he did so, an excruciating pain shot through his body. He fell to the ground, hardly able to move a muscle.

'Stay there, alien,' barked a voice above him. 'Do not move.'

Malcolm did move and the pain returned, more intense than before, forcing him into a foetal position. After a moment, he managed to look up to see the tall man standing over him, holding the black rod, ready to strike again.

Bloody hell, thought Malcolm, *it must be some sort of electronic cattle prod.*

The pain eased and he managed to gasp, 'Who are you?' hoping the rod wouldn't be used again.

'I am Talon of Copanatec,' said the tall man, 'and who are you?'

'You speak English?'

'I speak all languages, alien. I ask again, who are you?' said Talon, pointing the black rod closer to Malcolm's chest.

'You don't need to use that thing,' said Malcolm, raising a hand to protect himself. 'My name is Malcolm Kinross and my wife's name is –' He stopped and rose to his knees, looking around to see what had happened to Lucy. 'Where is my wife? What have you done with her?'

7

'She is a chosen one and will serve at the temple,' said Talon, smiling for the first time at Malcolm's confusion. 'Do not concern yourself, alien. She will serve us well ... and so will you, if we let you live.'

'What the hell are you talking about, you crazy butcher?' shouted Malcolm, getting to his feet. 'Bring my wife back –'

He felt the rod prod him forcefully in the chest. This time pain and shock overcame him and he fell unconscious at Talon's feet.

*

Malcolm woke up to find he was crushed together with twenty, or so, of the village men in what he took to be the cage he had seen earlier. From what he could see through the wire mesh on his side, they were now on the open deck of what appeared to be a very large craft, and they were powering through a turbulent sea towards an unknown destination!

Behind them, in the fading light of nightfall, he could see the outline of a rocky coast and wreckage-strewn beach. Beyond the beach was the jungle they had just left, but he recognised none of it as part of the Yucatan he had worked in for so long.

As he stared at the rapidly retreating coast, Malcolm was aware of something unpleasant in the air around him. He realised it was the stench of fear, and men being sick where they lay. It was overpowering, but worse than that, was the fear at what might have happened to Lucy.

My God, he thought, *how did we end up in this nightmare?*

Chapter Two

The Cell

The clanking of a heavy chain being dragged across the stone tiles of the passageway woke Malcolm from the sleep he had craved all day.

'Why can't you let us sleep, you rotten scum?' he muttered, turning over on his side for the umpteenth time. He buried his head between his hands to try and keep the groans from the prisoners and the other sounds of the night from penetrating his sleep, but there was to be no peace for Malcolm tonight.

A key rattled in the lock of the ancient ironclad cell door. It slammed inwardly against the rock wall, as three men, shackled together at the ankles, were shoved onto the earthen floor.

One of the two Terog guards escorting them took a couple of steps into the cell, his whip arm stretched out in front of him. He snarled and grunted as the prisoners, dazed and frightened by their new surroundings, tried to rise awkwardly to their knees, while the other guard stood by the door.

Malcolm raised his head to see what was happening. He saw the guard's whip, split into three metal-tipped ends, slash the air above the men, forcing them to lie flat on the floor. One of them tried to rise up again, but the whip caught him across the shoulders, drawing blood as the metal tips hooked into his flesh.

'Stop it!' shouted Malcolm, getting to his feet. 'Can't you see he's had enough!'

The guard grinned, a twist of skin below his left eye making him squint, but he said nothing as he jerked the whip away from the man's back, causing him to scream. He motioned to the other guard to remove the prisoners' shackles, and then they left, relocking the cell door behind them.

Malcolm, with the aid of a walking-stick he had managed to fashion from a piece of driftwood, hobbled over to the prisoners to see what he could do to help, if anything. But it was too late for the man who had been whipped. He was dead – one of many since Malcolm had arrived in this hellhole.

'Pigs!' he spat after the guards. 'That's what they are – bloodthirsty pigs!'

As he stood there staring helplessly at the dead prisoner, he felt a tug at his sleeve, pulling him away from the body. He turned round to see a small figure with brown leathery skin and twinkly eyes by his side. It was his friend Harry, beckoning to Malcolm to let the others in the cell deal with the dead man and the new prisoners.

Harry wasn't his real name, it was Harimon, but Malcolm had found it comforting, somehow, to call him by a name he was familiar with on Old Earth. Harry was a Salakin, a member of one of the old ruling tribes of Amasia, the land in which a timecrack had deposited Malcolm and Lucy so many months ago – how many, he had no idea. The concept and *feeling* of time was different here; his watch had been taken from him and there was no calendar or other way of marking the passage of time. His clothes had also been taken from him and replaced with the rough cloth navy tunic and trousers that all the prisoners wore, although he had been allowed to keep his desert boots, which was a small mercy.

He stared at the poor devil lying on the floor. Another death, crushing the hopes of the prisoners of any chance of escape from this godforsaken place.

And Lucy, where was she? He hadn't seen her since Talon had said she would be taken to serve at the

temple. What did he mean ... to serve? And the boys ...
what will happen to Archie and Richard?

'Come, Malcolm, the others know what to do,' said Harry, breaking into his thoughts, urging him into the corner of the cell they both shared as their living space. 'They will cover the body with bed-grass until we can take it to the sea tomorrow.'

Malcolm nodded. It was what the guards did with the prisoners who didn't survive the daily torture of forced labour; they simply threw the bodies over the wall into the sea.

He sat down on his sleeping pallet of bed-grass, thinking he had been lucky that Harry had taken him under his wing. In fact, he supposed he had been lucky on two counts:

First, when he came to realise that the prisoners were expected to rebuild and maintain the huge seawall that surrounded the city, he knew his leg would let him down and that would be the end of him. But he had approached and persuaded Talon, that because of his archaeological restoration experience, he could be useful to him. Talon had listened, then agreed to let him supervise one of the seawall labour gangs. They had implanted a language chip, allowing him to communicate with the other prisoners, but few of them were inclined to talk as they tackled the back-breaking work the guards demanded, even less so when the whips were used.

The second, was when Harry had befriended him in the cell and made living space, such as it was, for them to share. But more importantly, Harry had become his tutor and mentor, explaining, for example, why Talon had called him 'alien'. It was because Malcolm was a New Arrival in this strange world of timecracks and ancient tribes, and Talon saw his kind as inferior, only useful as slave fodder to be used in the service of Copanatec.

Every night, to maintain his sanity, Malcolm would lie on his pallet and follow a ritual of remembering life on Old Earth: Lucy, his family, friends, professional colleagues, his career as an archaeologist in the Yucatan, and finally his incredible journey to this new world. He would gaze at the black, rock-faced ceiling of the cell, lit only by the dim light of a single vallonium lamp, and his thoughts, once again, would drift towards his sons, Archie and Richard, wondering what they were doing right now.

Part Two

The Yucatan

Chapter Three

Grimshaws

'This really is a most extraordinary request, Professor Strawbridge, as I'm sure you will appreciate,' said Dimwiddy, poking a rubber tipped blue pencil a little deeper into his left ear. His pale face twisted sideways, momentarily, before resuming its usual hangdog appearance. 'The boys have been back at Grimshaws for less than six months, after an absence of nearly a year and a half – and you propose to take them out of school again?'

Archie watched with fascination as the headmaster struggled with whatever it was he was trying to dislodge from the inner depths of his ear. Finally, Dimwiddy – or Dimwit, as he was better known to the students at Grimshaws – dropped the pencil on the rosewood desk he was sitting behind and looked pointedly at the professor for an answer.

'Yes, Headmaster, I fully understand that what I'm asking may seem a little unusual, but I can assure you, I asked for this meeting only because I believe it to be absolutely essential that Archie and Richard spend a few days with me at the Facility in New Mexico.'

'Well, I must admit, I'm mystified by what you say,' said Dimwiddy. 'What with past events, especially, that of Miss Peoples not contacting us directly with her reasons for not returning to Grimshaws, it makes me wonder what is actually going on, eh?'

If only you knew, thought Archie. He turned towards Richard and raised his eyes, as if to say: *When are we getting out of here?*

They had been sitting in Dimwiddy's office for nearly thirty minutes, with Uncle John trying to explain why they had to leave for New Mexico again, but without actually revealing any important information. As he'd said, shortly after they returned from Mount Tengi: 'Boys, everything that we have been through on New Earth must remain Top Secret while we continue to develop our links with Dr Shah at Mount Tengi. You must give me your word on that.'

Archie and Richard had agreed, of course, but it had been nearly impossible to keep their promise, what with everybody at Grimshaws asking questions about where they had disappeared to for so long. They'd finally concocted a story about being out of touch in the Yucatan jungle with their uncle looking for their parents. Now it seemed it was about to come true.

'Well, no matter,' continued Dimwiddy, probably realising Professor Strawbridge was not going to elaborate on his reasons for Archie and Richard leaving the school again. 'The boys' tutor at extra studies has reported to me that they have made up a great deal of ground on their missing year; so I'm inclined to go along with your request.'

What! Who's he kidding? thought Archie. He glanced at Richard, snuggled into a corner of the old leather sofa they were both sitting on. Richard just shrugged and yawned, implying, if that was what old Dimwit thought, it was OK by him.

Archie had worked hard at extra studies, but no way had he made up for a year's work on top of his term classes. *No way.* And he knew Richard had worked even less, preferring to spend most of his spare time with the sailing club on the Fermanagh lakes that surrounded the school.

'Thank you, Headmaster, I'm very grateful for your support,' said the professor, rising out of his seat in front of the desk. He motioned the boys to his side. 'Archie and Richard will be with me for about ten days, part of it over the term break, so it shouldn't disrupt their studies, too much.'

'I hope so, Professor Strawbridge, for whatever it is you have planned for them, they cannot afford to waste any more time away from Grimshaws,' said Dimwiddy. He raised his eyebrows slightly, indicating that he knew there was more to this business than met the eye.

As they left the headmaster's office, Archie looked back over his shoulder. Dimwiddy was leaning over his desk with the blue pencil back in his ear, poking away furiously. *If he keeps that up*, thought Archie, *he'll clean out the other ear.*

*

Later that evening, in the hotel where he had stayed the previous night, preparing his notes for the meeting with Dimwiddy, the professor explained his plans for the journey. He had known that the headmaster would probably have reservations about allowing the boys to take an extended term break from the school, but he had been determined that Dimwiddy would acquiesce to his proposal. There was no other option; he needed Archie and Richard in the Yucatan.

'I booked a room here for the two of you, instead of staying at the school. It means we can travel together first thing in the morning, directly to the airport. So eat up, boys; this might be the last decent meal we'll have, at least until we reach the Facility. We have a long way to go.'

'I hope it doesn't take as long as the last time when we travelled with Marjorie,' said Richard, tucking into a generous portion of scampi and chips, his appetite as large as ever.

'I don't think so, Richard,' said the professor. 'I've just checked our travel itinerary, and everything seems

OK. We'll take the morning flight from Belfast International to New York, and then a connecting flight to El Paso. Chuck Winters will pick us up at the airport and take us directly to the Facility, hopefully without any delays.'

'Do you think we'll find it, Uncle John?' asked Archie, pushing his plate away. Unlike Richard, he didn't have much of an appetite when he had other things on his mind.

'The Transkal?' The professor frowned, his bushy eyebrows coming together to form a thick mat of hair. He had given the matter a lot of thought, but there were no easy answers. 'I think we have to try, Archie. Richard's attempts to reach your mother haven't worked, so we are left with Father Jamarko's suggestion that we try finding your parents by starting with their last known location in the Yucatan. Until something else turns up, that seems to be our best hope.'

The professor believed, like Archie and Richard that his sister, Lucy, and her husband, Malcolm, were still alive, despite the fact that they had been missing for over two years – of course, that was using Old Earth time.

Archie remembered the time when he had persuaded Richard to sneak out of Harmsway College in the middle of the night. His idea had been to try and contact their mother from the Transkal in the quadrangle and Richard had done it! He had gone into a trance and learned that their parents had been swept away by a timecrack from a Transkal in the Yucatan jungle, and that they were now being held captive in a place called Copanatec.

Since that brief contact and after their return to Grimshaws, Archie had asked Richard on several occasions to try again, through self-induced trances, to get in touch with their mother, but the results had been disappointing. The trances, such as they were, had only produced confusing glimpses of a stormy sea and a strange coastline; nothing that could be identified with any certainty as being part of the coast of Amasia

According to Father Jamarko, the old priest at the monastery in Timeless Valley, the legend of Copanatec told of a long lost city on the coast of Central Amasia that had been destroyed by a great flood, probably a tsunami caused by an undersea volcanic eruption.

'Can I ask you, Richard,' said the professor, 'if you feel that your trances are as strong as they were, or might they be weakening in some way?'

'I don't know if they're any weaker … it's just that they're not happening as often, and … well, they're not very clear when they do happen.'

'To tell the truth, Uncle John, we haven't tried as hard recently, because Richard didn't like the idea of us doing it together,' said Archie, looking sideways at Richard as if they shared some sort of secret.

'What do you mean … together?' asked the professor.

Richard stared at Archie, looking annoyed by what he'd just said. 'Well, yeah, it was getting embarrassing. Y'know, when we had to hold hands like Shaman-Sing showed us, to make the trances … deeper, somehow.'

'It worked, didn't it, back at Harmsway, when we got in touch with mum? *Didn't it*?' snapped Archie.

'Yeah, it did, but look what happened – we were the laughing stock of the college. They saw us holding hands and heard you yelling, all in the middle of the night. Everyone thought we were holding a séance or doing something really weird. And it was the same at Grimshaws!' complained Richard.

'OK, boys, I think I understand.' The professor studied the faces in front of him. He called his nephews boys, but in reality, with all that they had been through, they were young men who had grown up quickly, if not in years, certainly in spirit. Moving on to a new tack, he said, 'Once we're back at the Facility I want Richard to help us when we make contact with Dr Krippitz at Mount Tengi, to see if a link can be established between the Transkal in the Yucatan, when we find it, and wherever this Copanatec place might be. Ed Hanks, my chief engineer, has some ideas on this so he'll be going to the Yucatan to conduct tests for any unusual energy sources in and around the same area.'

He pushed his chair away from the table and gestured to a waiter to bring the bill. 'We have a long trip ahead of us, so I suggest we get some sleep.'

Archie nodded, but he was curious about something. He asked, 'I was wondering, Uncle John, why old Dimwit – sorry, I mean Mr Dimwiddy – didn't seem to mind too much about us leaving Grimshaws again?'

The professor's eyes twinkled as he looked at the two of them over the top of his glasses, 'Well, I suppose it might have something to do with the award of a grant by the Facility to Grimshaws towards a new sports hall.'

Chapter Four

Ed Hanks

'Hey, this is pretty cool,' said Richard. His gaze swept across El Paso International Airport as the Bell 429 helicopter flew over Airport Boulevard on its way to the Facility at White Sands National Monument. He turned to Archie, who happened to be thinking the same thing. 'I didn't know Chuck could fly helicopters, did you?'

'No, I didn't,' said Archie. 'I thought we'd be travelling in the pickup like the last time we were here, but this is something else.'

Archie was impressed. The Bell 429 was incredibly fast and spacious with a luxuriously appointed cabin that could hold up to eight passengers. The windows were large and would afford them panoramic views as they crossed over the vast expanse of white dunes.

'As a matter of fact, Archie, Chuck flies about a dozen types of fixed wing aircraft as well as helicopters.' As he spoke, the professor shifted awkwardly in his seat to avoid looking through the window next to him. 'Long before he joined us at the Facility, he was an army pilot for more than twenty years, mainly on special operations for the government. I can tell you we're very fortunate to have him working for us.'

Archie looked down at the sands, a little surprised by his uncle's nervousness and apparent need to keep talking to take his mind of the flight. Uncle John was a big bear of a man, a former Irish rugby international and the Director of Operations at one of the US Government's most secret projects, and yet he had his weaknesses, just like anyone else.

Nothing was what it seemed, thought Archie. Not even the world they lived in. How many people would believe there was another world: New Earth, in a parallel universe connected to their own through timecracks? And who would believe that throughout history – probably since the beginning, when mankind first appeared on the planet – that many of the people who had gone missing, never to be seen again, may have disappeared through a timecrack, ending up in another universe?

He glanced through the window as the helicopter suddenly nosed down towards a lonely highway snaking its way across the sands. Ahead of them, in the far distance, was the outer perimeter fence that marked the boundary line of EFTF, the US Government's foremost energy research establishment.

Patrolling the fence and approaching fast was a Comanche attack helicopter. Sleek, black and bristling with armaments, any one of which could blast them out of the sky, it drew alongside, its pilot waving with a thumbs-up, recognising Chuck and the Bell 429 as a friendly intruder. Chuck responded by communicating the daily security code permitting them access to the Facility. The Comanche acknowledged by banking sharply away to resume its patrol, leaving them to continue their journey.

A few minutes later, the Bell's engine pitch changed as Chuck adjusted the controls to prepare them for landing. To the professor it sounded as if the rotor was about to crash through the cabin roof, but he kept on talking: '... and Chuck received a warning that the Missile Range would be testing today. When that happens, the army set up roadblocks on the highway, so we had to use the helicopter today...'

The professor sighed, finally realising that no one was listening, and resigned himself to the rest of the flight. He closed his eyes until they landed at the Facility, near the entrance to the main building.

'Well, folks, we're here. I hope you enjoyed the trip,' said Chuck, looking over his shoulder. He grinned, knowing how much the professor hated travelling by helicopter.

'You know I can't stand flying in this thing, Chuck, so I would be extremely grateful if, in future, you would organise it so that we travel in the pickup. In any event, we don't want to inconvenience the army by having to obtain a special clearance for the helicopter, especially when they're testing, do we?'

'Of course not, Professor,' said Chuck, as they disembarked. 'I'll see to it, but I'd reckoned we didn't have much time to spare on this trip.'

The professor nodded, he knew Chuck was having a gentle dig at his phobia with helicopters but he ignored it.

'Yes, you're right. We need to make sure Ed has everything in place for the journey to Mexico tomorrow. Let's find him and see how his plans are progressing.'

They walked over to the main building and into the reception area where they collected ID tags. As Archie and Richard followed their uncle and Chuck through the checkpoints towards a metal door at the back of the building, Archie nudged his brother, muttering, 'Here we go again.'

'Yeah, I know. This could turn out to be a real pain,' grunted Richard.

'What do you mean?' asked Archie, surprised by Richard's reaction.

'Well, just look what happened to us the last time we came through here – we ended up in another world and nearly got killed!'

'But this time we're trying to find mum and dad. Don't you think it's worth the risk?'

Richard didn't answer. He turned away, refusing to make eye contact, leaving Archie bewildered and irritated, wondering what the heck was going through his brother's mind.

Up front, the professor had stepped into an open glass kiosk by the metal security door. He tapped his personal code onto a small touchscreen panel and waited as a narrow green ribbon of light zipped down the kiosk scanning him from head to foot. He explained: 'This is our latest security system, installed since you were last here. It scans eyes, teeth, bone structure and a great deal more. We believe it's foolproof, but we will be scanned again inside the corridor by the central security computer where all our personal access details have been stored – *including* yours, boys. If it detects any discrepancies in the ID profiles it will automatically imprison us in the corridor until a security team arrives to check us out.'

The computer cleared them and they moved through another metal door at the end of the corridor onto a terrace that overlooked the DONUT. The aptly named, unimaginably huge, tyre-like machine that was the heart of the Facility, reaching down into the depths of the earth directly below them.

The boys crossed the catwalk to the spot where two years earlier, along with their uncle and Marjorie, they had been engulfed by a timecrack. Archie stopped for a moment to stare down at the hub of the machine where a large, shiny, bulbous capsule now hung suspended by thick steel cables. It was the new timecrack chamber, reached by an extendable gantry. About the size of a small bus, it sat like a spider at the centre of a vast metal web awaiting its next unwary visitor.

Archie experienced an inexplicable sense of nostalgia; a creeping sensation, like the low heat from the embers of a dying fire warming his skin. Marjorie's face came to him and he recalled all the times she had looked after them. He remembered the last time they had crossed the catwalk just before the explosion that sent them to New Earth, and now she was in Fort Temple where she had elected to stay and teach at Harmsway College. He missed her and wondered if he would ever see her again. He shook the thought away as someone called to Uncle John.

'Welcome back, Professor, it's good to see you.'

It was Ed Hanks, the chief engineer, standing at the end of the catwalk where it joined the far terrace. A small, serious-looking man, with a high forehead and long, grey, thinning hair tied into a ponytail, he was originally a research scientist studying quantum mechanics at Harvard University, but as he had also worked on laser fusion systems which were integral to the DONUT project, he had been quickly head-hunted by the professor into the Facility's energy research programme.

Now that they had established a link with Mount Tengi on New Earth, Ed's unique credentials allowed him to liaise with the scientists working on each timecrack chamber. And with the forthcoming trip to Mexico, another benefit that he was able to offer was his recreational interest in Mayan archaeology and his knowledge of the Yucatan peninsula.

'Thank you, Ed, it's great to be back. Is everything on schedule for tomorrow?' asked the professor as he stepped onto the terrace.

'Pretty much so, but if we head over to my office, I'll bring you up to date.'

Before they moved on, the professor pushed his glasses to the tip of his nose and glanced at his nephew.

'Are you OK, Richard? You know … feeling strange, or … anything?'

He was thinking of the last time he had crossed the catwalk with the boys when Richard had unexpectedly displayed his unusual sensitivity towards high-energy sources. But it was different now. Since the completion of the timecrack chamber in the middle of the DONUT they had gained total control of timecracks and any unexpected energy surges.

'No … I'm OK, Uncle John,' mumbled Richard.

'That's good,' smiled the professor. He patted Richard on the shoulder and led them off the catwalk.

*

Ed Hanks' office was situated on a section of the terrace overlooking the DONUT, where he had an overall view of all the work areas. They settled into chairs around Ed's desk while Chuck stood by a percolator and poured coffees for himself, Ed and the professor. He turned to the boys. 'Cokes?' They both nodded. He opened a small fridge and handed each of them a can of Pepsi.

'Right, Ed,' said the professor, accepting a coffee. 'Perhaps you would brief Archie and Richard on what we have planned for the next few days.'

'Well, before we get into that, I would like Richard to tell me more about the contact he made with his mother, when she explained how she and Malcolm disappeared from the Yucatan. Can you do that, Richard?'

'It's hard to remember, exactly … it was all kind of hazy,' said Richard, hesitating, trying to put his thoughts together. 'She was in … a kind of prison … I don't know. It wasn't very clear.'

'But, they were in a place called Copanatec, somewhere near the coast of Amasia on New Earth, is that correct?'

As a scientist and engineer, Ed was still finding it hard coming to terms with all that Professor Strawbridge had told him: that they could connect to another universe through timecracks, and the diversity of beings *actually living there*. He shook his head at the thought and stared intently across his desk at the fifteen-year- old, fair-haired boy who had the uncanny ability to see and communicate with this other world. He watched closely as Richard struggled to give him an answer.

'Yeah, I think so ...'

'And they were taken there by a timecrack from a stone called a Transkal, near the pyramid they had discovered in the Yucatan?'

'Yeah –'

'We've got to find the Transkal,' interrupted Archie, a little too loudly, but he was beginning to feel impatient. 'Father Jamarko at the monastery said we should start there.'

'We know that, Archie,' said the professor. He turned to his chief engineer. 'Ed has already made a start on that, haven't you?'

Ed pushed himself out of his chair and pointed to a large, framed map of Mexico on the wall behind his desk.

'Yes, I've been on several trips to see the pyramid sites in the Yucatan, and there's a guide I know who lives on the island of Cozumel. He's agreed to take us to the site your parents were working on. We'll meet him in Playa del Carmen, shortly after we arrive.'

They discussed their plans for another hour, Chuck confirming that he had all the travel arrangements in place, and then the professor made a surprise announcement.

'I won't be going, boys. With Ed away, someone has to stay here and look after this place. With all that's happening right now, at least one of us has to be on the site. Chuck has agreed to go in my place. He'll take care of any problems that might crop up.'

'You're going instead of Uncle John?' said Archie, surprised at the change of plan.

'Yep, I'll just tag along, in case you and Richard run into any suspicious characters or wild animals. From what I hear, it wouldn't be the first time,' winked Chuck, pouring himself another coffee.

Chapter Five

The Yucatan Plan

The message stumbled across the screen one word at a time, step by step like a drunken fool, so slowly that Ed felt like thumping the side of the Parasite capsule, a name given to it because it fed off the latent energy of the timecrack chamber. Its proper title was MVCS, the multiverse communication system, created by Dr Krippitz at Mount Tengi.

... are ... you ... receiving ... me? ... this ... is

... Doctor ... Krippitz ...

'Yes – yes I am here!'

Not normally an excitable person, Ed found it almost impossible to contain his amazement as the words appeared on the screen before him. Understandably, because of the time barrier that existed between their worlds, it took a little while for the message to come through. Nevertheless, he couldn't help his impatience. There were so many questions he wanted to ask. *So much he wanted to know.* He realised, of course, that since the professor's return with the boys from Mount Tengi, they had achieved much more than they could ever have imagined when they first conceived the idea of building the DONUT. It was now the core of the highly secret energy programme, capable of creating sun-like energy, but who would have thought it would also help to open timecracks?

'I have Richard Kinross with me, Dr Krippitz. Do you have any information for us?'

As he spoke, Ed knew his words would be transcribed automatically into text to appear on a similar screen at Mount Tengi. He waited as their response came through, slowly digitising into a message he could read.

We … are … prepared … to … receive … the … co-ordinates …

... Is … the … tracking … unit … ready? ...

As Ed checked the message again, he nodded to himself that he was satisfied with the transmission codes he had devised that would link him to the MVCS and the timecrack chambers on both worlds. He punched the codes into the communication pad and affirmed that everything was ready for their trip to the Yucatan to find the Transkal.

He waited again for their response. The message was brief.

... Excellent … we … will … standby …

... for … your … signals … end ...

This is incredible … just incredible, thought Ed, as he watched the flickering words fade from the screen.

He shook his head, almost in disbelief, at what he and Dr Krippitz had achieved. To date, seven travellers had made the journey to the chamber from Mount Tengi, and returned, without incident. The MVCS, in tandem with the chamber, had functioned perfectly every time – and, very importantly, he had received his first small consignment of vallonium to use in the tests while in the Yucatan.

Following him out of the Parasite capsule into a low-temperature control room, shivering and feeling a little irritated, Richard complained: 'He didn't ask me anything.'

'No, I'm sorry about that,' said Ed 'but it was necessary to have you there, just the same, in case he had any questions only you could answer.'

'Oh … I see.'

Not that Richard did. In fact, he couldn't understand what all the planning would achieve if Copanatec no longer existed, as Father Jamarko claimed. Yet … he *had* seen mum and talked to her while he was in the trance. But did Copanatec disappear *after* that, to become the 'lost' city that the old priest had talked about? He didn't know. It was just too confusing.

He hadn't experienced a trance for a long time, but the dreams had returned almost nightly, leaving him drained and tired the next morning. None of the dreams let him 'see', or gave any clue as to where his parents might be or whether they were dead or alive. Instead, the dreams were brief – sometimes frightening – showing only kaleidoscopic glimpses of people and places he had never seen before. It was all he could do to try and forget them when he awoke.

He pushed a flop of fair hair away from his brow as he realised Ed was speaking to him.

'Uh – what?'

'I was talking about the tracking unit, Richard.'

'What's that?'

'Ah, that is a very special piece of equipment. It's an advanced version of one of Mount Tengi's TTU's, the Timecrack Tracking Units that were developed by their scientists to help them locate timecracks out in the field. Your friend, Aristo, left us one on his last trip. It helped us to build a model that can be used here in our world, and, hopefully, when we find the Yucatan Transkal we will be able to link up with Mount Tengi – '

'Do you really think it will make any difference? Will it help us to find mum and dad?' Richard asked impatiently. He was getting tired of all this. *Couldn't they just get on with it?*

'We hope so. Part of the Yucatan plan is to see if Mount Tengi can send a traveller to somewhere else on Old Earth, and not just to the DONUT. It's an important test, Richard. If all goes well, it will be the first step to sending travellers back to their points of origin – or, even to other points in time!' Ed couldn't help but feel excited, as he thought of the enormity of what they were trying to achieve. 'Another part of the plan is to see if Transkals have any significant effect on timecracks. It seems as if they have a number of Transkals in Amasia, but here on Old Earth we know only of the one your parents discovered.'

Richard shrugged. He was beginning to wonder if he was just being *used* to further some big fancy scientific project. *Yeah, I bet that's it. Well, we'll see about that*, he thought.

*

Later, in the room they shared at the Facility, Archie and Richard were packing their bags for the trip to Mexico.

'Everything seems to be just one big 'If',' complained Richard, shoving a bunch of crumpled T-shirts into an overstuffed rucksack.

'What's that supposed to mean?' asked Archie, trying unsuccessfully to squeeze a pair of trainers into his own bag. 'Blast! I wish Marjorie was here to help us with this stuff.'

'Well, she's not, and anyway, we're probably wasting our time on this trip.' Richard kicked the rucksack to one side of the room and threw himself onto one of the bunk beds he and Archie had been sharing. 'Even Ed's not so sure; he keeps saying *if* this and *if* that. I'm telling you it's a waste of time.'

'Look, let's get one thing straight,' snapped Archie, suddenly losing his temper. He marched over to Richard's bunk and stood over him, feeling ready to explode. 'I don't know what's got into you lately, but we're *both* going to the Yucatan, and we're going to find the Transkal, and when we do, *you* are going to try your damnedest to get in touch with mum! *Understand*?'

Richard stared back at Archie, but said nothing as he watched his brother stalk out of the room and slam the door behind him.

Chapter Six

The Unlucky Guide

Waiting for the group from the Facility at a small private airfield outside Playa del Carmen, Juan Emilio Sanchez – more popularly known to his dwindling list of clients as Johnny – had a compelling urge to smoke the cigar he kept twirling between the fingers of his right hand, the other hand counting the remaining dollars in his pocket. He resisted the temptation, knowing it wasn't permitted to smoke anywhere on the airfield; presumably in case he blew himself up. Mightn't be such a bad idea, he thought, considering the way his luck had gone recently.

That stupid cow of a woman getting herself stuck in the hatch of the submarine was unbelievable. Tourist submarines had been operating around Cozumel for years, taking tourists to visit the barrier reef, without any problems. Not until the American señora had lodged herself in the stern hatch. *How could that happen? How big could she be?* She had been trapped, unable to move up or down, for twenty-four hours. *Twenty-four hours!*

With the submarine tied up to the tender, the crew had erected a tent over her to stop the sightseers goggling and taking photographs. Her companion, a retired nurse, had tried using suntan oil, grease and any other lubricant that came to hand, but the señora hadn't budged an inch.

What he didn't understand was how she had got through the hatch in the first place. *Had she increased in size while she was down there?*

She must have lost weight with all the pushing and shoving, for without warning, and a sudden release of wind the pushers didn't appreciate, she'd popped out of the hatch, just like a champagne cork, taking the tent with her.

The US tabloids had had a field-day with headlines and cartoons proclaiming: *Mystery Missile Launched From Mexican Sub! ... Caught in the Hatch! .... Up, Up and Away! ...*

And now the señora's irate daughter was suing the submarine company for two million dollars. *For very painful embarrassment and unlawful captivity!* And they, in turn, had refused to pay him nearly three months' commissions *and* were suing him! How in the name of all the saints could they blame him? Was he supposed to weigh and measure everyone who booked a trip?

He chewed his unlit cigar and watched the helicopter land on the helipad. His client, Señor Ed Hanks and two young men jumped out onto the tarmac, ducking low below the spinning blades.

If anyone had told Juan Emilio Sanchez, of the now defunct Sanchez Tourist Trips agency, that these two young men would cause him a great deal more trouble than the señora in the submarine, he would have exploded with laughter.

*

'Who's the character with the cigar?' asked Archie, pointing to a small stocky-looking Mexican, wearing an unmissable, bright orange shirt over sky-blue trousers. He was standing by a battered-looking ten year old Chevy school minibus, waving a straw hat in their direction.

'That gentleman, Archie, is our guide, Juan Emilio Sanchez. He's better known to the tourists as Johnny.' Ed waved back and led the boys across the tarmac to meet him. Chuck stayed behind to check the unloading of the luggage and equipment from the helicopter, before transferring each piece carefully onto the minibus.

'Welcome back, Señor Hanks, I am most pleased to see you again,' said Johnny. *How true*. His exorbitant fee for the exploration into the Yucatan jungle would be paid without quibble. He didn't like taking advantage of such a generous client, but unfortunately his present circumstances dictated a new scale of fees. Especially to find a lost pyramid (although, if truth be told, this particular pyramid was not lost, it had just been ignored for a long time), and to take them to a mestizo village that had hired labour to the two missing archaeologists.

Johnny Sanchez was a mestizo through his father's bloodline of mixed Spanish and American Indian blood, an ancestry that could be traced back to the Spanish Conquest in the sixteenth century. His knowledge of the area was extensive, and he knew the village that Señor Hanks was seeking, for it was rumoured throughout the Yucatan to be cursed. After the pyramid had collapsed two years earlier, killing some of the mestizos working for the archaeologists, many of the inhabitants had become frightened and left the area, but he'd heard that a few of the Mayan workers had stayed behind, reluctant to leave a place they had lived in all their lives.

A story had been spread by some, that an angry god had destroyed the pyramid because it had been desecrated. Superstitious nonsense, he knew, but the tourists loved the stories, and, more importantly, added dollars to his fees.

'Hello, Johnny, it's good to see you, too. This is Archie Kinross, and his brother, Richard. It's their parents who went missing during the expedition I told you about.

'Buenos dias, señors, I am delighted to meet you.'

'Hi,' said Archie.

'Yeah' grunted Richard, staring at the minibus.

While Ed and Johnny discussed the plan for the trip, the boys wandered around the minibus, taking a closer look at the bodywork.

'You know what this reminds me of?' said Richard.

'What?'

'The Bonebreaker.'

'Yeah, you're right.' Archie thought of the flying vehicle that Aristo had flown to rescue them from the Sacred Temple before the mountain collapsed. It had saved their lives. 'Well, if it's anything like the Bonebreaker, I'll be happy enough to ride in it.'

*

After Chuck and Ed had loaded the luggage and equipment into the back of the minibus – Ed was particularly careful with the handling of the heavy rucksack and the long cylinder attached to it, which he secured to the roof rack – they left the airfield and Playa del Carmen behind them.

Johnny informed Ed that they would stay overnight in his mother's haçienda in Valladolid. 'It is a popular guest house and many tourists stay there. You will be well looked after, and it will give me the opportunity to speak with Father Higgins at the church. He runs the mission for the Maya here and he knows the area well. He will tell us more about the site you are looking for.'

During the drive from the airfield, Chuck had been listening carefully while Ed and Johnny chatted about the trips they had made in the past and he was curious to know more about the guide. He was responsible for everyone's safety, and he'd promised the professor he would take extra care of the boys. That included checking out everyone they were involved with, especially an intriguing character like Juan Emilio Sanchez.

'Tell me Johnny,' said Chuck, sitting behind the driver. 'Your name is Mexican, but do I hear a touch of up north there, somewhere?'

Johnny tilted the rear view mirror to get a better look, feeling a little surprised. He tended to maintain a local accent, thinking it more appropriate to his business, but the man in the mirror with the serious eyes who looked like a cowboy, did not sound like a tourist.

'You are very perceptive, señor. My mother is from New York. She met my father there when they were both at art college. They married in New York and I went to school there for several years, before they decided to return to my father's home in Valladolid.'

'And your mother and father run this haçienda … guest house, we're staying in?'

'My mother, yes, but my father rarely sets foot in the place. You see, he is an artist who is concerned about the Indians and their culture; it is a way of life that is disappearing and he is trying to preserve it in his art, which he sells in a gallery in Playa del Carmen.'

'I never knew that, Johnny,' said Ed, who was fascinated by anything to do with the Mayan culture. 'You and your mother must be very proud of him.'

'Maybe so,' said Johnny, chewing an unlit cigar. 'But I can tell you this: My father has been in the Guatemalan jungle with an Indian tribe for more than five years now, and when he finally comes home my mother will probably kill him.'

Ed was shocked. 'But why? What has he done?' he asked.

'My father is a lousy cook,' said Johnny, pulling the minibus alongside the front of a small cantina just off the main road. 'He was trying to make an albondigas soup, but he burned the kitchen down instead. It was my mother's pride and joy, and it was only one week old. I think it may be the reason he has stayed in the jungle so long.'

Chapter Seven

The Mark

Following the others, Richard hopped out of the minibus onto a hard-packed sandy surface and looked warily at the ramshackle, corrugated iron structure that seemed ready to collapse at any moment. Half a sign: CISCO'S, hung vertically by a single nail over the entrance – the other half: CANTINA, lay on a set of steps leading into the bar.

Archie shook his head and stared. A rust-stained scooter, without wheels, had been abandoned to a nearby cactus patch adding to the overall impression that the whole place was in urgent need of some much-needed maintenance. The cantina itself, set back from the road on a scrubby plot of land, had been hacked out of the surrounding jungle, but was now in danger of being reclaimed by the dark green creeper that covered the rest of the building. A slate-grey tarpaulin stretched over a large hole in the roof was held down by a TV cable leading to a satellite dish, and a large, concrete block. A pall of road-dust, stirred up by the minibus, drifted lazily across the entrance.

'I'm not going in there – it's a dump,' complained Richard, hanging back behind Archie.

'Suit yourself and stay here if you want, but it's far too hot and I'm thirsty.'

Archie left him, stepping over the broken sign to go inside. He followed Johnny and the others to a beer-spattered table near the door. An old Indian with a face like carved mahogany, sat quietly at a table before an open window smoking a cigarette. Flies buzzed noisily over an uncovered plastic tray of tortillas on the bar counter, killing any thought of food that Archie might have entertained.

A skinny, dark-skinned youth approached the table. 'Buenos dias, señors, what can I get you?'

They ordered drinks all round, including a Coke for Richard, who was still outside.

'This one of your regular stops, Johnny?' asked Chuck. He had seen some rough bars during his military service overseas, but this place matched the worst of them.

'I'm sorry we had to stop here, señor. It is not a place I normally bring my clients, but it's very hot and I thought you might like some cold drinks before we go much further.' He nodded in the direction of the toilet area. 'But I would suggest if you need to go, you wait until we get to Valladolid.'

Archie looked across to a beaded curtain that screened the entrance to the toilet beside the bar. The flies were still buzzing around the tortillas and he felt his stomach lurch as he stood up. 'I think I'll take Richard's drink out to him.'

'Good idea, Archie. We'll finish our drinks and join you outside in a few minutes. It'll be getting dark soon and we need to be on our way,' said Ed. He looked to Johnny who nodded in agreement.

The skinny waiter had returned to the table with the drinks. Archie lifted two Cokes by the neck and went outside onto a wood deck veranda where Richard had made himself comfortable on an old hammock. He was pushing himself back and forward with one foot against the veranda rail, hands clasped behind his neck.

'Here, take this,' said Archie, handing over the Coke. 'You're right, this place is a dump.'

'Thanks.' Richard reached out and took the Coke. He rolled out of the hammock and placed it on the floor, while he pulled off his T-shirt and wrapped it around his neck. He lifted the drink and downed half of it without taking a breath, some of it running down his chin.

'Make the most of it,' said Archie, 'I don't think we're staying here too long.'

He was about to warn Richard not to try the food when he heard a sudden commotion inside the cantina. He looked through the window, directly behind the hammock, to where the old Indian had been sitting but was now standing and pointing at Richard. He seemed to be agitated about something.

'What the heck is wrong with him?' said Archie.

'I dunno,' said Richard, 'he looks crazy to me.'

Inside, Chuck rushed to the window thinking that the boys might be in trouble. Seconds earlier, the Indian had unexpectedly jumped to his feet knocking over his chair, waving his finger and growling like an old dog.

'Es la Varita Inmortal!'

Chuck understood some Spanish, but he couldn't make out what the Indian was saying. 'Johnny, what's this old guy so worked up about?'

Johnny shook his head and grabbed the Indian by the arm. 'Que dice usted? What are you saying?'

'*El tiene la marca de la Varita Inmortal*! He has the mark of the Immortal Wand!'

The Indian was shaking, with anger or fright, no one could tell. Johnny picked up the chair and made him sit down, but the Indian was still muttering, and now he was pointing through the window. He said something that made Johnny stare in Richard's direction.

'What did he say?' asked Ed, who was on his feet and anxious to get away, but curious to know what was going on.

Johnny ignored him and went to the open window. 'Richard, excuse me, but would you come here, please?'

'Sure, what's wrong?' Richard stood closer to the window and peered into the shadow of the cantina, wondering what the old Indian was shouting about.

'Can I have a look at your shoulder, please?'

'What for –'

Johnny and Chuck were pushed to one side by the Indian as he pointed at Richard's shoulder. It was obvious that he was trying to make them understand something. Chuck looked closely and saw what it was that seemed to upset the Indian so much. On the back of Richard's shoulder was what seemed like a small, triangular-shaped mark with a vertical bar in the centre. Above the apex, was a rough-looking circle. The overall pattern had the appearance of an old tattoo, faded but still recognisable as a distinct shape.

Chuck turned to Johnny and handed him some money. 'Here, take this and buy the old guy a bottle of Tequila. Maybe it'll quieten him down a bit.' He went outside to where Archie and Richard had left the veranda, moving to the bottom of the steps to avoid the Indian's gaze.

'Sorry about all that, Richard, but he seems to have settled down now,' said Chuck, pushing his Stetson back as he glanced at Richard's shoulder. 'Mind if I take a closer look?'

Richard shrugged and pulled the T-shirt away from his neck. 'Sure, why not.'

'I can't figure it,' said Chuck, as he studied the mark. 'What could it be that would get the old Indian so worked up?'

'I dunno,' said Richard, shrugging his shoulders. 'I've never seen it, have I?'

'It's only a birthmark, he's always had it,' said Archie.

'Well, it's not like any birthmark I've ever seen,' said Chuck, his thumb and forefinger stroking his moustache. 'It's more of a regular design, like a tattoo — '

'It's *not* a tattoo!' snapped Richard.

'OK, pardner, I hear you,' smiled Chuck, backing off with his hands raised in self-defence. 'Let's forget about it. It's time we were back on the road.'

*

They left the cantina a few minutes later. Johnny looked back to see the old Indian sitting at the window, watching them, as he started up the minibus for the drive to Valladolid. *What had the strange mark meant to him?* Maybe Father Higgins would know. He made a mental note to ask him when he visited the mission.

Like Johnny and Chuck, Archie also wondered about the significance of Richard's birthmark, if that's what it was, but what else could it be? He'd known about it for years, of course, but he'd never given it a second thought. After all, he had one himself: a small splotch, more like an ink stain, on his right foot. But Richard's appeared to have a definite pattern, not an irregular patch, like most birthmarks.

A distant memory came back to Archie of an almost forgotten holiday, when the family had spent a day swimming and fooling around at the seaside in Donegal. Mum would carry him on her back as they raced to meet the white-crested waves come crashing onto the beach, and with yells of delight, they would tumble into the water, laughing. As his memory of the scene became clear, it was then that he saw it again.

The mark.

His mother had had one like it on her shoulder.

Chapter Eight

Haçienda Paz

Archie remembered the colonial city-town of Valladolid as an afternoon coach stop about halfway between Merida and Cancun, during a school field trip to visit the Mayan ruins of the Yucatan. Because of his parents' reputation as internationally famous archaeologists, the teacher had expected him to show a lot more enthusiasm when the class trudged through the old churches and the museum in Valladolid. It had been far too hot and the teacher's dreary monologue on the many ancient artefacts discovered in the Yucatan had left him almost numb with boredom.

Let's face it, he thought, *how many teenagers are really interested in that stuff?*

It was OK when his parents came to visit and they told him about where they had been and the wonderful things they had seen, but that was about *them*, not just about stone statues and things that they had dug up somewhere. He looked at Richard asleep beside him in the back of the minibus. He's fifteen now, would *he* be interested? Archie grunted at the thought of it. It was hardly likely, knowing that Richard wouldn't have the patience to open a book, let alone listen to a lecture on stones and bones from a dozy old teacher.

Valladolid had been settled during the Spanish Conquest and it was near Chichen Itza, probably the most famous of all the Mayan archaeological sites, but that was about all Archie remembered. They had arrived in darkness and he didn't recognise any of the streets or buildings they passed through on the way to Johnny's mother's place.

'Well, señors, we are here,' said Johnny. He drove to the end of a broad avenue lined with impressively

46

large houses and turned into an equally impressive paved driveway. A stone pillar was engraved: HAÇIENDA PAZ.

Chuck whistled softly as the minibus stopped in front of a stunning marble portico, leading to a set of double oak doors. 'Some place, Johnny. Your mother must run a very successful guest house.'

'She does very well, but it's my father's paintings that pay for all this.'

A concealed overhead lamp switched on and one of the oak doors opened wide as Archie and the others stepped onto the portico. A slim woman, in her fifties, with a tumble of curly brown hair and hardly any make-up, confronted them. Dressed in a blue denim shirt hanging loose over pink cotton trousers, she walked barefoot with the appearance of an attractive, aging hippie holding on to her past. She waved two arms, covered in gold and silver bangles, to greet them.

'Welcome to the Haçienda Paz, gentlemen. I see that in spite of losing his last clients, Juan managed to find his way here.'

'I didn't lose any clients, it was all just media stuff,' protested Johnny.

'Whatever it was, it's the talk of the Yucatan, *and* in the US, I hear. Anyway, what took you so long getting here?'

'Ah … we had to make a quick stop at Cisco's Cantina on the way here …' mumbled Johnny, turning away quickly '… I'd better get the luggage unloaded.' He hurried back to the minibus, avoiding his mother's incredulous stare.

'What in Heaven's name made you take these people to that flea-infested pit?' she called after him. 'Wait – don't tell me, I don't want to hear. It's the sort of thing your father would do.'

47

Sighing, she looked to Archie and Richard, as if noticing them for the first time. 'And who do we have here?'

Ed introduced them and then Chuck and himself.

'Well, my name is Jessica Sanchez, but my friends call me Jess – anything else makes me sound old and fusty. I'm the owner and general factotum around this place, and as you probably realise, Juan's mother, although he seems to have lost his name as well, somewhere along the way.' She gave Johnny a pointed look, which he ignored, as he brought the luggage up onto the portico.

She draped her arms over the boys' shoulders and guided them through the door into the haçienda's main hall. There were gold and jade framed paintings everywhere: on the walls, on easels, and on top of a grand piano in the middle of the lobby, a portrait featured Jessica in a magnificent evening gown. Chuck stopped to take a closer look at the painting.

'Don't pay any attention to that,' said Jessica. 'It was a long time ago, and probably the last time I wore a dress. My scallywag husband thinks it's his best work and insists we keep it there. Now, let's get you all settled into your rooms and then we'll see about getting you something to eat. Pedro will see to anything you need.' She nodded to a young Indian boy standing by the piano. 'Snap to it, Pedro, and help Juan with the luggage. We don't have all night.'

Jessica Sanchez might be described by some people as a loud American, and although she had lived on the Yucatan peninsula for nearly thirty years, she still retained traces of her New York accent. It was obvious she liked to speak her mind, but Archie was attracted to her and guessed that her bark was worse than her bite, that she liked to get things done quickly, *rapidamente.*

And that suited him: he didn't want to waste time either.

She led them into a beautifully decorated hallway with a richly detailed mosaic floor. The hallway led to the bedrooms and its walls were covered with more paintings, many of which depicted ancient Mayan ruins and different aspects of the Indian way of life.

'Amazing, there must be a fortune in art in the haçienda,' said Ed, standing closer to take a better look at an oil painting of El Castillo, the great pyramid at Chichen Itza.

'You think so?' said Jessica, in a business-like tone. 'Well, if you see something you like, put your money on the table and you can take it with you.'

'What about this one?' asked Richard. He was staring at a painting of a great flat-topped pyramid in the middle of a jungle. It was a typical Mayan structure, but instead of the temple building used by the priests for their ritual practices, very often found on the flat top, there was a golden column throwing dazzling rays of white light across the jungle canopy.

'You want to buy it?' smiled Jessica, her voice teasing him a little .

'No ... no, it's just that ... I thought I'd seen it before ... somewhere,' muttered Richard.

'My father painted it many years ago,' said Johnny, ignoring the irritated look from his mother at the mention of her absent husband. He had just joined them after helping Pedro leave the luggage in each of their rooms. 'It's one of a series he was going to complete called *The Lost World*, but we never saw any of the other paintings. They may have been painted here in the Yucatan, or in Guatemala, for all we know. It was a subject he used to discuss with Father Higgins at the mission, so he could probably tell you more about the paintings, if you're interested.'

'I would hardly think Richard is interested in old buildings, Juan,' said Jessica, sounding a little impatient with her wayward son. 'More likely a shower and a decent meal is in order, and then he can look at the paintings, if he's so inclined.'

*

Later that evening, having consumed a huge meal of *Pollo Pibil*, a delicious dish of baked marinated chicken served on banana leaves, everyone agreed it would be a good idea to retire to their rooms and get an early start in the morning.

'What was it about that painting you seemed so interested in?' asked Archie, glancing across to Richard in the other twin bed.

'I'm not sure … it sort of reminded me of the building I saw in the trance when we contacted mum from the Transkal at Harmsway.'

'You mean, in Copanatec?'

'Yeah, I think so.'

Archie's thoughts went back to the time he'd seen the city of Copanatec in the trance he'd shared with Richard. It had been in the middle of the night at Harmsway College when he'd coaxed Richard into trying the meditation technique that Shaman-Sing had taught them in Maroc, or the Screaming Forest as many of the inhabitants in Timeless Valley called it. He remembered only too clearly, mum's voice when Richard had made contact with her:

We are in a place called Copanatec …

A place where she and dad were being held prisoner. In a city on a strange island, where the city and its people were constantly under threat from the sea. The buildings and its inhabitants had appeared to belong to a distant past, not unlike what he had seen in the Sacred Temple before it was destroyed.

Back at Harmsway, shortly before travelling back to the Facility, Father Jamarko had said that the legend of Copanatec told of a city that had been lost to the sea somewhere off the coast of Central Amasia, and yet his mother had told Richard that was where they were. Archie felt like crying out in frustration at the task they had set themselves. Even with all the people and resources that Uncle John had put at their disposal it seemed like a hopeless venture.

'Do you think we'll be able to reach mum again?' asked Archie, a little tentatively, knowing that Richard was reluctant to talk about it.

'I dunno. I still have dreams, but nothing that makes much sense.'

That was true, thought Richard. He did dream a lot, but it was more than that. When the dreams and trances did happen, they left him feeling stressed out and sort of hung-over. Sometimes they were so frightening he never wanted to sleep again.

He knew how desperate Archie was to make contact with mum again – they both were, but Richard was frightened of what he had seen, and what they might yet discover.

'Maybe when we find the Transkal, we'll get through again ... I dunno ...' Richard tailed off, not sure what else he could say that would make Archie understand or share his fears on what might lie ahead.

Later that night Richard drifted into a deep sleep and dreamt again.

The trees were so close together he couldn't force a way through. The canopy above so dense, he couldn't see the sky. All around him, the sounds of the forest were getting louder as someone or some...thing, approached. He backed away, but he couldn't escape.

The forest was his prison, and the trees formed the bars of his cell.

The trees parted and two arms reached out, as if seeking help. It was an old Indian, with blood seeping from sightless eyes, coming slowly towards him. Richard tried to run, but he was trapped by the trees, the Indian almost touching him.

He woke up screaming. Archie was trying to hold him down while someone pounded on the bedroom door.

Chapter Nine

Lords of the Cloud

'How is Richard?' asked Ed.

'He's OK. He was sleeping when we left,' answered Archie. 'Jess said she would look after him until we returned from the mission.'

'That's good,' said Ed. 'Those blood-curdling screams of his in the middle of the night had me on the edge of my bed. God knows how he must have felt.'

Ed was right. When Archie had woken up last night to find Richard sitting upright with his arms outstretched trying to back away from some unknown horror, it had scared the wits out of him. Richard was screaming over and over that an Indian with bloody eye sockets was trying to drag him into a dark forest.

It was only when Jessica arrived clad in her dressing gown, holding a mug of herbal tea which she forced Richard to drink that he'd finally calmed down. She had been startled out of her sleep on hearing the dreadful screams. Guessing that one of the guests was having a nightmare after the evening meal and downing too much Tequila, she'd made her special herbal tea, concocted for just such an occasion. It usually worked a treat on her more adult guests, but she hadn't expected to see Richard in such a state.

Archie looked through a patch of clear glass on the dust-covered window at the side of the minibus, as Johnny drove them slowly past a sixteenth century Franciscan church. An Indian wearing denims and a battered-looking sombrero was sitting on a stone step at the entrance offering a colourful piece of pottery to a female tourist while she took a photograph of the church. He turned away from the window and thought about Richard's dream. He didn't know what to make of it – if it meant anything at all – but it did look as if Richard's dreams were just as disturbing as ever.

He was convinced that Richard was trying to ignore the power that he possessed, a special power that allowed him to 'see' through dreams and trances, things that other people couldn't see. He knew it was upsetting for him. Why, he didn't really know, but as long as mum and dad were missing Archie was determined to persuade Richard to use his power to find them – while he still had it.

Now, shortly after breakfast, in the bright Yucatan sunshine and gathering heat, Johnny was driving them to meet Father Higgins at the Mayan mission church. Chuck had elected to stay behind to check their equipment and to phone Uncle John at the Facility to give him an update on their progress, such as it was.

They arrived at the white-washed front of a stone building on the outskirts of Vallodolid. A *ramada,* a pole and thatched roof shelter at the side of the building protected a small group of Mayan women from the blazing sun. They were weaving purses and handbags from some sort of fibre while children played on the stone steps before a set of rough-hewn timber doors leading into the church. Directly above the doors an empty bell tower hinted at an impoverished community.

'Juan Sanchez! How are you?'

The soft tone of a western Irishman caught Archie's ear as they walked towards the open timber doors. He recognised the accent as being similar to that of the history teacher back at Grimshaws. The voice belonged to a tall, well-tanned, lean figure dressed in jeans, old Nike trainers and a military-style shirt with lots of pockets. Short-cropped, grey hair completed the military image, but it was the intelligent, deep-seated, green eyes that grabbed Archie's attention. He didn't look like any sort of priest that he had seen before, thought Archie, but they didn't always wear black robes, he supposed.

'I've been expecting you, Juan – oh, I'd forgotten, its Johnny these days, isn't it?' The green eyes twinkled as Father Higgins greeted his visitors. 'And these gentlemen are the searchers for the lost pyramid you told me about on the phone?'

'Yes, Father, they and two others are staying at the Haçienda Paz. They are anxious for more information, and I have suggested you might be able to help them.'

After the introductions they went inside the church where the air was cooler and the light from narrow side windows high above them cast rippled shadows across several rows of plain wooden benches. Faded wall murals and an altar that had once been painted gold, added to the sense of neglect that pervaded the interior.

They sat facing each other on two of the benches near the open doors where a couple of the children played hide-and-seek.

'I'm sorry the church is not looking its best these days,' said the priest, his right hand gesturing to the church around them, as if to apologise for its poor state, 'but there is little money available to keep the place in good repair.'

'Does the Church not support you here?' asked Ed, thinking that the building, somehow, displayed a sense of abandonment.

'Ah … I see that you are not aware of my … let us say … special circumstances?'

'No, I can't say that I am,' replied Ed.

'Well, it's common enough knowledge around here, and beyond, but Johnny has obviously exercised some discretion, which is a rare quality these days.' The priest smiled at Johnny, then continued: 'Mr Hanks, I'm told that you are a scientist, but I gather that your presence here in the Yucatan is not necessarily a scientific one?'

'That's correct, Father. I am a scientist – and an engineer – involved in energy research for the U.S. Government. I also have a great personal interest in the ancient Mayan people's technology and their amazing stone cities. I've visited many of the well-known sites such as Uxmal and Chichen Itza, but my main purpose here is to help Archie,' Ed glanced at Archie sitting quietly beside him, 'and his brother find the site near the pyramid where their parents disappeared.'

Father Higgins nodded thoughtfully. 'Well, we have something in common, Mr Hanks, but I will explain my own position first, and then I will help in any way I can in locating the site you seek. It shouldn't be too difficult, though, as the story of the Kinross archaeologists' disappearance is well enough known to the local Maya.'

He stood up and walked towards the altar. Spreading his arms, he said, 'You know, this place was once a Franciscan church, long before I arrived here.'

'What do you mean?' asked Archie, totally mystified. 'What sort of church is it now?'

'Well, you see, Archie, although I'm called 'Father', I'm no longer a priest – at least, not to my order. I'm afraid we parted company a long time ago.'

'Which order were you with?' Ed inclined his head towards the people outside the old mission building. 'Are you not working with the Maya here in this church?'

'I was with the Jesuits; and yes, I am working with the Maya, but on *their* behalf – *not* the Church,' said the priest. He walked around the altar, stopping to rest his hands on the bare marble surface. 'I am over seventy years of age, and for more than thirty of those years I have been in the Yucatan, and in all that time, I have never lost my fascination for the Maya and their pre-Columbian past. I came here independently, to learn more of the history of the Jesuits in the Yucatan. Unfortunately, my superiors felt that I had lost my way and become too close to the Maya and their beliefs. It was true. I had, and so they decided I should return to Europe. I refused. I felt that my life could be better spent helping these people, and so I became an outcast from my Church – but I have no regrets.'

'And this ... building?' asked Ed.

'Ah, well.' Father Higgins smiled, as if about to tell a secret. 'The old mission was abandoned by the Franciscans a long time ago. I took possession of it on behalf of the Maya, the mestizos – and all the other people who make up this part of the Yucatan. All are welcome here. We've been here for more than twenty years now, and in that time we have built a small crafts business creating products for the tourist industry. Johnny's mother, Jess, as well as running the Haçienda Paz, helps us by negotiating with the market dealers throughout the country. She is a remarkable woman and we greatly appreciate her involvement.

'As well as our little business venture, I minister to the needs of the people, including teaching them a little English and history, when they take the time to learn.'

Archie was intrigued by what he heard, from a priest who was no longer a priest, but acted like one. He wondered if he would be able to help them find his parents.

'Father ...' Archie hesitated, not knowing what he should call him.

The priest understood. 'Just call me Father, Archie, everyone does. Now, what is it you wish to ask me?'

'Uh ... well ... it's just that I wondered if you'd ever heard of a place called Copanatec?' It was the first

57

thing that came into Archie's head. He hadn't meant to broach the question so quickly, but it had slipped out.

It was a shot in the dark – and it hit home.

'Yes, as a matter of fact I have. Well, to be more precise, I've heard of the Copanatecs – the *people,* not the place.'

'What! You have?' Archie was stunned. He hadn't expected such a positive response.

'Yes, but I don't know a great deal. As I mentioned, I teach a little history, mainly pre-Columbian, and during some of my researches into the ancient tribes of the Yucatan, I discovered some strange marks and symbols, called *glyphs,* on great stones deep in the jungle near the area you intend to visit. The glyphs hinted at a race of people who may well have lived in the Yucatan over twenty thousand years ago. Some of my Jesuit predecessors, before the order was expelled from Mexico in 1767, made reference to them and called them the Copanatecs.' He stopped for a moment and looked curiously at Archie. 'Not much is known about them, Archie. How did you come across the name?'

What could Archie say? He was sworn to secrecy by Uncle John not to reveal the existence of New Earth or any connection with it. Not until the work between Mount Tengi and the Facility was completed would they announce to the world that a link to another universe had been discovered. And he certainly couldn't tell Father Higgins that he had asked the same question of another priest in another world!

'I'm not sure,' said Archie. 'I think my parents must have mentioned it. But my brother sometimes has these dreams and trances … he sees and hears things that really happen. It was in a trance that he saw our mother in a place he thinks was called Copanatec.'

'Very strange,' said the priest. He felt that Archie was holding back, not telling him the whole story, but maybe that was the way it had to be. As a priest, he knew that everyone had secrets and they could not always be revealed. 'And tell me, Archie, does your brother still have these dreams?'

'Yes, Father, he had one last night.' Archie told him of Richard's dream that had awakened everyone at Haçienda Paz.

'Mateo!' exclaimed the priest.

'Who?' asked Ed, surprised by Father Higgins' reaction.

The priest stepped away from the altar and sat down again. He sighed, clasping his hands in front of him, and said, 'It is truly a strange world we inhabit, my friends. Early this morning I had word from the Maya that the old shaman, Mateo, died last night. He belonged to the village near the site that you seek.' The priest's deep-green eyes studied Archie's face as he explained the significance of what he was saying. 'He was very old and had been suffering from some sort of diabetic disease which had led to his eyes bleeding. When I went to see him a few weeks ago, he had become totally blind.'

'Do you think … it was the Indian Richard saw in his dream last night?'

'It would seem so. Mateo was very distressed during his last days and kept repeating his concern that he was the last of his line.'

'What did he mean?'

'It's hard to say. You see, Mateo was unusual in that he was a white Indian, not albino, but truly white. He had his followers among the more superstitious here in the Yucatan, including some of the Maya and mestizos. They lived as a group aside from the other villagers who were wary of their beliefs. The followers thought his white skin was a special sign, a blessing from the deity they believed in. He would preach to them of an ancient tribe that lived in the Yucatan long before the time of the Maya, and the Olmec before them, who go back over three thousand years. He referred to this ancient tribe as *The Lords of the Cloud.* It was a tale he told many times and I've sometimes wondered if there was a connection to the Copanatecs, but I've never discovered any evidence to support it.'

'Father…' Archie hesitated before he asked, '…did Mateo have a strange mark on his shoulder?'

Father Higgins leaned forward, obviously surprised by Archie's question. 'Now, how would you know about that?'

Surprised by the priest's reaction, Archie explained the incident that took place at Cisco's Cantina, and then to Ed's astonishment, about how he thought there was a connection between the marks on his mother's and Richard's shoulders.

'Well, what you say is all the more remarkable, for Mateo did have such a mark. He referred to it many times, especially when he spoke to his followers. It was his belief that it was the mark of his tribe in this world and the next – whatever he meant by that.'

The Lords of the Cloud – the Transkal – could there be a link? Was that why Richard had dreamt of the old Indian – that they had something in common? What possible connection could there be between his family and Mateo? Archie shook his head in frustration. There were so many questions he wanted answered, but nothing he had heard so far seemed to make any sense.

'Father, we have to find the site, it's the only chance we have of finding what happened to my parents,' said Archie, almost pleading.

Father Higgins nodded and said he understood Archie's anxiety. He thought that although the pyramid and the archaeological site may not have been visited since the disappearance of his parents, it shouldn't be too difficult to reach.

'In fact, I know a young boy who was at the site at the time of the excavation. He does a little work here at the mission and I teach him English in return.' The priest hesitated, as if recalling the events that had taken place at the pyramid. 'When Johnny told me of your quest, I remembered Manuel had been there when the storm came and part of the pyramid collapsed. Some of the villagers were killed and he escaped. He doesn't like to talk about it, but he has promised me he will meet with you and tell you what he knows.'

They left the mission with Ed promising the priest they would look after the boy during their search for the pyramid and the Transkal.

Chapter Ten

The Mexican

Early the next morning, a twelve-year-old Indian boy, carrying an old straw shopping basket, arrived at the Haçienda Paz. His name was Manuel, and he had that uncertain look about him that children sometimes display when dealing with grown-ups.

Jessica knew Manuel well, and to help put him at his ease she introduced him to Archie and Richard first, before meeting the others. Ed and Chuck were helping Johnny load the minibus with their camping gear and food containers, along with the equipment Ed needed to carry out his scientific tests at the pyramid site.

Archie held out his hand, remembering what Father Higgins had said the previous day: *It seems that Manuel felt some remorse for fleeing from the site after your parents disappeared, and he has spoken little of it since. They had been good to him, and though it is more than two years, he still feels shamed by his behaviour.*

'Hello, Manuel. I'm Archie and this is my brother Richard - but don't mind him, he's still half-asleep and not in a very good mood.'

Archie side-glanced at his brother standing a little behind him, looking sullen with his hands shoved deep into his pockets, seemingly uninterested in the preparations for the trip to the pyramid. Ever since his nightmare two nights ago he'd hardly said a word to Archie, or anyone else.

'It's OK for you,' grunted Richard, 'I can't get to sleep here; it must be the heat or something.'

'Yeah, maybe,' said Archie. He didn't believe it for a minute. Richard had tossed restlessly in his bed last night and seemed to be dreaming about something, but wouldn't admit it. At least he hadn't ended up screaming like the previous night. But his morose attitude was getting on Archie's nerves, and the sooner he snapped out of it the better.

'OK, pardners, all the stuff's on board,' Chuck called out. 'Let's go.'

Johnny packed everyone, and some extra provisions supplied by Jessica, into the minibus until there was hardly room to move and then switched on the engine. He waved to Jessica as she stood in the shade of the portico, quietly watching them as they drove down the driveway.

*

As they left the outskirts of Vallodolid on the road towards Merida, Manuel handed over to Archie the old straw shopping basket he had brought with him. It was filled with pieces of broken pottery and little stone statues, probably of little value, but lying on top were three leather-bound notebooks that had been damaged by rain, leaving some of the pages stuck together.

Archie recognised the handwriting and the precise line drawings that were so typical of his father's notes. When he was much younger, his father, having returned from another one of his trips to some far-off, mysterious country, would come into the bedroom and tell Archie and Richard a fantastic story about where he had been. After they fell asleep he would leave a cartoon he had drawn on the bedside table, which they would discover the next morning. The drawings would always depict the boys doing something silly or adventurous, like riding on the back of an alligator, skiing down the side of a pyramid, or racing polar bears across an island of ice. They had become a treasured collection and were now stored at their home in Ireland.

Archie's heart skipped a beat as he held the notebooks that were the last direct link to their father before his disappearance. Would the notes help them to discover what had happened at the site? He didn't know. Someone else would have to decide that.

As they sped along the road to Merida, Archie gave the straw basket and its contents to Ed. 'Maybe these might help us,' he said.

Holding one of the notebooks, Ed turned to face the young boy sitting directly behind him. 'Tell me, Manuel, how did you come by these?'

The boy bowed his head slightly before answering, 'I went back to the pyramid last year, señor, to look for souvenirs that the *turistas* might buy. I wanted to help the mission, but I did not think that the old books would sell, so I kept them in my room.' Manuel hesitated, and then said, 'I am sorry if I have done wrong, Señor Ed.'

'No, not at all, Manuel. You did the right thing,' said Ed, nodding his approval.

'Do the notebooks tell us anything?' asked Archie.

'It's too soon to say. Quite a few of the pages are in poor condition, probably due to the storm Father Higgins told us about. I'll be able to take a closer look after we set up camp.'

*

Johnny turned the minibus off the main highway onto a narrow road that cut through a patchwork of cornfields, passing several small houses partly hidden by low stone walls. Fifteen minutes later they stopped outside a cantina in the main street of a large village.

A group of about twenty roughly-dressed Indians, some carrying machetes strapped inside wide leather belts, eyed them curiously. They stood between the cantina and three dust-covered pickups, one loaded with camping gear and an assortment of picks and shovels. A short, grubby-looking individual, displaying a large, well-fed belly, left the group and approached the minibus.

'That's Rafael, the man I arranged to meet here,' said Johnny to Ed, as they stepped out of the minibus. 'He is supplying the men and equipment we'll need at the pyramid site.'

'An interesting-looking dude,' said Chuck, as he and the boys joined them. 'I take it he doesn't sweat himself too much on these jobs?'

Johnny grunted, shoving an unlit cigar into his mouth. 'I've never known him to do a day's hard work, but then he doesn't have to. He's Mexican, not Maya like the rest of the men. His family came here many years ago after the Caste Wars ended in 1915, and now he's the richest farmer around here. He owns half the village and lets his money do the work for him, so like him or not, he's the man we have to deal with. I've dealt with him many times – and he is expensive – but he has never let me down.'

'*Ah! La guia de turista de submarine!* The submarine tourist guide!' laughed Rafael, his arms widespread in welcome. 'We have been waiting for you.'

Johnny ignored the 'submarine' taunt as he and Ed met Rafael in the middle of the dusty street. He knew the stories that had been told around the Yucatan about his recent misfortune, but he no longer rose to the bait. Instead, he said, 'The men who wish to go to the pyramid are here, Rafael, as we arranged. This is Señor Hanks, the leader of the expedition.'

'Buenos dias, Señor Hanks, you are very welcome to our humble village. My men are ready to go with you, but first there is the matter of my fee, eh, señor?'

Archie watched with the others as Ed and Johnny entered into what seemed to be a heated discussion, with lots of hand movements flying around. Ed handed over some money and the Mexican slapped him on the shoulder as they parted company.

'The man's a thief!' complained Ed, as they all climbed back into the minibus.

'What happened?' asked Chuck.

'He doubled his fee,' said Ed. 'He says his men wanted more money because it's dangerous to go the pyramid now. Something to do with the old shaman's burial, apparently.'

'Mateo's followers must have taken his body to the pyramid,' muttered Johnny, switching on the engine.

'Meaning what, exactly?' asked Chuck.

'Meaning, señor, that there are some who still believe the pyramid to be a holy and sacred place, not to be disturbed by outsiders. There are not many of them, but they may cause trouble.'

'And what do *you* think? You are our guide after all,' said Chuck, wondering if Johnny was up to the job.

Johnny shrugged his shoulders and chewed his cigar for a moment. 'They are a superstitious lot. Who knows what they will do?'

'We don't have any choice,' said Ed, feeling annoyed over his dealing with Rafael. 'We're already here and we only have a few days to carry out our search before the boys return home. Anyway, I've paid over the money and Rafael has more than enough men to deal with any problems, so I suggest we get moving.'

*

The three pickups and the minibus ploughed their way along a dirt road that gradually narrowed after a couple of miles, forcing them to come to a halt at a point where the dense jungle undergrowth had reclaimed part of the road. Their route had skirted the village where, according to Manuel, some of Mateo's followers still lived.

'They will not be pleased that we are going to the pyramid,' said Manuel, his soft voice filled with fear.

'Don't worry, Manuel, we'll not be staying here any longer than is necessary,' promised Ed, but he could see that the boy was not entirely convinced.

A shout from the lead pickup ahead caught his attention and he went with Chuck to see what was happening, leaving Johnny behind with the boys.

'What is it?' called Chuck.

'We are in luck, señors. See, a path has been made for us already,' grinned Rafael, pointing to a dark opening in the undergrowth.

Chuck looked at the Mexican as if he were the last man on Earth he would want to follow down any path, but he knew they had no choice. He turned to Ed.

'Well, pardner, it looks as if this is where the search begins.'

Chapter Eleven

The Burial Trail

The lead pickup had stopped at a large rock at the end of the road that marked the edge of a small clearing that fronted the jungle they were about to enter. Rafael was pointing towards a break in the expanse of spear-like ceiba trees where someone had evidently widened an old trail. Machete marks were still fresh where the grass and bushes had been slashed on both sides of the path. Although the sun was bright the path was in shadow and cave-like.

'That is where we go in,' said Rafael, grinning as usual, through a mouthful of large, tobacco-stained teeth. 'It is the trail that will take us to the pyramid and the Big Stone you seek, eh?'

'You're right, Rafael,' said Chuck, 'so let's get your men up here with the equipment, double-quick. And make sure they don't damage anything – OK?'

He turned to Ed. 'Maybe you should keep an eye on these guys while they sort things out.'

Ed nodded agreement. He liked the way Chuck seemed to move up a gear, to take charge, and he especially liked the look on Rafael's face when he realised that Chuck was someone not to take lightly.

'Good,' said Chuck. ' It's nearly noon, and it's getting hot, so let's get this bunch of boys moving.' He pushed the brim of his Stetson forward to shade his eyes, and walked back alongside the line of pickups to the minibus to tell Johnny and the boys what was happening.

'Well, Archie, are you and Richard ready for this? It's going to be a little rough in there – and who knows what we'll find, once we start?' He smiled and rubbed a hand through Manuel's hair. 'But I think we have someone here, along with Johnny, who'll keep us on the right trail. That right, Manuel?'

Then he left them to go with Johnny back to the pickup where Ed was supervising the unloading of his equipment into separate loads for the men to carry.

Archie watched Chuck, wondering: *What was it that he was trying to tell them? What did he mean, 'that it might get a little rough in there?'* Or was it just his military background preparing them for the unexpected?

Rafael walked past him, muttering something about interfering gringos, on his way to speak to some of his men.

Archie laughed. 'Well, I think Chuck's sorted Rafael out!'

'Yeah, everything's just great,' said Richard.

'What's up with you?' said Archie, turning quickly to face Richard.

'Nothing, I just want to get started, that's all,' said Richard. 'C'mon, Manuel, let's go get our things.'

Archie frowned for a moment; his brother's sarcasm seemed out of character, but he put it down to the rising humidity and noonday heat. He followed them to retrieve their belongings from the minibus, then they joined Chuck and the others at the pickups, now a hive of activity with Rafael's men loading equipment onto their backs. Two of the men were ready with the generators and fuel lashed into a stretcher-like cradle they would carry between them. The rest of the men would transport tents, bedding, food, water and all the gear needed for several days stay at the pyramid site.

Ed had taken possession of his rucksack with the silvery metal cylinder, nearly four feet in length, attached to it, and was now hitching it onto his back. Archie watched him spread his legs until the weight settled across his shoulders, ready to join the line of men forming on the trail.

'I wonder what's inside the tube that Ed has on his back?' said Archie.

'I don't know,' said Johnny, 'but whatever it is, it looks as if he's the only one who will be looking after it.'

An hour later they were ready to leave the clearing. The minibus and the pickups were locked and secured, until their return from the pyramid site, which Ed reckoned would take at least two to three days.

Chuck had taken charge and organised the men into sections, with himself, Rafael, and two of his men using machetes at the head of the column to lead the way. The boys, along with the main body carrying the equipment would make up the middle section. Johnny and Ed, with two more men, would bring up the rear.

As the column moved into the jungle, Rafael started shouting at the two men with the machetes, slowly slashing with practised strokes at the undergrowth on either side of the dirt path.

'What's he yelling about?' said Archie. Like Richard and Manuel, he carried a backpack containing some personal stuff and he was already feeling the humidity. He was anxious to get to the site as quickly as possible.

'The men are arguing with him that they are trying to be careful. They do not want to cause damage to the ceiba trees,' said Manuel. 'The trees are sacred to the Maya and they do not want to bring bad luck on themselves. Rafael is telling them they have to make the path wider to get the equipment through.'

'Oh, I see –'

'That guy's a real jerk,' said Richard. 'I don't think we should be going in there.'

'What do you mean?' demanded Archie. He couldn't believe what Richard had just said, now that they were so close to the pyramid. 'We *have* to go, it's our only hope of finding mum and dad!'

'I've heard some of the men talking – they say the place is dangerous and we shouldn't be going to the pyramid. That's what Manuel has been trying to tell you.'

Archie remembered the translation chips that had been implanted during their time at Castle Amasia. He touched his neck, feeling the slight rise under the skin. He had forgotten that it automatically translated all languages into his own – even here on Old Earth. It was probably why Richard had understood the Mayan dialect, but it hadn't dawned on him that he also understood.

'Leave Manuel out of it, he's been through enough already, without you making him feel worse!'

The brothers stared at each other, their tempers threatening to get out of hand, when Chuck arrived between them.

'What's going on here? You're beginning to sound like the men griping back there. So what is it?'

'It's nothing,' said Archie. He felt his face redden as Chuck waited for an answer.

Richard stood silently, his eyes shifting uneasily away from Chuck.

'It didn't sound like nothing, but whatever it is, keep it under control. We can't afford to have arguments out here in the jungle.' said Chuck.

He waited, but there was no further response from either of the boys. He didn't know what it was, but there was something going on here that gave him the feeling that trouble lay ahead. He cast the thought aside and said, 'OK, let's go. I'll take up point with a couple of the men to clear the trail. Ed and Johnny will stay at the rear. You boys stay in the middle of the column. Call out if you have any problems.'

A few minutes later, the column started along the path that would take them to the pyramid.

*

Archie trudged along the dirt track, taking occasional sips from a water bottle attached to his belt. The sounds of the forest were all around him: colourful macaws squawking loudly, spider monkeys screeching, and a host of other animals he couldn't name.

Manuel walked beside him, while Richard trailed behind, silent and moody, obviously still annoyed at the exchange of words between them back at the clearing.

'They found many pieces there, and Señor Kinross was very pleased when they found the Big Stone. He said it was most important because of the writing on it,' said Manuel, explaining excitedly what he remembered of his time at the dig before the blue cloud arrived over the stone.

'It was then that *Chac* took them ... before I ran away ...'

Manuel seemed to be in his element when in the jungle, thought Archie, telling everything he knew about the pyramid and the excavations at the dig, but when he spoke of the blue cloud and his belief that it was Chac the thunder god, he became upset.

Archie knew better; it had been a timecrack that had taken his parents, not some mythological figure from Indian folklore.

'Don't worry about it, Manuel, it wasn't your fault they disappeared. Let's face it, if you had stayed there, you would have disappeared, too!' said Archie. 'The important thing now is that we reach the Big Stone and maybe we can find out what happened to my parents.'

'No problem, Archie, I will find it for you,' said Manuel, confident they would reach the site soon and that he would help his new friends find their parents. He was an orphan living with his grandmother in the village, and when Señor Kinross and his wife had come to find workers for the site they had been kind to him. Yet he had run away when they were in trouble. It was a shame he would not repeat.

Suddenly a horrible scream rent the air followed by loud shouting from some of the men, bringing the column to a stumbling halt.

Johnny and Ed moved quickly from the rear to join the boys in the middle of the column.

'What's going on up there?' Ed was panting from the heat and the extra weight of the cylinder on his backpack.

'I don't know. Wait here while I see what is happening,' said Johnny, dropping his backpack to the ground.

He pushed his way through the Indians in front of him, to the head of the column. Archie dumped his backpack beside Johnny's and followed him.

Chuck was standing with his Stetson in one hand, scratching his chin with the other. 'What in creation is that?' he growled.

'Ugh! That's disgusting!' Archie drew in his breath, as he and Johnny joined him.

They were staring at a zapote tree. Skewered to the trunk was a large cat with an iron spike driven through its open jaw, revealing a row of vicious yellow teeth. It had been gutted; its chest and belly lying wide open to a seething mass of flies crawling through the carcass.

A short distance away Rafael was shouting at the two Maya who had been at the head of the column. Both men were pointing at the tree and chanting

Balam! Balam! It was clear they were frightened and reluctant to move any further.

Chuck called out to them, 'What is it, Rafael? What's got them so spooked?'.

'Ah, señor, it is a bad thing,' said Rafael, pointing to the butchered cat. 'They say Mateo's people have declared that the way to the pyramid is now a sacred burial trail.'

'What's that supposed to mean?'

'It means, señor, that the *balam,* the jaguar, is a warning that the trail must not be used. Mateo's body was taken to the pyramid this way. We must find another trail.'

'And just how long is that going to take?' asked Chuck, donning his Stetson and crossing his arms across his chest.

'Who knows, señor?' said Rafael, spreading his arms wide, as if he were not at fault. He pointed again towards the cat pinned to the tree where streaks of blood had stained the bark. 'You see? They have taken the heart of the jaguar as a sacrifice to help Mateo's spirit leave this place.' He shrugged. 'It may take another day to find a new trail.'

Chuck sized up the fat Mexican standing before him. He had a pretty good idea that Rafael didn't go along with the men's superstitions, but was bargaining on more money the longer they stayed in the jungle.

He turned to Johnny, beside him. 'What do *you* make of all this?'

'This is not a good situation,' said Johnny. The cigar he was chewing flicked up and down nervously as he took in the sight of the gutted cat. *This was not the type of guide work he had contracted for.* 'That's a jaguar – it's a protected species in the Yucatan. It's crazy what they've done to it' ... he hesitated ... 'I think maybe we should find another way.'

'No, that will take too long!' cried Archie. 'We have to go on!'

'I agree,' said Ed. He had just joined them, still carrying his backpack. 'We don't have the time to explore the area for alternative routes; besides, I've already paid Rafael some of his money and if he wants the rest he'd better get us to the pyramid, sooner rather than later.'

Chuck looked straight at Rafael and smiled. 'Well, there you have it, pardner, if you want the rest of your money, you need to get us there soon – *comprende?*'

Without warning he moved and grabbed one of the machetes from the Indian nearest to him. Before anyone realised what he was doing, he made several slashes at the head of the jaguar, releasing it from the tree. A few swift kicks and the carcass was lost in the undergrowth.

Turning to the shocked faces of Rafael and the Indians he said, 'OK, let's get these men moving again.'

As he pushed and organised the men into their sections, Rafael looked venomously at the *gringos* who had dared to threaten him by withholding his money. He turned his anger on the Indians, snarling at them to move their lazy backsides, otherwise *they* would not be paid. It was enough to overcome their fear, for they had little or no income, except for the work he could give them.

Archie was relieved as the column started moving forward again along the trail, but he had a feeling that their troubles were far from over.

Chapter Twelve

The Site

Later that afternoon, the column reached the pyramid site. Night fell quickly in the Yucatan and soon it would be dark, so it was imperative that they set up camp as quickly as possible.

Archie set down his backpack along with Manuel's and Richard's, while Chuck, further along the trail, called Rafael, Johnny and Ed together to decide how the camp should be laid out.

He was tired, hot and sticky, and his water bottle was nearly empty. He would have paid any price to have an ice-cold drink in his hand right now. But he was quietly thrilled as he stood on a small hill beside the trail overlooking a shallow valley filled with rocky outcrops and lush vegetation.

Manuel had confirmed that they had reached the area of his father's dig, but it had been two years since, as a young boy, he had left the site in fear and panic, and now the place had been virtually reclaimed by the jungle. A profusion of colourful wild flowers and tall ferns had spread right across the dig, concealing any sign of the trenches that had been excavated – and the Big Stone, now known as the Transkal.

But above the treeline, Archie could see the outline of what seemed to be a column, or pillar, on a flat top of grey stone jutting into the fading light of the Yucatan evening sky. It's fantastic, he thought to himself. A magical place that his parents had discovered, but also a place that had taken them into captivity and unknown danger.

'Do you think you can find the Big Stone, Manuel? It looks as if it could take weeks to clear this place.'

'Yes, it is over there, not far from the pyramid.'

Archie tried to follow Manuel's pointing finger, but all he could see was a forest of small trees and giant ferns stretching all the way to the base of the edifice. In the distance he could see a freshly cut track disappearing into the trees. It was a continuation of the burial trail that Mateo's followers had used to take his body to the pyramid. From what he had understood of the fearful whispers of the men in the column as they marched to this place, Mateo would be entombed so that his spirit could join his ancestors, the 'Lords of the Cloud' – whatever that meant.

'I hope you're right, otherwise, we'll run out of time, and we can't afford to do that.'

Further along the trail some of the men were slashing and hacking at thick undergrowth, clearing an area for the campsite while others sorted the power cables and light units that would link to the generators. Archie watched them for a few minutes, and then looked around, realising that his brother was no longer with them.

'I wonder where Richard is,' he said, wiping some sweat from his brow with the back of his hand.

'I think I know,' said Manuel, and before Archie could stop him, he dashed back down the hill onto the trail, yelling, 'I will find him for you.'

'Hey, take your time – I'll go with you,' Archie called after him, worried that young Manuel was becoming too impulsive in his eagerness to please. I'll have to keep an eye on him, he thought, before he gets himself into trouble.

*

Richard gazed up at the pyramid soaring above him, its ancient top partly destroyed by a fierce storm two years earlier, with large moss-covered stone blocks now lying scattered around in the vegetation like Lego bricks. The burial trail led to the only exposed area on this side of the huge edifice; the forest had long ago overgrown the base stones until only the upper steps could be seen.

Directly above his head, the steps led to an entrance leading into the tomb's interior; where they'd brought Mateo, he thought. Archie had told him what Father Higgins had said about the old shaman, but he hadn't the slightest idea what it all meant.

He sat down, his fingers following the outline of one of the short steps, the warmth of the stone running through his skin. He realised that he was probably sitting near Mateo's body, but in spite of the awful nightmare at Haçienda Paz, he didn't feel frightened, just a tingly sort of feeling that ran down his spine, making him shiver.

Richard hadn't told Archie, or anyone else, where he was going, and he knew they would be angry with him for being here on his own, but he didn't care what they thought. Something had drawn him here that he couldn't explain. It was the same feeling he had experienced when he saw the painting in Haçienda Paz.

'Richard!'

Startled by someone calling his name, he turned to see Manuel running up the trail towards him.

'Richard you are here! I told Archie I would find you,' smiled Manuel, looking pleased with himself. 'I thought you would be here, looking for the Big Stone.'

'Well, I'm here, but I haven't found the stone.'

'I know where it is.'

'OK. So where is it?'

Manuel clambered up a few more steps, gesturing to Richard to follow him. He stopped and pointed to an area in front of them, about two hundred feet in the distance, where traces of a mudslide could be seen. It ran from the far corner of the pyramid; a deep, brown streak, several yards wide, running scar-like through the thick vegetation in the direction of the new campsite.

'What's that?' asked Richard, climbing another few steps to get a better look.

'When the rains came, it brought the great mud river through here. It flowed past the pyramid down to the Big Stone,' said Manuel, shaking his head at the memory of the destruction it had brought. 'It was the only place we could find to stay out of the mud.'

Richard could see clearly how the mud river had coursed its way to the low-lying land of the original campsite, two years earlier. A torrent of fast-flowing mud had swamped everything before it, carrying rocks and stones that now lay baked into a new landscape.

According to Manuel, they would find the Transkal in the middle of the mudslide, marked by a jumble of fallen trees and new growth, a short distance from the line of trees beyond which Rafael's men were setting up camp. Richard saw how easy it would be to reach the Transkal from the campsite.

He heard shouts coming from the trail. He turned to see Chuck and Archie waving to him as they climbed up onto the pyramid steps.

'Hey, you two! What are you doing up there?' Chuck called out. With larger feet and wearing heavy hiking boots, he was finding it difficult to negotiate the narrow steps that had been built by a race of people long ago, obviously with much smaller feet than himself.

'We found the place of the Big Stone, señor. See it is not far from here,' said Manuel, pointing a grubby finger towards the mudslide.

'You have? Where is it?' cried Archie, but before he could say anything else, Chuck placed a hand on his shoulder, motioning him to stay quiet for a minute.

'OK, that's good news; but look, I don't want you boys going off on your own. I want everyone where I can see them, or at least tell me where they're going to be. Do you understand?'

Richard stared into the distance and said nothing. Manuel said he understood and would take them to the Big Stone when everyone was ready.

'Good,' said Chuck. 'Now let's get back and tell Ed what you've found. It'll be dark soon and he'll want to get his equipment ready for the morning, when we set out to find this stone of yours.'

Chapter Thirteen

Under Attack

Archie lay wide awake on the camp bed listening to the sounds of the forest. The screeching, squawking, chirping, from monkeys, birds, insects, and God knows what else, had kept him tossing and turning most of the night. Only a few moments earlier he thought he'd heard something moving and growling somewhere near the tent. *A jaguar?* He hoped not, that it was just his imagination getting the better of him, but whatever it was, he knew there was little likelihood of him getting back to sleep.

He switched on the battery lamp and looked across to the other beds. Both Richard and Manuel were fast asleep under their mosquito nets, hardly moving in the early morning heat of the tent. To heck with this, he thought, no point lying here staring at nothing. Slipping out from under his net, he pulled on a blue T-shirt, then his khaki trousers and field boots, quickly sprayed on some insect repellent and went outside.

Although it was the beginning of the hot season, the dawn approaching made the morning air pleasantly warm and silky. He looked up and saw the last of the stars in a fading night sky. A new day was about to begin and Archie wondered what, if anything, they would discover.

The steady beat of one of the generators caught his attention and he saw that a power cable, supported by a row of poles, now ran to the centre of the campsite. The cable fed several small lamps inside wire cages and underneath one of them, kneeling on a length of canvas in a circle of light, Ed was tinkering with the silver cylinder he had carried so protectively along the burial trail.

'Hi, Ed,' said Archie, coming up behind him. 'You're up early.'

'What the – ' Ed sprung to his feet, dropping the screwdriver he had been using on to the canvas. 'Oh, it's you, Archie, you gave me a fright.'

'Sorry, I didn't mean to scare you. It's just that I couldn't sleep, so I thought I might as well get up and do something.'

'Don't worry about it, I had the same problem. I decided it was time I got this thing ready for the Transkal – when we find it.'

'What is it?'

Ed picked up the screwdriver and tapped the piece of equipment he had been working on, an enigmatic smile appearing on his face.

'*This*,' he said, 'is probably the most valuable bit of hardware on the planet – certainly it is the rarest.'

Archie stared at him, then the unusual-looking apparatus in front of him. The silver container was set to one side of what looked like a three foot high model of a lunar landing module he had built when he was younger. Three telescopic legs had sprung out from its sides allowing it to stand freely, with two antenna-like rods protruding from the top. A series of numbers and symbols ran across the face of a touchscreen on the side of the module, replicating the information from a laptop Ed had been using.

'Why is it so valuable?' asked Archie, bending down to take a closer look at the module.

'It's a prototype Timecrack Field Unit, Archie – an extremely advanced version of a TTU, the Timecrack Tracking Unit that Aristo, and others since, have used on their journeys from Mount Tengi. This machine contains a one inch cube of vallonium, which as far as I know, is the only piece of the mineral on our planet. You know what it is, of course?'

'Vallonium! It's the stuff used to power the timecrack chamber at Mount Tengi and nearly everything else in Amasia. But how did you get it?'

'Dr Shah arranged for your friend Aristo to bring it to us on his last trip to the Facility, along with a set of plans that enabled us to build this particular unit to use at the Transkal.

'But ... but what does it do?' Archie was struggling to understand how this strange-looking machine would help them find his parents. 'How does it actually work?'

Ed paused for a moment, understanding how difficult it must be for Archie to appreciate what he and the scientists at Mount Tengi were trying to achieve. He'd had a number of discussions with them and Dr Shah and, combined with his own explorations in the Yucatan, he now had a theory that might explain the timecrack phenomena.

'I think it's like this,' he said. 'When our universe came into being after the Big Bang, tremendous forces were released, which we are still experiencing today.' He hesitated for a moment, gathering his thoughts, before continuing excitedly. 'I believe that timecracks were a natural part of those forces which came into existence at the beginning of time as we now know it. They act as portals to other universes that were also created at the same time as our own; and they are still a part of the natural order that we have yet to fully understand. With the information Richard has provided so far, I think we can assume that whoever built the Transkals, somehow understood how these forces worked and positioned the stones according to their own calculations. Timecracks are apparently attracted to high energy sources and this TFU has been designed to detect them.'

'Then what?' Archie was beginning to feel a tingle of excitement running through him, and was anxious to know more.

'The professor has arranged with NASA to place a geostationary satellite in orbit above us – it should be up there now. Whatever information we pick up at the Transkal, this little toy will transmit it through the satellite to the Facility... and then to Dr Shah and his team.'

'What will they do with the information?'

'I'm not entirely sure, but part of the evaluation process will be to use the data to see if it's possible to send timecrack travellers back to their point of origin.'

Archie nodded. He remembered Dr Shah's speech at the Meeting House in Fort Temple when he talked about undesirables arriving in Amasia through timecracks and how his work would help to send them back home.

'But how will it help us to find mum and dad? How – '

Before Archie could finish his question, a horrible, agonising scream pierced the air.

'What in Heaven's name was that?' Ed turned quickly, trying to source where the scream had come from.

'Look. Over there!' said Archie. He pointed towards the centre of the campsite where some of Rafael's men had built a campfire and cooking pit.

Two of the Indians had been preparing their own early breakfast before the others arose and now one lay across the campfire with what looked like an arrow sticking out of his back. The other was brandishing a machete above his head and shouting crazily at some unseen presence in the surrounding trees.

Archie and Ed were joined by Chuck and Rafael, both hurriedly half-dressed, having run immediately from their tents, after hearing the scream.

'What the hell's going on here?' demanded Chuck, then he spotted the Indian waving the machete and the other one lying across the campfire.

He dashed over, followed by the others. He called out, 'Help me with this man!' Ed helped him drag the Indian away from the fire. Fortunately, it had only just been started and wasn't fully lit. They could see that the lower part of a jacket the Indian had been wearing and the top of his denims had both been slightly scorched, but no worse than that. The arrow hadn't fully penetrated the man's flesh, stopped by the thick leather of the jacket.

'He'll be OK,' said Chuck, breaking off the top half of the arrow. 'Get –'

'Aaahhh!'

Suddenly Rafael screamed and clutched his shoulder. A rock fell at his feet followed by a hail of smaller stones, narrowly missing the rest of the group. An arrow flew over their heads, plunging into the side of a tent.

'We're under attack!' yelled Chuck, turning to Rafael. 'Are you all right?'

The Mexican nodded, rubbing a hand over his shoulder, where he was struck.

'Good. Get your men into the edges of the jungle and tell them to stay under cover until they hear from us. You come with me while I figure what we're up against.'

The camp was in an uproar as the rest of the Maya, alerted from their sleep, cried out to each other in confusion. Johnny appeared, pushing some of them to one side, stopping when he saw the injured Indian.

'Holy saints, what happened to him?'

'Later. Get the medical kit from my tent and see what you can do for him. Can you handle that?'

'Yeah, but –' Johnny was about to object that he wasn't a doctor, until he saw the look on Chuck's face. 'OK, I'll do what I can.'

'Good.' Chuck turned to Ed. 'Kill the generators and the lights – not that it matters, now that first light is nearly here, then give Johnny a hand.'

There were no more stones or arrows; it might have been a hit and run attack, but Chuck was taking no chances. As he left them, pulling Rafael with him, he shouted: 'Archie, look after the boys and stay under cover.'

Archie could hardly credit the chaos around him. The Indians were yelling, waving machetes, as they moved cautiously into the trees. It must have been Mateo's followers, he thought, angry because they had used the Burial Trail and ignored the jaguar warning. It was frightening and he wondered if their attackers were still out there somewhere waiting for another chance. It was pretty primitive, but stones and arrows could still kill them.

Richard , with Manuel, came up beside Archie and pointed to the injured man being carried on a makeshift stretcher by Johnny and Ed to one of the tents.

'What's happening?'

Archie stared at him. 'Don't tell me you slept through all this?'

'He did,' said Manuel, 'I had to wake him.'

Archie shook his head in disbelief. 'Well, just in case they come back, Richard, you should know that we were under attack by bandits. But don't worry, I'll wake you if they do.'

*

With Rafael and four of his men, Chuck checked the entire perimeter of the campsite, kicking himself that he hadn't posted more guards during the night. What would his old army buddies have thought of that, he wondered. He looked around, but there was no sign of the attackers, just breaks in the undergrowth where they had hidden.

'Where did you get your hands on that?' Chuck glanced at the weapon in Rafael's hands. It was an AK-47 using 7.62 ammo, probably made at the Arsenal factory in Las Vegas. No doubt, like many other weapons, it had made its way into the hands of one of the many drug cartels in Mexico. 'I didn't expect to see one on this trip.'

'I meet with many bad men in my business, señor, and I need friends I can trust,' laughed Rafael, 'and *this* is my best friend.'

'I don't think you'll be needing it. I'm pretty sure this was a one-off to warn us against trespassing on this site. There's no sign of Mateo's followers – they're long gone.'

'Cowards, superstitious savages, that is what they are,' grunted Rafael. He waved the AK-47 towards the trail. 'When I return to their village, my friend and I will deal with them.'

'Whatever you say, pardner, but meantime I need you to cover our backs while we look for the Big Stone. Do that and I will see that your fee is doubled again. Deal?'

Chuck knew how Rafael worked – it was all down to money. And if that was what it took to protect his people, so be it. Being attacked was the last thing he'd expected, and he hadn't made provision for it, except for his own personal weapon, an old Colt police handgun that he had stashed away in his own backpack. He was going to make sure he didn't make any more mistakes he would live to regret.

A wide grin creased the Mexican's sweaty face. *Now the gringo is speaking my language,* he thought. 'It is a deal, Señor Chuck.'

Chapter Fourteen

The Mudslide

Chuck stared at the radio transmitter for a moment, shook his head, then left the tent to find Ed, who was probably preparing his equipment for the hike to the Transkal.

He had just been in touch with the professor at the Facility, knowing how anxious he would be about his nephews' safety in the middle of the Yucatan jungle. Chuck sent him updates on the expedition's progress twice daily, but on this occasion he had said little about the attack, playing it down as a minor skirmish with the local Indians. A full report could wait until later. For now he had another concern to deal with.

'How's it going, Ed?'

The engineer looked up from the heavy duty rucksack he was packing. It was sitting on the ground beside the long cylinder, the TFU, and some other pieces of equipment. He pulled at his grey ponytail, frowning as if trying to remember something he might have forgotten.

'I think we're ready to go. Just carrying out a last-minute check on our stuff.'

'Good. The sooner you can move out, the better. I've received a weather warning from the Facility that a hurricane is building out in the Gulf and heading our way.'

'What! I thought the forecast we were given said it would cross the Gulf into the US?'

'Nope. The guys at the Facility reckon it's building faster than predicted and turning towards the peninsula, so we need to move soon.'

'How long have we got?'

'Best estimate is thirty-six hours but I wouldn't depend on it. Just get your data and transmit as fast as you can. We want to be out of here before the storm hits.' Chuck hesitated, then said, 'And I don't want to take any chances on Mateo's followers having another go at us on the way back.'

They arranged that Ed and Johnny, along with the boys, would make the journey to the Transkal, with four of the Indians to clear a path. Chuck, and Rafael with the rest of his men, would cover their flanks and rear until they returned to the campsite.

*

Archie pushed an overhanging branch to one side as he trod carefully behind Acat and Chiccan, two of the Maya with them clearing the tangle of dense undergrowth up front. It swung back, brushing the side of Richard's head and shoulder, but not causing any harm.

'Hey, watch it!'

Archie looked round, gesturing with his hands that he couldn't help it.

Johnny, walking beside him, grinned at Archie's reaction. He whispered, although he hardly needed to, with the sounds of the jungle all around them, 'I don't think your brother is too happy being here.'

'I don't know what's wrong with him – probably just the heat,' said Archie, knowing it was more than that, with Richard making it pretty obvious that he would rather be somewhere else. He couldn't understand why Richard didn't show more concern, but he wasn't going to let it hold him back from finding what had happened to their parents.

He trudged on, stepping over thick, moss-covered roots that disappeared into dense thicket. The tree canopy directly above was so thick the sunlight could hardly penetrate the branches. In the darkness his fear of snakes – even thinking of them made him shudder – kept his eyes darting back and forth through the undergrowth for anything remotely snake-like.

Manuel kept pace with Chiccan at the front, advising him on the most likely trail to the Big Stone, but they proceeded slowly as the Indian tried to avoid damage to the tall, spear-like ceiba trees, held sacred by the Maya, as he slashed a way past them. Further on, the trail led them through an old plantation of zapote trees, decorated with deep criss-cross patterns cut into the bark, where locals at one time had extracted the sap, *chicle*, used in chewing gum.

Acat moved ahead of them, stopping to point at one of the zapote trees. '*Balam*,' he called to Chiccan. Claw-like scrapes on the bark had caught his attention.

'A jaguar has made its mark on the tree,' Johnny explained to the group. 'It's something that the big cats do –'

'Yeah, that's just great,' muttered Richard, looking around, half-expecting a wild animal to come bursting out of the trees. 'I knew we shouldn't have come here. It's too dangerous – and the Indians know that.'

'For crying out loud – give it a rest, Richard!' Archie felt he was reaching breaking point with his brother, but before he could say anything else, Ed interrupted him.

'Don't worry, jaguars are night animals. If there is one around, it'll be lying in the sun, having a siesta.'

Richard didn't look entirely convinced, but he said nothing more as they prepared to move on.

*

The group had only moved another fifty yards or so along the trail, hacked out by Acat, Chiccan and the other two Indians, when they came to a large outcrop of rock.

It was a dead end.

'Now what do we do?' Archie stared up at the moss-covered rock, huge ferns and wild orchids growing in profusion along its base. 'Can we go around it?'

'We do not have to,' said Manuel. 'I know this place – it is the top of the cenote where the children of my village used to swim; before the great storm brought the mud.'

'And is there a path?' asked Ed, dropping his rucksack along with the TFU at his feet. He stretched his arms out wide to relieve the ache and stiffness where the straps had bitten into his shoulders.

Manuel nodded. He pointed to a rocky nose-like projection about thirty feet into the undergrowth along the base.

'There is a way to the top, up through the rock.'

Ed didn't hesitate. 'OK, that sounds good to me. Johnny, tell these men we need to clear a path to that rock.' He looked up. They were in a small open patch now, the forest canopy behind them and he could see traces of smoky, grey cloud gathering across a bright blue sky. 'The weather is against us, so we need to move quickly.'

The four Indians started slashing a path through ferns as tall as themselves; sweating, muttering to each other, their machetes rising and falling like oars dipping in and out of a rough sea. They were not happy at being so close to the Burial Trail that they had been warned not to use, and were anxious to return to the campsite and the others as quickly as possible. Wasting little time, they soon cleared a path to the base of the rock that Manuel had shown them.

'Look!' cried Archie, pointing towards a crevice that split the rock face all the way to the top. 'There's a set of steps!'

'See, I told you,' shouted Manuel, pushing past them to reach the crevice. Ancient steps that had been carved out of the rock, twisted upwards through the narrow fissure for about thirty feet, wide enough for Ed with his heavy rucksack and equipment. A minute later, Manuel stood at the top, gesturing to the others below to join him, obviously excited by what he could see.

Archie couldn't wait. He quickly made his way up the tight twisting steps, finding small openings for his fingers in the rough rock to help him maintain his balance on the slippery stone, worn smooth by countless feet. He was followed by a moody and reluctant Richard, who seemed to withdraw more into himself the closer he sensed the presence of the Transkal.

As he left the last step behind him, Archie saw clearly for the first time the pyramid that his parents had discovered. Some of the stone blocks below the flat top had broken away from the edifice and crashed to the ground directly below, probably long-covered by dense undergrowth. But in spite of the damage, the great structure, with its unusual gold-flecked column on the flat top, continued to dominate the landscape around it.

It was a heart-stopping moment for Archie as he joined Manuel at the edge of the rock. The pyramid with its strangely carved column, which made it different from the other flat top pyramids he had seen in the Yucatan, seemed to rise slowly before him, reaching upwards to a darkening sky, leaving him silent for a few moments to think about his mum and dad. This was the area where they had worked the dig:

exploring the pyramid, excavating the trenches, recording everything they found in their notebooks.

His father's notebooks. He suddenly remembered – Manuel had found them here, but Ed had them now. Had he read them? Had he found anything useful that might explain their disappearance? His mother had mentioned the Transkal during the trance at Harmsway, but that was all he knew about this place.

There was nothing left to see of the actual dig or the trenches his parents must have excavated, for a massive mudslide had coursed a snake-like path from the side of the pyramid towards the remains of a building further away. Mostly hidden by the thick undergrowth of the jungle on the edge of what might have been a paved square, glimpses of tall columns and a pediment could still be seen through the clinging creepers that now covered the building. The mud had continued its relentless journey through the dig, with nothing escaping its onslaught until it reached the rock where Archie stood. As his eyes slowly scanned the site he began to visualise an outline of the square, formed by the pyramid, the building and the edges of the jungle – and then he was drawn to its centre.

'There it is,' said Manuel. He pointed towards to what appeared to be a pile of stones in the middle of the mudslide, a couple of hundred yards from the cenote.

It was the Transkal.

A slurry of mud and gravel had poured around and over it, partly covering the stone but most of it was still exposed. From what Archie could see, it looked like the one in the Harmsway quadrangle – the trough in the middle and the strange figures and symbols chiselled into the round edge of the stone seemed to be the same.

'So that's it. Doesn't look like much from up here, does it?' said Ed. He and the others had lined up beside Archie and Manuel to view the stone that was the purpose of their journey. He nodded to himself. 'I think I see what happened here.'

'What do you mean?' asked Archie.

'From what Manuel has told us, we are standing over what may be one of the biggest sinkholes, or cenotes as they are known in the Yucatan – it's where he and the children used to swim. As you probably know, there are no rivers or lakes in the Yucatan; the whole place is one massive area of limestone riddled with underground caves and large caverns. There are places like this all over the peninsula and it's where the people get their water from.'

'That's right,' agreed Johnny. 'I used to take tourist groups to the cenotes before visiting the ruins at Chichen Itza, but I didn't know about this one.'

'Well, anyway, what I think may have happened here is that when the mudslide came, it was channelled past the pyramid and through the low-lying land out there and down into the sinkhole below us.'

Ed could visualise the place, seeing the basin-like area as a meeting place where an ancient people came to market their crops and, perhaps, worship at the pyramid. And he could understand the fascination that this hidden land must have held for Malcolm Kinross and his wife.

He looked up at the gathering storm clouds, and smiled grimly. 'If we don't want to get caught in another one, we'd better keep moving.'

The way down to the rough terrain of the mudslide was easy enough, but they had to watch their footing on the hardened mud ridges as they made their way to the Transkal. Ed and Johnny led the way, the Indians hanging back behind the boys, obviously unhappy at being so close to the pyramid.

Archie kept an eye on his brother, watching for any sign of distress or unusual behaviour, but Richard seemed OK, saying nothing as he listened to Manuel chattering almost incessantly about the landscape and how it looked before the mudslide.

When they reached the Transkal, Ed immediately began setting up his equipment. He asked one of the Indians to clear away some of the mud beside the stone to give him a flat base to place the TFU. Once the legs were extended, the unit positioned and stabilised, Ed switched it on.

'This will take a few minutes. Once I have everything keyed in, I'll be able to hook up to the satellite,' he paused and grinned, 'provided the professor's friends at NASA have it in place. Then you and Richard can stand by while I programme the coordinates here – after that, we'll just have to wait and see what happens. That OK with you?'

Archie nodded. He knew this whole trip was about tracing and tracking timecracks and that Richard's special power – no matter how reluctant he was to use it – might help them do just that, but it was also about finding their parents. It was all highly experimental and no one had any idea what would happen, if and when, the TFU made contact with a timecrack.

He looked round and saw that Richard had climbed onto the Transkal, while Johnny and Manuel walked around the edge examining the carvings on top of the stone. He was about to join Richard when he heard Johnny call across to them.

'Over here!'

He was looking closely at one of the carvings, his finger tracing the outline in the stone. Archie leapt up onto the top of the mud-streaked stone to see what it was that had caught his interest.

'Look at this – it's the same mark as on Richard's shoulder!'

Sure enough, there it was. Although the stone was very old and weather-worn, Archie could see that it was the same mark: a triangle with a vertical bar in the centre and a flattened circle above the apex. He couldn't understand it – what did it mean? What was it doing amongst all the other carvings on the Transkal?

He turned to ask Richard what he thought, but what he saw shocked him. Richard had gone deathly pale, his eyes were wide open with horror, his arms outstretched as if he were trying to ward off some fiendish demon.

It was then that Richard started screaming.

*

At first, the Transkal welcomed him.

He felt its power reaching out as a friendly embrace, with no warning of what was to come. The stone felt solid and safe, and from its position in the middle of the arena he could see the edifice as it was long ago. Great towering white columns tapered towards a massive pediment, its triangular expanse containing a vertical wand with what might be described as a cloud above the apex. Below, on the steps a column of white-skinned men entered the edifice through tall golden doors carrying a golden casket; priestesses in white robes followed behind, their heads bowed, as if in prayer.

This was the temple of the Copanatecs.

The scene slowly faded to be replaced by a series of dream-like visions of events that had taken place in the sacred temple over the millennia.

The Copnatecs were long gone, unknown by others on the peninsula who came after them. Later, a pyramid would be built over the temple by a new people, the Arnaks, who would violate the stone with their sacrifices and worship new gods, never understanding its true purpose.

Richard saw these events as if played back to him in old newsreels, but soon something more sinister began to form around him. It became very dark. Images of people he had never seen before began swirling around him in a violent maelstrom, reaching out as if they wanted to welcome him into their company.

A familiar figure approached; the sightless eyes, the blood-stained cheeks had returned to haunt him. Mateo swept across the Transkal, both arms outstretched towards Richard.

It was then that he started screaming ...

*

Oh no, not again! thought Archie.

He dashed across the stone and, in spite of Richard's flailing arms, dragged him away from the centre of the Transkal.

'Give him to me,' shouted Ed, reaching up to grab him.

The rain and the thunder came so unexpectedly, it startled all of them. Day was turning to night and the Indians were shouting and pointing towards the pyramid. A blue cloud with a pulsing inner light was rapidly approaching the Transkal.

'Oh, my God, it's a timecrack!' yelled Archie. 'We've got to get out of here!'

He turned to see where everyone was. The Indians were running back towards the cenote. Ed had his arm around Richard and was pulling him away from the Transkal. Johnny was still on the other side near the carving he had been looking at, but there was no sign of Manuel.

Archie called out to Ed, 'Where's Manuel?'

'Behind you in the – '

Without warning, there was a mighty clap of thunder. A blue cloud descended so quickly and disappeared again that Archie could hardly believe he had seen it. He blinked and looked again, but Johnny was gone.

He looked down and saw that Manuel was lying face down in the trough, his arms over his head as if trying to protect himself from the rain which was now falling heavily in great drops over the stone.

'Get out of there, Manuel. We have to leave here, fast!'

Archie reached a hand down to help him out of the trough, but he seemed to be frozen stiff, frightened and unable to move.

'Manuel, get up! We have to go!'

But it was too late. Another thunderclap roared above them and the bright yellow light intensified as they were sucked into the timecrack.

Chapter Fifteen

The Notebooks

'Let's get on with it, Ed' said Chuck. He was sprawled across an old leather sofa in the professor's office, but his laid-back appearance belied his true feelings about their journey into the Yucatan jungle ten days earlier. 'I'm still not clear about what happened back at the pyramid.'

'Neither am I.' A grim expression on the professor's face said it all. As far as he was concerned the expedition to the Yucatan to find the Transkal had turned into a total disaster. Not only had he lost Archie to a timecrack, along with Manuel and Johnny Sanchez the guide, but Richard was now recovering in the Facility clinic under the watchful eye of the formidable Nurse Buckley.

He looked at the two men who had returned from the expedition with the news he had least wanted to hear. 'Look, I'm not blaming either of you for what happened, but I need to know exactly what took place down there, where we stand now and what our options are, before we make another move. So, Ed, you've been in touch with Krippitz, what's the latest news there?'

Ed glanced up from the leather-bound notebook he was holding. He was sitting in a matching leather club chair opposite Chuck, a deep frown creasing his high forehead. Lack of sleep and his long, iron-grey hair, normally tied in a neat ponytail, now hanging loose around his collar, gave him an unusual, out of character, dishevelled look.

'Well, Professor, you may not be apportioning blame but I have to accept that what happened at the Transkal was, in part at least, my fault.'

'How so?'

'To put it bluntly, the Timecrack Field Unit is too damned powerful and I should have known that. I designed it based on the information Dr Shah's engineers sent me, but I had no idea how much energy such a small amount of vallonium would unleash. In fact, I now know that the cube of vallonium we used in the TFU could supply the energy needs of a city like Chicago for a year!'

'My God!' The professor stared at Ed in disbelief. He put a hand to his head and thought of the vallonium they had used in the construction of the new timecrack chamber in the centre of the DONUT. 'We should have known ... we should – '

'No point in kicking yourself, professor – or you either, Ed,' said Chuck, rising from the sofa to move to the percolator on a stand near the door to pour some coffee. 'It's easy being smart after the trouble's done and dusted. I'm not too happy about my own part in all this, but the big question is what do we do now?'

Ed sat back in the chair, feeling a little better by what Chuck had just said. Deep down, he realised that what had happened at the Transkal wasn't totally his fault, but he knew that rushing into some sort of rescue plan could lead them into an even bigger disaster.

He shuddered inwardly at the memory of the timecracks descending upon them so unexpectedly, so rapidly. Ed remembered looking up from the TFU to see Archie struggling with Richard, pushing him off the Transkal into his arms, urging them both to run. He had managed to get Richard behind a large rock at the edge of the mudslide before dashing back to the side of the great stone, just in time to see Johnny looking up in amazement as the cloud approached. One minute he was there, the next ... he was gone, as if consumed by the cloud. It was at that moment, he sensed that the TFU was the problem: not only was it sourcing and tracking timecracks – it was attracting them! Throwing himself onto the ground as another blue cloud approached he had crawled to the unit and pulled a cable free, disconnecting the power pack. But it was too late for Archie and Manuel – they too had disappeared.

He shook the memory aside and looked at the professor. 'You asked me about Dr Krippitz. Well, there is some good news; some of the data reached him before I shut the TFU down, so he was able to follow the timecrack traces back to Amasia. From what you've told me, you would expect them to end up in the Exploding Park.' Ed allowed himself a small smile before continuing. 'One did – it was Johnny! They're processing him right now at the place you mentioned ...'

'Yes, the New Arrivals' Centre,' said the professor, reflecting for a moment on his own experience there. 'That is good news, but what about Archie and Manuel, any news of them?'

'Not yet, I'm afraid. There was a second trace, but it seems to have terminated in an area known as the South Amasian Sea. Krippitz says that Brimstone has asked a colleague, Sunstone, in a port city called ... Zolnayta, I think, to carry out a search.'

The sea. John Strawbridge was a big man, in every sense, but for a brief moment he seemed to have shrunk in stature. The thought of his nephew being lost at sea was too much for him.

He stood up and walked to look through a window overlooking the Facility's garden. He remembered how Marjorie, the boys' tutor who had elected to stay on New Earth, had so much admired the unique landscape they had created here. The morning sunlight glistened on small coloured pebbles at the edge of an artificial lake where a gardener was attending to a row of Beaked Yucca trees, alongside a path that led to the clinic. He stayed there silently for a few moments, keeping his thoughts to himself before turning to face Ed again.

'Is there anything else we need to know?' he asked.

'Maybe you don't want to hear about this now, but there are some curious items in the Kinross notebooks which young Manuel recovered from the dig your brother-in-law was working on.'

'Don't hold back, Ed. I want to hear everything you've come up with.'

Ed moved to the front of the professor's desk and placed the notebook he had been holding in front of him. He pointed to one of the open pages.

'This particular notebook is one I've been checking over the past few days. I scanned and sent copies of all the drawings Kinross had made, along with photos I'd taken of the Transkal and the pyramid, to an old friend of mine at the British Museum in London. He was one of the archaeologists on the team that carried out the investigation into the Crystal Skull forgeries a few years ago. I phoned later and asked him if he had ever seen anything like them before.'

'What did he say?'

'He said he hadn't, but would get back to me if he found anything of interest.' Ed ran a finger over two slightly smudged black ink sketches. 'However, after I spoke to him I noticed these particular sketches. There's a little water damage to the pages, probably due to the storm, but the images are clear enough.'

The professor adjusted his glasses on the tip of his nose to take a closer look. The two roughly drawn sketches each displayed a triangle with a vertical bar in the centre and a flattened circle above the apex.

'That's the mark on Richard's shoulder!' said Chuck. He had finished his coffee and joined them at the desk. 'Even the old Indian back at the cantina recognised it. But what does it mean?'

Ed nodded as he remembered the incident in the Yucatan. Johnny had taken them to a ramshackle cantina for drinks where the Indian had become agitated when he saw Richard's mark.

'I don't know, Chuck. What I can tell you is this: all the marks are connected in some way –'

'*All* the marks? How many are there?' asked the professor. He was beginning to feel more than a little confused with what Ed had told him so far.

'That's what I was about to explain. This notebook reveals that Kinross had discovered a new kind of pyramid, and what he describes is intriguing, to put it mildly. In fact, he claims to have found the ruins of a much older structure, possibly tens of thousands years older.'

'But ... the Mayan pyramids ... they only go back about three thousand years, don't they?'

'That's the current thinking, Professor,' said Ed. 'During my trips to the Yucatan, I learned that the Maya built two types of pyramid: one was used by their priests for sacrificial rituals, but the other was not meant to be used as such, only to be worshipped, to honour one of their gods. Both types were similar in construction; with four steep stepped sides and flat tops. They were tall enough to be seen protruding through the jungle canopy. Not only did they act as landmarks for the Maya, but possibly, as they were also excellent astronomers, as observatories. The platform at the top of the sacrificial pyramid very often had a small building or temple where the priests would carry out their ritual ceremonies, which, as you know, could be pretty gruesome.'

Ed hesitated for a moment, collecting his thoughts, before continuing: 'Kinross mentions all of this in the notebook and describes the interiors of several Yucatan pyramids he has investigated in the past. They were similar in that they had doorways into mysterious passages that apparently led nowhere, and staircases that the priests would use to reach the top of the pyramid. All of this is fairly well documented, archaeologically ... but this is where it becomes ...' Ed stared at the notebook for a moment, spreading his arms as if searching for the right word , '... unbelievable.'

'What do you mean?' asked the professor.

'Well ... he writes about the pyramid that Manuel led us to. He'd found a way into heart of the pyramid and found a huge cavern-like space, unlike anything he had ever seen before. An inner building had collapsed leaving only a ruin, but from what he could see with the aid of the torch he was using, it had been built much in the style of an early Greek temple. He mentions that there was a pediment that had shattered when it crashed to the ground from the columns that once supported it, but there was enough of its typical triangular shape still intact to see that it contained the vertical bar and the flattened circle above the apex. It was an architectural symbol that the people, whoever they were, would have seen above them as they entered the building.'

Ed stopped for a moment, waiting for a comment. When none came, he continued, 'The other thing he mentions about the pyramid, but with everything that was happening ...' He shrugged his shoulders. 'Well, it's something I didn't notice at the time. What he points out is that, instead of a temple, the flat top of the pyramid supported a stone column with several glyphs carved into its face. There were traces of gold around the carvings, probably for decoration, but most of it had long since disappeared, possibly to be recycled for other uses, who knows? One of the glyphs – or the mark, as we know it – is also on the Transkal. There are other mentions of the mark here, but unfortunately the rest of the pages are water-damaged, so we can't make out the rest of what he's written.'

The professor sat down again behind his desk and ran a hand through his hair, obviously more perplexed than ever. 'Let me get this right. This mark on Lucy and Richard, whatever it is, has also been seen on the old shaman, Mateo, and now you say on ancient stonework, possibly thousands of years old. What in Heaven's name can it all mean?'

'I can't say, but my friend at the British Museum did say he felt that the pyramid and the inner building were built by different civilisations, separated by a span of thousands of years, certainly long before the pre-classic period which goes back to 2000 BC. He couldn't tell me much more, except that the glyphs on the Transkal were an unusual mixture of different styles of carving, as if one race had supplanted the other, by putting their own messages on the stone.'

Ed sat back in his chair and watched as the professor and Chuck tried to take in what he had just said. He cast his mind back to what Father Higgins said when he and Archie had visited him at the old mission in the Yucatan: ...*The glyphs hinted at a race of people who may well have lived in the Yucatan over twenty thousand years ago* ... He didn't know what to make of it, but all the information they had so far was beginning to point to a link between the Kinross family and a race of highly civilised people that may have existed at the end of the stone age.

*

Chuck made his way through the garden to the Facility clinic. He nodded as he passed the gardener still tending the yucca trees. After listening to the discussion between Ed and the professor, his mind was now fixed on a course of action he knew he had to take. But he needed more information and he was hoping Richard could provide it.

He didn't feel any sense of guilt by what had happened in the Yucatan – he'd experienced his share of failed operations during his time in the military, but it was something you assessed and learned from, then you put it behind you and moved on to the next task. And that's what he intended to do.

After all that had occurred at the campsite and the Transkal, the return journey along the Burial Trail back to the pickups had proved uneventful. With no sign of Mateo's followers threatening them again, Rafael had made a great show of bringing them back safely. No doubt, trying to justify his double fee, thought Chuck.

Looking back on it, when the attack came it had probably been no more than a few young hotheads trying to prove how brave they were. He wondered if Rafael would carry out his boast that he would deal with them. No matter, as far as he was concerned it was now ancient history and he had other things to worry about.

He arrived at the clinic, entering through a set of stainless steel and glass doors to be met by a tall, athletic-looking, dark-haired woman leaving the reception desk, clutching a clipboard. Attractively dressed in a crisp white uniform, she possessed a piercing blue-eyed look that made it clear, as the charge nurse, she brooked no nonsense from visitors.

'Good day, Mr Winters. Here again to see Richard?'

Chuck nodded. Why was it, he thought, every time he spoke to Nurse Buckley he had the unsettling feeling of being interrogated? 'Yes, Nurse, if it's all right with you I would like to see him for a few minutes.'

'Well, make sure it's no more than a few minutes. He's still recovering from the stress over whatever it was he encountered in Mexico, and we don't want to see him suffering a relapse.'

'I understand. Is he OK now?'

'It's hard to say. Dr Wells, his psychiatrist, thinks his condition is linked to worries about his family, and when he comes to terms with whatever it is that's bothering him, he will be fine. That's all I can tell you. So please, don't go upsetting him.'

'I wouldn't dream of it, Nurse Buckley. I'll treat him like a little puppy-dog.'

She stared at him for a moment, then said, 'I hope so. He's out on the veranda, same room as before.'

Chuck made his way to a room at the end of a short corridor and found the door ajar. He knocked and walked in. A young Mexican nurse was making up the bed, fixing the sheets and fluffing up the pillow. She recognised him from his previous visit and nodded towards the open patio door leading to a stone-paved veranda. 'He's out there, señor.'

Chuck smiled at her, 'Thanks, Nurse, I'll only be a few minutes.' He stepped out onto the veranda to find Richard sitting at a white plastic patio table, tapping the keys on a laptop.

'Hi, pardner, keeping yourself busy, I see.' said Chuck. He had lapsed into his folksy, cowboy style of speaking when dealing with young people, but he was about to realise that Richard was no longer the boy he once knew. He dropped his Stetson on the floor and pulled up another chair to the table.

'I was Googling stuff about dad. I'd never really thought much about it before, but now ... well, it's just that ...' the words trailed away and Richard went silent. He was quiet for a moment, looking at the laptop screen. Chuck said nothing and waited. 'He was ... I mean ... he's really famous. There's a lot here about him ... and mum, too. They both discovered a lot of things in Mexico, but I never paid any attention to it before.'

Chuck listened quietly, observing the boy in front of him. It sounded as if Richard was getting to grips with what had happened to his parents, perhaps for the first time. And, maybe, his peculiar ability to get in touch with them. He let him talk a little more, then said, 'Look, Richard, I know you've been through a lot recently, what with your parents' disappearance – and now, Archie and Manuel. But it's something I intend to deal with.'

'What do you mean?' Richard stared at him, his eyes suddenly wide open. 'What can you do?'

'I'm going to Amasia, Richard, to find them – all of them. There is nothing I can do here, and the professor has finally agreed to let me go. But you may be able to help me ...'

'How can I help?'

'I hate to ask, and I'm pretty sure the medics around here would have my scalp, if they knew what I'm about to say. But you're the strongest link we have to finding where they've all disappeared to. That's why I'm here – to see if you can still get in touch, to give me some idea where they might be.' Chuck hesitated, then asked, 'What about it – can you help?'

Richard stood up and walked into the bedroom. The nurse had left and the room was tidy again. He picked up an old exercise book from his bedside table and took it back out to the veranda. He opened it and showed it to Chuck. The pages displayed several rough sketches of what looked like a large building with columns in front and a pediment on top.

'I feel a lot better now, but I still have the dreams. I drew these because it's what I see in most of them – I think it's where they are.'

Chuck stared in amazement at the sketches Richard had made. It was virtually the same ruined building inside the pyramid that Malcolm Kinross had drawn in his notebook. But he had also drawn one that was identical to the painting he had seen in the Haçienda Paz.

'Archie was right. He kept telling me we had to find mum and dad, but I was scared. When I have a dream or go into a trance, I usually see something horrible; something really scary ... and it frightens me ... I feel as if it's happening all around me. Now Archie's gone ... and it's my fault.'

'I don't think so –'

'I have to go with you!'

Richard's sudden outburst startled Chuck. 'That's impossible. The professor would never allow it.'

'You'll never find them without me, and I can't help you unless I go.'

Chuck watched the eyes and the features on Richard's face change, as if a new landscape had suddenly come into view. No longer the sulking, petulant teenager, but a young man who had seemingly come of age. Obviously Richard's time in the clinic had given him a chance to reflect, to come to some personal decisions about his role in all that had taken place in the past two years. They were quiet for a moment, both of them considering what needed to be done, but it was obvious to Chuck what the next step would be.

He nodded, 'OK, Richard, I'll talk to the professor and see what can be done.'

*

It took forty-eight hours and some persuasion from Chuck that it was their best option. In fact, that it was their only realistic option of getting in touch with

Archie or Malcolm and Lucy. And finally, after a clean bill of health from the clinic that Richard was as fit as he would ever be, the professor, very reluctantly, gave his permission for Chuck and Richard to go to Amasia.

On the day of the journey, the professor stood beside Ed at the Parasite capsule, the inter-dimensional monitoring system that would track the journey between the two timecrack chambers. Watching the technicians and engineers going about their myriad tasks as Chuck and Richard entered the timecrack chamber, he turned to Ed.

'Richard is the last of the family. I just hope to God I've made the right decision in allowing him to go.'

Part Three

Port Zolnayta

Chapter Sixteen

The *Serpent*

A huge wall of black ocean hung ominously above the fishing vessel, threatening to send hundreds of tons of seawater crashing down onto the wheelhouse.

'Hold fast, Bran, this is a big one,' grunted Captain Abelhorn, spitting a gob of tobacco juice into a spittoon near the head of the wolftan lying at his feet. He took a tighter grip on the wheel as it tried to spin through his thick, gnarled hands. Bran looked up at the sound of his name, growling as if he understood.

'Don't worry, Captain, nothing will shift that beast of yours while you're on the wheel,' said Orlof. He grabbed the brass rail next to the wheelhouse door, ready to brace himself against the onslaught of the giant wave about to bear down on them. 'This is the worst weather we've had in years – I don't know how much more we can take –'

'Keep your wits about you, Orlof! The *Serpent* will see us home, no matter what the Amasian throws at us.' Abelhorn glared at his next-in-command, not taking kindly to his words. 'I just hope you and the men have both the hatches well secured. We've netted our best catch of hoopers this season, and I'm not in a mind to lose them.'

His keen eyes, deep-set in weather-beaten leathery skin, framed by shocks of long, thick white hair, peered out through the wheelhouse window at the forward deck towards the hatches. Below in the freezer compartments were stored the large hooper fish, worth their weight in gold on the Port Zolnayta fish markets. He saw the heavy nets lashed across the hatches for extra protection and nodded his approval, just as the wave hit them.

He held the wheel tight as tons of foaming white water washed over the *Serpent* as it climbed, then crested the giant wave, before plunging into the trough to face the next one. Above the roaring of the sea he could hear peals of thunder, unbelievably louder than anything he had ever heard at sea. Moments later, ragged lightning streaked across the sky, illuminating the boiling water pouring over the bow and onto the hatches, before rushing through the scuppers back into the ocean.

Orlof was right, thought Ablehorn, there hadn't been anything like this storm for years. Waves bigger than any building on the Zolnayta dockside and the terrible sound of the sea were warning him that at any moment they could be swamped by a rogue wave and lost without trace. His only comfort was the faint hum and throb of the powerful vallonium engine telling him that all was well down below. He had replaced the old engine two years earlier to obtain more power and save fuel, but still he wondered would it be enough to get them back safely to Zolnayta.

Suddenly, a booming clap of thunder followed by a strange blue-yellowish light swept across the forward deck, making the hatches and fishing gear stand out in sharp relief. It lasted only a split-second, but in that instant everything changed. They were no longer in a pitching sea; the ocean was as calm as a millpond and no longer threatening to capsize them.

'What's happened, Captain?' whispered Orlof, worried by the strangeness of it all. 'What happened to the storm?'

'I'm not sure, but I'd wager a hundred dolans we've just been on the receiving end of a timecrack.'

'What do you mean?'

'This is the second time I've seen a storm settle like this. Years ago when I was a young crewman on one of the early vallonium boats the same thing happened then. It's a freak of nature – '

'Grrrrrr ...'

'What is it, Bran?' Abelhorn watched as the wolftan raised itself to look through the wheelhouse window. The little clusters of three ears on each side of its great head were twitching as it pressed a wet nose against the glass. He patted the beast and stared down at the forward deck, wondering what it sensed. 'What is it you see down there?'

The sea was calm and the *Serpent* was rolling gently, now that the storm seemed to have passed over them. But he knew it might only be a temporary lull in the weather. He'd been about to tell Orlof of timecracks and how most people believed that they usually occurred up north in the Exploding Park, but less predictably, they did occur elsewhere, sometimes at sea. Old mariners told fantastic stories about timecracks – how they calmed the ocean during an angry storm, was one often told in the dockside taverns. But he had a theory that the boat's engine with its powerful vallonium core might have something to do with it – like lightning directed to a metal rod.

As Abelhorn mused on the possibilities of vallonium and lightning, Bran growled again, making him peer more closely at a couple of objects that seemed to be caught in the net stretched over one of the hatches.

'Take the wheel, Orlof. Something seems to have been washed on board – I'm going down to see if any damage has been done.'

He left the wheelhouse, making his way down metal steps onto a wet and slippery deck. When he reached the second hatch he was satisfied that the cover was still intact, but sprawled across the net was the last thing he expected to see. He climbed up onto the hatch to take a closer look.

What in thunder has the sea offered up to us? he wondered.

Joshua Abelhorn had every right to be surprised, for at his feet was not a fish from the depths of the Amasian Sea, but a young boy, apparently unconscious. He heard a cry and saw at the far end of the hatch another body trying to rise to its knees. The body stood up, rather shakily, facing him, and to his astonishment, Abelhorn saw that it was another young man.

Chapter Seventeen

The Amasian Sea

Archie clutched at his clothing, squeezing droplets of water through his fingers.

Why am I so wet? he wondered.

It was so cold, he couldn't stop shivering. His head was throbbing and his legs were wobbly – for some reason, the ground under his feet seemed to be shifting from side to side, as if he were on some kind of fairground ride.

Then he remembered.

He and Manuel had been caught in a thunderstorm, and then a timecrack when it descended on the Transkal, moments after Johnny had disappeared from the far side of the stone.

But where had the timecrack dropped them?

The light was poor and it was the light wind whipping at his wet clothes that was making him feel so bitterly cold. He moved forward, trying to keep his balance, but his foot caught on something and he fell to his knees. He reached out and gripped what felt like a rope; then he looked more closely, and Archie saw that he was holding onto a section of a very large net stretched out before him. It was only then that he noticed the overpowering smell of fish, the taste of salt in the air and the sound of waves slopping nearby. A lamp flickered in the distance, revealing a figure behind a large, glass window that seemed to dominate the upper part of a small block-like structure. Lightning flashed overhead, illuminating the structure and the surrounding area.

It suddenly dawned on Archie what he was looking at – it was a wheelhouse.

The timecrack had landed him on a fishing boat!

The boat heaved as a large wave came over the port bow, throwing Archie off balance again. He struggled to his feet, bracing himself to stay upright against the boarding sea. Wiping his eyes to clear away the spray, he saw Manuel lying on the net, several yards away. Standing over him was a dark, broad-shouldered figure, wearing a flat, peaked navy hat, a thick ribbed sweater and rubber boots.

'Hey, Manuel ... Manuel!' He called out again, but his words were lost in the wind. He staggered across the net, almost crouching, until he reached Manuel and the man, now kneeling beside him.

'Is he all right?' Archie shouted to make himself heard above the roar of the sea, stumbling against the man as the boat suddenly rolled to one side. 'Who are you? Where are we ...?

'Keep your questions for later. Your friend is alive, but we need to get him inside. The storm is building again and the sooner we're out of it, the better.'

The man lifted and cradled Manuel in his arms, then made his way alongside the hatches back to a door below the wheelhouse. He nodded towards a metal handle recessed into the side of the door.

'Open it and make sure you close it tight, once we're inside.'

Archie gripped the handle and levered it up until it was vertical, then pulled it open. As soon as they were safely inside, he pushed the handle back down until it was horizontal again.

'Good, now let's find this young lad a bunk.'

They were in a narrow passageway with three cabin doors on either side. Through an open door at the end, Archie could see pots and pans hanging on a rack above a cooking range. The galley, he supposed.

A skinny, pale-faced man, wearing a badly stained white apron, poked his head through the doorway. 'What's up, Captain?'

'Get yourself out here, Daniel, and give me a hand with this lad – he may be hurt,' said the man, shouldering his way into a small two-berth cabin, where he laid Manuel on the bottom berth.

'Beg your pardon, Captain, but if you want any dinner tonight, you'd better let me get on with it,' grumbled Daniel. 'This storm has already held me back with the veg.'

'Stop your moaning and see to the lad.' The captain turned to Archie and stared at him for a moment. 'New Arrivals, no doubt.' He put up a hand as Archie tried to say something. 'Not now. I have to get back to the bridge, or God knows where we will end up. We'll talk later when the storm eases.'

He left them, calling over his shoulder, 'And Daniel, get them some dry clothes, or they'll freeze to death.'

'He's a bleedin' joke, that man,' mumbled Daniel. He started to examine Manuel, who was still unconscious, but beginning to groan and move his arms. 'Fisherman, cook, medic ... and now he wants me to sort out your bleedin' wardrobe.'

In spite of the seriousness of their situation, Archie couldn't help grinning at Daniel, muttering and complaining, while he carefully inspected Manuel for signs of injury.

'Sorry,' said Archie, 'but ... are you a nurse ... or something?'

'Just like you, mate, a New Arrival. Except I arrived on land, not in the middle of the bleedin' ocean. Been here three years now, most of it on the *Serpent*, doing whatever the captain needs done.'

'You're English?'

'London, Hammersmith, if you want to know.' He held out a hand. 'My name is Daniel Bannerman, what's yours?'

'Archie Kinross, and that's Manuel. Is he going to be all right?'

'I'm no doctor, mate, but I was an ambulance driver back home, so I know a bit about first aid.'

'Oh, I see.'

'Your friend is going to be OK, I think. No sign of anything broken, just a nasty looking bump on the back of his head, probably happened when he hit the deck.'

'What do we do now?'

'A couple of pills and a few hours rest will see him all right until we get into port. And now, as the captain said, we have to get you some dry clothes. Go into the cabin opposite and you'll find some stuff in there – just take what you need. I'll see to your friend. Throw your wet things on the floor and I'll deal with them later.'

Archie nodded, feeling relieved that Manuel was going to be OK. He went into the cabin across the passageway to discover piles of clothing on both bunks, along with life jackets stacked in a corner, and a jumble of what seemed to be electronic parts strewn across the floor. He shook his head at the mess and started searching through the clothes. He found a cotton T-shirt and a navy ribbed sweater like the captain's, and a pair of heavy denim trousers that were a reasonable fit. His own trekking boots from the Yucatan were OK, but he felt a lot better with a pair of fresh woollen socks.

An unexpected roll of the boat threw him against the cabin wall, reminding him that he needed to find out where he was, and, more importantly, the boat's destination.

An hour later, after a shower in a small washroom next to the galley, and a meat stew served up by Daniel, Archie found himself climbing up a companionway to see the captain. As he stepped through the wheelhouse door, Archie was confronted by the sight of something he had last seen in the Screaming Forest.

A wolftan.

It growled as Archie stared at the huge head twitching side to side, glancing at Abelhorn as if expecting an order.

'Lie down, Bran, he's a friend.'

The beast seemed to understand, returning to a spot near the wheel.

'I never expected to see a wolftan on a fishing boat,' said Archie, keeping a wary eye on Bran as he approached the captain.

'Maybe so,' said Abelhorn, his eyes peering into the darkness as he held the wheel steady. The *Serpent* rose and dipped as she ploughed through a series of breaking waves crashing over the bow; but the boat was heavy with a full hold of fish, making her more stable and easy on the helm. 'And I didn't expect to find two young men on my deck in the middle of the Amasian Sea.'

'The Amasian Sea!'

The words were out of Archie before he realised he needed to be careful what he said. As a New Arrival he wouldn't know the name of the sea, or anywhere else for that matter. The captain was unlikely to know about the top secret timecrack programme at Mount Tengi that could now return New Arrivals back to Old Earth. It was still an experimental project in its early stages and its results had yet to be made public.

'You've heard of it?' asked Abelhorn, turning to face Archie, a curious look on his face.

'I've never been here before,' said Archie, truthfully. 'I was surprised to hear the name. How far from land are we?'

Abelhorn turned his gaze to the sea again. Foam-streaked waves broke the blackness of the ocean, and although he could feel the pounding of the sea against the hull, he knew they were through the worst of the storm.

'The storm's easing. A day should see us into port.' He glanced at Archie for a moment, taking in the confident bearing of the young man now standing beside him. The mop of dark curly hair that lay across his brow, above strongly chiselled features, reminded him of his son, lost at sea four years earlier. Suddenly, as if he had just made up his mind about something, he called out,' Orlof, get your hide over here and take the wheel. I'm going down below with the lad for a hot drink. I'll send a brew up to you – just make sure you stay steady on this course.'

Orlof, a short, stocky man with closely-cropped grey hair and the deeply-lined features of a seasoned mariner, nodded and took the wheel while Abelhorn led the way down the companionway, with Bran loping closely behind. Archie followed them into the galley and saw two men sitting at a narrow wooden table; both were wearing thick flannel shirts tucked into long rubber leggings, braces hanging at their sides.

'Right, lad, I'd better have your name if I'm going to introduce you to these two scoundrels,' said Abelhorn, smiling as he sat down on a bench opposite them. 'Set yourself down here.'

'Uh ... yes, I suppose so,' said Archie, taking a place beside him. The two crewmen were looking him over, as if he were an alien from outer space, which in a sense he was. 'My name is Archie Kinross, and my friend's name is Manuel.'

'Good, that'll do for a start.' Abelhorn nodded towards one of the crewmen. 'Meet Quig, our mainliner.'

Archie found it hard not to stare at Quig, for he had a vicious-looking, crescent-shaped scar that curled around his right eye and ear. He learned later that Quig was descended from one of the ancient farming tribes of Amasia, but had elected to become a mainliner because of the money that could be made fishing for the giant hooper fish. His job was to cast thousands of feet of mainline chain baited with small fish on steel hooks attached along the length of the chain, into the sea. Afterwards, if they had a successful drop, he and the other men would haul the mainline in, killing the hooper fish with a stun gun. Then the fish would be gutted, cleaned and stored in the ice compartments that made up a large part of the hold..

Unfortunately for Quig, on a previous trip through a raging sea, the mainline had jumped off the drum, lodging one of the hooks into the side of his face. Instinctively, knowing that he could be hauled into the sea by a running mainline, Quig had ripped it out, almost dislodging his eye and cheekbone. The scar was the result of Daniel's emergency handiwork.

'Hi ... nice to meet you ...' said Archie. He felt very much out of place here, not knowing what to say, or what to expect from these people.

Quig stared at him, but said nothing.

'And this fine-looking fellow is Tinkey, the fastest bait man you ever saw,' continued Abelhorn. He reached across to the middle of the table for a tall stone jug and poured two glasses of a dark, honey-coloured liquid, one he handed to Archie.

Tinkey was a small, handsome young man with the deep, brown eyes and coffee-coloured skin common to the Salakins, the dominant tribe in Amasia. Thin and wiry, he reminded Archie of Captain Hanki, the commander of the Fourth Lancers, who had rescued him, along with Richard, Uncle John and Marjorie, from the dinosaurs in the Exploding Park when they had first arrived in Amasia. It was Tinkey's job to bait the hooks on the mainline with small fish as it reeled off the drum towards Quig.

'It's Sticklejuice!' Archie coughed and spluttered, as the fiery liquid caught the back of his throat. Earlier, when he had been in the galley on his own, Daniel had served up a salty stew and it had left him thirsty. Now he had taken a large gulp from the glass before he realised what it was. He put it down and with the back of his hand wiped several drops from his chin.

Tinkey laughed out loud and said, 'It's a seaman's drink, not the monk's tonic they serve to children.'

'That's true,' said Abelhorn, 'but tell me something – how did you know it was Sticklejuice?'

'I'm not sure what you mean,' said Archie. This wasn't true; he had a pretty good idea what Abelhorn was asking, but he needed time to think before he said any more.

'Well, Archie, let me put it this way. It's obvious you and your friend are New Arrivals. Nothing unusual about that, it's happening all the time; although, in my experience, it doesn't happen too often in the middle of the ocean.' Abelhorn stopped for a moment to drink some Sticklejuice, then continued. 'But what I don't understand, Archie, is how a New Arrival who has never been here before knows about Sticklejuice? As far as I know, it's unique to this world. And earlier, it seemed as if wolftans and the Amasian Sea were not unknown to you. How can this be, I ask myself.'

Archie held the glass of Sticklejuice cupped in his hands, gazing into it as if it were a crystal ball, but there was no help there. He was on his own and he was caught somewhere between saying nothing and telling the truth. His face felt flushed and he could feel the three of them staring at him, waiting for an answer.

'You're right, I have been here before. Well ... not here in the sea but to Amasia ... the Exploding Park, to be exact.'

Abelhorn was incredulous. 'You have travelled through *two* timecracks?' He thought for a moment. 'But that must mean ... that, somehow, you were able to return to your own world, and now you have arrived here a second time!'

'Yes, that's about it,' said Archie. He put his glass back on the table, not sure what to say next, but he was saved by Daniel coming over to the table.

'The boy's awake, Captain, but he's nervous and frightened and keeps asking where he is. I gave him some stew, but he hasn't touched it. I think Archie had better see him and explain things.'

Abelhorn stood up and nodded to Archie. 'Very well, we'll talk later in the morning. There is more I would like to discuss with you, but you had better attend to your friend.'

'Yes, I think I'd better,' said Archie, grateful for the extra time to think about how he was going to answer Ablehorn's questions.

He made his way to the cabin he was sharing with Manuel. He found him sitting on the bottom bunk, arms wrapped around knees close to his chest. His eyes were wide open with apprehension until Archie stepped into the cabin.

'Archie! Where were you? What has happened to us? What –'

'Whoa, Manuel, take it easy. Just listen for a few minutes and I'll explain.'

Manuel was frightened and confused by the strange surroundings in which he found himself and he kept interrupting as Archie tried his best to make him understand that they were on a fishing boat in another world.

'There is nothing we can do until we land. And we have to trust that Captain Abelhorn will get us there safely. Then I have to find a way to contact Dr Shah at Mount Tengi. I know he will help us to return home.'

Manuel considered all that Archie had told him, but he was still confused and worried about what would happen.

'Is this new world the place where your parents are?'

'I think so, but I don't know exactly where. It's something I intend to find out.'

He had a lot to think about, but there was nothing to be done until the *Serpent* reached port.

'Let's get some sleep, Manuel. I've a feeling we're going to need it.'

Chapter Eighteen

Approaching Port

The next morning, the sea mist that had been the *Serpent's* constant companion for the past few hours began to thin as a blazing vermillion sun made its way across a purple-blue sky, revealing a distant shoreline. To the north, a series of tall, white water spouts rose above the ocean, like a magical fountain reaching for the sky, before returning to crash against a spiny barrier of black rock, barely visible above the waves.

'What's that?' asked Archie. He leaned against the grab rail next to Captain Abelhorn on the helm, while he peered through the wheelhouse window to get a better look at the spectacular water display. 'It looks pretty rough over there.'

'The Dragon Banks,' said Abelhorn. 'When the sea is calm you can see its black spine, but on a night like last night you want to give it a wide berth, or you'll be like many a poor soul and sent to a watery grave.' He turned his head and spat a gob of tobacco juice into the spittoon. Archie flinched at the sound of spit hitting the copper container. 'I know, I know ... it's a dirty habit, as my granddaughter keeps reminding me, but I only use it when I'm on the helm. Helps me concentrate.'

Archie averted his eyes from the spittoon and turned his gaze back to the banks. 'Have there been many shipwrecks out there?'

'A few, but nothing like the White Waters further to the south,' said Abelhorn. For a brief moment, Archie detected a pained expression appearing on the captain's face. 'No sane man should go there if he wants to keep his boat safe.'

'Why is that?' asked Archie, wondering if he meant the White Waters or the Dragon Banks.

Abelhorn ignored the question. Instead, he pointed towards the shoreline. 'The banks mark the approach to Port Zolnayta; keep them well to starboard,' he said, pointing to the right of the ship, 'and you're on course for the harbour.'

Archie nodded but said nothing. His mind was still preoccupied with what he and Abelhorn had discussed shortly after he had entered the wheelhouse an hour earlier. A disturbed night listening to Manuel tossing and muttering in his sleep had forced him to leave his bunk early, get washed and dressed, then make his way to the galley where Daniel served him a breakfast of bread and spiced meat along with a large glass of fruit juice.

'That's all I can offer you, mate. At this stage of the trip there's not much in the stores to choose from,' said Daniel. 'What about your friend – is he having breakfast?'

Archie took a gulp of his juice, then shrugged. 'I don't know. He's still asleep, but I'm not sure it's doing him any good. He seems to be very restless.'

'I'll keep an eye on him,' promised Daniel, placing more meat on Archie's plate. 'But there's not much more I can do. He might have concussion from that knock on the head. If so, we'll be into port shortly and the doc at the clinic can check him out.'

Archie nodded and agreed that was all they could do. He ate his breakfast and looked around the galley. There was no sign of the crew. Tinkey, Orlof and Quig had already eaten and left to take up their duties.

'We sailed short-handed this trip,' said Daniel, discarding the apron he was wearing 'So we all have to pitch in to prepare the fish crates for unloading at the dock. I have to join them. Just take your time and I'll see you later.'

That's OK, thought Archie. It suited him to be on his own for a little while, at least until he figured out how much he should tell Abelhorn. Slowly, he finished his breakfast, then placed his plate in the dishwasher next to the sink, along with others left by the crew. He made his way to the wheelhouse, zipping up the navy and yellow storm jacket he had found in the cabin store. It was a little big for him but it kept out the sharp wind blowing across the *Serpent*.

He told Abelhorn most of the truth. How he and Richard, along with Uncle John and Marjorie, had arrived in Amasia. He recounted the adventures and the many dangers they had faced, including the destruction of the Arnaks' Sacred Temple, and their time at Harmsway College. Finally, their return to the Facility on Old Earth, but because of his promise to Uncle John and Dr Shah, Archie couldn't tell him the whole truth.

Remember, Archie, Uncle John had said, *that until all the tests on sending New Arrivals back to their point of origin are carried out – one hundred per cent successfully – then everything we have seen and done at Mount Tengi, must remain top secret.*

As it turned out, much to Archie's surprise, Abelhorn was familiar with much of his story.

'Yes, Archie, I may be out of touch when I'm at sea, but I do read the *Amasian Chronicle* when I'm at home.' He smiled at Archie, saying, 'Much of what you have told me was reported in the press at the time. I must admit, I thought a lot of it was sheer imagination – but now you are here on the *Serpent*, telling me the same story. No doubt, this is the start of another adventure, eh?'

Archie stared at him, amazed that his previous visit had become public knowledge. He said nothing more, reckoning that he'd said enough already.

Chapter Nineteen

The Auction Shed

Two stocky, Salakin dockers caught the heavy aft and bow lines thrown to them by Orlof and Quig. Quickly and expertly, they secured the lines to two of the iron bollards that lined the edge of the dock, while Abelhorn brought the *Serpent* smoothly alongside the huge, grey granite blocks that formed the bulk of the dock and most of the buildings on the dockside.

Once the lines were secured, Abelhorn shut down the vallonium engine and the command console which provided him with the essential information he needed while at sea. He stepped outside the wheelhouse with Archie to the open bridge where they watched Tinkey and Daniel clear the netting from the hatches, in readiness to open the hold for the unloading of the giant hooper fish.

Abelhorn called out: 'Tinkey, as soon as you're finished there, man the crane and be ready to lift the crates. The rest of you, go below and start crating the fish.'

Grunts of acknowledgement drifted back to the bridge as the men made ready to carry out their tasks. Abelhorn turned to Archie and grinned. 'They're tired but they'll soon have plenty of dolans in their pockets to put a smile on their faces.' He explained: 'Trawlermen share the profits of every catch; and on this trip we were short-handed, so it means that their share after the fish auction will be that much bigger.'

'Is there a demand for hooper fish?' asked Archie.

'Demand?' snorted Abelhorn, his eyes widening. 'Our catch will be sold within minutes of the auction shed bell being rung.'

He described how fishery agents, representing buyers from all over Amasia, kept offices on the docks. As soon as the unloading from a trawler commenced, a great bell housed in a tower above the auction shed would ring, alerting the agents that the auction was about to begin.

They continued to watch as Tinkey climbed into the cab of the dockside crane, held for use by the trawlermen. He settled himself on a metal bucket seat and started the task of lowering the cable with its double-loop slings into the hold. The rest of the crew in the hold were furiously packing the gutted fish into ice, held in six foot length orange crates. After packing, a sling was placed around each end of the crate, with Orlof yelling: 'Haul away!' Tinkey would hoist the crate out of the hold and swing it over onto a flatbed railcar which when fully loaded, would be shunted by a small engine along a narrow gauge railway into the auction shed.

By now, the bell had been rung and the agents, acting on behalf of bidders from all over Amasia, including hotel and restaurant owners, cannery operators and exporters, as well as a few local businessmen, had started the frantic process of bidding for the highly prized hooper fish, known to all Zolnaytans as the 'Prince of the Seas'.

Abelhorn was right. Within minutes of the final flatbed entering the shed the last crate from the *Serpent's* hold had been sold.

*

It was also about that time when the first bomb exploded.

'What was that?' The words were no sooner out of Archie's mouth when the loud boom of a second explosion hammered at his ears.

A great pall of dirty, grey-black smoke was billowing across the end of the auction shed, as well as a much larger cloud of smoke and debris spilling over the dockside rooftops from a large, white building several streets away.

Alarms began to shriek throughout the city, while men and women poured out of the offices and warehouses that lined the streets of the dock area. Suddenly, as if echoing the first explosions, another two boomed loudly in the distance.

'Captain Abelhorn, what's happening out there?' Archie had to shout to be heard above the cacophony of alarms and panic-driven screams arising from the people running along the dock.

'I don't know, Archie. There were warnings and threats from the rebels before we left, but nobody expected anything like this.' He pointed to the white building where the smoke continued to spread over narrow crowded streets. 'It looks as if they have bombed the Town Hall.'

'Rebels? What –' Before Archie could ask what he meant, loud shouting reached them from the deck, near the hatches.

It was Daniel. He had climbed out of the hold to join Orlof and Quig at the rail, all of them now watching in amazement as the crowd below them swept past the *Serpent*, seeking safety away from the explosions.

'Captain! Look!' Daniel was pointing towards someone caught up in the middle of a group of people, clawing and pulling, to get past each other. It was a young girl struggling to reach the gangway. Even amongst a panicking crowd she was a striking figure.

Her hair was a golden-reddish colour, cut short with little strands sticking up like bursts of flame on a coal fire. A large, black hoop, decorated with little gold stars, pierced her left ear, matching perfectly the black rings on each of the fingers of her left hand. A black pinstripe blouse, black trousers and black calfskin boots on a slim figure completed the image of someone trying to make a statement about herself, thought Archie. He wondered who she was.

As if in answer, Abelhorn gasped: 'My God, it's Kristin!' He gripped the rail and yelled back to Daniel: 'Get her out of there! Bring her on board now!'

But the Londoner was too slow. As he started for the gangway his foot caught in the netting from the aft hatch, now piled to one side. By the time he freed himself, Archie had taken his place.

He had seen from the bridge that the girl was in danger of being seriously injured. She had been pushed to the ground by the crowd fleeing past her in their panic to get away from the dockside buildings, one of which was now in flames. As she tried to get to her feet a burly docker knocked her down again.

'Watch where you're going, you big lump!' she screamed after him, greenish-grey eyes flashing angrily. She struggled to her feet, a little groggy, her clothes now covered in patches of grey ash.

Wasting no more time, Archie left the bridge and hurtled down the gangway onto the dockside.

'Here, give me your hand,' he yelled.

'Leave me alone! Who do you think you are?'

'I know who I am,' snapped Archie impatiently. 'Captain Abelhorn wants you on board the *Serpent* before you get hurt'. She backed away and glared at him as if he were mad. 'You're in danger here, so let's go!'

Before she could object, he grabbed her by the elbow, pulling her across to the *Serpent* and onto the gangway.

There were no more explosions. Except for a few stragglers still exiting from some of the warehouses, most of the crowd had fled into the streets leading away from the end of the dock. Several men in dark green uniforms had appeared, setting up a cordon to prevent anyone entering the dock area.

Archie and the girl reached the deck where Abelhorn and Daniel were waiting for them. The girl wrenched her arm away from Archie's grip.

'Take your hand off me! I don't need anyone pawing over me!'

'Hey, I was only trying to help,' said Archie, beginning to feel that he should have left her to Daniel.

'Yeah, well go and help someone else.'

Archie stared at her in disbelief, speechless at her bad temper and lack of gratitude. He turned away from her for a moment and looked at the clouds of smoke now hanging over parts of Port Zolnayta. He began to wonder how he was ever going to get out of the mess that the timecrack had landed him in.

Chapter Twenty

Kristin

'Don't worry, mate, she seems to be in one of her better moods today,' grinned Daniel, spreading his arms out wide towards the girl. 'Welcome aboard, Kristin, meet Archie, your rescuer.'

'I didn't need rescuing – I was all right.'

'Yes, we could all see that,' teased Daniel. 'You were doing just fine, down on your knees – for the second time.'

'If you don't shut up, I'll –'

'That's enough you two. Let's just be thankful that you're safe and sound, Kristin,' said Abelhorn. 'And, yes, it might be appropriate if you thanked Archie for helping you down there. It was beginning to look ugly.'

'Why should I? I don't know him.'

Abelhorn raised his eyes in exasperation.

'Why? Because it's the right thing to do when someone tries to help you.' He gave her a measured look which warned her to keep her tongue in check, then said, 'Archie, this is my granddaughter, Kristin. She will help you and your friend settle in with us for a night or two, until we decide what's to be done about you.' He smiled at the two of them, before adding, 'You'll get to know each other, soon enough.'

Archie looked at him, surprised, they hadn't discussed where he and Manuel would stay. He had just assumed he would sort things out after they arrived in port, probably by trying to get in touch with Dr Shah at Mount Tengi. But obviously, until that happened, they needed somewhere to live. At least that problem was settled, but he wasn't sure about living under the same roof as Kristin, and by the look on her face, she felt the same way.

A loud shout from the dockside startled them. They turned to see who was calling.

'Captain!'

The voice came from the end of the gangway. Two men, lean and muscular, dressed in green battle dress and black berets, stared up at the *Serpent*. They were taller than the average Salakin or Arnak and stood behind an older, balding man wearing a badly stained white, factory coat.

'Captain Abelhorn! The army is here. They want everyone away from the dock and the shed, but I need to give you your sales file before I leave.'

Abelhorn excused himself and hurried towards the gangway. After the clamour of the crowd going in and out of the auction shed during the bidding there was now an eerie stillness, a quietness punctuated only by an occasional shout or scream from the few remaining people evacuating the surrounding warehouses. Thick smoke was pouring from the shattered glass of a window at the end of the shed, its swirling tendrils drifting towards the *Serpent* as he stepped onto the dock.

The old man, visibly upset, handed over a brown folder, his hands shaking as he gesticulated towards the shed. Abelhorn stared at him for a moment, then spoke to one of the soldiers. When he joined the others on the *Serpent* his face was grim.

'That was old Andrew who looks after the sales office for the auction with Lieutenant Isula of the Southern Army Division. Isula has closed the dock until further notice ...'

Abelhorn looked upset, and he said nothing for a moment.

'What is it, Captain?' asked Orlof.

'Three people were killed in the explosion ... including my friend, Ben, who worked with Andrew in

138

the sales office. Others have been reported killed in the Town Hall and many have been injured. Damn them! What can they expect to achieve by such madness?'

'It's the rebel Arnaks, isn't it, Captain?' said Daniel.

'That's what they think. The army are searching the city to see if they can trace any of them.'

Rebel Arnaks. Archie felt a shiver run down his spine as he remembered the events in the Sacred Temple when Richard was nearly killed as a sacrifice by the rebel leader, Prince Lotane. Barely escaping with their lives after the temple had been destroyed inside the mountain he had hoped he would never see or hear of the rebels again. *Now they were here in Port Zolnayta!*

'Lieutenant Isula has directed us to leave the *Serpent* and the dock area immediately. He says he will impose a curfew during the hours of darkness, so we need to batten everything down and secure the boat before we leave. Orlof, you see to that with Quig and Tinkey, then make your way home. I'll contact you later. Daniel, I think you had better attend to the boy and get him to the clinic, then –'

'No problem, Captain,' interrupted Daniel, nodding towards the dockside.

Archie looked. Behind an army troop carrier were two sleek, white and red striped vehicles with tinted glass windows. Like most forms of transport in Amasia they were wheel-less, their vallonium power units allowing them to hover silently. An injured woman, her legs covered in blood, was being escorted to one of the vehicles by a soldier.

'The ambulance service,' said Daniel, approvingly.

'Good,' said Abelhorn. 'Archie, please go with Daniel and help him with your friend.' He turned to his granddaughter, standing quietly to one side with her arms crossed. 'Kristin, I'm sorry that you got caught up in this trouble today, but it was good of you to come here to welcome us home.' He waited, but she said nothing. 'Look, I know it must be lonely at times with your mother working in Sitanga and me at sea, but she will be home soon and we will all be together again.'

At that moment, the wolftan joined them, sidling up to Kristin, encouraging her to stroke its neck. She laughed out loud as the beast thrust its great head up against her chest, almost pushing her over.

'Bran, stop that,' she cried delightedly, obviously enjoying its attention. Turning towards her grandfather, she smiled. 'I'm sorry, Papa. It's OK, it was just the crowd pushing and shoving that annoyed me.'

'Well, we needn't worry about that now. The army is in control and I expect they will be here for a while. What I want you to do is go with Daniel when he's ready, and the two of you take Archie to the house and show him the spare room. Will you do that for me?'

'I suppose so,' she said, although not very enthusiastically.

'That's settled then,' said Abelhorn, nodding grimly. 'Now I must hurry and finish my business with Andrew before the army close the shed completely.'

Archie watched him leave, a sad figure with Bran loping silently beside him. The dockside buildings were practically deserted except for the soldiers checking that each one had been evacuated. He turned his gaze towards the end of the dock. It landed on a small group of figures being ushered through the cordon patrolled by the army. One of the figures was wearing a sand-coloured trader's robe, traditionally worn by those who travelled the ancient trade routes of Amasia.

*

The man who wore the robe stopped at the cordon and looked back at the *Serpent*. A few minutes earlier, along with the crowd fleeing from the auction shed he had passed a young man helping a girl to her feet. For a brief instant he had almost stopped to take a closer look, his astonishment at recognising one of the two boys who had caused him so much trouble, nearly getting the better of him. But he couldn't afford to stop; not until he was well clear of Port Zolnayta and the city boundary. The curfew would soon come into effect and the army would be everywhere with their security checks.

Anton Cosimo took one last look at the boy whose brother was responsible for the death of his half-brother, Sandan. He turned away, swearing to himself he would see the two of them dead.

Chapter Twenty-One

The Bombers

A short time later, Anton Cosimo arrived at a tavern on the side of a narrow, country road snaking its way up into the hills that surrounded the suburbs of Zolnayta. He drove the hovercart into a yard at the rear of the building, found a parking bay next to a similar cart and extended the stabilisers, before switching off the engine. The hovercart was a small, two-seat vehicle powered by a vallonium engine, with enough space to carry sample goods to display to potential buyers and was used by most traders who sought to do business in the towns and cities of Amasia.

The hovercart was the perfect cover for Anton, and one he used regularly, ever since joining the rebel Arnaks, shortly after arriving in Amasia. Not that he worried about the army recognising him, they knew little or nothing about him, but having killed a Lancer during his escape from Snakespass Ravine, he was well aware that he was still on that force's wanted list.

He pulled the cowl of the robe away from his face and entered the tavern by a rear entrance. His eyes scanned the faces of the men drinking at the bar, and of those sitting at tables in the middle of the room, before landing on a man sitting by himself in a small cubicle. The man, the driver of the cart Anton had parked beside, was also dressed in a sand-coloured trader's robe, as were several others in the tavern, a well-known hostelry frequently used by travellers to Zolnayta.

As he approached the cubicle he gestured to a nearby waiter to serve him before sitting down. He observed that no one sat near who might overhear what they had to say.

Nevertheless he spoke quietly. 'Well, my friend, you are well?'

'As well as can be expected.'

Anton nodded. It was the answer he needed to hear if all had gone to plan. 'That is good, but tell me, Nitkin, did you experience any problems? You seem a little unsettled ...'

They were interrupted by the waiter bringing to the table a large platter of cold meats, along with plates of bread and a jug of local wine, which he placed between them. There was no menu – the same meal was served up to everyone, and had been the practice for as long as anyone could remember. Anton threw some dolans on the table and waved the waiter away.

'As I was saying –'

'I know what you said,' snapped Nitkin. 'Everything went as you planned it, but why do we waste our time here? Our task is done and we should be far gone from this place.'

Anton smiled and pushed the platter towards his companion. 'One thing I have learned during my time here is that you never know when your next meal will be served. Eat up, my friend, and when it is dark then you can leave. Remember, it is a long journey you have ahead of you.'

'What do you mean – are you not coming with me?' said Nitkin suspiciously, ignoring the food. 'Where are you going? Are you leaving me, now that the soldiers will be swarming all over Zolnayta?'

'Do not trouble yourself. This place is well beyond the city boundary and will not be subject to the curfew. General Branvin does not have the manpower to cover the city *and* the country properly. So, as long as you and your friends stay in the hills until I call you, you will be safe enough. In the meantime, it is necessary that I meet with Talon alone to proceed with the next stage of our plan.'

'The Slave Master!' gasped Nitkin. 'Is he already here?'

'Quiet you fool! Do you want the whole tavern to hear our business?' hissed Anton. 'Where he is does not concern you, but you can be assured you will know soon enough.'

He chose a strip of meat from the platter and chewed it slowly as he supped at his wine. Bright Amasian sunlight poured in through a window high in the wall behind him, cruelly illuminating the features of the man opposite him. He observed, perhaps for the umpteenth time, how ugly his companion was: small and thin – as most Arnaks were – with sallow skin that emphasised yellow broken teeth and the contours of a shattered nose from some previous encounter. He possessed an evil temper which was directed with a fierce passion towards the Salakins and New Arrivals, who now occupied most of his homeland, Hazaranet. It was a temper Anton found very useful as it had taken little to persuade Nitkin when it came to bombing the citizens of Zolnayta.

After the death of the rebel Arnak leader, Prince Lotane, and the destruction of the Sacred Temple, the rebels, hunted high and low by the Lancers, had retreated to their stronghold deep in the mountainous region of Arnaksland, also known to the Salakins as the Darklands. Leaderless now, they had been ready to give up their dream of regaining Hazaranet, dispersing back into the scattered tribes of Amasia, but had not reckoned on the ruthless ambition of Anton Cosimo.

For as he had done with the rebels during the New European wars on Old Earth, he would build an army dedicated to creating a new empire under his leadership, only this time he would succeed. And it was the fortuitous meeting with Talon, the Slave Master, which had unexpectedly brought the promise of achieving his dream, even sooner than he had hoped.

*

Two months earlier, returning with a raiding party along a stretch of dunes on the south coast, Anton had ordered Nitkin and his men to stop at the approach to a large fishing village. The raid on the poorly defended armoury at the ancient fort further along the coast had been a significant success, with a haul of much needed supplies and weapons, including several cases of explosives, now added to the rebel arsenal.

'We will wait here until Deeway reports that the path around the village is clear,' said Anton, snapping his fingers at one of the rebels. 'Be quick, we can't risk staying here too long.'

As it happened, Deeway returned more quickly than expected. Running back along the path, he cried out breathlessly,' There are soldiers outside the village – and there are strangers on the beach!'

'Quietly, Deeway, what is it you have seen?' demanded Anton.

'Something bad is happening in the village. Strange men with whips are herding the male villagers down to the beach, and there are soldiers hiding in the dunes watching them.'

'Soldiers? How many?'

'I do not know. Six, maybe more.'

Anton nodded. He had twenty men with fresh weapons, so the soldiers would be no problem, but who were the strangers? He thought of his options for a moment, then faced the rebels. 'Check your weapons, we will see what danger these men pose to us.'

'Why don't we take another path to the hills?' asked Nitkin, fearing what might lie ahead of them.

'We cannot take the risk of the soldiers picking up our trail and following us to the camp. We have to deal with them, but first we will see who they are watching, and why. Choose four men to guard the supplies. You and the rest will come with me to the village.'

Minutes later, the rebels had positioned themselves on a ridge of dunes between the village and the beach. Unfortunately, one of them, in his anxiety to confront the enemy, fired a shot from the laser rifle he had recently liberated from the armoury, hitting a soldier who now lay screaming on the ground.

'You bloody fool, stop firing!' cried Anton, who had hoped to arrive without being seen, but it was too late. Soldiers and rebels alike were now shooting wildly at each other. Panic had broken out amongst the men who were chained together and trying to drag each other behind the rocks on the beach. Their guards had deserted them and taken cover in the tall clumps of dune grass below the ridge, while a tall man, his face strangely tattooed, stood his ground and stared in the direction of the pitched battle taking place at the top of the dunes.

Soon it was all over. The soldiers and two of the rebels lay dead, their weapons beside them. Anton grunted at the stupidity of the carnage that lay around him, but it was of no consequence, he had seen men die before and it meant little to him, only that it served his purpose.

He grabbed Nitkin, who was cowering in the grass beside him, by the shoulder and hauled him to his feet. 'Look there, who is the strange one with the marks on his face?'

'I don't know his name, but I have heard tales of such a man. He must be the one who raids the villages along the coast, and inland, looking for slaves. For what purpose, no one knows, but it has been happening for a long time. It must have been him the soldiers were waiting for – the Slave Master.'

Anton stepped forward and looked towards the sea. Low black clouds screened the horizon, darkening the sky, while the roar of the waves crashing onto the stony beach replaced the sounds of the battle. Further out, at the end of a wooden jetty used by the village fishermen, an unusually large amphibious landing craft was connected by a wide gangway.

He was surprised to see the tall man beckoning to him. 'Interesting ... He wants to see us, Nitkin, so let us oblige him. Place your men on the ridge, and tell them if there is any sign of trouble from the strangers, to open fire and kill all of them. They now know how to use their weapons – just make sure the fools don't hit us.'

Nitkin nodded. He stepped nervously through the bodies lying around him, giving the order before they descended to the beach.

The tall man, his face tattooed with small feathers, wearing a yellow robe and carrying a long, black rod, greeted them. 'I am Talon of Copanatec. I do not know you, yet you have killed our enemies. I must ask you why you have done this and what you hope to gain?'

'I am Anton Cosimo and this is my lieutenant, Nitkin of the Arnaks.' He pointed towards the ridge where the rebels lay hidden. 'It was an accidental meeting, but the soldiers are our enemies, too.'

'Ah, I see. I know of the *rebel* Arnaks, and their claim to the land of Hazaranet,' smiled Talon, as if the claim amused him. 'Perhaps, then, we can be of mutual assistance in the future?'

'Perhaps, but we would need to discuss what it is we want from each other, don't you think?' As Anton spoke, he wondered what possible benefits a slave master could bring him.

In due course, another meeting was secretly arranged and it was at this meeting that Anton was promised something so astonishing that he realised it was priceless beyond measure, if it were true. Even his desire for the secret vallonium process and other riches paled into nothing beside the promise.

In return, Anton and the rebels would attack Zolnayta and its port, and any other target that would draw General Branvin's forces away from the towns and villages along the coast, leaving them to the mercy of the Slave Master.

*

As Anton reflected on his meetings with Talon, a burst of angry shouting erupted at the end of the bar, disturbing his reverie. He called the waiter, a chubby red-faced man who waddled slowly to the cubicle. 'What is wrong there?'

'It's just one of the customers shouting at the news on the viewer,' said the waiter, shaking his head. 'He is angry at the madness that has taken place today ... There were people killed ... it is a terrible business.'

Anton nodded as if in agreement and stood up to take a closer look. As he watched, different scenes of the bombings appeared on the screen, but he had spotted something else that made him swear inwardly to himself. It was a shot of the boy he had seen earlier, now standing with a girl leaning on the rail of a trawler near the auction shed.

'Yes, but there are those who will answer for their deeds, my friend,' said Anton to the waiter, a cruel smile masking his true meaning.

Chapter Twenty-Two

Portview Terrace

'This is your room' said Kristin, leaning on the door with her shoulder. 'You have to give it a bit of a shove sometimes.'

Archie wasn't surprised. From what he had seen of the house so far it wasn't only the door that needed attention. He put the palm of his hand on it and pushed. The door opened slowly, the hinges resisting with a mournful groan as it swung inwardly to reveal a large, dark and forbidding room.

'Just a drop of oil needed, I think,' he said.

'I suppose so. Doesn't matter much anyway – hardly anyone goes in there, let alone sleep in it. At least, not since Daniel left,' said Kristin, stopping near the door as Archie stepped inside. 'He stayed here for a while.'

'There's a lot of stuff.'

'Yeah, my father kept a lot of his junk in here. Daniel left some things as well, not having any room in his own place.'

'Oh, where does he stay now?'

'Above old Flint's place at the top of the street.' She shrugged as if she couldn't care less where Daniel lived. 'Why do you want to know?'

'I just wondered, that's all.'

She shrugged again, 'Who cares where he lives.'

Archie stared at her wondering what it was that made her so surly. He looked around the room, about to ask her where the bed might be, but she was walking back towards the staircase.

'The kitchen's at the back of the house if you want anything to eat,' she called over her shoulder, 'or you can go up to Flint's.'

'Huh ... thanks for that,' he muttered to himself. And what exactly is Flint's place, he wondered.

After they'd seen Manuel into an ambulance to take him to the clinic, Daniel, carrying an old canvas grip over his shoulder, walked with Kristin and Archie through the narrow sloping streets that surrounded the harbour. As they went further from the dockside it became obvious where the port district ended and the city of Zolnayta began. Although the city was very old, the port was even older, its streets joining the Boundary Road where the newer and taller buildings stretched into the distance.

'Too much like London for my liking,' was Daniel's opinion. 'Driving through it every day in the blood wagon was a bleedin' nightmare. The old port's the place to be as far as I'm concerned – or it was until they bombed the place.'

'Do you think it'll get worse?'

'Who knows? It's up to the army to sort it out – or maybe they'll bring the Lancers in to deal with it. They did it before up in Fort Temple, didn't they?' Daniel had said teasingly, casting a glance in Archie's direction.

Archie hadn't responded, not really wanting to talk about had happened then, at least, not until he'd been in touch with Dr Shah at Mount Tengi.

A short time later, they'd arrived at Portview Terrace, an old three storey house on a cobbled street that led up to a junction with the Boundary Road. Daniel had left after seeing them to the door, saying he would call in later, once he'd put his gear away.

Kristin had shown him the room at the top of a winding staircase and then left him to settle in any way he saw fit. As he looked round the room, which was mostly in darkness except for a sliver of light coming through a heavily draped window, Archie had the creepy feeling he was in some sort of mausoleum. He went over to the window and drew one of the drapes aside, allowing a flood of light into the room. He blinked as his eyes widened in astonishment at what lay around him.

Kristin was right, there was a lot of junk. There were open chests and assorted boxes packed with clothing and other stuff that had spilled out onto the floor. Piles of books were stacked precariously on the edge of a large round table next to an old garden bench that had collapsed under the weight of a rust encrusted anchor. One wall was totally covered with paintings and faded photographs of ships and sailors, all of them covered in a film of dust. On the opposite wall someone had tacked a number of sea charts and land maps of places which Archie didn't recognise, and on the floor beside him were coils of rope and an empty wooden barrel with STICKLEJUICE stencilled across it.

But there was one thing missing. There was no sign of a bed – where was he supposed to sleep?

He looked through the window and studied what lay behind the house. A flagstoned courtyard gave access to the street through a wide archway at the side of the terrace. Beyond the courtyard was a large, obviously untended, garden burdened with weeds and forgotten trees. Long grass encroached onto a gravel path leading to an outbuilding that had been painted black with a semicircle of gold stars around a door Kristin was about to enter. What was that place, he wondered, *a witches' hideaway?*

A sudden shout drew him back to the door.

'Hey, is anyone around?'

Archie went to the top of the staircase and looked down. It was Daniel just inside the front door.

'I'm up here.'

'Thought so. Hang on, I'll come up,' said Daniel bounding up the steps two at a time, joining Archie to walk back to the room. 'Left you to it, has she?'

'More or less. I've been trying to figure out where I'm supposed to sleep – and Manuel too, if he's coming back here.'

'There's another room adjoining this one.' Daniel walked over to the side of the room to another drape partly covering a side wall. He hauled on it to reveal a hidden door. 'This is a suite with a couple of bedrooms and a communal bathroom on the other side. Another door from the bathroom leads onto the hallway and a room at the end that Manuel can use. Kristin's parents used the suite when they lived here, but that's a while ago now.'

'What happened to them?'

'Her mother works in one of the factories in Sitanga, secretary or something, and her father, the captain's son ... well, no one really knows. They say he was a bit of a dreamer, always talking of treasure and lost lands and that sort of nonsense. Anyway, it must be nearly four years ago now that he and a friend of his decided to head into the White Waters in search of some lost island that he had read about. It was a big boat, I hear, but it was never seen again. It happened before my time, so I don't know much about it. All I can tell you, mate, is that no one in their right mind wants to sail into the White Waters if they're thinking of coming back alive.'

'What happened after he disappeared – I mean ... to this place?' asked Archie, looking around the bedroom he was going to sleep in.

'Kristin was at boarding school, but after her father disappeared, she became hard to handle, apparently, so she came back here to the captain. And from what I hear, there was no love lost between Kristin and her mother. It was a tough business all around.'

'And then you moved in?'

'Well, I was with the girlfriend on the Big Wheel in London, having a great time when the timecrack struck. I tell you, mate, when I saw all that light, I thought I'd bought it.'

'I know how you feel,' said Archie feelingly.

'I suppose you do. Don't know what happened to the girlfriend, but I ended up in the Exploding Park, then a spell at Brimstone's New Arrivals' Centre – you know the place, I hear?' Daniel grinned. He remembered Archie back on the *Serpent* having to explain to the captain that he had been through *two* timecracks.

Archie just nodded, letting Daniel continue his story. He was anxious to find out as much about Zolnayta as possible – anything at all that would help him decide what he was going to do next.

'Well, you know how it works. When Brimstone heard that I'd been an ambulance driver, he decided to send me straight to the hospital in Zolnayta. But it was a nightmare trying to find my way around the place. Luckily, I met Captain Abelhorn when he came into the hospital for a check-up and I was detailed to bring him back here after he'd had some treatment. We got talking, and as they say, the rest is history. He was looking for crew, so he offered me a job for twice the money I was getting, *and* room and board. It was no-brainer, so I took it, and no regrets, so far.'

'But you moved out?'

'It's a big house, way too big for me. I stayed for a couple of months until I found my own place above Flint's.'

Archie had a feeling that maybe Kristin had something to do with his leaving, but it was none of his business. Instead, he asked, 'What exactly is Flint's?'

'It's a coffee house, and I've an apartment above the place,' said Daniel. 'It's a good place to eat if you don't want anything too fancy. That's one of the reasons I called; thought you might want some grub. I don't expect Kristin will be serving anything up.'

'Well, she did mention I could use the kitchen.'

'That's typical of Kristin. Her motto is 'each one to their own', or so she told me before the last trip.'

'She's a bit ... weird, isn't she? I mean ... the way she dresses ... and the way she talks, and that place out there with the stars on it?'

'That's her studio. The captain let her fix it the way she wanted, after her father disappeared – to help her get over it, I suppose.' Daniel shrugged and stared out the window for a moment. 'She sees herself as an artist, and that's the way she expresses herself. Calls it *expressionism,* but it means nothing to me, mate. Art's not my thing.'

'Does she stay here on her own, when you're all away on the *Serpent*?' asked Archie. 'I mean ... it *is* a big house.'

'No way. Flint's wife looks after the place and sleeps here when the captain's on a trip.' Daniel sighed, as if he'd said enough. 'Look, let's go and get something to eat. I'm starving.'

Chapter Twenty-Three

Sunstone

They sat at a bay window overlooking the street, watching the passers-by go about their business, while the fat man served up another helping of the delicious seafood stew. His huge belly, supported by the edge of the table, forced him to stretch out his arm to ladle the stew from the tureen onto their plates.

'The best food in the port,' he boasted. 'Isn't that right, Daniel?'

'Without a doubt, Flint. Not only the port, but the whole city as far as I'm concerned. Certainly better than mine on the *Serpent.*'

Flint left them to their meal, his chubby red face beaming with pride at the compliment.

'His heart's as big as his belly and he's as generous as they come,' smiled Daniel, as he watched the fat man waddle a course through the tables back to the kitchen. 'He let me have the apartment upstairs when I didn't have a dolan in my pocket, and was prepared to wait for his money until after my first trip. Of course, the captain vouched for me, but still, not many would do it.'

Archie's mouth was full, so he just nodded. He dipped another slab of bread into the rich stew, wiping the plate clean to savour every last drop. With all the excitement that had taken place, he hadn't realised how hungry he was, but as he pushed the plate away, he was unable to eat another bite.

'He's right, the food here is pretty good,' said Archie. He slouched back on the chair, wondering if he should ease his belt a notch or two.

'Well, I hope there's enough left for the captain,' said Daniel, his eyes glancing out to the street. 'I don't think he's had a decent meal since supper last night.'

They both looked through the window to see Abelhorn striding up the street, the wolftan loping ahead of him, as he approached the entrance to Flint's. A black cat sitting at the door humped its back and hissed, before leaping into the street to escape their presence. Bran ignored it, choosing to lie on the pavement, the great wolfish head resting on the stone doorstep while Abelhorn marched on into the dining room.

Daniel pushed a chair towards him. 'Have a seat, captain.'

Flint was about to return to the table with the tureen, but Abelhorn, sitting down wearily, with the look of a man who has had a long day, waved him away. 'Forget that, I'll eat later.'

Looking surprised, Daniel said, 'What's up? Is there something wrong?'

'It's the army. They've found an unexploded device in one of the buildings on the dockside.' He sighed, obviously frustrated at the day's developments. 'They've cordoned off the whole area and extended the curfew while they continue the search. It means I can't get anywhere near the *Serpent* until they check out all the buildings in the port, and God knows how long that will take.'

He shook his head, then called to Flint to bring a jug of Sticklejuice to the table. 'Might as well enjoy a glass,' he muttered. Then more loudly: 'Damn those rebel Arnaks! What do they think they're going to achieve with this madness?'

Rebel Arnaks. Archie could hear the confusion and anger in Abelhorn's voice, and, in a way, he felt the same. This was the second time he had unexpectedly been transported to Amasia by a timecrack, *and* the second time he had got caught up in the middle of something that involved the Arnaks.

The crazy priest, Prince Lotane, the leader of the rebel Arnaks, had chosen Richard as a sacrifice to the Arnak god, Zamah, but it was Lotane who had died during the sacrificial ceremony when the mountain caved in, destroying the Sacred Temple.

Richard had escaped to join Archie who, with the others, had been searching for him. They had run for their lives to reach a chasm created by a previous eruption, centuries earlier. Two men had chased them, one grabbing Archie's leg as they crossed over a collapsed marble pillar, acting as a makeshift bridge. It was already shaking itself loose from the edges of the chasm as mighty forces below them threatened to bring the mountain down. Richard reached the other side safely, but it was a near thing for Archie, and if it hadn't been for Brimstone, he never would have made it. The androt, with his enormous strength, had held the bridge until they were safe, but as soon as he released his grip the man trying to hold onto Archie fell away into the depths of the abyss. Richard told him later, the man who died had been the one who had kidnapped him from the monastery.

As he thought back on that day, when he looked across the fiery chasm at the other man, Archie remembered well the look on his face. He was not an Arnak, but European in appearance, and if looks could kill, Archie would have died on the spot.

But that was then. What was going on now? Were the rebels trying to bomb Zolnayta and the port into a war between the Arnaks and the Salakins? And did any of this matter to him?

What did matter was the task he had set himself from the beginning: To discover what had happened to his parents, and to do that he had to find the mysterious city of Copanatec. But without Richard's help, he had little idea where to start. Although his brother had shown a strange reluctance recently in finding their parents, it had been his only real hope that Richard would be able to contact their mother again and pinpoint exactly where they were.

'You look worried, Archie,' said Abelhorn, turning an eye in his direction. He poured himself another measure from the jug, smiling grimly. 'If it's the bombing, I wouldn't concern yourself. I don't think the rebels will be coming after Flint's place just yet.'

'No, it's not that. I was just thinking about what I'm going to do next. I need to get in touch with Dr Shah at Mount Tengi – after that, I'm not sure what's going to happen.'

'Sorry, I should have told you. Before I left the port, I was in touch with Sunstone at the castle; he wants you to see you in the morning, so I imagine he will do what needs to be done.'

'Sunstone? You mean, like Brimstone at Castle Amasia?'

'That's the idea; he deals with New Arrivals who turn up here in the south, but he also has responsibility for the Lancers' recruitment depot at the castle. He processes the new recruits and sends them onto the academy in Fort Temple.'

'I see. But I was also wondering about Manuel – if he was alright?'

'Yes, Archie, I checked there as well. He'll be discharged in the morning. I'm sure Daniel will pick him up and bring him to the house ... eh?'

'No problem, Captain, I'll order a cab in the morning,' said Daniel.

*

As they sat at the window discussing the day's events, none of them noticed the young man observing them from a pavement cafe across the street. He wore a patterned robe, marking him as a member of one of the many ancient tribes that made up the outer regions of Amasia. There were many young men like him from the tribes seeking work in Zolnayta, but Deeway was not one of them. He was here for one purpose only, and that was to find the boy and report on his movements.

Sipping a herbal tea, Deeway congratulated himself on how easy it had been to trace the one that Cosimo sought. The captain of the *Serpent* was well known around the port and a few discreet questions had soon led him to Portview Terrace. Within minutes of arriving at the house he had seen the boy leaving with his friend to walk the short distance to Flint's, and a little while later the captain arrived.

He had no idea why he had been set such a task, but he knew that Cosimo would be well pleased with his report.

*

The next morning, after a short run into the city's hospital district, the hovercab dropped Daniel at the entrance to the casualty clinic.

'You continue to the castle, mate – Sunstone is expecting you, first thing. When you're ready to come back, just go to the rank outside and the cab will be waiting for you. Meanwhile, I'll see Manuel settled in back at the house ... OK?'

Nodding, that everything was fine, Archie lay back into his seat as the driver, an elderly thin man, a Salakin by the look of him, drove on to Castle Zolnayta. He wouldn't admit it, but he was nervous about meeting

159

Sunstone; not knowing what might happen to him when they met, left him feeling a little uneasy.

Would it be like Castle Amasia? Would he have to be 'assessed' again, then sent somewhere ... 'suitable'?

No! There was no time for anything like that. He shook his head at the thought. Now that he was back in Amasia, there was only one thing that mattered, and that was finding Copanatec and his parents.

But how? What should he do next?

His thoughts were interrupted by the driver, suddenly pointing through the cab's glass dome towards a huge grey stone building in the distance. 'Look, young sir! We are nearly there.'

Only now did Archie realise they were climbing steadily along a modern road cut into the side of a mountain. The other side fell away steeply into a wooded valley through which a wide river coursed its way to the Amasian Sea.

'It looks a long way down,' said Archie, trying to ignore the sensation of vertigo as he looked into the valley.

'Ah, we have nothing to fear, my friend.' The driver grinned, reaching out a finger to stroke a little blue and grey statuette bolted to the dashboard in front of him. It was the figure of a bearded man wearing a robe, sitting on a rock. Carved from stone, it was obviously some sort of religious figurine. 'Not while the holy one from my village is with us.'

I hope you're right, thought Archie. From his time at one of the Harmsway College classes he remembered that public hover vehicles were restricted to less than two feet above the road, and the valley floor was a lot further down than that.

However, they arrived safely to enter a large public square fronting Castle Zolnayta . The driver brought the cab to a stop by a low brick wall overlooking the valley. Archie exited through the cab's sliding door and walked across to a water-filled moat, filled by a stream emanating from the side of the mountain.

He was stunned by the sheer size of the place. A bridge across the moat ended directly in front of the main gate which was dominated by tall, drum towers on either side. Towering curtain walls extended, as far as he could tell, all the way round the castle, making it a heavily fortified fortress. A bronze plaque beside the bridge stated that the castle, situated on a massive rocky outcrop above the mighty Shana River, was over two thousand years old, and had originally been built as a defence against foreign invaders using the Shana as a gateway to the southern lands of Amasia.

In some ways, the history of this place and the ancient castle sites he had seen on Old Earth, when visiting his parents on their field trips, were pretty much the same, thought Archie. Not surprising, really, not when you think of all the Earth people brought here by timecracks.

'Sir ... I was told by your friend that you will be here for at least two hours.' The driver pointed to a parking bay, shaded by a row of trees further along the low wall. 'I will return and wait for you there.'

Looks like Daniel had pretty good idea how long he would be there, thought Archie. 'That's OK. I'll see you there when I finish.'

He left the driver and made his way across the bridge, feeling a little apprehensive as he approached the open gate. A soldier armed with a laser pistol strapped to his waist stopped him as he reached the gatehouse. Small and wiry, with a broad, dark-skinned face, he spoke with a sharp accent. One of the 'good' Arnaks, Archie guessed.

'Your business here?' demanded the guard.

'I've an appointment to see ...' Archie glanced at the note Captain Abelhorn had given him after breakfast, to make sure he had the name right. 'Er ..., Sunstone the Protector ... he's expecting me.'

The guard took the note and studied it, then gestured towards a side door leading into the gatehouse. 'In there. The office will check your appointment.'

Three well-worn stone steps led him into an unexpectedly modern office, where a stern-looking woman, wearing glasses with very thick lenses, stood behind a marble-topped counter. She peered at his note as if it might be a forgery.

'Sit there,' she ordered. 'I'll see if he's ready to see you.'

Archie went over to a row of wooden chairs positioned directly below a large notice board. Curious, he chose to stand and read the various leaflets pinned to the board. Some described a variety of events that would take place in Zolnayta during the coming weeks, including one that made him smile: A challenge cup zimmerball match between Zolnayta City and Harmsway College Zimballers would be held in the city stadium sometime next month. As he pondered whether any of his old friends from the college would be playing, another notice suddenly caught his eye.

The Ancient Lands of South Amasia

An illustrated talk on the pre-history of

South Amasia will be given by Father

Jamarko of the Fort Temple Monastery ...

Father Jamarko is coming to Zolnayta!

The priest was one of only two people – not counting his mother – who had been able to tell him anything about Copanatec. The other had been another priest, Father Higgins at the old Mayan mission church in the Yucatan. He read the rest of the notice. Apparently Father Jamarko would be giving his talk in the castle museum, situated on the ground floor of the keep, in two days' time. Near the bottom of the notice was a small map showing part of the southern area of Amasia, including the coast, but it was impossible to read all of the names or details shown as another notice overlapped it.

'Mr Kinross!' The woman at the counter called out to him. 'Sunstone will see you now at the keep.' She put down the com, the communications system they used in Amasia, and pointed through a wide arched window to the main castle building, a granite-like stone, five-storey structure, on the far side of a grand courtyard. 'That's it, over there. He will be on the ground floor outside the museum hall.'

Archie nodded his thanks and left the office to walk across the courtyard. He felt a quiet thrill as he passed a row of bright scarlet, torpedo-like, machines parked outside the keep. They were Spokestar Specials, the flying machines used by the Lancer squadrons on their patrols over Amasia, reminding him, all too clearly, of his encounter with the dinosaurs when he and the others first arrived in this new world.

An armed soldier, standing on the landing of a stone and wood staircase, looked down on him as he approached the entrance to the building. Two figures, conspicuous by their difference in height, stood outside; the smaller one, obviously excited, was grinning and thrusting a clenched fist in the air. The tall one had his back to Archie, and it remained that way as his head swivelled one hundred and eighty degrees to face him.

Ugh! Archie had hated it when Brimstone at Castle Amasia had swung his head around like that, and he didn't like it any better here as the flesh and metal head stared at him. Sunstone looked exactly the same, except for the red, knee-length tunic he wore, but there was something else, which surprised him. A hint of a smile?

'Archie Kinross, I believe. Welcome to Castle Zolnayta. I am Sunstone the Protector for the territory of Zolnayta and its citizens. I – '

'Archie, I have been accepted for the Lancer Academy! Look – my certificate!' The small figure waved a sheet of paper in the air, not thinking in his excitement, that he had interrupted the protector.

As Sunstone's head swivelled again to look at the new recruit, Archie suddenly realised it was Tinkey, Abelhorn's bait man from the *Serpent*.

'Tinkey, please leave us. You have your certificate of acceptance, and in due course you will be notified when it is time to travel to the academy in Fort temple.'

The young Salakin, looking sheepish and suitably embarrassed, mumbled an apology, before dashing off in the direction of the gatehouse, clutching his certificate.

'He looks pretty pleased with himself,' said Archie, not really sure what he should say.

'Yes, he will no doubt celebrate with his friends this evening. He is one of the few to be accepted this year, but more may be required if the attacks on Zolnayta continue,' said Sunstone, looking up to the soldier above him. 'As you can see with the security precautions we have taken.'

It was only then that Archie saw them: a string of soldiers spread along the length of the wide ramparts on top of the high curtain walls that encompassed the castle. As he took in the extent of the fortifications, two Lancers, each wearing the distinctive red and black uniform and carrying a matching helmet, nodded as they left the keep on their way to the Spokestars.

'I can't imagine the rebels attacking this place,' said Archie.

'Perhaps,' said Sunstone, 'but no one would have imagined them bombing the city and the port, either. Their purpose and tactics are still unclear, so we need to be prepared.'

'Are the Lancers looking for the rebels?' Archie watched as two of the Spokestars rose slowly from the courtyard ready to exit the castle.

'This is only the recruitment centre and active squadrons are not usually based here. However, present circumstances dictate their presence.'

'Do they – ' Archie was about to ask if the Lancers had any idea where to look for the rebels, but Sunstone raised the palm of his metal hand in front of him.

'Enough. I don't think you are here to discuss our military preparations, Archie Kinross, are you?'

'No, not really. Captain Abelhorn sent me here to find out what I should do next.'

'Yes, I spoke with him yesterday. He explained how you came to be on his boat on his return from the fishing grounds. It is very unusual for someone to be transported twice to Amasia by a timecrack.'

'I know, but if you speak to Dr Shah at Mount Tengi, I'm sure he'll explain everything ... I mean, on how it happened.'

Sunstone stared at Archie for a moment, his crystal-clear eyes not unlike Brimstone's, then turned to enter the keep. 'Come, the sun is brighter now and it may be too hot for you here.'

Archie followed him into a large, well-maintained, medieval-style hall. Paintings adorned the walls and glass exhibit cases displayed artefacts describing the history of the castle. They moved to a sofa by a patio window overlooking the courtyard. An armed soldier passing by, gave them a nodding glance.

'This is the main hall leading to the museum. There is no need to go to my office as our meeting will be brief, and I need to attend to other matters as soon as we finish. Let us sit here, and you will forgive me, if we go over your situation as quickly as we can.'

'Yes, that's OK with me,' said Archie. He sat down, relieved that the meeting wasn't going to be dragged out all day, remembering all the tests and stuff he had had to endure at the New Arrivals' Centre, when he and the others had been taken to Castle Amasia. 'But does that mean I don't have to go through assessments or anything like that?'

'No, there is no need for such procedures. Let me explain what has happened since my meeting with Captain Abelhorn. After he left, I communicated with my cousin, Brimstone, and Dr Shah at Mount Tengi.'

Archie couldn't help grinning at the term 'cousin'. During his orientation classes at Harmsway, he had learned that three strange beings had landed in Amasia, centuries earlier. They had entered by way of a cosmic portal from an unknown dimension, long before their own world and its remaining inhabitants had been left to the destructive forces unleashed by a dying star. The beings were known as androts, indestructible life forms, creatures of simulated flesh and highly advanced technology, whose only purpose was to serve their masters.

With the knowledge that the end of their world was coming, the scientists during the coming millennia built spacetime craft to carry as many of their inhabitants as possible, along with the androts, to escape to other life-supporting worlds. But of all the thousands of craft that were sent, only one was known to have survived.

When the three androts appeared in Amasia, they were recruited by the Elders, the governing body of all the territories once known as Hazaranet. The androts were given the names, Brimstone, Sunstone and Firestone, to be protectors, each with special duties and the responsibility of a city, reporting directly to the Meeting House of the Elders.

In time, they became popularly known as the 'cousins', and now Archie was sitting with one of them, again.

'You are amused?' asked Sunstone.

'No!' said Archie quickly, embarrassed at the idea of causing offence. 'No, I was just pleased that I don't have to go through all the assessments and tests again.'

The crystal eyes scanned him for a moment, then Sunstone glanced at a sheet of paper he had been holding.

'This is a copy of a report I received from Brimstone. It states that you passed all your tests satisfactorily, qualifying you for citizenship, so there is no question of you repeating the same tests.'

'That's good news,' said Archie, slumping back into the sofa. He hadn't realised how tense he was until that moment. He breathed out a sigh of relief.

'Yes. All that is required at present is to make preparations for you and your friend to be transferred to Mount Tengi, but that will take a day or so due to the security position.' Sunstone stood up, ready to leave. 'Now, I must return to my office.'

'Uh ... Can I ask you something?' Archie pushed himself up from the sofa, flicking strands of dark hair away from his eyes.

'What is it you need to know?'

167

'It's just that I saw a notice about Father Jamarko giving a talk in the museum this week and I was wondering if I could meet him? You see, we met when I was on a school trip to the monastery, and ... well, I would like to ask him something.'

Sunstone expressed no difficulty with Archie's request. As an androt the concept of a surprise question would not occur to him, the answer would be based on whether he could make an adequate response, or not. He suggested that as Father Jamarko would be arriving early the next day to prepare for his talk, it might be best to meet him then.

*

Archie crossed the bridge and made his way over to the trees by the parking bay. He recognised the cab, but saw no sign of the driver. There was a young man standing by the low wall, looking strangely flustered and brushing patches of dust from his clothes.

As he approached the parking bay, Archie's sixth sense warned him that there was something terribly wrong here.

Chapter Twenty-Four

A Narrow Escape

Archie glanced into the cab, then around the square, but there was no sign of the driver. Something was wrong, something he couldn't quite put his finger on – and the tingly feeling he had running up and down his spine was telling him to take care. It was when he took another look through the open door of the cab that he realised what it was that had disturbed him.

'You are ready to leave?'

The voice startled him. He turned quickly to face the man who had been standing near the cab. Archie stared at him for a moment, noting his face was flushed and that he was breathing heavily, as if he had been running hard. Streaks of greyish-brown particles of dirt and sand clung to the black shirt and trousers he wore, despite obvious attempts to brush them clean. He put his hand on Archie's arm.

'Please, get in. We will go now.'

'Hey, wait a minute,' said Archie, pulling his arm away. 'Where's the driver? He said he would be here to pick me up.'

'I'm afraid he was unable to be here. He sent me in his place to collect you.' With his breathing back to normal the man smiled, gesturing to Archie to get inside the cab. 'Please, we should leave now.'

Archie pointed inside the cab to the dashboard. 'What happened to the little figure?'

The man bent over to take a closer look. He looked confused by Archie's question. He shrugged, saying, 'It is nothing, it has always been like that.'

An alarm sounded inside Archie's head. Now he knew something was seriously wrong. He'd noticed that the little figurine was missing, with only a jagged

169

edge of the base still fixed to the dashboard. But what concerned him even more were the blood-like marks that stained the base; and something else had caught his eye. A crumpled up robe with a distinctive, purple chevron pattern lay on the floor in front of the driver's seat.

He suddenly remembered where he'd seen it before, or one remarkably like it. When he had sat in the window bay of Flint's with Daniel and Captain Abelhorn, he'd seen a man sitting at the pavement cafe across the street wearing a similar robe. At the time he'd thought that they were being watched, but dismissed it as his imagination getting the better of him. But what if it were the same man now facing him?

In the split second that his brain processed this information, Archie came to a decision.

'It's OK, I'll walk back,' he said.

'No! It is too far, I will take you,' said the man, once again trying to grip Archie's arm.

'Hey, let go! I told you I'm not going with you.'

Archie wrenched his arm away from the man's grasp and started walking quickly towards the bridge back into the castle. He had no idea what he was going to do, just that he needed to get away as far as possible from the man and the cab. A sudden shout made him look over his shoulder. The man was waving at an old hovercart that had entered the square.

Now what? wondered Archie.

The answer came soon enough. The hovercart stopped near the moat, blocking his approach to the bridge. A man he never expected to see again stepped out of it, appearing in front of him like a spectral figure in a nightmare ready to haunt him. His stomach tightened into a knot at the memory of their last confrontation, making him ask himself what it was that this man wanted from him.

In the weeks and months following their return to Old Earth, Uncle John, as well as continuing his energy research programme at the Facility, had, in conjunction with Shah and Krippitz at Mount Tengi, pursued the work of ensuring safe journeys for travellers between the two timecrack chambers. One of the original travellers, Aristo, who had helped rescue Richard from the cavern, was now a regular visitor to the Facility, escorting new travellers and acting as a liaison officer for the scientists and engineers in both worlds.

During one of his visits he had brought news of the Lancers' efforts in trying to capture the two men responsible for killing one of their own and stealing a Spokestar, and who had assisted Prince Lotane in his attempt to sacrifice Richard in the Sacred Temple. The Lancers had learned from some of the captured rebels that one of the men, New Arrivals, had fallen to his death in the chasm while chasing Richard, supposedly a sacrificial Shamra child. But the other man, known as Cosimo, had escaped and was now suspected of being the rebel Arnaks' new leader.

Archie had paid little or no attention to any of this, not thinking any of it would ever be relevant to him. But from the description Aristo had mentioned at the time, passed on from the Lancers' investigators, the man now blocking his path to the castle, might well be Cosimo. The same man he had seen on the other side of the chasm, moments after Brimstone had saved his life.

But if it's him, why is he here? Why is he still after me?

As much as he wanted the answers to these questions, Archie wasn't about to stay and find out. Both men were walking quickly, trying not to draw attention to themselves from the few people wandering through the square, but they started to pick up the pace as soon as they realised he was about to make a run for it.

'Deeway, you fool, don't let him get away!' shouted Cosimo.

Archie looked around for help, but no one seemed to be paying any attention to them. The soldier at the castle gate was busy dealing with another visitor and up on the ramparts two soldiers had their backs to him, talking to each other.

Would you believe it? A castle full of soldiers and Lancers and not one able to help him!

There was no other way out of the square, except over the low wall alongside the parking bay. Where that would take him, he had no idea, but it was his only option. He winced as he felt the bony clutch of someone gripping his shoulder from behind. Instinctively, he kicked back with his heel and felt it connect with something hard. There was a yelp of pain as the grip on his shoulder was released. He turned to see the man called Deeway, bent over, moaning and clutching his knee. There was nothing else for it; he sprinted for the wall and leapt over it, assuming the height of the wall would be the same on the other side. It wasn't. It was nearly six feet down to a rough, stony patch, thick with surface roots spreading out from the nearby trees, like snakes slithering through the undergrowth.

He hit the ground hard, falling forward with his arms crossed to protect his face. Instinctively, he rolled away from the wall into a thick clump of bushes before coming to a halt. Quickly, he checked himself for any injuries, but except for a few scratches, he was unhurt. He looked through the bushes, staying on his hands and knees while he studied his surroundings. He was on a steep slope, with dense shrub and tree cover all the way down to the river. There was no path, only small open areas of greyish-brown soil and scraggy weeds poking up through broken rock. A large fir tree stood back from the wall, its trunk wide enough to offer some sort of cover. He crawled across to it, keeping as low as possible behind the bushes, hoping they wouldn't see him. As soon as he reached it, he gathered his breath and slowly got to his feet to take a look through the overhanging branches. Yes, there they were, two faces staring down from the top of the wall, but after a moment, they disappeared.

Had they spotted him?

A light breeze prickled his skin, or was it fear? The knot in his stomach was still there, tighter than before. He held his breath and retreated a little further into the trees, worried that they were about to come after him. He lost his footing as he stumbled over what he thought was a thick root. His breath left him in a gasp of shock as he looked down to see that he had tripped over the leg of someone lying amongst the bushes. It was the driver, a deep gash across his forehead, eyes closed and as still as a corpse.

*

'Can you see him?'

Deeway shook his head, stretching himself as he leaned out over the wall to get a better look. There was no sign of the boy, and there was little he could say to stem the anger of his leader.

In furious disbelief, Cosimo stared down at the trees below him. Once again, one of the Kinross boys was about to escape his clutches, and yet he had been so close to catching him.

'How could you let him get away, you idiot? He was in your hands!'

Deeway said nothing. He had contacted Cosimo straight away, once he realised the boy would have to return to the square after he finished his business in the castle. Unfortunately, things had gone badly wrong when he approached the cab driver, pretending to be a friend of the boy. He'd tried to get into the cab to wait for him, but the driver was having none of it, saying that he had no instructions to pick up anyone other than the boy.

Angrily, Deeway had forced his way into the cab and in the scuffle that followed, the driver's head had struck the figurine, snapping it off its base, causing him to bleed profusely and fall unconscious. Seeing blood pour from the head wound had panicked Deeway into dragging the driver out of the blind side of the cab and over to the wall, to hide him out of sight on the other side, but he had misjudged the height of the wall and the weight of the driver. The body slipped away from Deeway's grasp to plunge to the ground, landing awkwardly on the neck and shoulders. When he reached the driver he knew there was little he could do but hide him amongst the trees. His plan to snatch the boy and hold him until the leader arrived had been ruined by the stubbornness of the old Salakin, and now he would have to suffer the new leader's anger.

'Should I go after him?' he asked.

Barely able to contain his frustration, Cosimo looked to the castle walls where he sensed that one of the soldiers was paying too much attention to them.

'Forget it. We must leave before the soldiers decide to investigate what we are doing here.'

'But I could –'

'No! I do not want to hear any more!' exploded Cosimo, his rage suddenly overwhelming Deeway. Then just as quickly, he calmed himself, realising that one or two people in the square had turned to see what was happening.

He gripped the young rebel by the sleeve to steer him away from the wall, when he noticed that Deeway's clothing was different.

'Where is your robe?' he demanded.

'It was covered in blood. I didn't want to be seen wearing it ... so I left it in the cab ...'

Cosimo shook his head, wondering what else the rebel might have left behind that might provide leads for the Lancers' investigations into their activities. There was no time to retrieve it; with the soldiers' curiosity aroused they could delay no longer. They hurried to the hovercart, narrowly missing a couple of sightseers as they sped away from the square.

*

Archie kneeled down by the side of the body to take a closer look. Small insects were scurrying around an open head wound that was clogged with dirt and blood. The head was lying awkwardly to one side as if someone had tried to force it into an unnatural position away from the neck. Feeling nauseous and ready to retch, Archie placed the palm of his hand on the Salakin's chest, hoping to feel some sign of life, but there was nothing, not a beat.

Not sure what else he could do, he stepped back to the edge of the trees, hardly able to take his eyes away from the body before him. Suddenly, he heard a sound up above him. Worried that Cosimo and the other man might still be waiting for him, he moved slowly through the bushes until he could get a better look at the top of the wall. There was someone there, a face scanning back and forth searching for something ... *or someone.*

It was a soldier! Archie left the cover of the trees and started flailing his arms like crazy to attract his attention.

'Hey! Hey, you up there! I need help down here!'

He kept yelling until the soldier waved back at him. Moments later they were standing side by side, with Archie trying to explain how he had found the driver. The soldier looked at him for a moment, said nothing and then kneeled down to examine the body.

While up on the castle rampart the soldier had noticed a trader's hovercart arrive in the square; minutes later he heard the shouting. As he tried to see what was happening below him, he observed the two men as they dashed back to the hovercart and their hasty exit from the square, almost hitting a couple as they left. Their strange behaviour had made him curious, so he'd decided to investigate.

He shook his head as he looked closely at the wound and the peculiar slant of the head and neck. He stood up and turned to Archie.

'This man is dead, his neck is broken. Why are you here – and why were those men chasing you?'

'I told you. I don't know why they were chasing me. I had an appointment to see Sunstone at the castle and it was the cab driver who brought me here.' Archie looked down at the body of the old Salakin, thinking it might have been him lying there. 'When I came out of the castle, they attacked me. I'm sorry, I don't know any more.'

'Wait here, you may have more questions to answer when my superior arrives.' The soldier unclipped a radio com from his belt and made a call, walking over to the wall so that Archie couldn't hear what he said. He returned a few minutes later. 'Sunstone has confirmed your meeting, but you are to wait here until he has the area sealed and searched. He is sending out

Lancer patrols to find the hovercart. Later, I will take you to him to explain what happened here.'

Explain what happened? How could he, thought Archie, when he had no idea what Cosimo and his men wanted from him.

Chapter Twenty-Five

The Kitchen

'Bleedin' hell, mate, you're lucky you weren't killed!' said Daniel. He sliced a couple of rounds of bread from the long crusty loaf he'd brought with him from Flint's. Slapping on a thick slice of succulent roast beef layered with mustard, he made a sandwich and handed it across the table to Archie. 'Here, eat this, you look as if you could do with a bite.'

'Hmmm, this tastes good,' said Archie, hungrily. He hadn't had anything to eat since leaving early that morning to go to the castle, returning late in the evening to the house to find Daniel waiting with Manuel in the kitchen. Munching on the sandwich he gazed up at the ceiling for a moment. 'You're right, at one point I didn't think I was going to make it back here in one piece.'

Daniel frowned. He looked round to see Manuel fast asleep in one of the old leather armchairs beside the fireplace. He'd hardly said a word since leaving the clinic, with the doctor warning that Manuel had suffered a mild concussion and would need to rest quietly for a few days. If only! The past couple of days had been anything but quiet. Bombs exploding, people killed, soldiers operating a curfew, Lancer patrols searching for rebel Arnaks, and now the old Salakin cab driver had been murdered – and for what?

Months earlier, he'd read of the destruction of the Sacred Temple inside the mountain near Fort Temple and of the death of the rebels' leader, Prince Lotane, who, it seemed, had been one of the monks in the monastery. The local press had headlined the incredible story about the Lancers and Aristo the time traveller, and how they had rescued two boys from the collapsing mountain. It was yesterday's news and most people, up until now, had paid little heed to the rebel problem. Yet here was Archie in front of him – not a boy, but a young man not much younger than himself – caught up in some sort of trouble again. And if the rumours now spreading throughout Zolnayta and the Port were to be believed, the rebels had returned, posing an even bigger threat.

So what was the connection between Archie and these events – where was it all leading?

They sat facing each other across the long wooden table, a platter of freshly prepared beef sandwiches and a jug of non-alcoholic Sticklejuice set to one side – although the stronger juice would probably appear when the captain arrived. It was a supper time habit Daniel had developed when he was a lodger, knowing that when Mrs Flint wasn't around neither the captain nor Kristin would bother to prepare anything for themselves, yet in the hours approaching midnight there was always someone prowling around the kitchen looking for something to eat.

Truth be told, outside of his time at sea, and even though he was no longer a lodger in the house, being in the kitchen was the place Daniel liked best; somehow it gave him a sense of belonging and being part of the family. 'New Arrival sickness' some people called it.

Chewing on a piece of beef, he asked, 'Have you *any* idea why the men were after you?'

'Not really ...' Archie hesitated, not sure what he could tell Daniel that would make sense, without breaking his promise to Uncle John not to reveal what was taking place at Mount Tengi. But as Captain Abelhorn had told him back on the *Serpent*, much of what had happened on his last journey was already public knowledge. 'You know about the last time I was in Amasia, don't you?'

'Yes, I do,' smiled Daniel. 'It was front page news in the *Chronicle* at the time, but I don't think the whole story was told, was it?'

'Maybe not. I heard it was about the Arnaks trying to reclaim their land and that there was an attempt to obtain the secret of the vallonium process, but what I can tell you is that my brother was held prisoner inside the mountain and nearly killed there.'

'Yeah, I read that the rebels were practising some sort of ancient Arnak sacrifice in the temple. Crazy buggers if you ask me.'

'Well, I'm certain that one of the men who chased me at the castle today was the same man I saw in the Sacred Temple when it collapsed.'

Daniel's eyes widened in disbelief. 'Are you sure?'

'Positive. He almost caught up with me in the mountain and now he's after me again –'

They heard the outside door that led into courtyard slam shut as someone stepped into the kitchen. It was Kristin. She was wearing an artist's smock over the black outfit she usually wore; it was covered in so many different splotches of colour it was hard to tell what the original colour might have been. Smudges of black and red paint on her brow indicated she had been working in her studio, although it was late in the evening.

'Looks like danger follows you around.' She'd obviously heard the tail-end of their conversation as she came into the room. 'Remind me to stay clear the next time you decide to make a trip somewhere.'

She walked over to the table and grabbed a sandwich, took a bite and then dropped heavily into the other armchair near Manuel, who suddenly woke up to her presence.

Archie glared at her, tempted to say something rude. Instead, he said, 'Don't worry, I doubt if we're going anywhere together.'

'Oh, and where are you going – back home?'

Daniel laughed. 'Don't let Kristin get under your skin, Archie, she's pretty good at it.'

'Huh, I suppose I got under yours!' she snapped, turning away from him.

His face reddened, obviously annoyed by what she'd said. He lifted the bread knife and cut a few more slices of crusty bread, but said nothing. Something had happened between them, but it was plain that Daniel wasn't prepared to talk about it, at least, not at the moment. The silence was broken by Manuel who was now wide awake and looking around him, as if lost and confused about his surroundings.

'Archie ...'

'What is it, Manuel, are you all right?'

'My head aches ... and my eyes ... they do not see very well ...'

'You had a bad knock, but you'll be OK, isn't that right, Daniel?' said Archie.

Daniel agreed. 'They told me at the clinic, Manuel, you'd suffered a concussion and you will have a few symptoms, but there's nothing serious to worry about. The doctor gave me some tablets for the headaches, so I'll give you couple before you go to bed, but the main thing is to rest up for a while.'

They were interrupted by a shout from the hallway and a door slamming shut. This time it was the front door leading to the street.

'Is there anyone about the place?' called a voice approaching the kitchen.

The door opened and Captain Abelhorn strode in with Bran trailing behind him. He went straight over to a tall cupboard, opened it and lifted out a bottle of

Sticklejuice Reserve. Archie remembered Finbar the Guide at Castle Amasia telling him it was the best that money could buy, but it was also the strongest Sticklejuice available. The captain picked up a glass and sat himself at the table while Bran stretched across the front of the dying embers in the fireplace.

Abelhorn poured himself a large measure. 'Anyone care to join me?' he asked. He rubbed his eyes and the skin above his cheeks before lifting and swirling the honey-coloured liquid around the glass before taking a sip. Only Daniel might have joined him in drinking the fiery juice, but it was too strong for his taste.

'You look tired, Captain, were you at the shed all this time?'

'No, Daniel, the dock is still cordoned off to all but the army. I was at Ben's home this evening, paying my respects to his family.' He shook his head and took another sip, obviously greatly saddened by his friend's death. 'It has been a great shock to them and they simply cannot understand why such savagery has taken place in the dock area.'

'Is there any news about who was behind the bombings?' asked Daniel.

'Not yet. Lieutenant Isula and Sunstone also called to pay their respects, which was kind of them, but they had no information beyond the rumours sweeping Zolnayta that it was the work of rebel Arnaks. Although, God only knows what the rebels would hope to gain by such fiendish acts.' He tossed back another measure of Sticklejuice, his eyes landing squarely on Archie across the table. 'And you, young man, from what I hear, seemed to have become engaged in another of your strange adventures.'

Archie heard a snigger behind him. He turned quickly to see Kristin smiling as she took another bite from her sandwich. He glared at her before turning again to face Abelhorn.

Feeling that he was being accused of something, he said, 'If you mean the business at the castle today – '

Abelhorn waved a hand to silence him. 'Sunstone told me the whole story. You gave him a statement, I gather, about what happened to the cab driver.'

'Yes I did, but I don't know *why* it happened.'

'Well, it would seem that you've got yourself into *something* that those men want.' Abelhorn closed his eyes and for a moment Archie thought that the Sticklejuice had got the better of him, but he opened them again and said, 'Sunstone also tells me you want to return to the castle tomorrow to see a Father Jamarko. Is that correct?'

'Yes, I want to – '

'I don't need to know why you want to see him, Archie, but while you are in my care, I'm not taking any chances with your safety. So I've asked Sunstone that he send one of his Lancers to take you to the castle.'

Archie hadn't really given much thought to how he would return to the castle, which was pretty stupid if Cosimo and his men were still looking for him. He glanced towards Daniel who nodded as if to remind him how close he had been to being caught and maybe ending up like the poor cab driver.

'Thank you, I …' he tried to thank Abelhorn, but it didn't really matter, for the captain had drunk the rest of his Sticklejuice and fallen fast asleep.

Chapter Twenty-Six

Father Jamarko

Unable to stop thinking about Father Jamarko and the last time they had met in Harmsway College, Archie kept tossing and turning until the top sheet was damp with sweat and in a twist around his ankles. He had hardly slept for the past hour or so, his thoughts constantly returning to what the old monk had advised him in Miss Harmsway's office. With a sudden jerk he freed his feet from the sheet and swung himself out onto the floor, knowing there was no point staying in bed any longer. He wasn't going to sleep, so he might as well plan what he was going to say to the old monk.

Jamarko had told him that finding Copanatec and his parents might best be achieved by going to the place where they were last seen. Well, they had trekked into the Mexican jungle and with Manuel's help they had found the Transkal, but look where they were now! The timecracks had struck without warning, separating him from Richard who, in spite of his strange reluctance to use his power, had gone into a trance when he climbed on to the great stone. Within seconds he was shaking, his arms outstretched in front of him as if to protect himself from some unseen presence. One look at him and it was obvious Richard had seen something that had badly frightened him.

But what was it that had caused him to scream and act so strangely?

When Archie had struggled to get Richard off the stone his brother had been almost manic as he pushed him towards Ed who had managed to drag him away from the influence of the Transkal. That was the last he had seen of them. Hopefully, they were safe and had made it out of Mexico and back to the Facility, but without Richard he had lost his best chance of finding Copanatec. So what was he supposed to do now?

He looked around the room. A stream of early sunlight poured through the courtyard window, illuminating a framed chart that hung on the opposite wall. He walked over and examined it more closely. It seemed to be a fairly modern chart showing the central and southern Amasian coastline dotted with a string of names, but nothing remotely like Copanatec.

Scores of islands, large and small, were scattered off the coastline like beads from a broken necklace. Looking carefully at the edge of the chart where it met the frame he saw a name he did recognise: THE WHITE WATERS. It was the place Captain Abelhorn and Daniel had warned him about, the sea area where Kristin's father had disappeared. Why was it so dangerous, he wondered?

'Archie ...?

He turned round. It was Manuel, wearing only his underpants, standing at the end of his bed in the far corner of the room. They were in the suite of rooms Daniel had shown him shortly after he arrived. A separate bedroom was available at the end of the hallway, past the bathroom, but he'd forgotten he had decided to share the suite in case Manuel needed him.

'Hi, Manuel, you sleep OK?'

'No ... my head hurts ... I don't think I slept very much ...'

'Look, why don't you lie down again and I'll go to the kitchen and see if I can find some aspirin, or something, OK?'

Manuel nodded and sat down on the end of the bed without saying anything. He looked around the room as if seeing it for the first time, lifting a hand to shade his eyes from the bright sunlight that seemed to be bothering him. Then like a little puppy he curled up into a ball and closed his eyes.

Archie watched him for a moment, moving to the chair beside the bed where, a few hours earlier, he'd dumped a pair of jeans, T-shirt and trainers, which Daniel had managed to procure for him. Dressing quickly, he called over his shoulder, 'I'll be back in a minute.'

He hurried down the staircase, but as he stepped through the kitchen door he stumbled over Bran, lying stretched out on his side, across the stone floor. The wolftan took no notice, hardly moving as Archie tried to keep his balance.

'That's good, he trusts you,' laughed Abelhorn. He was sitting at the table they'd shared last night as if he'd never left the kitchen. 'Otherwise you'd be on your back with his teeth at your throat.'

'Glad to hear it,' said Archie, remembering only too well his experience in the Screaming Forest when the Rooters and the wolftans had dealt with the Arnaks. 'I wouldn't like to get on his wrong side.'

Abelhorn nodded. 'You're right about that, there's not many would get the better of him.' He got up from the table, plates of bread crumbs and the empty bottle of Sticklejuice still remaining, a reminder of their conversation only a few hours earlier. 'Sorry about the mess. Mrs Flint will be in shortly to do the cleaning, and then she'll prepare breakfast. While we're waiting, I'll make us some coffee – God knows, I could do with a mug of something.'

Archie smiled. The captain was probably suffering from too much juice, and he looked as if he hadn't slept that well either.

'Thanks, I'd like that, but I came down to see if there were any headache tablets. Manuel's not feeling too great – he seems to be suffering the after-effects of his concussion, but I'm pretty sure it's the time differential that's affecting him as well.'

'Ah, I'd forgotten how New Arrivals can suffer the time sickness. In fact, it took Daniel quite a while to adjust when he first came here, but he's well settled in now.' He went over to a shelf near the kitchen door and lifted down a flat white box. Opening the lid he fingered through the contents to find a blister pack of white tablets. Returning to the table he pressed a couple into Archie's hand. 'Here take these and give them to your friend with a glass of water. Daniel will be in later and he can look in to see how he's feeling.'

Nodding his thanks, Archie took the tablets and water back to the bedroom, where he found Manuel partly awake and still lying on top of the bed. Making him take the tablets, and assuring him he would feel a lot better, Archie explained he had to go to the castle to find out from Sunstone when they would travel to Mount Tengi, in all probability to be sent from there to the Facility. But to avoid any confusion in Manuel's mind, he kept the real reason to himself: that he wanted to ask Father Jamarko if he had discovered anything more about the lost city of Copanatec. And, more importantly, if there was any prospect of finding it.

*

After a quick shower, and breakfast with Captain Abelhorn, Archie was in a Spokestar Special on his way to Castle Zolnayta. Flown by a young Lancer, who turned out to be an older brother of Tinkey the bait man on the *Serpent*, Archie marvelled once again how smooth and silent these machines were as the Spokestar made its descent into the castle courtyard.

Sunstone was waiting for him as the Lancer brought the machine to hover in front of the steps leading into the castle. The canopy slid back, allowing Archie to climb out and drop the short distance to the ground.

'Welcome, Archie Kinross. You have recovered from your unfortunate experience here yesterday?'

'Yes ... I'm OK. Daniel and Captain Abelhorn have been looking after me ... I'm fine, thanks.'

'That is good. Now, if you will follow me, I have arranged your meeting with Father Jamarko to take place in my office. Both of you will have privacy there and it should be sufficient for your purpose.'

Archie smiled at how precise and formal the androts could be, but at least you knew where you stood with them. No 'back doors' or double meanings, as his mother used to say about some of her colleagues in the archaeology faculty where she'd worked in New Mexico.

'That's great – hey, wait for me!'

Sunstone was already striding away across the main hall towards a corridor alongside the museum before Archie had a chance to say another word. He had to hurry to catch up with him.

'In here,' said Sunstone, stopping at a door halfway along the corridor. They entered a large room, empty of furniture except for several leather-backed wooden chairs placed around a circular marble-topped table.

Archie remembered Finbar the Guide telling him that the androts didn't eat, drink or sleep, and if it weren't for the Elders and the sensibilities of the people, they probably wouldn't wear clothes. The lack of adornment in Sunstone's office reflected the simplicity of their virtually indestructible existence.

Uncle John had discovered through Dr Shah, that the androts, named by an early Council of Elders as Brimstone, Sunstone and Firestone, had been appointed as protectors of the main cities in Amasia. They had arrived on New Earth during the final days of their dying planet, in a universe known as the Ninth Dimension, when immense forces had been released, thrusting them through a timecrack and across the dimension barrier.

Everything they needed for survival was contained within their flesh and metal bodies, created by the masters of their world, aeons earlier. It explained why there were so few furnishings in the office, provided solely for the benefit of visitors.

As he thought about what he'd been told about the androts, Archie experienced the strangest sensation. It was as if a window into his mind had suddenly opened and, just as quickly, closed again. He turned to see Sunstone looking down at him, with that same odd hint of a smile he'd noticed before.

He's telepathic.

Archie had forgotten what Richard had told him about Brimstone and the Vikantus, and later, when Dr Krippitz, at the meeting at the Gladden Plateau, had explained further: that the androts possessed limited powers of telepathy. It was how Brimstone and Targa, the Vikantu, had discovered that Richard was being held prisoner in the Sacred Temple.

Had Sunstone read his thoughts?

Feeling annoyed at the possibility, Archie was about to say something, but Sunstone forestalled him as they approached the table.

'Good morning, Father, this is Archie Kinross who requested the meeting with you.'

Father Jamarko had hardly changed since their last meeting at Harmsway College; the long grey beard and twinkly blue eyes, along with the brown robe he wore, the features that Archie remembered best. Sitting at the table, Jamarko gestured for him to sit opposite.

'Ah, I remember you well. The young man with so many questions!'

Archie sat down. 'I'm afraid I have some more, Father – '

'I found it, Father; it was in the museum map room!'

The interruption came from a monk, holding his robe by the hem, as he rushed into the room past the androt, to place a long roll of ivory-coloured parchment on the table.

Sunstone gazed down at the monk standing in front of him. 'I will leave you to your meeting, Father. Please call me if you need my service.'

Jamarko sighed as he shook his head, watching sadly as Sunstone strode towards the door. He had little experience in dealing with the androt cousins, but he liked to think they should be treated no differently to themselves.

'Really, Felipe, a little less haste would be in order. I know the androts do not share the same feelings as us, but the formalities should be observed.'

'But ... Father, I found the map you were looking for! It was in one of the drawers of the old map cabinets, just as you suggested it might be,' said the monk, pointing an ink-stained finger at the rolled-up parchment.

'Yes, I thought it could well be in one of the cabinets,' said Jamarko, smiling at Felipe's enthusiasm. 'I knew they had an extensive collection of maps and charts covering the history of central and southern Amasia – it's why I wanted to give my talk here.'

Looking to Archie, he said, 'I am sorry, you have not been properly introduced to my librarian, Felipe Santos. He is now in charge of the monastery scriptorium, and the new library collection generously donated to us by his family – in addition to the new building to house the collection.'

Archie glanced up. The librarian's lean, clean-cut features and olive complexion gave him the appearance of someone from a Mediterranean background, and a wealthy one by the sound of it.

'Hi, I'm Archie Kinross.'

The monk nodded, but said nothing.

'Felipe, this is the young man I told you about,' said Jamarko, his eyes closing for a moment, brow furrowed. 'At our previous meeting, Archie expressed great interest in finding the lost city of Copanatec.'

'But, Father, as I've said before,' said Felipe, sounding a little impatient. 'There is little solid evidence, outside of Elmo's letters, for such a city.'

'I know, I know, but ever since Archie raised the possibility of such a city, or a land, still being in existence, I have trawled through many ancient texts to find such evidence – and, I suspect, that is why he is here today?'

'Did you ...' Archie suddenly found himself breathing more deeply at the thought of what he was about to be told '... find anything?'

Still sitting, Jamarko stretched out both of his hands to lift a thick leather- bound book from the middle of the table. It was obviously very heavy, slipping through his fingers as he tried to hold it. Archie stood up quickly, reaching out to push the book across the smooth marble table-top towards the old monk's fingertips.

'Thank you, I'm afraid age is beginning to restrict my movements a little,' said Jamarko. He lifted the richly embossed gold and silver cover to reveal a printed page displaying several columns of strange symbols above a small map. 'To answer your question, Archie ... yes, I did find something. In fact, within these pages the name, Copanatec, is mentioned by Elmo in

the course of his journey through the ancient tribal
territories of Amasia.'

Chapter Twenty-Seven

Elmo's Journal

Archie's eyes were riveted on the book as he and Filipe moved round the table to stand beside Father Jamarko, all of them drawn to the map and the strange-looking symbols. The map was a roughly drawn sketch of an ocean and a rugged coastline, but the faded brown ink and other faint colours made it difficult to read.

Leaning over the table to take a closer look, Archie shook his head. 'I can't make head nor tail of it – where's it supposed to be?'

'This is Elmo's Journal,' said Felipe. 'It is a collection of letters – and a number of rather obscure drawings like this one, which we have yet to place in a modern context. The letters were sent to the monastery, sealed in stone jars, several thousand years ago, when Elmo was reporting on his attempts to set up missions in the old tribal lands of Amasia. They were chemically treated to preserve the pages and bound in this journal by my predecessors, as recently as the last century. I came across it when Father Jamarko asked me to catalogue our older manuscripts for the new library.'

'What ... what do the symbols mean ...?' Archie's mouth suddenly felt very dry. He peered closely at the map and symbols again, not quite believing what he was looking at.

There were four columns, four symbols in each, all of them meaningless to Archie – except one. In the third column was one he had seen before. It was the mark on Richard's shoulder ... and on his mother's ... the small triangle with a vertical bar in the centre, surmounted by a circle. It was also the same mark he had asked Father Higgins about when he and Ed Hanks had visited the Mayan mission church in the Yucatan.

'They refer to the drawings Elmo made in his letters,' said Felipe. 'We cannot be sure of their meaning, but I believe they represent some sort of code –'

'A code!' Archie shook his head in frustration – why did everything have to be so complicated? 'But doesn't it say in the letters what they mean?'

'Perhaps.' Felipe sounded irritated by the question. 'The letters are written in a language that Elmo and the early Amasians used at that time. We have not fully transcribed –'

Jamarko raised a hand in protest. 'I would remind you, Father Felipe, I have now spent some considerable time with this book, and I do have some understanding of what the letters contain. In fact, as you should be aware, it is central to my talk tomorrow on the early history of Amasia and its towns and people. It is also why I arranged to meet this young man today. It was his question on Copanatec, in the first place, that inspired me to carry out the research for my talk.'

Looking suitably chastened, Felipe said nothing.

Turning to Archie, Jamarko gestured that he sit beside him. 'Now, tell me, what is it that seems to concern you about the symbols?'

'It's this one,' said Archie, pointing to the triangle, 'I've seen it before.'

'You have?' said Felipe, plainly astonished. 'Where –'

Jamarko raised a hand again. 'Let him finish.'

Archie hesitated for a moment, but feeling a surge of relief that he could share his frustration and concern about finding his parents with someone who might be able to help him, he told the old monk about what he had learned at the mission in the Yucatan. How Father Higgins knew about Mateo, the shaman, with the same mark on his shoulder, and that the Indian professed to be a descendant of an ancient tribe of white-skinned people – possibly connected to the Copanatecs.

'I've seen it on the big stones. My father named them Transkals – like the one in the Yucatan .'

Jamarko frowned. 'And you say that the ancients may have arrived from this place ... the Yucatan?'

'Yes, Father Higgins said Mateo referred to them as *The Lords of the Cloud.*'

A nodding glance between Jamarko and Felipe told Archie they were aware of something he'd just said. They were silent for a moment as Jamarko turned the pages of the book, stopping at one of the white card inserts where he had made notes on the letters.

'Ah, here it is. The translation is not complete, but this letter mentions Elmo's contact with fishermen from a coastal village who refused to supply his mission with fish. They claimed that all of their catch had to go to the white-skins in the stone city.'

'Copanatec!' gasped Archie.

'He does not mention the name of the city in this letter, but ...' Jamarko leafed over a few more pages to look closely at another white card, '... yes, here it is. Elmo says he visited another village where terrible loss of life had occurred. From what we have translated so far, it would seem that the village was attacked and all the men taken –'

'Taken? What does he mean?' asked Archie.

'I do not know. The text is not clear, but this is what may be of interest to you. When Elmo spoke to the women and children who were left, they said the evil ones from Copanatec had taken them.'

'Then it's true – it does exist! Do the letters say where Copanatec was located?'

Archie's mind was beginning to reel with the significance of what Father Jamarko was telling him. That Copanatec *had* existed in the past – but what about now?

'No, but you must remember, Archie, these letters are more than five thousand years old. We have yet to complete our work on the journal, and up to now, this is the only mention of Copanatec that we have found. However, there is something that did catch my attention.'

'What is it, Father?' asked Felipe.

'Well, it is very strange, but one of Elmo's drawings shows a coastline between central and southern Amasia that no longer exists.'

Felipe and Archie stared at him, waiting for him to explain.

Jamarko smiled at them. 'It's not unusual to see coastal erosion over such a long period, but a very large land mass seems to have disappeared.' He pointed to the map Felipe had brought to the table. 'Felipe, you'll have to find some weights to hold the map flat.'

The young monk nodded and left the room. He returned a few moments later with four thick books clutched to his chest. 'These should do. I noticed the bookcase in the corridor when we arrived earlier.' He spread out the map across the marble table-top, placing a book on each corner to prevent it rolling up again.

Rising slowly from his chair, Jamarko studied the map. It was obviously very old. Made from sort of yellowing fabric, its edges were frayed with threads hanging loose over the margins. Stained by grubby hands sometime in the distant past, it was protected now by a transparent sleeve, a label with a reference number attached to its edge.

Stroking his wispy, grey beard, he muttered to himself, 'Yes, it's as I thought.' He pulled the heavy, leather-bound book nearer to the map, leaving it open at the page with the drawing and symbols. 'Look, this part of the coastline – they are very alike.'

On the large map, Archie and Felipe watched him as he traced a finger around a long peninsula that jutted out into the Amasian Sea. At the end of the peninsula, a symbol, three concentric circles, had been drawn in red ink. In the book, although it was much smaller, the drawing included the same symbol.

'You're right, they both look the same, but what do the circles mean?' asked Archie.

It was Felipe who spotted it. 'They're cities! This is a map of the land of Hazaranet and its people, the Zamahonites, and where they lived. You see! There are more circles further inland.'

'Very good, Felipe,' said Jamarko. He pointed to one of the columns of symbols in the book. 'And, also ... we see it here.'

Archie looked, but he didn't understand. 'So the symbol represents a city, but I'm not sure what all of this means, Father.'

The old monk, still standing, was a little unsteady on his feet as he turned away from the table. 'Let me have your arm, Archie, I want to show you one last thing that may help you on your quest.'

Curious as to what Jamarko meant, Archie supported him as they walked slowly to the other end of the room, followed by Felipe.

Although, Sunstone required little in the way of furnishings for his office, he had seen the importance of one very necessary item when he held meetings with the Lancers in this room. It was a huge, large-scale modern map of the whole of the Amasian continent, covering most of the end wall. In the greatest detail, it encompassed all of the north, central and southern territories, as well as the Amasian Sea.

They had to stand a little way back from the map to see all of it clearly. Holding himself steady on Archie's arm, Jamarko pointed to the coastline. 'What do you see?' he asked.

At first, Archie couldn't focus on anything in particular. Running south from Port Zolnayta there were hundreds of place names: small and large estuaries, coves, harbours, fishing villages, all of them marked quite clearly until the border between central and south Amasia was reached, where there was a stretch of unnamed territory.

Then he saw it – or to be more precise, he didn't see it. The coastline on the old map of Hazaranet no longer existed on this modern map. The peninsula with its red concentric circles had disappeared, and in its place Sunstone had pinned a yellow card with three lines of black print. It described a group of tall grey-black rock formations that rose out of the sea off the southern coast. They were referred to by seamen as 'Hell's Pillars', and were in an area known as the White Waters.

Chapter Twenty-Eight

The Emergency

The sudden appearance of Sunstone and the sound of his urgent stride across the room to where Archie and the monks were still examining the wall map gave warning that something was wrong.

'I am sorry to disturb you, Father Jamarko, but I have to ask you to finish your meeting.'

'But why ... what has happened?'

'There are reports coming in of explosions having taken place in Zolnayta – at least two citizens have been killed. I have also been informed that a suspicious vehicle has been abandoned at the bridge approach to the castle.'

'My God! What in Heaven's name is going on?' gasped Felipe.

Sunstone's crystal eyes glowed brightly for a moment. It was an androt brain indicator when information input was being processed. He continued: 'I do not know, but I have just received a message that the vehicle contains a bomb. All civilians will have to remain at the rear of the castle until it is dealt with. However, I have arranged for Archie Kinross –'

'Just call me Archie, if it's OK with you ... everyone else does,' said Archie. He knew that the androts tended to be formal when communicating with others.

Sunstone's eyes glowed again. 'It is ... OK – but we must move quickly now. A Lancer is waiting to take you to Portview Terrace, while it is safe to do so.' As they prepared to leave, he turned to the monks. 'I have placed a guard at the door, so please wait here until I return.'

Jamarko's frail hands reached out to clasp Archie's right hand. 'It was good to meet you again, young man.

I hope what you have learned here today will help you in your search for your parents.'

'I hope so, too, Father. Thank you for taking the time to see me.'

As they left the room, Archie's mind was in a whirl with what he had learned from Jamarko. Copanatec had existed thousands of years ago, but there was no trace of it now on the modern maps, so how was he going to find it? After his experience with Richard on the Transkal at Harmsway he had no doubt in his mind that the city still existed – but where? He was beginning to think that there was only one choice left to him but he had no idea how he was going to do it.

A soldier wearing a khaki and brown combat uniform, unlike the soldiers' uniforms he had seen at the port dockside, held a short stubby rifle across his chest as they passed him in the corridor. Sunstone led the way until they reached an emergency exit that opened onto a huge area of the courtyard at the rear of the castle that was hidden from public view.

'This way, Archie,' said Sunstone, threading a way through several armoured vehicles of a type Archie had never seen before.

The courtyard was a hive of activity with soldiers and Lancers attending to their respective machines. A row of Spokestars, with Lancer pilots and soldiers ready to leave the castle, hovered in front of them. As they hurried onwards a loud explosion rumbled across the courtyard; seconds later, a smoky cloud swirled slowly into the air above the wall. A siren sounded as a soldier dashed past the Spokestars, barking orders to a group of men to follow him to secure the main gate.

'That must have been the bomb you warned us about!' cried Archie. 'What do we do now?'

'General Branvin's men are dealing with the emergency. My concern is to get you out of danger and away from the castle.'

Well, that's something I go along with, thought Archie. He wasn't frightened – at least, not yet, but he realised he had ended up in the middle of a strange set of unfolding events, making it difficult for him to carry out a decision he had just made.

'Follow me,' said Sunstone, his head swivelling to the rear to make sure Archie was still with him. He hurried past an armoured vehicle to one of the smaller Spokestar Specials to speak to a Lancer, already climbing into the cockpit

'Tinkey, this is your passenger.'

'Archie!' Tinkey was grinning from ear to ear as he turned to greet them. He was wearing the uniform of the Sixth Lancers, with the matching red and black skull helmet under one arm. Obviously excited, he said, 'I am to take you to Captain Abelhorn –'

'Quiet, Tinkey,' ordered Sunstone. 'Please prepare to leave immediately.' His head swivelled towards Archie. 'Tinkey is still a trainee, but he is fully qualified to fly this Spokestar. During the emergency he is the only one available to take you to Portview Terrace.'

'That's OK,' smiled Archie. 'I'm sure he'll get me there in one piece.'

'Yes, that is essential,' said Sunstone. 'Also, I must explain that in two days' time it has been arranged that you and your friend, Manuel, will be transported to see Dr Shah at Mount Tengi. I will confirm the departure time as soon as the emergency has been dealt with –'

'No, not me,' said Archie. 'I won't be going.'

Sunstone's crystal eyes flashed momentarily as they scanned Archie's face. It was as if he was computing the information to make sense of what Archie had just told him.

'I believe I understand,' he said. 'You do not wish to travel to Mount Tengi at this time – you plan to do something else.'

'That's right. There is something that I need to do before I see Dr Shah.'

Chapter Twenty-Nine

Archie's Plan

The next morning, Archie walked into the kitchen to find Abelhorn at the cooking range. Bran, his little ears twitching as he entered, lay stretched out nearby. The aroma of spicy meat filling the air, made him realise how hungry he was.

He had gone straight to his room after Tinkey left him at the house, not bothering to make any supper, his mind too restless to think about food. There had been no sign of Abelhorn or anyone else, and he guessed that Kristin was probably in her studio. Daniel had left a note to say that he'd taken Manuel to Flint's for a meal, which left him on his own for most of the evening. That was OK, because although he'd told Sunstone he wasn't going to Mount Tengi with Manuel, he hadn't really planned what he was going to do next. His instinct was to stay put and find out more about the coastline and where Copanatec may once have existed and, for that, he needed a plan.

He'd spent most of the time in the junk room checking the charts and maps tacked to the wall. The coastlines on each of them were the same as the big map on the wall of Sunstone's office. None of them displayed any sign of the peninsula or any of the symbols Jamarko had shown him. The only thing he noticed was something written in pencil in the margin directly below the border between Central and South Amasia. Above a line drawn directly from the coast out to sea towards the area known as the White Waters were two words. They were faded and partly smudged, but still clear enough to read: 'ask Quig'.

Quig. That was the name of the captain's mainliner on the *Serpent* – why was his name there? The question was still buzzing through his head as he stood in the kitchen.

'You're up with the birds this morning, Archie,' said Abelhorn. He swirled a piece of fat around the meat as it sizzled in the pan he was holding. 'Did you not sleep well?'

'Not really – I mean, it wasn't the bed or anything,' said Archie quickly. 'It's just that ... Well, I've a lot on my mind at the moment.'

'A lot on your mind!' Abelhorn shook his head. 'I'll grant you one thing: for someone so young, you seem to have ended up in a lot of scrapes. Here, sit down and try this.' He walked over to the table and dished up a plate of meat from the pan, along with a reddish nutty-looking mixture. 'Dinosaur, rhino, I don't know what exactly. It's some sort of spiced beef sausage from the Riverlands up north. It goes well with the fried beans.'

'It tastes really good,' said Archie. He munched the sausage and beans hungrily, although he couldn't help thinking about the Richard's near-death encounter with the dinosaur in the Riverlands. Was this it on the plate?

Abelhorn placed a couple of mugs of hot tea on the table and sat down. He smiled. 'Wash it down with this - it'll set you up for the day.'

They sat quietly for a few minutes while Archie finished his breakfast, then Abelhorn said, 'It's probably none of my business, but it's very obvious there is something troubling you. If you want to talk about it, I'm more than willing to listen.'

Archie pushed his plate away and took a sip of the tea. 'There is something ...'

'What is it?'

'The maps up in the room next to the bedroom. There's one with Quig's name on it. I wondered if you knew anything about it.'

'Hah,' snorted Abelhorn, 'you mean my son's treasure map!'

'Treasure map?'

'Yes. The fool thought he had found evidence of a treasure trove somewhere in the White Waters. It was madness; no one can go into that sea and expect to survive.'

'What happened to him?'

Abelhorn looked at Archie with piercing blue eyes above a broken nose that had never set properly, while he pondered the question. He sighed. 'No one really knows. Nathan was last seen at Quig's village, accompanied by a stranger. They spent the night there questioning one of the villagers about an old chart they'd brought with them.'

'Like the one upstairs?'

'No, it wasn't a map. Apparently it was a very old chart of the White Waters, carried by the stranger. According to some of the villagers there was an island marked on it, but Quig said no one had ever seen such a place; although, mind you, there are countless legends about that part of the Amasian Sea. It's a volcanic area and no man in his right mind would sail in that ocean.' His brow furrowed as he cast his eyes down, as if visualising his son sailing there. 'But some have and were never seen again.'

'But ... why did Nathan go to the village? Who was the stranger?'

'I don't know, Archie. It was only after we came back from a fishing trip that Quig heard about Nathan's visit. When he was declared missing we went to the village, but it was too late – neither of them were seen again.' Abelhorn hit the table with the flat of his hand, his voice rising. 'I'll tell you this, whoever the stranger was, he filled my son's head with nonsense about treasure ... and Nathan paid dearly for it.'

Archie flinched. He had never seen the captain so angry, but he understood how he must feel. 'I'm sorry, I didn't mean to ... uh, upset you ... I was just curious about the map.'

Abelhorn waved a hand. 'No, don't be concerned. I'm the one who should be sorry ...' He shook his head. 'I'm afraid that after all this time the wound has not healed. But, tell me, why such curiosity about the map?'

What do I tell him?

This was all becoming too much to handle by himself, thought Archie. He needed to talk to someone about what he should do next. If only Richard or Uncle John, maybe Chuck or Ed, were here to help him. But, not counting Manuel, he was here on his own. He had thought about going back with Manuel and getting in touch with the Facility through Mount Tengi, but he was convinced that, somehow, he was closer to finding the truth about his parents by staying here. In any event, he could give Manuel a message for Uncle John.

Abelhorn was staring at him, waiting for an explanation. Archie shrugged, realising he had to confide in someone. If he was going to ask for help there was probably no better person than the captain.

For the next hour, Archie told him about his parents and how they had disappeared and about Copanatec. The captain sat quietly, sipping mug after mug of tea, while Archie related all that had happened on his first journey to Amasia: The dinosaurs, Aristo and the Lancers, Brimstone, the Rooters, Harmsway College, and finally, his brother's escape from Prince Lotane and the Sacred Temple. But hardest of all to explain were the Transkals and Richard's ability to communicate from them. That they had actually spoken to their mother in Copanatec.

'My God, it is hard to believe ... and you say ... your father is there, too?'

'I think so, but we never heard anything more,' said Archie. He didn't want to discuss his brother's strange reluctance to pursue the search for their parents.

'It is an incredible tale, and now you and Manuel will go to see Dr Shah at Mount Tengi tomorrow to continue your search, is that it?'

'No, not exactly,' said Archie, hesitating for a moment, not sure how to explain what he had in mind. 'I'm not going with Manuel. He has to go back, but I'm afraid I can't say what will happen when he gets there. I promised not to reveal what they do at Mount Tengi.'

Abelhorn nodded. 'I understand. There are many rumours about that place, but it's of no concern to me. What *does* concern me, is what you intend to do by staying here. Can you tell me that?'

'Yes ... I'm going to find Copanatec. Well, at least I have to try, and I can't do that by going to Mount Tengi.'

'I see,' said Abelhorn, his eyebrows rising slightly, 'and how do you propose to do that?'

'By going to the area marked on your son's map upstairs. It's the same place that Father Jamarko told me about. There may be some sort of evidence of Copanatec ... I don't know, but I've got to try.' Archie tried to describe what the old monk had shown him in Sunstone's office, when a thought occurred to him. 'Maybe Nathan was looking for the same site – maybe he was told it was the site of the treasure?'

Abelhorn pushed himself away from the table, startling Bran as his chair scraped across the flagstone floor. He stood up, looking thunderstruck at the suggestion Archie had just made. 'Copanatec ... the White Waters ...could Nathan have been searching for your lost city? No, I can't believe anything could exist in that sea. It's madness to think of it!'

'But it might be possible,' insisted Archie, 'it might just be possible.'

'What is it? What is it you want to do?' A note of impatience, anger, had crept into the captain's voice.

'I think I should go to Quig's village, maybe I can learn something there. Can I do that? It ties in with everything I've heard so far, and if I can speak to the -'

The kitchen door slammed open and Daniel walked in, clutching a large carton against his chest. 'Morning, Captain, brought some stuff from Flint's for breakfast – ' He spotted the empty plates as he rested the carton on the table. 'Oh, looks like you've beaten me to it. You must have been up early.'

'Thanks, Daniel, it'll do for later. Pour yourself some tea and join us, I want to ask you something,' said Abelhorn. 'Archie has been telling me his plans for staying with us for a while longer.'

'You're not going to Mount Tengi in the morning?' said Daniel.

Archie shook his head.

Abelhorn answered for him. 'He's not – only Manuel. He can explain to you his reasons later, but he wants to go to Quig's village and I want you to take him there. I can't do it, I have the *Serpent* to attend to and I have to find someone to replace Tinkey.'

'You'll have a bit of bother there. Another bomb went off in the city last night and there's trouble down at the dock with some of the men trying to break the curfew.'

'Dammit. I don't know what these rebels want, but no one is stopping me getting on the *Serpent*.'

'That's the spirit, Captain,' said Daniel. He turned to Archie. 'Well, whatever your plan is, just let me know and I'll organise it.'

208

'Can we go tomorrow, after Manuel leaves?'

Daniel grinned. 'In a hurry, are we?'

'We'll leave it at that, 'said Abelhorn. He nodded to Archie as he got ready to leave the kitchen, Bran by his side. 'Remember, there's been nothing heard of Nathan for four years, so I don't expect you'll learn anything new.'

*

As the captain made his way into the hall, Kristin stood outside the back door a little while longer, but nothing more was said that interested her. She had listened to the newcomer, Archie whatever-his-name-was, tell his story to grandfather and it was just too fantastic to believe, not even half of it. But what had it to do with her father looking for treasure? Did they believe he was still alive? And where was this place ... *Copanatec?*

She was only eleven years old when her father had disappeared, and since then Mrs Flint had looked after her and her grandfather, when he was home from sea. Shortly after the disappearance, her mother had left to work in one of the factories in Sitanga, or so she'd been told. But one night she'd overheard Mrs Flint tell Daniel that it was a nervous breakdown that had caused her mother to leave. She had been in a sanatorium for a while, and now she was working on a factory assembly line checking machines of some sort. Mrs Flint said she wasn't herself anymore – whatever that meant – and she wouldn't be coming back to Portview Terrace, anytime soon.

When she tackled her grandfather about her mother, all he would say was that he hoped it wouldn't be too long before she came home, and that she was not to worry. And when she'd asked Daniel to take her to Sitanga to find her mother, he'd refused and told her

209

quite sternly not to be doing anything behind her grandfather's back.

Well, maybe they wouldn't let her see her mother, but Daniel was not going to stop her finding out what had happened to her father.

She marched back to her studio, determined that whatever Daniel and Archie were up to, if it involved her father, she would be part of it.

Chapter Thirty

Marcie

'I'm sorry, Manuel, but I have to stay here. I need to find out what happened to my parents – you understand, don't you?'

It was late in the evening and they had just finished a meal of fried fish cakes and bread chips dipped in a spicy herb sauce, prepared earlier by Mrs Flint. They sat on the sides of their beds in the room they shared, washing down the last of the meal with glasses of Sticklejuice (the non-alcoholic kind) from a stone jug on the floor. Archie had elected to have their meal in the bedroom so he could talk privately with Manuel and Mrs Flint said she didn't mind as it gave her a chance to tidy the kitchen.

Manuel had been pronounced fit to travel by a doctor from the hospital who had called in during the afternoon to see him. But it was obvious to Archie that Manuel was still unwell and not fully recovered from his concussion, and probably a little frightened by the strange circumstances he found himself in. His face was pale, the dark brown skin now an unhealthy hue, the eyes less twinkly than before, betraying the anxiety he felt about travelling alone to Mount Tengi.

'But, Archie, I do not know this place you want me to go to ... I think it is better I stay with you.'

Archie shook his head. 'I understand how you feel, but it is important that you do this for me. And you will not be on your own; Tinkey will take you there and be with you all the time until you meet Dr Shah.' Archie smiled at the sad face in front of him. 'You do want to help?'

Manuel nodded, shrugging his shoulders in resignation, not fully understanding what it was that Archie expected of him.

'All you have to do is take a message to him that will explain everything. After that, Dr Shah will arrange for you to get you back home to Mexico, but you also need to get the message to my uncle, Professor Strawbridge. Is that clear?'

Archie hated putting his young friend in this position, knowing how confused Manuel must feel, but he felt he had no other option. His plan, such as it was, consisted of he and Daniel going to Quig's village to discover what he could about Copanatec, and that was still a shot in the dark. While he was about that, there was no way he could be responsible for Manuel tagging along ... *who knew what lay ahead?* Besides, if the message got to Uncle John and Chuck, as well as Dr Shah, they might be able to help him in some way. There was nothing else for it – he had to try.

*

The next morning, Archie and Daniel watched from the patio outside the kitchen door as Tinkey manoeuvred the Spokestar in the restricted space available to him. He turned slowly as he prepared to make his ascent over the house. Manuel sat in the rear of the cockpit, his face a picture of sadness and dejection, as if he had been condemned to serve a prison sentence.

'Not looking too happy, is he?' said Daniel.

'No, he's not,' said Archie. 'He thinks he's being abandoned, but it's better this way. He's not fully recovered, and I can't really bring him with me –'

'Now that you mention it,' said Daniel, suddenly sounding serious, 'seeing I'm the one that's going with you, maybe you can bring me up to speed on why we're going to Quig's place?'

Archie sighed. He'd expected that at some stage of the journey to the village he would have to explain to Daniel what he was trying to find ... A *clue to the existence of a long lost city called Copanatec.* It sounded crazy, but what else could he tell him?

As they watched the Spokestar disappear from view, Archie turned to Daniel. 'It's a long story, maybe I can explain on the way to the village, if that's OK with you?'

'Suits me, mate. I have the captain's hovervan out at the front, so we'll go as soon as you're ready.'

*

Kristin squeezed into a corner between one of the *Serpent's* large fenders and a roll of tarpaulin, swearing to herself as a fingernail cracked on a broken link of heavy chain. 'Freak this!' she muttered, as she tried to make herself more comfortable by stretching her legs across the tarpaulin. Hearing Daniel and Archie approach the van, she held her breath, hoping they wouldn't look in the back before leaving. As they climbed into the cab, she breathed a sigh of relief. Whatever it was they were looking for, there was no way they were leaving her behind.

*

The hovervan was a large, heavy duty vehicle with a wide cab and three bucket-style seats. Daniel sat in the middle, a hand resting on the T-shaped steering control, the other tracing a route on the dashboard touchscreen. With Archie beside him, they were soon cruising along the Amasian Coastal Highway, the sea on their left and a vast stretch of densely wooded forest on the right.

'I didn't get a chance to thank Captain Abelhorn for the use of the van,' said Archie, 'but I didn't see him before we left the house.'

'Don't worry, he's happy enough to do it, although I suspect he's as curious as I am to see how this trip works out. Anyway, we only use the van when we have to transport stuff to the *Serpent*. That's where the captain is now. He left early to see Lieutenant Isula to ask him if he can get ready for sea and, believe me, he'll be in a foul mood if he can't get on board.'

'You're heading back to the fishing grounds?'

'As soon as we get a replacement for Tinkey, we'll be away,' said Daniel, suddenly pulling out to overtake a line of small traders' hovercarts.

'Will Quig be going too?' asked Archie. He was beginning to wonder what he would do next, if he learned nothing from Quig. Maybe this trip is just a waste of time, he thought.

'Of course, he's our mainliner, the best one around. We can't sail without him,' laughed Daniel, at the idea of it. He glanced at Archie's face, beginning to redden. 'Look, if he can help you, I'm sure he will. He may not be the prettiest guy to look at, but he's a good man to have on your side.'

Archie nodded. His thoughts dwelt on what lay ahead of them as he watched the white surf pound the greenish-black rock that formed much of this part of the coast. Earlier, he had repeated his story to Daniel, just as he'd told it to Abelhorn the previous day.

Daniel had listened, seemingly bemused, but said little, except to say that he shouldn't expect too much when they met Quig: 'He's a quiet one at the best of times, so just bear that in mind when we get there.'

They travelled on for another hour, or so, before Daniel pointed towards a tall grey stone, pencil-like building sitting proudly on a rocky islet, white spray crashing all around the rocks at its base.

'We've made good time. Look, there's the lighthouse beyond the harbour wall,' said Daniel. A few minutes later he brought the van to a stop at an open space by the wall. On the other side was a narrow stone jetty with a few small fishing boats tied up alongside, but no sign of life.

The road separated the harbour from rows of quaint postcard-style cottages, surrounded by flower-filled gardens. Stone-walled fields ran up to the edge of the forest which covered much of the mountain range they had followed from Zolnayta. More cottages and low walls, all built from the ubiquitous grey stone that seemed to characterise the area, dotted the slopes of the mountainside.

'Pretty sort of place, isn't it?' said Daniel, as he let the van hover for a moment. He checked the oncoming traffic, then crossed the road to make a turn onto a stony track that would take them up the mountainside. He said, 'Quig lives by himself in a hamlet near the top; let's hope he's there.'

'Isn't he expecting us?'

'The captain tried to call him, but he couldn't get a reply. I decided to make the trip anyway – I was free, so why not?'

'Oh ... I see.'

Daniel smiled, sensing Archie's disappointment. 'Don't worry, he won't be far away.'

He cut the hoverdrive shortly after they left the track to park on a paved square encircled by a cluster of cottages. Several women with young children playing nearby watched as the hovervan settled on the edge of the square. One of them, a tall figure with dark, shoulder-length hair, wearing a leather apron over a green blouse and rough work trousers, stood by a waist-high, stone-built, barbecue pit. She was shaking a large skillet over the hot stones, sending a rich aroma of fried fish into the air.

Daniel called to her as he hopped out of the cab: 'Smells good, Marcie.' He nodded to Archie to join him as he walked over to the barbecue.

'Daniel!' The woman pronounced it 'Dan-yeel', in a slightly West Indian manner, thought Archie, as she set the skillet to one side, before rushing to meet them. 'Why didn't you let me know you were coming?'

'Sorry, Marcie, it was a last minute decision. We did try to get in touch with Quig, but we couldn't reach him. Is he here?'

'The radiocoms do not work well here, but you are here now and you and your friend will eat with us, yes?'

'I'm afraid not –'

'But you must,' said Marcie, 'the fish is good today. It has just come from the harbour and there is plenty for everyone.'

'OK, I suppose we can stay for a little while,' said Daniel, shrugging his shoulders. He glanced at Archie, as if to say it would cause offence if they refused.

'It's OK with me,' said Archie. After last night's meal with Manuel he hadn't felt like having any breakfast before they left the house, but now with the smell of fried fish drifting across the square, his stomach was beginning to grumble.

Marcie smiled. She put an arm around his shoulders and with the other she gestured to Daniel to follow them. She led them to a long wooden bench by the barbecue pit where one of the women quickly set two extra places. 'Good. Now you can tell me your name, and while we eat you can also tell me why you and Daniel have come all this way to see my brother.'

*

Kristin fumed as she stepped down from the toolbox she'd been standing on. She had stacked it on top of the pile of chain, allowing her to reach the air vent at the rear of the cab. By placing her ear against the vent she had been able to listen to nearly everything that had been said, but with the toolbox wobbling from side to side it had been a precarious position to be standing still in for so long. Now her neck, back and legs were aching as she sat down on the tarpaulin to try and stretch her limbs as best she could in the confined space.

Alone with her thoughts she went over the story Archie had told Daniel.

'Freakin' weird,' she thought. But she was beginning to wonder if Archie's quest to find his parents might also help her to find out what had happened to her father.

*

With the meal finished, the women cleared the dishes away from the table while Marcie listened to Archie explain that he hoped her brother, or someone who knew this part of Amasia, might be able to help him uncover information leading to the existence of an ancient city known as Copanatec. His parents had disappeared through a timecrack and he hoped to find them there.

'I do not know of such a place. Like you, I am from your world –'

'What! I didn't know that,' exclaimed Daniel. 'I thought you and Quig belonged to one of the old tribes of Amasia?'

'Yes, that is true of Quig and his family, but I arrived here as a young girl, found by his parents in the fields of their farm. They adopted me and I became his stepsister.'

That probably explains the accent, thought Archie, nodding to himself.

'Oh, I didn't know ...' said Daniel.

'It does not matter.' She spread her arms wide and looked to the children playing in the square. 'I am very happy and Quig has been good to me, but he is hardly ever here. Either he is at sea or he goes to our farm in the hills.'

'And where is he now, Marcie?'

'He left yesterday to go with the men to the village of Elam to pay their respects to the Man of Dust. She shook her head. 'It is foolishness, I think, but it is something they do every year.'

Archie's eyes widened. 'What is the *Man of Dust*?'

Marcie stared into the distance for a moment, before answering. 'I am not certain. It was something that happened during the time the evil ones came to Elam –'

'Who are you talking about, what evil ones?' asked Daniel. He sounded perplexed by what he was hearing.

'Those who come from the White Waters to raid the villages of the south are known to us as the evil ones.'

Chapter Thirty-One

The Pendant

Archie and Daniel glanced at each other, and then to Marcie. *A Man of Dust. The evil ones.* What did she mean?

Sensing their confusion, she continued: 'I'm sorry. I can only tell you what I have heard from the people who pass through here. It is said that strange beings rise out of the sea and attack the villages of the south. They take all the men, leaving the women and children to rebuild what is left of the homes that have been destroyed.'

'That's terrible,' said Archie. 'But why – what happens to the men?'

'No one seems to know,' said Marcie, a touch of sadness in her voice as she remembered the stories she had been told. 'Quig said that the men of Elam were taken into the White Waters and never seen again.'

'Yeah, I think I remember Quig and the others on the *Serpent* talking about all the mysterious things that happen in this part of the world,' said Daniel, 'but I put it down to the stuff that sailors always talk about – you know, superstitions and legends, things like that.'

'I might have thought so, too, but when they came to Elam, which is only a day's distance from here, then I knew the stories were true.'

'But what about the soldiers, can't they do something?' said Archie. 'And what about the Lancers, surely they can find these ... *evil ones* ... or whatever you call them?'

'The Lancers do not patrol so far south. It is up to the army to do that,' said Marcie, shaking her head, her voice full of contempt when she mentioned the army.

'Until now, there have been too few soldiers sent to help the villages when these things happen.'

Archie watched as she reached for the gold chain she wore around her neck, her fingers rubbing the surface of a golden disc-shaped pendant encrusted with small red and blue stones, her lips mouthing silent words, as if in prayer.

He said, ' Until now ...?'

She nodded. 'Yes, the army wanted to send in a large force after a group of soldiers were killed near one of the villages on the coast. It is said that General Branvin was very angry, and at a meeting of the Elders, he demanded a free hand in finding those responsible. But now Quig thinks that he has to deal with the explosions in Zolnayta, and he may not have enough soldiers to do both.'

Unless ... *the evil ones and the rebels were one and the same ...* thought Archie.

He stood up, peering at Marcie's pendant. She was running the gold chain and disc through her fingers, as if handling a string of rosary beads. On one side of the disc, the coloured stones shimmered in the sunlight, on the other a faint design could be seen.

He asked, 'Can I see that?'

'My pendant? Of course.' Looking surprised, she pulled the chain over her head, placing it in his hand.

Archie stared at the stones for a moment, then turned the gold disc to the reverse side. It was flat, smooth, with an emblem-like design etched into the gold surface. He caught his breath when he realised that what he had noticed a moment earlier, was in fact an image he had seen before.

He was stunned to see it – here in another world, in another dimension, in a small, remote village perched on the side of a mountain he had never been to before – a piece of gold bearing the mark he had seen on his brother's shoulder. The same mark on his mother and the same one that Father Higgins had confirmed that the old shaman, Mateo from the village in the Yucatan, had possessed. And yet again, carved into the stone surface of the Transkal he had been standing on, before being engulfed by a timecrack.

What did it all mean?

Mateo had told Father Higgins his mark was that of an ancient tribe known as *The Lords of the Cloud*, a tribe that belonged to *two worlds*. Could he have meant Old Earth and New Earth? But what then did the mark mean to his family? He ran his fingers through his hair in frustration. It was like finding pieces of a jigsaw puzzle scattered all over the place, but without the picture on the puzzle box cover to help him put it altogether.

'What is it, Archie?' asked Daniel. Both he and Marcie were staring at him, waiting for him to say something.

'I'm sorry,' said Archie, handing the pendant back to Marcie. 'I was surprised to see this. The design on the back is unusual and it's .... well, I've seen it before.'

They looked at him blankly for a moment, not knowing what he meant. Having come this far, he realised he had better explain to Daniel what the mark might mean. That it might be part of the answer to what had happened to his parents.

'It sounds pretty crazy to me,' said Daniel, after listening to Archie for a few minutes. 'But maybe we can find out a bit more about the pendant.' He turned to Marcie. 'Can you tell us where you got it?'

Replacing the pendant around her neck, she said, 'Quig gave it to me. He believes it possesses powerful magic. I do not know if it does, but it is the first piece of jewellery I have ever been given. I would not like to lose it.'

Daniel smiled. 'Don't worry, I don't think Archie wants to take it, but maybe you can tell him where Quig got it?'

She shrugged, gesturing with her hands that she knew very little. 'What can I tell you? He gave it to me four years ago shortly after he returned from Elam. Our men had gone there as soon as they heard of the attack, but they were too late to help the men of Elam. They had been taken. All they could do was to help the women and children rebuild their homes.'

She looked over her shoulder, admiring, as she had countless times, her neat stone cottage with its flower-covered front wall next to the others that bordered the square. An old fear gripped her, as it had many times since Elam. *Could it happen here?* She shook the awful thought away as her fingers stroked the pendant.

'It was when they went to cut wood, one of the evil ones was found lying in a ditch in the forest. He had been badly injured, no one knows how, except that he had a deep wound in his side which had become infected. Quig and the others brought him to a cottage, one of the few with its walls and roof still intact, leaving him there until they decided what to do with him. Some wanted to kill him there and then, but Quig argued they needed to keep him alive to question him about the attackers – who they were and where they came from.'

'Good thinking,' nodded Daniel. 'What did they discover?'

'Nothing. It was too late. The evil one never recovered ... but something very strange happened when he died ...'

'What was it?' asked Archie. He could hardly contain himself; was he on the verge of learning the meaning of the pendant and its mark?

'At the very moment he died, a golden glow appeared, like a shimmering cloud it covered his body from head to toe. Quig said it lasted several minutes, then it faded away. When the glow vanished all that was left ... was dust ... and this pendant. All those who witnessed it were terribly frightened – they were convinced they had been in the presence of one of the gods.'

When Marcie finished her story, Archie asked when Quig would return. She replied that the men believed they had to appease the god who might appear again with the evil ones to seek revenge for his bodily death, by destroying more villages, including their own. And so it was, at this time every year, the men went to Elam to pay their respects to the Man of Dust.

'I hope he and the men will come back tomorrow, but for the past four years they have stayed to carry out repairs and whatever needs to be done. There are few able-bodied men left in Elam to do such work.'

Archie nodded that he understood. He turned to Daniel. 'Can we go to Elam ... please? I need to see where the pendant was found – the mark means something and I need to know what it is.'

*

Daniel had given into Archie's plea, but as it was the better part of a day's journey he said they would have to stay overnight. They would return to Zolnayta the following day. He explained, 'The captain will be needing his van to transfer gear to the *Serpent*, so we can't stay that long.'

Marcie prepared a basket of food and drink for the journey. Later, as she walked with them across the square, she pointed towards the hovervan. 'Who is that?'

As they stared, they saw a figure dash from the undergrowth at the edge of the forest and into the back of the van. Despite being dressed in a black roll neck sweater worn below a black tank top, black trousers tucked into black boots, it was the red spiky hair that caught their attention.

Kristin!

Daniel took off like a rocket, racing across the square with Archie close behind. He reached the van's rear door and whipped it open.

'What are you doing here?' demanded Daniel.

Kristin was standing behind one of the large boat fenders adjusting the belt on her trousers. She glared at him then turned away to fix her clothing.

'I had to take a leak – OK?'

Daniel's face reddened. 'You know what I mean. What are you doing here in the village?' As she turned round to face him again, he realised she had hidden herself in the van and been with them since they left Portview Terrace. 'Bleedin' hell, Kristin, you've been with us all the time. Why? What is it you want?'

She made her way to the door and jumped down onto the square just as Marcie joined them.

'I want to find my father, that's what I want!'

'What makes you think he's here?'

She tilted her head towards Archie. 'I heard him talking to grandfather in the kitchen yesterday and what he told you on the way here. If it's OK for him to go looking for his parents, then it's OK for me, too. I know my father is alive and I'm going to find him.'

Daniel shook his head. 'This is crazy. We have to stay over in Elam and we'll not get back to the house until tomorrow. You'll have to go back. Besides, the captain will be looking for you.'

'No, he won't. He's staying on board the *Serpent* tonight. I heard him tell Mrs Flint he'll not be back until tomorrow.' Kristin stood defiantly, with her hands on her hips, grinning. 'So it's OK then, isn't it?'

Archie could see Daniel was exasperated by Kristin's stance, but he realised that if they took her back home they would have to make another trip to Elam, and when would that be?

Shaking his head, Daniel had come to the same conclusion. Pointing towards the basket Marcie was carrying, he said, 'Looks like we're going to need more food, if you can spare it.'

Chapter Thirty-Two

The Body

Marcie waved to Archie as the hovervan rose slowly, ready to leave the square. He was at the side window, Kristin at the other, while Daniel sat in the middle control seat, studying the secondary road on the touchscreen that would take them to Elam.

Archie returned the wave, then said to Daniel, 'How long will it take us to get there?'

'Hard to say. Marcie said it takes a day, but the villagers use the old wheel drives, and from what I can see on the screen it's about three hundred miles from here.' He shrugged as he steered the van out of the square onto a road that ran along the base of the mountain, leaving the village and Marcie behind them. 'Maybe four hours or so. We can't go too fast on this road; it gets narrower the further we edge into the forest, and there are a lot of twists and turns before we reach Elam.'

Archie nodded. He knew that hoverdrive engines were governed and restricted to travelling a few feet above the ground. They made for very smooth driving, but only the Spokestars were allowed to fly over Amasia. He had learned while on the orientation class at Harmsway College that there wasn't even an airline. The Elders, who controlled the country, had decreed that for security reasons, all public and private transport systems were confined to the surface of land and sea, only the Lancers would fly the skies over Amasian territory.

'Four hours!' groaned Kristin. She was munching a mouthful of bread roll from the basket of food and bottled water on her knees, provided by Marcie before they left the village. Ravenous since climbing into the van she had hardly eaten a bite until now.' Not another four hours in this thing,' she complained out loud.

'Stop whingeing, or you can get out and stay with Marcie until we get back,' said Daniel, his tone making it clear it was no idle threat. 'No one asked you along, so it's up to you whether you stay or not.'

Kristin stared at him and said nothing. She ate her bread roll and kept her eyes on the road ahead, but Archie could sense her resentment at what Daniel said.

Great, he thought, *that's all I need: These two quarrelling all the way to Elam.*

Funnily enough, the tension between them reminded him of Richard, back home on Old Earth. They had argued, but it was always a transient thing, that it wouldn't last, forgotten until the next time. He thought about the last time he saw Richard: He had pushed him off the Transkal in the Yucatan into Ed Hanks's arms, and hopefully, he had saved him from harm, before the timecrack struck.

As they travelled onwards, bright glassy sunlight split the trees to reveal a landscape of open fields and dense woodland. Ancient, grey stone walls, crumbling in places, were the only clue to any form of civilisation, past or present. The road itself, packed stone and gravel, constructed for use before the arrival of modern hover vehicles, displayed a variety of weeds, only held back by the passage of regular wheeled transport.

Three hours later, Daniel began to reduce speed as the road narrowed and became little more than a track, with trees so close the branches were sweeping the sides of the van.

'We've had it,' announced Daniel, coming to a halt. 'This is as far as we go. We're only going to get stuck if we try to take the van any further.'

'What are we going to do?' asked Archie.

'There's more than a couple of hours of daylight left and as far as I can tell, we're only a mile or so from the village. That gives us plenty of time to walk there.'

Kristin stared at him. 'You want us to walk –'

Archie quickly interrupted her before she had a chance to start an argument with Daniel. He asked, 'What about the van?'

'We just passed a small clearing back there,' said Daniel, pointing to a break in the trees behind them. 'It should be safe enough there until we get back.'

*

After parking the hovervan behind a clump of trees on the edge of the clearing, Daniel walked back to the road to where Archie and Kristin were waiting for him. 'That's it,' he said, 'nobody can see it from here.' He returned to the van and checked that each door was properly locked. 'OK, let's see if we can make it to Elam before it gets dark.'

Starting down the road, his long, loping gait set a fast pace that had Archie and Kristin almost running to keep up with him.

'Hey, will you slow up – aaoow!' Kristin let out a yelp as she tripped over the edge of one of the flat, stone slabs that made up this part of the road. 'Look, my boots are ruined!'

Archie stopped beside her as she pointed to the scuff marks on the toes of her black boots. He grinned at the look of concern on her face. He said, 'You'll be lucky if that's all you have to complain about by the time we leave Elam.'

Little did he realise how prophetic his words would prove to be.

Daniel called out to them, over his shoulder, as he continued his stride along the road. 'C'mon you two, we don't want to be caught out here when it gets dark.'

They arrived less than an hour later at a point where the road narrowed towards an old stone block archway that framed the entrance to a short tunnel. What little daylight was left could be seen at the other end, highlighting a small building in the distance.

'Is this it?' asked Archie, his eyes scanning the interior of the tunnel and the high tree-covered ridge above it.

'I don't know, mate, I've never been here before, but from what I remember of the van's screen map I guess that's the village on the other side.'

Daniel led the way through the tunnel, but stopped when he heard a stifled scream behind him. Turning quickly, he saw Kristin standing with her hands almost covering her face. Archie was down on one knee examining something lying in the shadow at the side of the tunnel. He shook his head. He had walked right past whatever it was that had caught Archie's attention.

He called out, 'What is it, Archie?' but there was no answer.

He sighed, turning back to have a look at what seemed, at first glance, to be a pile of old sacks or rags gathered at the side of the tunnel – except for the hand which now lay exposed by the short, broken branch that Archie had picked up from the floor of the tunnel to pull back what appeared to be a jacket sleeve.

'I noticed this,' said Archie, using the branch to point towards a silver object lying near the hand. It was a short, highly polished dagger reflecting the remaining light that managed to filter its way into the tunnel.

'Bleedin' hell, it's a body!' gasped Daniel. He knelt down as Archie, not wanting to use his hands, used the branch to pull a hood away from the head of a young man. He faced sideways towards them, revealing eyes wide open by the shock of sudden death.

'Do you know him?' asked Archie

'No idea – probably one of the villagers. But what's he doing here? Why has he been left like this?'

'It's hard to tell, but it looks as if he was trying to defend himself ... obviously not very successfully ...' said Archie. 'But look!' He shuddered as he stood up, pointing the branch at arm's length towards a deep wound between the neck and the shoulder. The blood had congealed along with some soil around the wound to form a dirty gaping mouth.

Archie dropped the branch onto the ground near the dagger, turning to one side as he felt a sudden wave of nausea about to overtake him. He held the back of his hand across his mouth until the sickening sensation passed as quickly as it came. Feeling better, he pointed to the end of the tunnel, 'I think we need to be very careful when we approach the village.'

Daniel nodded his agreement, then turned to see Kristin who had stepped back as far as she could, away from the body, to the far side of the tunnel.

'Are you OK,' he asked.

She held her arms tightly crossed against her chest, her eyes flickering between him and the body. 'Did someone kill him?' she asked, her voice almost a whisper.

'It looks like it. We'll have to go into the village to try and find out what happened here.'

'Are you going to leave it ... here?'

'We're not in a position to do anything about burying the body, if that's what you mean. We'll have to leave that to the villagers.'

Archie left them, walking slowly out of the tunnel to get a better look at the building they had seen earlier. He let his eyes adjust to the failing light until he could see that there were other small buildings clustered together against the skyline. In the middle of the cluster, a bright light, slowly getting brighter, caught his attention.

Daniel and Kristin joined him.

'What's that light – is it Elam?' asked Kristin.

'Probably,' said Daniel, 'but it's hard to tell from here what it is.'

'I think it's a fire,' said Archie. 'While I've been watching, it's been getting bigger and brighter.'

'Maybe it's a bonfire, or a barbecue or something,' ventured Kristin.

'Only one way to find out,' said Daniel, striding out once more onto the road. 'Let's go.'

Chapter Thirty-Three

The Man of Dust

Quig drew back from the opening, fearful that the two Terogs searching through the tall grass and bushes would look up and see him. He held his breath as he tried to maintain his cramped position in the hollow of the huge tree. Although he was small, he was broad and stocky, giving him little room to stretch out in the space he now occupied. Caused by years of disease and decay, the hole was about twenty feet above the Terogs who were circling the base of the tree as they continued their search. Parts of the thick creeper, crawling snake-like up the ancient trunk, were hanging loose where he had hauled himself up to gain access to the hole. He prayed they wouldn't notice. The opening gave him a clear view of the Terogs, but the tree was unsafe and he was in danger of being discovered if more of the rotten wood broke away under his weight.

It was the hour before daylight when he and his friend, Tomis, had been forced to make a run for it, but they were spotted by one of the Terogs standing guard near the road leading out of Elam. Quig knew the area from his previous visits to the village and immediately ran for the cover of the trees, but Tomis had panicked at the sight of the guards with their crossbows and made a dash for the tunnel, a short distance away at the end of the road.

Moments later, after he climbed the tree into his hiding place, he'd heard the shouts, then the bloodcurdling scream.

Tomis! – Had he been caught?

He shook his head at the thought. Was he going to be the only one not in the hands of the evil ones?

The last time they had come to Elam, they had arrived without warning in the middle of the night. Elisha, his betrothed, the women and the children and the men were all fast asleep when they were attacked. Most of the men had been taken; the others, including Elisha, had been killed.

Every year since the attack, Quig and his friends had come to Elam to pay their respects to the mysterious one they called the Man of Dust – one they suspected of being a god. They had dutifully placed his remains in a beautifully crafted stone urn created by one of their own stonemasons and built a small altar in the community hall where it had reposed until now. After paying their respects to the urn they stayed, as always, to help the women and children with the general maintenance of Elam's cottages and buildings, carrying out repairs wherever necessary.

Only this time they had stayed too long.

The evil ones – now known to Quig as the Terogs - had returned to find a man they called Tenoch. A Lord of the Clouds, they said, easily recognised by the golden pendant he wore. They had heard about the Man of Dust and realised it must be Tenoch, one of their own, missing after the last raid on Elam.

Quig had shown them the urn, hoping they would respect the villagers' efforts in looking after the ashes and leave without causing the village any more harm, but they had become very angry when told there was no pendant. Quig was too frightened to tell them the truth that he had taken it and given it to Marcie.

For two nights and a day the Terogs had rampaged through Elam searching for the pendant, destroying buildings and killing anyone who stood in their way. Quig feared that if they discovered what he had done, the Terogs would go to his village and continue their destruction.

Three of his friends were dead, killed when they tried to prevent a Terog entering one of the cottages to set it alight. The other men from his village, chained, and held along with the women and children of Elam, were in the square in front of the community hall, while he and Tomis had managed to escape into the loft above the hall. There they had stayed, too frightened to move, not knowing what to do – until they heard the crackle of burning wood and saw the wisps of black smoke filtering through the floorboards.

The hall was on fire!

Terrified by the thought of being trapped in the loft they had smashed their way through the slates between the rafters of the roof, allowing them just enough space to climb out onto the gutter. It led directly to a downpipe that fed rainwater into a large waterbutt next to a rear exit behind the hall. Worried they might have been heard descending the downpipe, they immediately dropped to their knees after jumping from the waterbutt and onto the path that encircled the building. Running with their bodies bent low they made for the long grass and wild gorse that surrounded much of the village. But as Quig took the lead to try and reach the road that would take them out of Elam they were seen by one of the Terogs.

That was hours ago, before daylight. Now as night approached, he was on his own with at least two of them searching for him. The shouts of the Terogs become more distant as they extended their search through the forest close to the road leading to the tunnel. He breathed a sigh of relief as he risked stretching his cramped limbs to ease the ache in his back.

After a while, he crept carefully out of the hollow onto a branch and reached for a creeper to help him stand upright. He peered through the gaps in the trees and across the tops of the bushes and long grass, all the way to the road and the tunnel. The heads of the Terogs – still only two of them – were bobbing up and down as they sought their prey when some movement near the entrance to the tunnel caught his eye.

The light was fading, but he recognised the tall, thin figure in front of two others striding up the road towards Elam – and towards the Terogs!

It was Daniel and the captain's granddaughter – and the stranger from the sea. What were they doing here?

From his vantage point, Quig could see that if the Terogs left the cover of the forest to return to the road they would immediately see Daniel and his friends.

He had to warn them.

There was a path through the forest which some of the villagers used as a shortcut to reach the tunnel when leaving Elam. If he could get to it quickly enough he would intercept Daniel before the Terogs did. Checking to see if they were still searching the forest – and they were – he left the safety of the tree hollow and ran as fast as his short, stocky legs would allow him, towards the path.

*

Archie was still shaken by the discovery of the body in the tunnel and his mind churned with questions as to how it came to be there. He was nervous about what lay ahead and what they might be walking into. The fire he had seen earlier had died down, with only vague tendrils of smoke curling into a starlit sky over the cluster of buildings on the horizon. But his eyes were suddenly drawn to another fire sparking into life in one of the other buildings, close to the end of the road.

They all saw it. Daniel stopped dead in his tracks, raising his right hand in a sign to halt, but Kristin walked past him, her curiosity taking her a few steps further along the road that now ran uphill to Elam.

'Kristin, wait,' called Daniel, 'we need to be careful. We don't know what's happening there.'

'You're right,' said Archie, coming up beside him. 'There is something seriously wrong around here. First the body in the tunnel and now fires breaking out all over the place.'

'Yes, I know, mate, but the people in the village probably need our help –'

'Hssssttt!'

'What was that?' Daniel turned quickly in the direction of the sound coming from a break in the forest beside them.

'Look!' Archie pointed to a dark figure standing behind a tree on a slope alongside a narrow dirt track that ran to the edge of the road.

The figure stepped out onto the track, gesturing to them to come to him.

'It's Quig!'

Daniel with Archie close on his heels ran to the slope and up the track to where Quig had retreated behind a tree.

He's trying to stay out of sight, thought Archie. *But from what?* It was obvious that the mainliner from the *Serpent*, whose scarred face might frighten others, was himself very frightened.

'What is it, Quig? What are you doing out here?' asked Daniel.

'I would ask you the same.' Quig was breathing heavily and leaning against the tree, his eyes darting between them and the road. 'But no matter; you must leave this place!'

'But why? What's happening in Elam?'

'The Terogs ... the evil ones, they came back ... some have died ...' He clasped his chest, breathing deeply, nodding towards Elam. 'And now they are burning the rest of the village.'

Archie, thinking of the body in the tunnel, asked, 'I don't understand, why did they come back?'

'They came to find one of their own ... the one who became dust.' Quig shook his head, still confused by what he had witnessed that day. 'We cared for the Lord of the Clouds and gave his dust to them, but they were very angry when they didn't find the pendant.'

Archie stared at him, hardly believing what he'd just heard. The evil ones – Terogs, or whatever they were called – had come for a Lord of the Clouds and the pendant with the strange mark. He felt a tingling sensation in his spine, a feeling that told him he was close to finding out what had happened to his parents.

Archie wanted to ask him more: Did the Terogs come from Copanatec? Had he heard anything about such a place? He was about to put the questions to him when the shrill, piercing scream from the road forced his attention away from Quig.

Kristin!

He suddenly realised they had left her alone on the road when they dashed up the path to see Quig. She was on her own – now something was happening to her!

Pushing Daniel aside, he raced back down the path to a narrow ridge overlooking the road. He stopped for a moment to take in the scene before him. Kristin was down on one knee with her hands outstretched to protect herself from the threat of a crossbow aimed at her head. It was held by a squat, heavily-built figure, while another, wielding a whip, grabbed her shoulder, forcing her to her feet.

237

'Get your freakin' hands off me!' Kristin screamed and clawed at the hand of the Terog trying to hold her. 'Get away from me!'

The Terog responded by throwing her to the ground, raising his whip ready to strike.

Without another thought, Archie hurled himself from the ridge straight into the Terog's chest, forcing him to drop the whip. Rolling over as he hit the ground and then back onto his feet, Archie tried to grab Kristin to make a run for it, but as he reached out to grip her arm he saw the other Terog swing the crossbow directly towards him. Another scream and oath from Kristin made him look round to see her lying on the ground with the first Terog's boot firmly placed between her shoulder blades.

There was no sign of Daniel or Quig, but as he looked up he saw more Terogs approaching quickly from the burning village of Elam. Reinforcements, he thought. They must have seen what was happening and sent help. It looked as if he and Kristin were on their own to deal with this situation.

*

'What are we going to do?' whispered Daniel, keeping his head low in the grass.

'There is nothing we can do – look!' Quig nodded towards the Terogs. They were carrying vallonium torches to light up the road as they hurried towards their comrades.

Daniel, with Quig behind him, had crawled through the grass and shrubbery covering the slope until they could position themselves to see what was happening on the road. It was dark now but the Terog's torches made it easier to see what they were going to do next.

Shocked by what he was witnessing, Daniel watched as Archie and Kristin were pulled to their feet, their wrists manacled with short chains and then dragged to stand between two lines of Terogs. Grunts and shouts along with the sound of whips cracking over their heads accompanied them as they were force-marched into Elam.

'We can't just leave them,' said Daniel desperately, as the Terogs and their prisoners disappeared out of sight.

'There are too many of them,' said Quig, 'and you saw how they were armed. What can we do against such men? They have already killed some of our people and they will kill again.' He lay silent for a moment, thinking of his friend Tomis, and what Daniel had told him about the body he had seen in the tunnel. He said, 'We must seek help quickly before they return to the White Waters. If we do not leave now, your friends will never be seen again.'

'Bleedin' hell, what am I going to tell the captain about Kristin?'

It was the first thought that came into Daniel's head. Even though it wasn't his fault that Kristin had stowed away in the van, he knew the captain's anger would explode when he heard what had taken place here.

But Quig was right: there was nothing they could do. Only the army could deal with this situation. They would have to get to the van and make contact with the soldiers as soon as possible. He turned round as Quig pulled at his sleeve, murmuring that they should leave. Daniel nodded his agreement, taking one last look towards Elam before following him on another route through the forest, away from the road and a Terog who had been left behind to guard the tunnel.

*

Archie pulled again at the chain between his wrists, but it was useless. There were no weak links and he was only making the grazes on his wrists worse. He gave a sigh of frustration and looked around the square where he now sat, along with Kristin and the villagers. It was dark, but the flickering light cast by the burning remains of the cottages and buildings that surrounded the square let him see the groups of women standing huddled together in the distance, crying and calling out to the men and boys beside him.

He realised that only the men from Marcie's village and the boys of Elam were held in the square, separate from the women.

He smiled as he had a sudden thought.

'What have you got to smile about?' snapped Kristin. She was sitting opposite him, her arms clasped to her chest, trying to keep warm.

'I was just thinking you should be over there with the women.'

'What do you mean?'

'It's your hair, and your clothes. The Terogs must think you're a boy, otherwise you wouldn't be here –'

Kristin squealed at him. 'Who do you think you are, saying that –'

'You must be quiet!' hissed a man sitting near her. He nodded towards one of the Terog guards flicking a whip as he walked around the square. 'They are quick to anger if they suspect trouble.'

'I'm not causing trouble!'

'He's right, Kristin. We have to be careful what we say and do if we're going to get ourselves out of this mess,' whispered Archie.

The man had introduced himself earlier when Archie and Kristin had been herded into the square to join the others. His name was Roni and he was the only man left in Elam after the first attack. He explained how he had been working on his boat in the harbour four years ago when the Terogs arrived. 'I was spared then,' he said, 'but now ...' He had raised his shackled hands to the sky and said nothing more, until now.

'What will happen to us?' asked Kristin quietly. For the first time since Archie had known her, she sounded frightened.

He shrugged, not knowing what to say to her. He was tired, hungry and cold; the dying fires that had consumed the buildings around them cast very little warmth across the square where they now sat, wondering what was going to happen to them. The air was laden with smoke; he could smell its sooty texture, taste it on his lips, so thick it made him want to spit.

He looked around the crowded square as a scream split the air behind him. It was one of many he had heard since arriving in Elam. Dozens of men, besides Kristin and him, were there, and the Terogs were not slow to use their metal-tipped whips on anyone they thought offered the slightest provocation. The very sight of their thick, yellowish features and red-rimmed black eyes was enough to inspire fear in anyone.

Roni kept his voice low as he spoke to them. 'I think we will leave as soon as their leader returns. He left soon after they arrived here – to where I do not know.'

'Who is he?' asked Archie.

'I know nothing of their language, but the Terogs called out to him as he left. They called him Talon.'

Chapter Thirty-Four

The Hidden Valley

Cosimo looked at his guest sitting opposite, across a breakfast table bearing the remains of a meal they had just eaten. He was intrigued by the little grey and black feathers tattooed on his face, from brow to chin, around piercing dark brown, almost black, eyes. A work of art, he thought, but more likely a design to bring fear to his enemies.

'Thank you for your hospitality last night, Anton,' said Talon, 'it was a very entertaining evening.'

'I never thought of the punishment detail as a form of entertainment, but I'm glad you enjoyed it,' said Cosimo, smiling at the description.

He poured each of them another glass of ale. It was the preferred drink of the Arnaks; a strong intoxicating beverage they brewed in one of the large caves near the river which ran the length of the valley. The water they needed for the process was scooped up by a waterwheel into the pipes that fed the caves where the rebels lived and slept.

'Perhaps not an entertainment, but I appreciate its effectiveness in maintaining order amongst your men.' Talon took another sip of his ale, then gestured with the glass a sign of his approval. 'Excellent. But tell me, what was the nature of their crimes, the men who were punished?'

Cosimo studied his own glass as he considered the question. Eight men had been reported to him, by Nitkin, his lieutenant, for various breaches of the laws he had imposed after he became leader of the rebel Arnaks. Another was Deeway who tried to capture the boy at the castle, but had failed. His 'crime' was leaving his robe in the hovercab, a careless act in

Cosimo's eyes, as it might have been a clue for the army or the Lancers to follow. But another reason, he knew, was that the boy who had escaped, continued to plague his thoughts as a business yet to be settled.

Deeway's punishment had been twenty lashes, strapped to the whipping post for all to witness. The other Arnaks had been given fewer lashes for a variety of minor offences, but one rebel had been given the ultimate penalty. The man had deserted the camp in the middle of the night, taking food and a weapon with him, both being commodities that were in short supply. He had been hunted down and brought before Cosimo the previous night, who had immediately sent the man to the whipping post to be garrotted. It was a form of strangulation he had seen practised in New Europe on Old Earth by the rebels there, who had found it to be an effective deterrent.

Cosimo explained why the men had been punished: 'I have over four hundred men in this camp and order must be maintained – with no exceptions. When Prince Lotane led them, they were a ragtag rabble of peasants and malingerers who could hardly wield the shaft of a brush, let alone a weapon. But now they know what is expected of them – and soon they will be a force that all of Amasia will fear.'

Talon laughed. 'I knew of Lotane and his dreams of restoring an ancient empire! That may yet come to pass, but he was not the one to make it happen. But you and I are very much alike, Anton. Now that you have the Arnaks with you and I have the Terogs, there are possibilities we should consider ... together.'

They were sitting on the veranda of a two storey log cabin that been built into the entrance of a large cave. The living area of the cabin, including two bedrooms and a large kitchen that extended into the rest of the cave, gave Cosimo the space he needed to keep his distance from the rebels he commanded. The cave was one of many dotted around the valley walls on both sides of the river. An ancient Arnak stronghold, it was once again a base from which the rebels could launch their attacks against the hated Salakins and anyone else they saw as their enemy. Protected by its natural surroundings the valley could only be approached through a narrow gorge on the edge of a wide river.

Deep in the forests of Arnaksland, the hidden valley had a plentiful supply of timber and water for most of their needs, but beyond hunting for fresh meat, there was little open space for growing food. The Arnaks had created numerous small allotments for their own use, but the rebel numbers had increased under Cosimo's leadership, putting ever greater strains on their food supply. Soon they would have to leave the valley and reclaim the land beyond they saw as rightfully theirs.

Far beyond the reach of General Branvin's army on the ground, they were unlikely to be seen from the air by any stray Lancer patrols. And in keeping with the Elders' edict, that for security reasons, no aircraft, besides the Lancers' Spokestars, would fly over the land of Amasia, it was unlikely anyone would find them in the deep tree-lined valley. But Cosimo suspected that his guest had plans for him to leave the safety of his retreat.

'You said something similar on one of the occasions we met,' mused Cosimo. 'In fact, each time we've met you alluded to such an arrangement. Perhaps, you would like to explain *exactly* what you have in mind?'

For a brief moment, their eyes locked together, like two chess masters trying to read the thoughts of the other, before making a move. In this case, it was Talon deciding how much he should reveal. He took another sip from his glass of ale before answering.

'I like your directness, so let me be equally forthright. But first, I think I should tell you a little about the Copanatecs and how they came to be in Amasia.'

Leaving his glass on the table, Talon stood up and went to the end of the veranda where steps led to the open ground in front of the cabin. The aroma of barbecued meat drifted through the air. A short distance away was another cave occupied by his phalanx of Terog guards, where two of them sat outside by a fire cooking a breakfast of freshly killed game. He pointed to the gorge where they had entered the valley a day earlier.

'Unlike you, Anton, I am not an alien. Beyond this valley is a land once peopled by countless tribes, including my own. Many of the tribes had their origins in your world, but mine had its roots in this one.' He touched his face as he recalled his youth. 'We were a warrior race known to all by our skin; this was given to me as a boy when I killed my first enemy.'

'Who were your people?' asked Cosimo. He was beginning to wonder where this history lesson was leading.

'It does not matter; it is more than 20,000 years since they existed as a tribe and now only a handful of us are left. But long before that time, the Copanatecs arrived from your world through the stones to establish a new kingdom in the coastal lands. One of many in a land that later came to be known as Hazaranet.'

'Stones – you mean like the one in the Sacred Temple where Lotane died?' Talon nodded. 'But I thought they were sacrificial sites –'

Talon raised a hand for Cosimo to be patient. 'No, that was not their original purpose. Since the beginning of time when all the universes were created there have been gateways connecting the worlds, and it has been the fate of countless beings to be transported between them. It was never the intention of the Copanatecs to journey to other worlds, but the unexpected arrival of timecracks gave them no choice.' He smiled. 'You know this, of course?'

Cosimo nodded. He and his half-brother had been the victims of such an event. If it hadn't been for the timecrack when entering Old Earth's orbit they could well be rotting in a prison in the middle of the Sahara. Although, Sandan might well have preferred such a fate to that of falling into the abyss in the Sacred Temple.

Talon continued: 'But the Copanatecs are a resourceful people and they came to learn many of the secrets of their universe. In the natural world, the occurrence of timecracks are unpredictable, but the ancient ones came to know that they are attracted by powerful energy fields, and that there were special places in their kingdom where such forces could be found. To control these forces they built the Chapac Stones alongside mighty pyramids and temples where the Lords of the Cloud could be worshipped.'

'And who are the Lords of the Cloud?' This was beginning to sound like the mumbo-jumbo Prince Lotane used to spout – and look what happened to him, thought Cosimo. But he realised Talon was telling him all this for a purpose, something, he sensed, that would be highly beneficial to him.

'They are the protectors of the Immortal Wand ...' Talon paused, as if the words were of great significance.

'And you are one of them?'

'No. I am known as one of the Defenders.'

'This is becoming confusing – why are you telling me all this? And what is the Immortal Wand?'

'It will become clear, and I believe, very acceptable to you. May I continue?'

Cosimo nodded. His curiosity aroused, he reached for the jug of ale and poured each of them another glass.

Accepting the drink, Talon said, '50,000 years ago the Copanatecs were a poor and primitive people, distinguished only by their height and white skin, but at some point during their long history they discovered something truly wonderful ... the Immortal Wand ... the giver of immortality ...' He paused again to watch Cosimo's reaction. 'Yes, Anton, it is unbelievable, but it is true. From that time on, the Copanatec Lords, and those whom they chose, became endowed with special powers; they and their descendants would forever bear the mark of the Immortal Wand.'

Talon reached below the neck of his robe and withdrew a golden chain. It held a gem-encrusted pendant with an unusual design on the reverse face. Displaying it before Cosimo, he said, 'This is the mark gifted to me by our First Lord, when he chose me to be a Defender.'

'A very impressive piece, I grant you, but what has it do with immortality?' Cosimo was becoming impatient and a tone of scepticism had crept into his voice. His inclination was to laugh out loud, but he did not want to insult his guest. After all, Talon had journeyed to the valley with important news and he had yet to hear it. 'Are you trying to tell me you possess the secret of eternal life?'

'Yes, Anton, I am.' Talon's eyes darkened, almost as black as the darkest night, while he considered his next words. 'Only the Lords of the Cloud and their descendants bear this mark on their skin as protectors of the Immortal Wand. Others who serve them well, like myself, are known as the Defenders. We are granted the pendant and the Blessing of Immortality by the First Lord, but the blessing must be performed on the eve of each person's great cycle ...'

'Or what?' prompted Cosimo, whose scepticism had abated as Talon told his story.

'Or ... we return to dust.'

Cosimo stared at him. 'You mean ... on the eve of each great cycle, the blessing must be repeated?' Talon nodded. 'How long is such a cycle?'

'I have been told you aliens call it a millennium.' Talon looked to the sky as a flock of birds flew overhead. 'I do not know, but the Lords calculate such things by the events of the stars. I am awaiting the fourth cycle.'

A millennium!

It was not often Cosimo was lost for words but, as he continued to stare at his guest, his amazement was obvious and profound. During his time in this new world he was aware that people lived a great deal longer than on Old Earth. Nitkin, his lieutenant, had admitted to being well over two hundred years old, and some of the other Arnaks claimed to be considerably more, but Talon ... *was he truly immortal?*

'You are trying to tell me that you are more than three thousand years old?'

'Yes, and it is the purpose of my visit to offer you the same prospect of immortality – that is,' Talon smiled at Cosimo's look of incredulity, 'if you wish to join with us?'

'You will forgive me, Talon, if I can't help thinking that this ... rather generous *offer* – the Blessing, you call it – is not without certain conditions?'

'Only that you continue to keep Amasia's army and the Lancers at bay while I, and my men, recruit the labour we need.'

Recruit? Enslave would be a more accurate description, thought Cosimo, but it was no concern of his – *or was it?* He said, 'I have not asked why you need to *recruit* so many men, but I have to admit I am curious – do you expect to go to war?'

'In a sense we are. At war with an enemy we cannot defeat,' said Talon. He paused for a moment, raising a hand to stay any more questions. 'The sea is our enemy, as it was in the past when it destroyed the land of the Copanatecs in the old world. Some of the people escaped to other lands, but many of the Lords managed to journey here through the stones, bringing the Immortal Wand with them.

'They built a magnificent city and a palace fit for the Lords of the Cloud to rule once again, over a new Copanatec and its people. But the land they chose was a wild and dangerous place on the coast of an angry sea, and in the time of my third great cycle a terrible cataclysm tore the earth apart, allowing the sea to overcome us until only an island – the land we now live on – was left.'

Cosimo listened carefully to Talon's story. Disasters were nothing new in any world and it mattered little to him what happened to the Copanatecs, but he was curious to learn more about them. He said, 'Is this why you take men from the villages – to rebuild your city?'

'No, the city will never be rebuilt, nor will we save the land; all will be lost when the sea finally returns to take Copanatec, as it has in the past.'

'You believe another disaster will occur – and yet you stay on your island?' Cosimo couldn't help laughing out loud, incredulous at the idea of waiting for the forces of nature to destroy the island. 'But that is madness!'

'It would seem so, but we stay for one reason only.' Talon returned to the table to look down at Cosimo, still sitting, drinking his glass of ale. 'During its passage through the pyramid after the ceremony of the Blessing, the wand fell into the depths of the earth when the Destruction came upon us and the sea swept over the city. The earthquake separated Copanatec from the mainland and the Immortal Wand was lost. For centuries we have searched for it, digging tunnels deep below the pyramid and beyond, while the White Waters continue to threaten our very existence. Every day we build and maintain the seawalls to stop the sea from flooding the tunnels'.

His eyes narrowed as he glanced at the pendant, the long claw-like fingers playing with the gold chain as it gleamed in the morning light 'So you see, Anton, we have no choice. Without the wand the Blessing cannot be given and the great cycles will come to an end. The Lords *and* the Defenders will cease to exist.'

Cosimo nodded. Now he understood why Talon had been raiding the villages. He needed the manpower to dig the tunnels and to build the seawalls that held back the sea.

But before he could respond to what he had just heard they were interrupted by someone shouting. The harsh guttural voice called again, loud and urgent, from the steps at the end of the veranda. It was one of the Terogs holding a communicator – a com similar to those used mainly by the army and the Lancers.

Talon strode down the veranda, his hand outstretched. 'Give me that and wait here!'

The Terog nodded, handed over the com and stood to one side while the rest of the Terog guard grouped below the cave waited expectantly for their orders.

Talon held the com to his ear. 'Did you recover the pendant?' What he heard from the person he spoke to did not please him. 'And you have the dust? Then take the men and destroy the village, and leave no one else alive!'

He gestured to the Terog to take the com. 'Get the men ready – we leave shortly.'

He had been expecting the call, hoping that the Terogs he had sent to Elam would find evidence of the missing Lord Tenoch and his pendant. Tenoch had disappeared four years earlier during a raid on the village, but recently rumours about a 'Man of Dust' in the village of Elam had been circulating among the prisoners working in the tunnels below the pyramid and others in the temple gardens. The rumours had been reported to Talon by the guards, saying the villagers now revered the man as a god. As soon as he heard the story, he knew it had to be Lord Tenoch, whose great cycle had obviously come to an end. But if the pendant had not been found, he knew he would have to answer to Lord Pakal.

Turning to face Cosimo, he said, 'I know you want power, Anton, and so do I. Together we can achieve much. Help me by keeping the soldiers and Lancers at bay until the wand is found and I will give you all the power you desire. Together, as immortals, we can forge an alliance to build a new empire in Amasia that no one will be able to resist! What do you say?'

Cosimo smiled at his guest's enthusiastic offer, knowing that he would have to tread carefully with such an ally, but he also knew that he could only progress so far with the rebel Arnaks. This was an offer he could not refuse. He nodded his acceptance. 'I think we can help each other, but I would like to learn more about this mysterious wand and its promise of immortality.'

'So be it. We will leave for Copanatec when you are ready.'

Chapter Thirty-Five

Copanatec

Once a city sitting proudly on a peninsula, penetrating spear-like into the churning waters of the Amasian Sea, Copanatec was now an island in the White Waters, its western shore dominated by towering basalt cliffs, the legacy of cataclysmic volcanic eruptions that had destroyed the landbridge to the mainland. White crested waves swirled and rushed past huge pillars of grey rock rising out of the sea near the shoreline, like giant fingers pointing towards a bleak, early morning sky. The mist that had hidden the island for most of the approach had disappeared.

Archie stared through the small, windowless porthole at the waves as they peaked and dipped before crashing onto the rocky coast, hardly believing that he was so close to the place where his parents were being held as prisoners.

But what now? How was he going to help them?

He and Kristin, along with the male villagers of Elam were also prisoners, all of them unshackled now for easier movement. Some were standing, crushed together in the middle of the cage, looking desperately forlorn, hardly able to come to terms with what had happened to them. Others, like Archie and Kristin, were crammed together on metal benches that ran alongside the sides of the cage which made up the best part of the stern of the ship. Only the sea air from the small open portholes above the benches afforded them any sort of relief.

Archie turned away from the porthole and looked down at Kristin sitting next to him. She was pale and seemed to be muttering to herself.

'Are you all right?'

Ever since the burning of the village and the massacre of those left behind she'd hardly said a word. When they marched out of Elam along with the villagers, they'd all heard the screams of the women and children being attacked as the Terogs, with ruthless determination, had gone into every building still left standing and set it alight until only smouldering embers remained. Afterwards, it was as if Elam and its inhabitants had never existed.

Some of the men had tried to stop and turn back. Yelling and pulling at the chains that shackled them together, they demanded to go back to the village to see what was happening, only to be savagely whipped back into line. One of them had dropped in front of Kristin, blood spurting from a bolt lodged in his neck. While she watched, horrified, the man had been unshackled and dragged into a ditch by the Terog who had fired the crossbow. After the killing there had been no further dissent as the column of prisoners and their guards marched to the coast. It was obvious they were now in the hands of a cruel, merciless force and any resistance would be foolish.

A short distance beyond the harbour, in a cove well-hidden below a high treeline, a strange looking oval-shaped craft with a wheelhouse near the bow and a long container-like structure that stretched all the way to the stern, had been drawn up onto a shingle beach. From its shape and the way it sat on the beach, Archie had guessed it was some sort of amphibian craft. Whatever it was, it was obviously the slave ship.

Now he was inside it.

He stepped down from the bench and stood in front of Kristin.

'Are you all right?' he asked again.

'Don't be stupid!' she snapped. 'No, I'm not all right. None of us are. We're in chains going to God knows where, and there's nothing we can do about it!'

Kristin was probably right, thought Archie. He looked around at the downcast faces of the men, who had clearly given up all hope of escape. He had no idea how they were going to get out of this mess. Certainly not while they were still caged in the slave ship. They would have to bide their time until they arrived in Copanatec and see what lay ahead of them.

*

As the slave ship rounded a point on the western headland, Archie, peering through the bars of the porthole and heavy sea spray, could see a group of figures moving along the top of a massive stone wall. Sailing closer to the island, he could see more clearly that the figures were hauling a wagon laden with large stones towards a spot on the seaward side where scaffolding had been erected against the wall. Planks laid across the top of the scaffolding held several men to receive the stones, ready to pass onto another group below them. As he watched, Archie could see there were several holes in the wall where the men were cementing the stones into place. They're repairing the wall to hold back the sea, he thought, just like the dykes he had read about in school.

Another L-shaped wall, a breakwater, stretched out to sea directly ahead of them, protecting the harbour against the worst of the White Waters.

'They are waiting for us,' said Roni, after climbing onto the bench to join Archie at the porthole. He nodded towards a line of armed Terogs standing on top of the harbour seawall inside the breakwater.

The slave ship made its way into the harbour until it came alongside a stone-built jetty. A gangway was run out on the port side, while a group of prisoners working on the seawall, ushered by the Terogs, rushed to make up the bow and stern mooring lines to the bollards on the jetty. Another group went on board to secure the fenders on the side of the ship.

'Looks like we've arrived,' said Archie.

He watched as two tall figures walked along the seawall. They came to a stop at the top of a set of stone steps cut into the wall. One of them, a stranger carrying a long rod, had unusual feather-like markings on his face, giving him the appearance of a fierce-looking bird, but it was the other figure who made him gasp out loud. 'I don't believe it! What the hell is he doing here?'

'Who are you talking about?' said Kristin. She stared at him, waiting for an answer.

Archie didn't hear her, his eyes were locked in disbelief on a man who seemed hell-bent on finding him, even here in Copanatec.

It was Cosimo, and he seemed to be on friendly terms with Birdface – as he now thought of the stranger. If so, and they were allies, the task of finding his parents and getting out of this place seemed even more unlikely.

Part Four

The Tunnels

Chapter Thirty-Six

Return to Mount Tengi

The door of the timecrack chamber slid silently into its recess as the two travellers stepped out onto the catwalk, directly opposite the lift that would take them down to the Timecrack Research Unit (TRU).

Watching them from his hoverchair, Dr Shah smiled broadly as one of the travellers raised the tinted visor to reveal the face of a boy he hadn't expected to see again. A catwalk engineer helped to remove the protective helmet, placing it to one side on a trolley next to the chamber door. He did the same for the other traveller, and then stepped inside the chamber to carry out an inspection. Both of the arrivals were wearing the new advanced version of the green, metallic fibre tracker suit, developed by the Mount Tengi engineers for timecrack journeys.

Pressing one of the symbols on the arm-pad of his hoverchair, Shah brought himself closer to the chamber. Despite his disability, he was an impressive figure. Stocky and broad-shouldered, he sported a walrus-like moustache and long white hair that blew freely around his head in the high wind that swept across the catwalk. He gave to the world, some would say deliberately, the appearance of a Viking warrior, reincarnated.

'Welcome back, Richard – look at you, you have grown much taller!' said Shah, his pleasure obvious at their safe arrival. 'And you, Aristo. No problems, I take it?'

'No, sir, nothing to report. Every journey between the chambers has been pin-point perfect, so far,' said Aristo, smiling. 'No need for these tracker suits, not like the first time!'

They both laughed at the memory of Aristo's first timecrack journey, which had almost ended in disaster when he had been propelled, accidentally, into Old Earth's distant past to the time of the dinosaurs. But the early prototype tracker suit had saved him by detecting a timecrack, enabling him to return to the Exploding Park in Timeless Valley. It was during his time in the park that he had met Professor Strawbridge and his nephews, Archie and Richard – and Marjorie, their tutor, who was now his wife.

Now head of the newly formed Timecrack Escort Group, Aristo, and other members of the group he would select, were to travel with and protect travellers during their journeys between the chambers at Mount Tengi, and Ameratsu, at the Facility on Old Earth.

'Perhaps not, Aristo, but remember that one of these suits saved you from being stranded in a very undesirable place. Once our programme of sending people back to their points of origin begins, the new tracker suits may well be the saving of many a traveller, once again. But enough of that – what about Mr Winters? Is he following?'

'Yes, another of the escorts is with him. He will be here shortly.'

'Excellent. Now, my young friend and I have a lot to catch up on. Haven't we, Richard?'

But Richard didn't hear him. His eyes were focused on the huge black-tiled structure that housed the timecrack chamber. When last here, on their return to the Facility, he and Archie had been so dazzled by the great, glowing silver sphere, they'd worn dark sunglasses to prevent them being blinded. Now a ten-storey black cube encased the entire sphere and its chamber.

He could sense the enormous power being drawn from the grid and the vallonium that made up most of the mountain, its influence coursing through him like an electric current.

His eyes flickered as strange images appeared unbidden, but such visions no longer held any fear for him. Not since his time in the clinic when he had come to terms with whatever it was that haunted his dreams, turning them into nightmares. He turned away from the images, sending them back into the mountain, or wherever they came from.

'Richard? Are you all right?'

'I'm sorry, Dr Shah, it's just that everything looks so different from the last time I was here.'

'Yes, there have been a number of advances in the timecrack programme, here in the chamber and the Parasite. We had realised for some time that the sphere was losing too much of the energy it drew from the grid – that's why it glowed so brightly. And so, shortly after you and Archie left here, we designed and built a series of containment shields inside the black housing you see.' Shah chuckled for a moment, 'Krippitz is delighted with the extra power he has access to; it's like a new toy he has to play with. Now let's go below for some refreshments and let you change out of that suit, while we wait for your colleague to arrive.'

*

Chuck followed the escort into Shah's office, helmet and tracker suit replaced by denims and checked shirt, the Stetson he usually wore carried in his right hand. He looked around a large room, the walls coated by sheets of paper covered with strange diagrams and a host of figures. On chairs opposite a wide desk sat Richard, Aristo and a spiky-haired, geeky-looking figure he later came to know as Dr Carl Krippitz.

Moving from behind the desk, sitting on a floating chair, Shah spoke to him.

'Welcome, Mr Winters, to Mount Tengi. Sit yourself down and join us. An uneventful journey, I hope?'

'Call me Chuck. Yes, it was – I've had more trouble crossing over the Mexican border than making this trip to another world.'

Shah laughed. 'Yes, I crossed that border many times, but that was long ago. Sixty years before you, by Old Earth time, I think.'

Chuck nodded. He had checked out Shah's background before leaving the Facility, and through his security clearance he had been able to access secret files that hadn't seen daylight since the end of the Second World War. He had discovered that Emil Shah had worked at Los Alamos with Robert Oppenheimer and a team of scientists on the Manhattan Project to create the first atomic bomb.

The results of the project were witnessed on a fateful summer morning in July 1945 when the bomb exploded and the Atomic Age was ushered into an unsuspecting world. But an unforeseen and inexplicable event had taken place, seconds after the explosion, when four of the scientists disappeared in a mysterious blue cloud when it descended onto their observation post, and just as rapidly, disappeared again. Despite an exhaustive search of the area, they were never seen again. Nobody could explain what had happened and in due course the event was hushed up, a memorial service held and the incident recorded in the archives as another tragic accident in the annals of war.

The scientists were long gone, thought Chuck, except for one and he was staring right at him.

'Yes, Dr Shah, a lot has happened since you and your friends disappeared from Los Alamos,' said Chuck.

'Ah, you have been doing your homework, I see.'

'Back at the Facility part of my job is to keep an eye out for anything unusual – and by the look of things there's plenty of that here.'

'I'm afraid you have come to us at a difficult time, Chuck. There *is* a lot happening here. As far as we can tell, the rebels are behind a series of bombings and killings across the country; they have attacked Zolnayta and its port, and only yesterday, they struck again in Fort Temple by blowing up the bus station!'

Richard flinched when he heard what Shah said, thinking of the time he had travelled from there on the Freebus.

'It sounds bad. Any word on Archie's situation?' asked Chuck. He didn't like the sound of what was going on and the sooner he got to grips with what was happening in this world, the closer he would be to finding Archie.

'Has anyone heard anything about him?' echoed Richard.

Shah raised a hand to stay any more questions. He nodded towards Krippitz, 'I think Carl can bring you up to date on what we know.'

Adjusting the thick-lensed glasses that had slipped to the end of his nose, Krippittz stood up and pulled a leather-bound notebook from the pocket of a three-quarter length, navy lab coat he habitually wore.

'At two minutes past three yesterday afternoon I met with –'

'Oh, for Heaven's sake, Carl, this is not a courtroom,' groaned Shah. 'Put the notebook away and introduce yourself to Chuck. Just give us an overview of what you learned from Brimstone.'

Richard grinned as Krippitz turned to Shah, looking offended at being interrupted. Not much has changed between these two, he thought.

'Yes ... Well, whatever you say, Emil,' said Krippitz. Putting his notebook away, he turned to face Chuck. 'My name is Dr Carl Krippitz. I am the chief scientist at the Evaluation Clinic in the Centre for New Arrivals at Castle Amasia. I am responsible for assessing arrivals and their suitability for remaining in Amasia – '

'Carl, will you *please* just tell us what Brimstone told you ...' said Shah. His eyes now firmly fixed to a spot on the ceiling.

'I'm only ...' Krippitz gave up what he was about to say when he saw the look on Shah's face. Instead, he said, 'Brimstone is the Castle Protector and I met with him yesterday when I delivered some assessments I'd just finished. During the course of our meeting, he mentioned that he had received a report from his fellow protector in Zolnayta about an incident involving Archie Kinross.'

'What!' Richard was out of his chair when he felt a hand on his arm restraining him. 'What's happened to him? Where is –'

'Easy, Richard, let's hear what the man has to say,' said Chuck. He stood up and placed his Stetson on the chair, then walked across to a framed map hanging on the wall. 'Does this show where this place Zol ... what do you call it ... is?'

'Port Zolnayta,' Aristo joined him and pointed to a place on the map, 'here, on the south coast. There have been a number of bombings in the area, probably caused by the rebel Arnaks – but it's unusual in that it's not their normal tactic. It's too well planned. Major Hanki of the Lancers believes the bombing campaign has been instigated by a new leader of the rebels.

Possibly a New Arrival called Cosimo according to information he's received.'

Chuck nodded. This was all new to him and he needed to learn a great deal more. He turned away from the map. 'Dr Krippitz, what was this incident concerning Archie? What can you tell us?'

'It would seem that there was an attempt on his life shortly after he met with Sunstone at Castle Zolonayta, but he managed to escape without any harm coming to him.'

'Thank God for that,' said Chuck.

'But ...' Krippitz hesitated, as if he was reluctant to say anything else.

'What do you mean, 'but'?'

'I'm afraid Sunstone reported that Archie and a girl, along with a number of villagers, were abducted by slave traders and they haven't been seen since.'

'Slave traders! What in creation's name are you talking about?'

'I can't tell you any more than that. It's all we have heard so far, but there were others with them and apparently they managed to escape. They were the ones who told Sunstone what happened.'

Chuck looked at Richard who seemed to be stunned into silence by Cosimo's name and by what they'd just heard. He cast his eyes back to Krippitz.

'And what's happening now? Is there a search going on for them?'

'I believe the army is scouring the area, but we have heard nothing more.'

'If we are waiting for General Branvin and the army to find them, we will be waiting a long time,' snorted Shah. He manoeuvred his hoverchair over to face the map. Pointing to a spot near the bottom of the frame, he said, 'That part of Amasia is like your jungles in South America and its coast is just as wild and treacherous.

Branvin has no idea how to deal with the rebels and the bombings; and at the same time find the slave traders who have been plaguing that coast for years. He's an incompetent fool!'

'I think I get the idea, Dr Shah,' said Chuck. He looked at the map again, for a moment, before turning to Krippitz. 'Where are these people now who escaped?'

'One of them, I believe, works on the trawlers in Port Zolnayta.'

Chuck stroked the moustache he had trimmed recently, then picked up his Stetson. 'Well, folks, I think Richard and I'd better get down there and hear how he managed it'

Chapter Thirty-Seven

The Quayside

Aristo took the Bonebreaker very slowly through the narrow gap that separated the black housing of the timecrack chamber from the vallonium grid interconnectors. As the TRU complex slipped out of sight below them, he retracted the six landing-pads, pointing the nose with its huge fender into the high turbulent winds that swept around this part of the mountain, the ancient steel plates of the Bonebreaker groaning like an old woman, the higher it rose.

Chuck grabbed his Stetson as the wind tried to whip it from his head and placed it between his feet. 'This is some machine, Aristo. The last time I was in an open cockpit, I was a kid learning to fly an old Stearman biplane.'

'You're a pilot?' asked Aristo.

'I don't do much flying these days, but, yes, it's in my bloodline, I suppose.'

'What do you mean, your 'bloodline?' asked Richard. He was strapped in the middle of three bucket seats behind the deep windscreen of the Bonebreaker, sitting between Aristo and Chuck. Behind them a short passageway led to the passenger and load bay in the rear.

'Well, I guess what I mean is that it goes back to my grandfather and the days of the barnstormers in the 1920's. That's only a few short years after the Wright brothers built and flew the first practical flying machine, and not that long after the end of the First World War.'

Richard looked at him curiously. 'What were the barnstormers?'

'They were the early stunt pilots. I know it sounds like ancient history, but in just over a hundred years of manned flight, those guys were there at the beginning. After the end of the war in 1918, a lot of the pilots had it in their blood to keep flying and when the government started selling the 'Jennys' – the Curtiss JN 4 biplane, that most US pilots had learned to fly in – for a couple of hundred dollars each, and bearing in mind they'd originally cost a few thousand to build, they bought them and kept on flying.

'Jobs were hard to come by in those days, so guys like Lindberg and the other pioneers of early flight flew across the country to small towns where most people had never seen an airplane up close and started selling tickets for a ride in the sky. They would land at a farm near the barn – hence the 'barnstormers' – and do a deal with the farmer to use a field as a runway. From there they would stage an airshow, carrying out all sorts of crazy stunts like wing-walking and anything else they could dream up to thrill the crowds. When the barnstormers flew in, the whole town would close down and declare the day a holiday.

'My grandfather – 'Cold' Winters they called him, for the cool and nerveless way he used to perform his stunts – finally retired when the government, along with the changing times, imposed new laws to curb the accidents and deaths that had taken place, not only to the pilots but to some of the people on the ground. By that time, my father who had grown up around all those incredible flying machines had also been bitten by the flying bug.'

'Did he become a barnstormer?' asked Aristo. His eyes bright with curiosity, he was enthralled with Chuck's story and the strange aircraft he described.

'No, it was all over by then, but he managed to get his hands on an old Stearman trainer biplane that had crashed into a field. A crop duster had been spraying that day, but he lost control of it and hadn't the skill to rebuild it, so he scrapped it. Luckily my father came across it and he decided to have a go at restoring it, but it took quite a few months to get it into shape to fly again. The Boeing Company had built thousands of Stearman Kaydets as a military trainer for the army and navy during the war, so it was no problem getting parts.'

'And he taught you to fly?'

'That he did. I was only fifteen at the time and to this day I remember my solo as the most exciting thing that ever happened to me – and that includes a lot of flying time since then. But this is a first, flying in a machine that's more like a tank than a plane.'

Aristo laughed as he adjusted a set of levers in front of him. 'Others from your world have said the same when they flew with me, but as I told Archie and Richard when they first saw the Bonebreaker: It was never meant to fly and was originally used many years ago by the Lancers to herd wild animals in the Exploding Park, until it was replaced by the more modern Spokestars.'

'Spokestars?'

Richard spoke up. He had been sitting quietly, sensing the strange power of the vallonium deposits that permeated Mount Tengi, but thankfully they no longer seemed to disturb him. 'The Spokestars are fantastic, Chuck. The Lancers fly them when they're on patrol over Amasia. They're like missiles, only you can ride in them.'

'Yes, they are nothing like the Bonebreaker, but they both use the same principle,' said Aristo. 'The vallonium units feed anti-grav power thrusters for vertical and horizontal flight.'

Chuck nodded as he settled back into his seat. 'Looks like I've a lot to learn about this world of yours.'

Aristo glanced across Richard to observe Chuck as he folded his arms and closed his eyes. Pulling away from the mountain, he wondered if this man had any idea what he might be up against in his search for Archie. Only time will tell, he thought, as he set course for the south coast.

*

'There it is,' said Aristo.

Through a darkening sky, and a hint of rain, he pointed a finger towards a collection of one-storey, grey stone buildings running the length of Port Zolnayta's quayside. Three trawlers lay alongside as cranes worked two of them, unloading crates of fish and ice onto the little flatbed railcars for their journey into the cold storage units inside the auction shed.

It had been a week since the bombings had occurred, but the presence of the army was still evident with two fully armed soldiers still patrolling the dock area.

'I'll put down beside the shed, in the parking bay,' said Aristo. He peered over the side of the cockpit as he brought the Bonebreaker over a large open area where the railcars were normally parked. He moved a lever to hover, ready to descend, when a loud *thanngg* startled all three of them.

He called out, 'What was that!'

'I don't know, but it sounds very like something I've heard too many times in the past,' said Chuck. He had taken the opportunity to catch up on some sleep during the flight. But now he was fully awake, looking cautiously down at the dockside.

'What do you mean?'

'You'd better take this thing out of here damned fast!'

'What – '

'Just do it! Someone down there is shooting at us!'

Another *thanngg* somewhere below them convinced Aristo to take immediate action. He turned the Bonebreaker and dipped the nose until it was facing into what he hoped was the line of fire, the wide, spoon-shaped nose fender ready to deflect any more shots. Chuck and Richard ducked their heads below the windscreen, while Aristo released his safety belt, allowing him to stand and get a better look at who was shooting at them.

'The stupid idiot,' he muttered. 'Doesn't he recognise the TRU badge?'

Down below on the dockside a soldier armed with a laser missile rifle was crouched near one of the railcars, about to take aim again when it was suddenly snatched from his hands. Standing over him was a burly, well-built man, obviously a seaman with his rubber boots and navy peaked hat. The soldier tried to get to his feet, but the seaman kept him on his knees with the rifle pointed at him while the other soldier ran towards them.

'Crazy fool,' said Aristo. He levelled out, pulling another lever to lower the landing pads, quickly picking a clear spot in the parking bay to land. 'We better get down there and help that man, before someone gets hurt.'

After the first shot everything had come to a halt on the dockside, the dockers and crane men scattering to take cover wherever they could. The seaman, Abelhorn, with the wolftan by his side, had been working on the deck of the *Serpent*, preparing to go back to sea. He'd recognised the TRU badge on the side panels of the

Bonebreaker as it hovered over the shed, but suddenly, confusion and panic had broken out when one of the soldiers patrolling the dockside fired his weapon. Without thinking about his own safety, Abelhorn, with Bran behind him, had dashed down the gangway to tackle the soldier, ripping the rifle out of his hands.

'You bloody fool, who the hell do you think you're shooting at?'

'Drop the weapon!' yelled another voice. 'Now, or I will fire!'

It was the other soldier, now aiming his rifle at Abelhorn. But the seaman refused; instead he pointed the weapon directly at the soldier still on his knees. Bran growled, a long reddish tongue slithering between yellow fangs, ready to sink into flesh if given the command.

'You fire and I'm likely to do the same, and Bran, here, will not take too kindly to your action. So I suggest you both come to your senses and stop trying to shoot innocent people.'

'That's right, soldier, you've fired on a government research craft, endangering the passengers. This will have to be reported to your superiors,' said Aristo, with as much authority as he could muster. He and Chuck, along with Richard, had just joined Abelhorn. He turned round and pointed to the Bonebreaker. 'Didn't you see the TRU badge?'

'No, we did not recognise your craft,' said the soldier. He looked nervous, unsure what he should do next, especially as the big seaman still held his friend's weapon. A wolftan with its hellish eyes and great drooling jaws stood nearby, ready to tear someone apart. He nodded towards the Bonebreaker. 'Only the Lancers fly the skies over Amasia – and that is not a Spokestar!'

A small crowd of men had ventured out from the warehouses to see what was going on. They were grouped together near Abelhorn when a figure marched through them. Like the soldiers, he was dark-skinned, wore green battledress and a black beret with the insignia of the Southern Army Division.

'Lower your weapons,' ordered Lieutenant Isula. 'That includes you, Captain Abelhorn.'

The soldier on his knees retrieved his rifle from Abelhorn and scrambled to one side, trying to avoid the lieutenant's angry gaze.

'Now, would someone like to explain what is happening here?' asked Isula. He looked around the group, but his question was obviously directed to Abelhorn.

'It would seem, Lieutenant, that the army is unable to tell friend from foe. No sooner is your curfew lifted we're now subjected to trigger-happy soldiers as well as the rebels and their bombs.'

One of the soldiers snarled an oath, about to say something, but a look from Isula put him in his place. He glanced across to the Bonebreaker and noted the TRU badge on the panel.

'Ah, the prestigious Timecrack Research Unit, I think? A very unusual machine, not known in this part of the world by my men ...' He let the excuse for their actions hang in the air for a moment. 'Perhaps, you could explain its purpose here?'

Aristo stepped forward and introduced himself, along with Chuck and Richard.

'Aristo ... Ah, the time traveller! I know of you. I have read of your work with Dr Shah at Mount Tengi and the TRU. Yes, I remember well the news of your first journey to the other world.'

'You do?' Aristo's eyes widened, surprised by Isula's reaction to his name. 'I didn't think anyone this far south would know anything about me.'

It was true that only the Lancers flew occasionally over this part of Amasia, security being in the hands of the army, and certainly, the arrival of a strange flying machine would have been an unusual sight for the citizens here. Perhaps, he thought, belatedly, he should have informed the army in advance of his visit to Port Zolnayta.

'We may be some distance from the centre of government, but we follow such news with great interest,' smiled Isula, his gaze sweeping across the faces of the others with Aristo, 'and, of course, all those also involved with the TRU.'

Aristo nodded at the obvious hint that Isula wanted to know more about what they were doing on the quayside. Introducing Chuck and Richard as New Arrivals, he explained that they had recently arrived to help in the search for Archie, who had disappeared along with the captain's granddaughter. It was why they were here; to discover what they could about their disappearance.

'Yes, there have been many such incidents on this coast. Unfortunately, we do not have the manpower to investigate all of them –'

'One or two, at least, would be a start!' snorted Abelhorn.

Isula ignored the interruption. Smiling, he said, 'I am sorry about the ... rather *warm* welcome you received, but we are still on high alert here, as no doubt, you will learn from Captain Abelhorn. However, I am here to help in any way I can. My quarters are at the end of the quayside, if you need me.'

He snapped his fingers at the two soldiers who quickly fell into step behind him, leaving the group standing near the *Serpent* to consider what he'd said.

'A pretty sharp customer, I would say,' muttered Chuck. 'Maybe he can help us.'

'Maybe,' grunted Abelhorn. He made his way back onto the gangway, with Bran at his heels. He called over his shoulder: 'You'd better come on board and meet Daniel, he'll tell you what happened to Archie and Kristin.'

Chapter Thirty-Eight

On Board the *Serpent*

Abelhorn led them into the galley where they saw a young, lean figure leaning over a long wooden bench with a bar of soap and a scrubbing brush.

'Glad to see someone is getting on with some work around here.'

Daniel grinned. 'Well, Captain, someone has to keep an eye on things while you play soldier out on the dock.'

'You saw what happened?'

'I did, but I saw you and Isula had things well in hand, so I came back here to tidy this place – in case we had visitors,' said Daniel, looking pointedly to the others behind Abelhorn.

'Aye, we have,' said Abelhorn, quickly introducing everyone to each other. 'And after that nonsense out there, I think a drink is in order.' He went across the galley and opened a locker to reveal a bottle of Sticklejuice. He lifted it out and placed it on the table with several glasses.

'Here, try this,' he said. 'It's the real stuff, not the tonic that most Amasians drink.'

Chuck took a sip and rolled his eyes as he tried the strong liquor, nodding his appreciation to Abelhorn.

'This'll match a good brandy any day, Captain.'

'So I'm told. You're welcome to take a bottle with you. You may be needing it, if you're planning to go after those savages, whoever they are.' Abelhorn's words cast a silence around the table. 'Yes, I was informed by Sunstone, our Castle Protector, of your impending visit. Apparently, Dr Shah at Mount Tengi asked for whatever assistance we could offer you while you're in Zolnayta.'

They were interrupted by Orlof, the *Serpent's* wheelman, joining them at the table. Abelhorn introduced him to the visitors, and then asked him if he had found a replacement for Tinkey.

'We can't go back to sea without a bait man, and Quig still hasn't shown his ugly face, so what have you come up with?'

'I talked to a bait man from one of the trawlers in the yard for repairs. He said he might give us a trip if she's in too long. I don't know what Quig's plans are – he's with Marcie at the village dealing with the aftermath of the massacre at Elam. When I spoke with him he seemed to be worried that the slavers might come after him.'

'What in Heaven's name would they want with him?'

'I don't know, Captain, but he said something about a pendant he had found in Elam.'

'Whatever it is he's talking about, it's a damned bad business,' said Abelhorn, pouring himself another large measure. 'Bombings, slavers attacking the villages, Kristin and Archie gone to who knows where. When is all this madness going to end?'

'What happened to Archie?' asked Richard. 'I mean ... where do you think he is?'

Since leaving the Facility and arriving at Mount Tengi, Richard had said little about his brother. He regretted not paying more heed to what Archie had asked of him, but it had been at a time when his dreams and visions had caused him nothing but pain and distress. Now they only occurred when he was ready to open his mind to another dimension. Something had happened to him during his time in the clinic; it was as if he had learned to switch off the kaleidoscope of crazy images that swirled through his head, to accept only what he *needed* to see and hear. But even then the visions were not always clear.

Shaman-Sing's words had come to him ... *'Remember, Richard, the mind is the universe within, but you are also part of the universe without. Understand that your world and all other worlds are connected. It is a journey you have already taken many times, and you will again.'*

Recalling the old shaman's words, Richard had tried to reach his mother again on a couple of occasions, only to witness strange scenes of a city and turbulent waters, before slipping away again into the realms of darkness, leaving behind a memory of meaningless chaos which he could not explain.

Abelhorn shook his head as he spoke, 'I don't know, Richard. I think you'd better ask Daniel your questions, he was the last to see him ... and my granddaughter.'

'I don't know what to tell you, mate,' said Daniel. 'The last I saw of him, he and Kristin were being dragged away by the Terogs. I couldn't believe what he did, jumping on those brutes to try and save Kristin.'

'Are the Terogs the slavers?'

'I suppose so. I've never seen them before, but they're a bleedin' ugly lot, I can tell you. They're not a crowd I want to see again, here or anywhere else.'

Chuck placed a hand on Richard's arm to stay any more questions. From what he'd heard so far, he realised that there was trouble ahead of them in their quest to find out what had happened to Archie and the girl. He explained to Daniel he needed to know about the Terogs: how many there were, where they came from, their weapons, and anything else that might prove useful in dealing with them.

'I can't tell you much more. It's really Quig you need to talk to. He was a prisoner of theirs before he managed to escape from them.'

Chuck nodded. There was no point in wasting more time here. He turned to Aristo, ' I think we'd better get back into that machine of yours. The sooner we get to this village of Quig's, and find out what he knows, the better.'

Richard couldn't agree more. After what Daniel had said about Archie attacking the Terogs, he was beginning to fear the worst about what could have happened to him.

Chapter Thirty-Nine

Richard and the Pendant

A tall woman, with strands of long dark hair swirling around her face, waved to them as Aristo brought the Bonebreaker to a rest in the centre of the square.

Chuck gripped his Stetson as the strong mountain breeze whipped through the cockpit. 'I guess that's Marcie waiting for us. Daniel said she would be here with Quig.'

Before leaving the cockpit, he scanned the square, a habit from his military days when entering unfamiliar territory. Considering the welcome they had received from the soldiers back at Port Zolnayta, he wasn't taking any more chances. As they left the Bonebreaker behind them, he noticed a man with a badly scarred face crossing the square from a nearby cottage to join the woman.

'Hi there, you must be Marcie,' said Chuck, introducing himself along with Richard and Aristo.

'Yes, I am. I have been expecting you, and this is my brother, Quig.' Knowing the purpose of their visit, her eyes lingered for a moment on Richard, as if she knew that the search for Archie would, somehow, centre around him. 'Daniel said you would have many questions, but please, I have prepared a meal for us and we can talk then.'

Ignoring their protests that they didn't want to put her to any trouble, she led them to the cottage Quig had just left. Ushering them through a narrow wooden door into an unexpectedly spacious room, they were met by dozens of brightly coloured, hand-woven cushions spilling onto the floor from nearly as many sofas and chairs. On the far side of the room was a cooking range that had obviously seen many years of use, with blackened pots in all shapes and sizes hanging above the range in an orderly row. A pan and its contents simmered, sending a beefy aroma across the room as she sat them down at a table near the range.

Richard, whose appetite was rarely sated, licked his lips at the prospect of a home cooked meal. He said, 'That smells really good.'

'You're hungry?' said Marcie, placing a dish of meat stew and vegetables in front of him. 'Well, there's plenty here for everyone. Eat your fill, there's more if you want it.'

She grinned as she watched Richard clear his plate before anyone else, ready for the same again. She was delighted that her food was appreciated and that the others also ate well, except for Quig muttering that he had work to do. He seemed anxious to leave and had hardly touched his plate.

'Don't be so rude, Quig,' scolded Marcie. 'Our guests have only just arrived and they have questions they wish to ask.'

A little embarrassed by Quig's obvious reticence to say anything, Aristo felt obliged to say something: 'You have a lovely place, Marcie. I've never seen so many cushions in one room, and the patterns ... they are stunning.'

'Thank you, I am pleased you like them. It is what I do ... I make and sell them to those who wish to buy ...' She hesitated for a moment, a look of sadness flickering across her face, betraying some inner thought. 'My friend in Elam used to help me sell the cushions to the other villages –'

'And now she's dead!' Quig's sudden outburst caught all of them by surprise. His eyes cast downwards, hands bunched into fists resting on the table, he shouted the words at Marcie.

'Hush, Quig, our guests should not be disturbed with such things. Elisha would not have you behave like this –'

'We were to be married – how should I behave?' He stood up, pushing his chair away from the table, ready to leave. 'I must go. The Terogs may come here, and it will be my fault if they do.'

Marcie's eyes widened. 'How can you say such a thing. Why would it be your fault?'

It was too soon for Chuck to fully understand the reasons for Quig's behaviour, but he recognised fear when he saw it. He had seen it on the battlefield, and afterwards when men were trying to come to terms with what they had seen and done in the name of war.

He said, 'Please stay, Quig, and tell us what you can about what happened in Elam. We are here to help in whatever way we can, as well as to find Richard's brother. Will you help us?'

Quig shook his head, as if unsure what he should do. In spite of the fearsome scar he bore, at this moment in time he seemed a sad and lonely figure. When he spoke, his words were directed to Marcie: 'What happened at Elam must not happen here. When the Terogs come to our village we must be ready for them ...'

'But why ... why should they come here?' asked Marcie.

Quig gazed around the table at all of them, speaking slowly and quietly, as if he were frightened by the very words he uttered. He told how four years earlier, when the men of his village heard of the attack on Elam, they rushed to help, but it was too late. All they could do was comfort those left behind and make whatever repairs they could. But as they cut wood to carry out the work they found one of the evil ones lying in the undergrowth, badly wounded. Some of the men carried him on a makeshift litter of roughly trimmed branches held together by twine, to a cottage that had been undamaged in the attack. There they laid him on a cot to take a closer look at his injuries, but they shook their heads when it became obvious that there was little they could do, for the wound was deep and already badly infected.

The men debated what they should do with the evil one. Some argued that they should finish him there and then for what had happened in Elam, but there were others who wanted nothing to do with more killing, saying that he was due for an early grave, anyway. As it happened, the decision was unexpectedly taken out of their hands by a very strange event that took place while they argued.

Quig stopped for a moment in the telling of his story, then said,' I learned later, during my capture, that the man we had found was known as Tenoch, a Lord of the Clouds. He was different from the ugly, yellow-skinned Terogs, with their foul tempers and deadly weapons. Tenoch was tall, slender and white-skinned ...'

He hesitated again, lowering his head over clasped hands, as if he wanted to forget what happened that day.

Encouraging him to continue, Chuck said, 'Quig, please try and remember what happened.'

'I remember only too well,' said Quig, lifting his head, eyes flashing angrily. 'It was while we talked of killing him that the golden smoke formed over Tenoch –'

'*Golden* smoke? You mean, like a cloud?' asked Richard, wondering if it was anything like the blue cloud of a timecrack.

Quig nodded. It was as if the sun had entered the room, he said. So terrified were they by the glowing mist that had suddenly appeared, that he and the men fled from the cottage, believing it to be the harbinger of an approaching spirit. Several hours later, more out of curiosity than bravery, he returned to the cottage to discover that Tenoch had disappeared. All that remained was dust and the golden pendant.

Intrigued by the story, Richard had the strangest feeling that he knew the golden smoke held some sort of meaning for him, but he couldn't quite put his finger on it.

'What happened after that?' he asked. 'Did you find out what happened to Tenoch?'

'Nothing is known about him, but a terrible storm raged through the land that night. The men believed it to be the angry spirit of Tenoch, warning them that the Terogs would return to avenge him.'

Chuck listened quietly, but couldn't help smiling at the superstitious interpretation that the villagers had put on the events of that night.

Quig didn't notice and continued: 'To make peace with him, we collected his dust and placed it in a beautiful urn we had one of our masons create from the local stone quarry. Since then, it had rested on a special altar in the community hall where the people from both our villages paid their respects to the Man of Dust. But it was not enough, and now it is my fault that the evil ones have returned.'

The anguish that crossed Quig's scarred face was painful to witness, his self-guilt obvious to all of them.

Mystified by what he'd heard, Richard said, 'You did nothing wrong, how could it be your fault?'

'Because when I gathered Tenoch's dust, I discovered his golden pendant and kept it for myself.'

Still confused, Richard asked, 'What's so important about the pendant? I mean, what's it like?'

'I don't know why the Terogs will kill for it – but Marcie now wears it around her neck.'

A sudden gasp from Marcie made Richard, Chuck and Aristo turn to see her clasping something inside her blouse. Slowly, she opened the top button and drew forth a gold chain until it was fully exposed.

She cried out in shock, her voice angry, as she pulled the chain over her head, throwing it onto the table towards Quig: 'You never said the evil ones had come back for this!'

The golden chain lay amongst the plates they had eaten from, its disc-shaped pendant, encrusted with small precious stones, glittering in a beam of light streaming through a nearby window, its links shimmering like little goldfish in a sunlit pond.

'I was going to give it to Elisha, but when you saw it and liked it so much, I let you have it ... and now she is gone because of it.'

'You must take it back to them – we cannot keep it here!'

'Are you mad? If they know I took it they will come here and kill all of us!'

'What have you done to us, Quig? We must get rid of the pendant before they come!' cried Marcie. Her eyes swept round the table in desperation, seeking some sort of answer to rid themselves of the danger from the Terogs. Suddenly she stared at Richard, as if something had just occurred to her. 'What was it that your brother knew about the pendant?' she asked.

'I don't know,' shrugged Richard.

He was sitting between Aristo and Chuck, transfixed by the pendant ever since Marcie had thrown it onto the table. He had sensed its power immediately, drawing him into its sphere of influence, sucking him into some unknown place, a place of mystery and danger.

He picked up the pendant and let his fingers trace the pattern of the coloured stones on one side of the disc.

*

285

Without shape or physical form, unseen and unknown, Richard entered a large, rectangular room. The walls were covered with long, rich red and gold drapes, hanging between pairs of tall marble columns that stood on each side of the room. The columns, each one resting on a huge golden plinth, rose majestically to meet a ceiling decorated with the stars and symbols of the multiverse. Bright sunlight slanted through a stained glass dome to fall on a great circular stone directly below. He recognised it as a Transkal, and in its shallow central trough, encircled by strange glyphs engraved into the stone, was the body of a woman dressed in a white robe

As he watched, several other women approached the stone, each one laying their hands on a glyph. They were the priestesses, each wearing a white robe bearing the image of a glyph matching the one their hands rested on.

The priestesses began to sing. The song was thousands of years old, its words sung only when they stood together by the stone to prepare one of their own for the journey to the next realm. The woman in the trough opened her eyes and smiled. It was Richard's mother. A golden mist seemed to leave her body, slowly enveloping the great stone until he could no longer see her.

The mist hovered over the stone for a moment and then began to spiral upwards to the dome. When the last trace of the mist disappeared, so had his mother.

He cried out ...

*

Richard felt someone pulling at his arm.

It was Chuck. 'What is it, Richard? What's wrong?'

Richard's eyes were closed for a few moments, his skin pale and fingers twitching as he held the pendant. He had just witnessed the golden smoke Quig spoke of earlier. He stood up and reached out for something that none of them could see. Chuck grabbed him by the arm and pulled him back into his chair.

Marcie and the others were startled by his behaviour, wanting to know if he was ill, or having some sort of fit.

Richard held the pendant next to his chest and looked at the others sitting around the table. They were gazing at him in silence, as if they expected him to say something.

'Sorry ... uh ... sometimes I get these ... well, like dreams ...'

'Dreams?' said Marcie, looking a little worried. More like a nightmare, she thought. Was it a kind of madness she had just seen? 'Is it an illness you suffer?' she asked.

'No ... no, nothing like that ... it's just –'

Chuck came to Richard's rescue, knowing how hard it would be for him to explain his trances. He held his hand out for the pendant. 'Can I see that?' He had a pretty good idea what had happened. It was what he had been hoping for: that through Richard's special power the path to finding Archie would be revealed.

As he held the pendant up to take a closer look, he smiled as he turned the disc through his fingers. 'Well, take a look at that, who would have thought we'd see this again.'

'What is it that you see?' asked Marcie, impatiently. She was becoming angry at knowing so little about the chain and pendant that Quig had given her; a gift she had treasured so much, yet it now threatened her and the rest of the village. 'What is it that everyone sees that I do not?'

Chuck showed her the strange design etched on one side of the disc. 'It's this, Marcie, we've seen it before, but we don't know what it means.'

She frowned as she studied the mark. It was not as pretty as the side with the coloured stones and it made no sense to her. She told how Archie had also been surprised to see it, but said it might help him to find his parents, although he did not explain how. Daniel had agreed to take him to Elam to see where Quig had found the pendant, but before they left they discovered that their friend Kristin had been hiding in the hovervan. They'd argued about leaving her behind in the village with Marcie, but eventually she went with them to Elam.

'And now they are in trouble.' She shook her head at the thought of all that had happened. 'I do not want this evil thing in the village,' she said, staring at Quig, 'you must take it away from here.'

Quig was about to protest, but Chuck held up his hand. 'Marcie, I understand, but I think it might be better if we deal with this. We need to go to Elam to see for ourselves what happened there. Will you let us take the pendant back to Elam, if Quig will show us the way?'

She looked to Quig, a little doubtfully for a moment, but he nodded his agreement. 'So be it, but then he must return here, for there is much to be done.'

Richard wondered what they were going to find in Elam. Would it help to explain what he had seen when he held the pendant?

Chapter Forty

Harimon

Under close questioning by Chuck, Quig explained what had happened in Elam and how the Terogs had taken Archie and Kristin from the road leading to the tunnel, back to the village.

'There was nothing we could do for them. They are killers,' growled Quig. 'They killed Elisha and my friend Tomis, and many others have died at their hands.'

Chuck listened very carefully, noting every detail that might prove useful once they got to Elam. Quig was obviously still very frightened by his experience at the hands of the Terogs, and was very wary about going back to the village. But he had a sense of guilt that he had been unable to help Archie and Kristin, and the others who had either died or been captured.

'I'm sorry for your troubles, Quig,' said Chuck, 'but with your help, we may be able to find them. I know we're up against a ruthless bunch, so it makes sense we take a few precautions when we get there, OK?'

They were sitting with Richard in the rear bay of the Bonebreaker while Aristo carried out a final check before leaving the village.

'I have to ask you, do you have a weapon you can use?'

Quig looked startled by the question. 'Only this.' He pointed to a sheathed knife strapped to a leather belt around his waist. 'It is one I use on the boat – it is very sharp.'

'Good. I've checked with Aristo and he says he has two paraguns, whatever they are, stashed in the cockpit,' said Chuck. He pushed the Stetson up off his forehead and smiled at the two worried-looking faces in front of him. 'Don't worry, I don't expect we'll have to use them, but it's always a good idea to know what our resources are.'

They heard Aristo call from the cockpit that they were ready to go.

'OK, Quig, you better sit up front with Aristo and help with directions to Elam. I'll stay here with Richard until after lift-off.'

*

Richard loosened the drawstring to open the little leather pouch Marcie had given him before he left the cottage. Slowly, curiously, he drew the chain out of the pouch, careful not to touch the disc-shaped pendant as it swung between his fingers. His skin tingled as he felt its power, urging him to stroke the disc, to enter its world – but if he did enter its world, *he* wanted to be in control, not like earlier in the cottage when he seemed unable to resist its influence.

'You OK with that thing, Richard?' said Chuck.

'What do you mean?'

'It's a fine looking piece of gold, but its more than that, isn't it? When you handled it back at Marcie's place you seemed to be in some sort of trouble when you were in the trance – or whatever it is you call it. Was it like the other times you told me about?'

'It isn't the same ... it's different, somehow.'

'Different, in what way?'

I don't know. It just is ... When I had the dreams I would see things, but that's all they were: dreams that I had no control over. The other times, when I was in a special place – like the Transkal or the DONUT back at the facility, it was like ... actually being in those other places, seeing and talking to people ...'

290

Richard frowned, trying hard to remember the dreams and trances he had experienced. They had all happened to him in so many different ways, it wasn't easy to explain. '... and then there was Shaman-Sing. He told me I could make myself reach these places and contact the people there, if I wanted to. Like practising a kind of meditation, I think.'

'Who's Shaman-Sing?'

'He's a holy man, Archie and I saw him the last time we were in Amasia.'

Chuck sighed and stroked his moustache. 'I don't know much about this sort of thing, pardner, but when I was with the military, I heard talk about army scientists experimenting with ESP and telepathy, stuff like that, but I don't think anything came of it. But what about the pendant – what's so special about it?'

'I'm not sure – it's a feeling I get from it. It's as if it's trying to *tell* me something ... and maybe I can use it to see things when ... I don't know ... maybe when ... *I* want to. In the same way that Shaman-Sing tried to teach me.'

Chuck thought back to the time when he went to see Richard in the clinic: that his 'gift' or 'power', whatever it was he possessed, might be the only way they would be able to trace Archie. Maybe the pendant was the answer.

'Well, Richard, if you can do that, it might just help us to find your brother.'

*

Chuck left Richard in the rear bay and went through the short passageway to the cockpit, to check on their progress towards Elam. The light was failing, but he could see they were flying low over dense, dark green forest, broken only by long, narrow, brown trails which probably connected the villages to each other.

'How're we doing, Aristo?'

'Quig says we are nearly there.'

Quig nodded. 'We will be there long before dark. There is a place near the village where we can land.' He pointed through the windscreen to a small clearing lying to one side of an old stone-paved road that was partly hidden by the overhanging branches of the trees. 'Look! That is where Daniel and his friends left the captain's hovervan. Perhaps you can land there?'

'I'll get closer and take a look,' said Aristo.

Chuck watched him bring the Bonebreaker lower, smoothly and slowly over the trees until it hovered over the clearing. It was a strange machine, but it reminded him of an old beaten-up Dakota he used to fly. Battered and frequently in the hangar for repair, it had never let him down when in the air and he'd loved flying it.

He said, 'Nice flying, looks to me you could drop down here?'

Aristo nodded, reached for a lever to extend the landing pads, ready to start his descent.

'I think I saw something down there,' said a voice.

It was Richard. He was standing in the passageway behind Chuck. A minute earlier he had been leaning over the side of the open rear bay, gazing across the vast expanse of the forest canopy, when he thought he saw something glinting as it moved through the trees near the edge of the clearing.

'Hold your position, Aristo,' snapped Chuck. He turned to Richard. 'What did you see?'

'I'm not sure.' Richard squeezed himself in behind one of the cockpit seats to get a better look. He pointed to a craggy outcrop of rock overlooking a small grassy clearing that lay to one side of a narrow stone-slab road. 'Over there, I thought I saw something moving in the trees behind the rocks. Maybe it was an animal ...'

Chuck scanned the area; a light wind rustled the leaves of the taller trees, but there was no other sign of any movement. He said, 'What do you think, Aristo?'

'It looks all right to me, but I'll set down closer to the road. That will give us a clear view of anyone out there.'

'Not if they're in the trees,' said Chuck. 'Let's get those paraguns out that you told me about.'

As soon as they landed, Aristo reached under the dashboard to unlock a black cabinet with a large red X stamped on the front panel. He keyed a code into a small brass tumbler lock which allowed the panel to slide down to reveal two black, stubby-looking weapons with short barrels and pistol grips.

'I wondered what was in the boxes back there,' said Chuck, referring to four similar cabinets he'd noticed in the rear bay.

'Yes, they were there for the Lancers in the early days when they used the Bonebreaker. They're empty now, except for this one.' He withdrew both paraguns, handing one to Chuck, flicking open a cover above the pistol grip of the other, revealing two switches: one yellow, one red.

'Only open this when you are ready to fire. Switch to yellow if you want to stun and disable a live target.'

'And the red?'

'Use it when you want to kill your target. It's the lethal switch.' He put his finger on a small cylinder attached to the barrel. 'This is the target finder, it's accurate up to half a mile or so.'

Chuck turned the weapon over in his hands. It was compact and felt easy to handle. He asked, 'What sort of ammunition does it use?'

'None, this is the latest and most deadly version of the weapon we used to use. It's a vallonium powered plasma weapon developed recently by Dr Shah's research people, and produced in Sitanga exclusively for the Lancers,' said Aristo, smiling. 'And for us, of course.'

'A plasma weapon? Back home, the army experimented with the idea, but they reckoned it would take a fusion reactor to power one of these things,' said Chuck. Shaking his head at the thought of what he was holding, he took a closer look at the paragun.

'Maybe so, but we have vallonium which is unique to Amasia.'

'It's like the one you used on the dinosaur in the Exploding Park,' said Richard.

Aristo laughed as he recalled his failed attempt to rescue Richard from the back of a runaway dinosaur – one of a pair of triceratops, maddened by their journey through a timecrack, that had landed in the park.

'No, Richard, these weapons are much more advanced than the one I used on the dinosaur –'

'Look!' Quig was standing, leaning over the windscreen and pointing to something across the clearing. 'There is someone there!'

The others looked up and stared towards the rocky outcrop but there was no one to be seen.

'Are you sure?' asked Chuck.

Quig shrugged. 'It is hard to say, but I think someone was watching us from the top of the rock.'

Chuck looked at him. Quig had the keen eyes of a seaman and if he said he'd seen something, then they needed to be careful. 'OK, let's go and see what's out there. Richard, you stay behind me; drop flat to the ground if I give the call.'

They climbed down from the cockpit, Chuck leading with Aristo and Quig on either side of him as they crossed the clearing. Richard trailed behind, his head swivelling side to side like a periscope, searching for anything that moved. The rock was bigger than he thought, much bigger as they got closer to the sheer face, broken by a deep wedge-shaped cleft near the top.

It was then that he saw it again. The same glint he saw from the Bonebreaker, something shiny moving in the cleft, pointing towards them.

He tried to yell a warning, but it was too late.

Aristo had gone further ahead to examine an old dry riverbed that ran parallel with the rock face about a hundred yards away. He stopped, as if he had walked into an invisible wall, clutching at his chest as he staggered forward before falling into the riverbed.

Chuck dived to the ground, calling to Richard and Quig to do the same. 'Stay flat,' he yelled, 'I'm going to try and reach Aristo.'

Richard hugged the ground as he watched Chuck crawl and weave his way through clumps of tall grass and loose rocks towards the riverbed. He rolled over the edge into a shallow depression about twenty inches deep just as something hit the ground behind him.

What was that? Richard lifted his head to try and get a better look. *A stick? An arrow? What was it?*

Another two of the 'sticks' landed on the edge of the bank as Chuck rose up out of the riverbed with the paragun held at shoulder height. He fired repeatedly at the cleft in the rock before taking cover again. For a moment there was only silence, until a skittering of stones falling down the rock face betrayed the presence of the sniper who had taken up a position inside the cleft. It was a Terog; he stumbled forward clutching a crossbow, arms flailing wildly as he plunged head first out of the opening to hit the stony ground at the bottom of the rock.

This is crazy, what have we got ourselves into? thought Richard. He shouted to warn Quig and Chuck as he spotted two more figures running into the trees to the far left of the rock, but they had already seen them.

'Quig, keep an eye on those guys,' yelled Chuck. 'Richard, quick, I need you over here!'

Richard ran to the edge of the riverbed, but stopped in his tracks when he saw Aristo lying silently on his back with one of the sticks in his chest.

'Oh, my God! ... Is he dead?'

'No, but he needs medical attention, fast.'

'What is it – an arrow?'

'No, it's a bolt. Whoever it was, was using a sniper crossbow. I've seen them used by a guerrilla group back in the States.' Chuck was on his knees, examining the wound around the bolt. There was hardly any blood, just the shaft with a fletch-like guide sticking out of the left side of Aristo's chest like a little flagpole. 'Richard, I saw a medical kit in the rear bay of the Bonebreaker. Get back there and bring me bandages, pads, whatever you can find, as fast as you can.'

Richard hesitated, shocked by the sight of Aristo lying so still on the riverbed.

'Go! We can't waste any time here!'

Feeling shaken, Richard didn't need to be told again. He turned round and sprinted as hard as he could back to the Bonebreaker. Scrambling up the rungs into the cockpit and through the passageway into the rear bay, he found the medical kit under one of the side benches, attached to the side panel. *Now what do I do?* He flicked back the catch and opened the cover. Besides the bandages and pads it was packed with little bottles filled with coloured liquids he didn't recognise. He looked more closely and saw that the kit was clipped to a bracket. *It'll be easier to take the whole thing to Chuck.* He unclipped it, placed it under his arm and raced back to the riverbed.

He dropped the kit beside Chuck just as Quig returned from the trees with another man. The newcomer, a small, wiry, brown-skinned man, dressed in a tattered brown – or was it dirt? – tunic and trousers, was carrying a crossbow with a shiny, silver sighting device at its tip. Richard guessed this was what he'd seen glinting earlier.

Chuck reached for the paragun.'Who's this?' he asked.

'This is Harimon of Elam,' said Quig, 'he was one of those taken by the Terogs when they first attacked the village.'

'And what's he doing here?'

'The Terogs brought him from Copanatec to help them find the pendant,' said Quig, looking grimly at Aristo's wound.

Richard reached into the pocket of the denim jacket he was wearing; he fingered the pouch with the pendant as he looked around the clearing. He asked, nervously, 'Where are they – the Terogs?'

Quig nodded towards the rock. 'There were three of them. That one is dead.'

'What about the others?' asked Chuck.

'They were holding Harimon in the trees,' said Quig. He hefted his knife for a moment, as if testing its balance, and then wiped the blade on the side of his trousers. 'They are no longer a threat to us.'

Richard shuddered at the thought of what Quig meant, but he had no time to dwell on it. Chuck laid the paragun to one side and gestured to him to get down beside him and Aristo.

' OK, Richard, open that kit and let's see what we have. Quig, keep an eye out for any other visitors.'

'Are you going to take it out ...?' asked Richard, pointing to the bolt.

Chuck shook his head. 'No, I don't know how deep it is or how close to the heart or lung it might be – it's safer to leave it in. I need to stabilise the bolt before we move him and get him to get to a hospital, pronto.'

'But he's the pilot ...' said Richard.

'I'll have to fly the Bonebreaker. I don't think it'll be a problem. He's breathing steadily, but we have to get him out of here as fast as we can.'

'I will stay,' said Quig.

Chuck had started to use some of the pads and bandages from the kit to pack around Aristo's wound to strap it in place before moving him. He looked up at Quig. 'What do you mean, 'you'll stay'?'

'Harimon wants to go back to Copanatec to help his friends – he says they are ready to fight, and they would rather die fighting than be slaves.' He pointed to the crossbow. 'We now have the Terogs' weapons. I will go with him.'

Richard heard the angry determination in Quig's voice. Back at the cottage Quig had been worried, frightened that the Terogs would attack his village, but now here with Harimon, he seemed ... different, somehow. *He had just killed a Terog – was that it? Was he now prepared to kill more of them? To seek revenge?*

As he listened to Quig, Richard felt the pendant growing warm in his pocket. The urge to hold the disc was growing stronger. He had the feeling it held a message for him. He took it out of the pouch and stroked the stones ...

*

The old man groaned as the rock slipped from his hands onto the tunnel floor between the rails of the narrow gauge track. As he lifted it again to heave over the side of the wagon that was about to trundle its way to the surface, the whip snaked out of the recess in the tunnel wall where one of the Terogs stood guard, watching the slave workers hammer, chisel and drill into the solid rock.

The whip was the Terogs weapon of choice when it came to inflicting pain and keeping the diggers in order. But this time the whip caused no harm to the old man, narrowly missing his fingers as he struggled with the rock, its metal tips ringing out as they struck the rim of the wagon as a warning not to be so careless. Next to him, Archie turned angrily, defiantly facing the Terog – it was a stupid thing to do, inviting only one reaction, but he couldn't help himself. The whip lashed out again, catching him on the shoulder, the sting of one its razor sharp tips causing him to yell out ...

*

'Archie!'

'Richard, what is it?' asked Chuck.

Quig and Harimon watched the boy from where they stood on the edge of the riverbed. He gazed back at them as if surprised to see them standing there.

'Archie ... I saw him ...' said Richard.

'Where?'

'I don't know, someone attacked him, but it was too dark to tell where it was. It was a ... rocky sort of place ... like a cave, or somewhere like that.'

Chuck shook his head. It was too little to go on, but before he could say anything, a low, painful moaning sound made him look down. Aristo was moving, his hand trying to reach across his chest to touch the bolt, but the effort was too much and his hand fell away to his side.

'We can't waste any more time – we have to get him out of here and into a hospital, pronto.' Chuck unrolled another couple of bandages, strapping Aristo's hands to his sides to prevent any movement. He looked towards the Bonebreaker as he stood up. 'Richard stay here and try and keep him still. I'm going to bring that machine over here and try and figure a way of getting Aristo into the loading bay without disturbing the bolt.'

'There's a ramp at the end you can lower for loading stuff. I've seen Aristo use it when collecting equipment for Dr Shah,' said Richard.

'Great, that'll make things a lot easier.'

A few moments later, Chuck was in the cockpit. Having flown many types of aircraft he had made a point of watching Aristo work the controls, meaning to ask him at some stage if he could fly the Bonebreaker. *Who would have thought it would come to this!* Keeping the landing pads extended he brought the machine slowly over to the riverbed and settled as close as he dared to the edge. He left the cockpit and went through to the bay to check the loading ramp. On one of the side panels a plate over a lever indicated the ramp control. He pushed it down and watched the ramp descend until it met the ground. He called to the others who had been watching him.

'Right, pardners, there's a roll of tarp in here. Let's get it out and we can place Aristo in it. It'll act as a stretcher and keep him steady while I fly this thing back to Zolnayta.'

A short while later the four of them, each one holding a corner of the tarpaulin, brought Aristo slowly off the ramp and into the middle of the bay, wrapping the stiff material around him to try and keep him stable for the journey back to the city.

'That's it, Richard, now we need to get moving –'

'I'm not going back. I have to stay here.'

'What do you mean?' Chuck stared at Richard, not understanding what he meant. He looked at Quig and Harimon, both of them had left the Bonebreaker and were now standing to one side talking to each other. 'They're going to Copanatec – you can't stay here on your own!'

'I'm going with them. Archie's in trouble and this is the closest I've been to him since the Yucatan, I can't go back now.' He held the pendant in front of Chuck. 'I can find him with this, I *know* I can.'

Chuck shook his head. 'It's too dangerous. We have no idea what's happening over there.' He looked down at Aristo, lying very still, then said, 'Whoever they are, these people are ruthless, you can see that. I don't want this happening to you.' But he knew from the look on Richard's face that he was wasting his breath. 'OK. If you have to, then stay here and use the pendant to try and get in touch with Archie, but I want Quig and his friend to stay with you until I return. As soon as I get Aristo safely to a hospital I'll get back here with the army or the Lancers, then we can decide what has to be done about Copanatec. Will you do that?'

Richard nodded. 'Yeah, I guess so.'

'OK, let's get Quig here.'

Richard waited quietly, nervously fingering the pendant in his pocket, while Chuck explained to Quig what they had agreed. 'He's impatient to find his brother over there, but I want you to stay here until I get back, OK?'

'We will wait in Elam, but we do not know if there are other Terogs in this place. If we have to move we will leave you a message there,' said Quig, pointing across the clearing to a distinctive, toadstool-shaped rock beside the road.

Chuck took a good look, memorising its position. 'OK, that'll have to do, but take the paraguns with you - and make sure you know how to use them - hopefully you won't need to.'

Quig nodded. A few minutes later, with a paragun slung over his shoulder, he and Richard climbed down from the cockpit and watched Chuck take the Bonebreaker up very slowly, turning to the north on a course for Zolnayta.

Chapter Forty-One

The Pyramid

Gritting his teeth against the burning pain of the cut, Archie clasped his shoulder where the razor-sharp metal tip of the whip had sliced through the rough cord of the tunic he wore. He took a step towards the grinning Terog – although, with his mean slit eyes and wide pig-like nose, which were the distinguishing features of the Terogs, it was hard to tell whether he was grinning or snarling. Sometimes he called the guards 'pigheads', which he thought was a more apt description.

'Try that again, you ugly bastard, and I'll –'

He felt a tug on the back of his tunic. He looked over his shoulder; it was the old man shaking his head, warning him not to say or do anything foolish. Not that it mattered. The Terogs didn't understand a word he said, and in spite of the translator chip in his neck he understood very little of what they said. It wasn't so much the language, but the way they grunted and snorted when they spoke, usually impatient and in anger, that made it impossible to communicate with them in any meaningful fashion. Not that any of the tunnellers ever wanted to get that close to the Terogs to carry out a conversation with them.

'I know, Daros, I know,' he muttered to the old man, 'don't make trouble, but I only wish I could use that whip on *him* for a change.' He turned away from the Terog to avoid any further eye contact, and stepped in between the tracks behind the wagon. 'I suppose we better start pushing before he decides to use it again.'

They gripped the edge of the loaded wagon and leaned into it to get it rolling. Ignoring the threatening stare of the guard, Archie pushed past him, taking deep breaths as he made the extra effort to keep the wagon moving forwards. From this part of the tunnel it was only a short distance to the entrance, but it was a hard push up a steep incline and Daros wasn't up to it.

'Ouch, that stings!' Archie reached inside his tunic to touch the cut as he pushed the wagon a little harder. It wasn't too deep. Luckily, the rough cord material of the tunic had stopped most of the metal tip touching his skin, but there was fresh blood on his fingers. He reached into his pocket and pulled out a piece of cloth that he used to wipe his face and eyes clear of the ever-present tunnel dust. He rolled it into a pad and pressed it into place over the cut.

'Are you all right, Archie?'

'I'm OK. Just let's get this thing up there.'

As they neared the top of the incline, Archie peered over the top of the wagon to get a glimpse of the entrance. It seemed to appear very slowly, like the sun rising above a distant horizon, but the sight of it every time they reached this point always lifted his spirits, to the extent that it spurred him to push just that little bit harder. It was that precious few minutes spent in the open, breathing in fresh air like it was his last that made it worthwhile.

Every hour of the day and night, each wagon was loaded with the greyish-black and red rock extracted from the tunnels and caves that honeycombed the earth below the pyramid, next to the gorge and the temple. Shafts had been driven down through the basaltic rock until there were more than a dozen levels of tunnels criss-crossing in every direction. Within the great temple was the palace of the Lords of the Cloud, and the high priests who controlled all aspects of life on Copanatec.

Hundreds of diggers and wagon operators like Archie and Daros, worked on every level below the two buildings. All of them worked twelve hour shifts in the claustrophobic darkness; their only illumination the small vallonium lamps attached to metal pegs spiked into the tunnel walls. Many of the men brought here from the mainland villages never saw daylight again. Literally entombed, they were worked until they dropped dead from exhaustion or tunnel-dust sickness, never having set eyes on the mysterious golden casket, the artefact that was the cause of their enslavement.

'What is the golden casket?' Archie had asked Daros, when he had first been paired with him to operate the wagons on the top level.

'None of us know, only that it contains something that belongs to the Lords of the Cloud and that it must be found soon,' said the old man, hawking a mouth full of spit and dust onto the tunnel floor. 'Hah! They say soon! I have been here many years and yet to see it.' He spat again, wiping his mouth with the back of a dirt-encrusted hand. 'Let us hope that it is found before you become old and sick from the dust disease, like me.'

That was ... what, a week ... more? God, I have to get out of here before I end up like him, thought Archie. He cast a glance at Daros coughing and wheezing beside him, putting in what little effort he could to push the wagon. It was obvious that he couldn't do this kind of work for much longer. *And what then?* But Archie knew the answer to that question. In the cell he shared with other prisoners, he'd heard the stories about those who had died in the tunnels. When his turn came, and by the look of him, it wouldn't be long, Daros would be taken to the end of the seawall in one of the wagons and thrown into the sea, just like the rock he had pushed for so many years.

And what about Kristin? Was she OK? Archie's mind went back to when he and Kristin had arrived on the island after their capture by the Terogs ...

During their journey through a turbulent, stomach churning sea, which they both thought would never end, they encountered a menacing, swirling mist so murky it effectively acted as a protective cloak around the slave ship. But the coastline had eventually appeared as they came out of the mist, drawing the prisoners to stare through the barred portholes of the cage at their first sight of the mysterious rocky coast, wondering fearfully what lay ahead of them. Huge columns of black basaltic rock rose up like chimney stacks at the tip of the island before gradually descending in giant steps into the sea. As they sailed further along the coast a harbour, hidden by an outer L-shaped breakwater, came into view as they slowly made the turn to go inside and line up alongside a stone-built jetty.

As soon as the bow and stern lines were secured to the bollards, the cage, which made up the rear of the ship, was opened and the villagers were prodded and manoeuvred onto a gangway that extended out to the jetty. Cracking their whips like circus lion tamers controlling a pride of lions, a squad of Terogs corralled the villagers into two separate groups on the breakwater below the seawall.

Archie and Kristin tried to stick together, but Kristin was snatched by one of the Terogs and forced into the other group. Archie saw her, briefly, turning and frantically waving back to him as she and the others were forced to climb up a set of steep stone steps cut into the side of the seawall. It was a moment he would recall many times in the coming days, a moment when he felt a sudden stab of fear that he would never see her again.

A tall yellow-robed figure, with a bird-like face, was holding a long, black rod, waiting for Kristin's group. Prompted by shouts from a Terog next to him, the villagers huddled together at the top of the steps. At this distance, Archie couldn't hear what was being said, but it was obvious that some kind of instruction was being issued by Birdface as he pointed his rod towards a line of wagons further along the seawall. As he watched Kristin's group of villagers make their way towards the wagons, Archie had a sudden gut feeling that Birdface was someone he would see more of in the coming days.

Later, Archie would learn from Daros that some of those who worked on the wall, the seawallers, prepared the empty wagons for the return trip to the pyramid. The tunnellers would then refill them with more rock, as countless others had done before them, and so the endless cycle would continue until the golden casket was finally recovered.

When it was the turn of Archie's group to climb the steps to stand before the tall, yellow-robed figure, Birdface announced himself as Talon, one of the Defenders dedicated to serving the needs of the Lords of the Cloud. The villagers were stunned by his appearance. Talon's forehead and cheeks, partly hidden by long black hair, were decorated with clusters of little tattooed feathers, a tribal honour bestowed on him when he'd reached manhood many centuries earlier. His eyes quickly swept over the group, surveying them as if they were no more than cattle intended for the slaughterhouse. Standing on a large block of granite, with the black rod held in his right hand, he looked like an ancient biblical prophet about to pronounce judgement, thought Archie.

They stood on top of the seawall. Over eight feet wide and three times as high, it was built with grey, black, and red basaltic rock, its top paved with squares of quarried grey granite. Running its full length was a narrow gauge rail track, approximately three feet wide, the rails shining from constant use.

There was no sign of Cosimo; he must have left before they climbed the steps, thought Archie. A raw wind with icy needles stabbing bare skin, made his eyes water as he tried to protect his face with the back of his hand. He looked towards the white crested waves crashing over the breakwater, before turning away from the wind to look inland to see a landscape of fields filled with scattered boulders and small rocks. Nearby, a cobbled road curved alongside the seawall. It led to a line of buildings about a mile away. As his gaze travelled to the end of the seawall he saw something that took his breath away.

He gasped, 'My God ... it's the Yucatan pyramid!'

When Manuel led him to the pyramid in the jungle that his parents had discovered, Archie realised its structure was different to the others in the Yucatan, and now he could see how similar it was to this one in Copanatec. During one of the school breaks he had spent with his parents on one of their archaeological digs in Mexico, his father had explained how the Mayan builders had constructed two types of pyramid, both possessed of steep stepped sides leading to a flat top. One type was complete with a small building on the flat top, very often used as a temple by the priests for ritual sacrificial ceremonies, while the other type of pyramid was not intended to be used. It was regarded solely as a sacred edifice, meant only to honour a god. The Mayan flat top pyramids were distinctively different to the later pyramids in Egypt with their smooth sides and pointed apex tips.

As he stared at the unusual tall column that had been erected on the flat top, Archie realised that his father had discovered a third type of Mayan pyramid, and perhaps not even Mayan.

'Quiet!' The voice commanded, making the villagers look in Archie's direction, wondering what it was he had said.

'Uh ... I'm sorry ... I just ...'

'Quiet!' repeated Talon. He looked at Archie a little more closely. 'You are an alien, how do you come to be in this company?'

What could Archie say? He hadn't expected to be noticed amongst the villagers, but he was taller and looked different. He said the only thing that might make sense to Talon, and stop him asking questions.

'I'm not sure ... I was caught in a storm ... then there was lightning ...' Archie shrugged. 'I don't know what happened, but the next thing I knew I was near the village, and now I'm here.'

'A timecrack,' said Talon, nodding as if he agreed with Archie's explanation. 'And tell me; what is your name, alien?'

'Archie Kinross.'

'*Kinross?*'

Talon frowned as he considered Archie's name, but before he could say anything more, he was distracted by a burly, bearded man shouldering a path through the men around him. He seemed to be agitated and muttering to himself as the men stepped aside to let him approach Talon, and the Terog guard beside him.

'What is it, villager, what troubles you?' asked Talon.

'I demand to know why you have brought us here.'

'You *demand* to know?' said Talon. He smiled as he stepped down from the granite block he had been standing on, gesturing to the Terog to stay behind him. 'It is quite simple. We have need of able-bodied men here on Copanatec, but you need not concern yourself with that. Your services are no longer required.'

The man screamed as Talon prodded him with the black rod, forcing him backwards over the rail track towards the edge of the seawall. Teetering on the edge, his arms flailing as he tried to keep his balance, the man shrieked as Talon prodded him again. The repeated bursts of energy from the rod lifted him off his feet to plunge down onto the rocks near the jetty.

The rest of the villagers were stunned into silence as they and Archie looked down in horror at the broken body now lying on the rocks ...

*

'Archie?'

'Sorry, did you ask me something?' Archie cast the memory aside as Daros spoke to him. 'What was it?'

'Your plan – I think, perhaps, we can do it today when they come with the empty wagon.'

They had reached the top of the incline where the tunnel entered a dark cavern-like space at the base of the pyramid. Archie turned to the old man who was now breathing hard, contributing little effort to pushing the wagon. 'Sorry, Daros, my mind was elsewhere. But look, I don't have much of a plan yet, beyond what I've already told you.'

'It may be so, but it is the first step.'

'What do you mean?'

Daros put a finger to his lips, cautioning him to be quiet as they approached the guard. 'We will talk outside.'

Chapter Forty-Two

The Seawall

They entered the cavern that had been carved out of the rock below the pyramid. As they left the tunnel they passed a Terog guard, but he hardly glanced at them or the rock-filled wagon as they made their way to the exit. Obviously bored, he waved them past with his whip onto another guard who would escort them to the exit and beyond to the seawall.

Nodding towards the guard, Daros whispered, 'Wait until we get to the seawall, then we'll talk. He will wait for us while we exchange the wagons.'

The rail track was one of two sets that ran parallel with a cobbled road that lay between the side of a large public square and the seawall. One track with the loaded wagons coursed its way to a long, sloping ramp that ran up the side of the seawall, while the other track allowed the empty wagons to make the return trip to the pyramid.

They continued past piles of large stone blocks and rubble that lay scattered along a narrow gorge between the pyramid and a massive, white stone temple that stood on the edge of the square. The sides of both buildings nearest each other had suffered enormous damage during an earthquake and were now separated by the gorge.

Archie pushed a little harder to take the wagon past the front of the temple where a series of broken steps fronted huge golden doors situated behind a row of six Ionic-style columns. Two of the columns had collapsed along with part of the pediment to form a barrier in front of the steps. It was the temple of the Copanatecs and the palace where the Lords of the Cloud lived and ruled their ancient society. A sacred place that had been partly destroyed by the earthquake and the flood that followed, many centuries earlier.

I can hardly believe this, thought Archie. *I'm in the actual place that Richard's vision had revealed to him.*

Not for the first time did he reflect on the incredible situation he found himself in. This very square was the scene that Richard and he had witnessed from the Transkal at Harmsway College, the last time they had landed on New Earth. He had heard his mother's voice then and Richard had spoken to her. She'd said they were prisoners, but had been unable to say exactly where she and their father were being held and it was driving him crazy not being able to do anything about it.

His eyes swept across the square to little groups of Copanatecs shuffling towards several rows of stalls displaying baskets of vegetables, presumably brought in from the countryside. Sometimes they would jeer at the slaves pushing the wagons, but today was a market day and the Copanatecs had better things to do.

'There they are,' said Archie, putting the frustrating thoughts to one side.

He nodded towards two seawallers standing beside a wagon on a turntable set into the end of the seawall. They were waiting at the top of the ramp that led down to a corner of the square. 'I hope they can tell me something about Kristin.'

Daros nodded, but said nothing. He was watching two men approaching them on the other track, pushing an empty wagon. As they passed, one of the men lifted his hand, the fingertips and thumb forming an 'O' next to his cheek.

'Why did he do that?' asked Archie, but again there was no comment from Daros.

Archie glanced at him; perhaps he was too old and tired to say anything. Daros thought he had a plan, but so far all Archie had was a gut instinct about what he might do next. Every hour of every day while he pushed the wagons, and every night when he couldn't sleep in the cell he shared with the other prisoners, his mind churned with thoughts of escape, his parents, and Kristin.

One idea he had, had come to him after Daros had taken him to the clothing store, a large cave carved out of the rock in one of the tunnels. He had been forced to exchange his clothes for a soiled navy tunic, trousers and leather boots, clothing once worn by another prisoner who no longer had need of them. They were allowed to wear scarves to keep the tunnel-dust at bay and, if the tunnel sickness was present, to prevent the sickness spreading to the other prisoners. It was then that the idea had begun to form when Daros said it made them all look the same.

'The Terogs are stupid. They cannot think for themselves, all they do is what Talon tells them,' said Daros. 'They do not see us as people; we are only numbers to them to carry out the tasks we have been given. Wherever we work, either on the seawall or in the tunnels, all they care about are the numbers. They must be the same at night as in the morning, unless one of us dies, and then that is a new count.'

If the Terogs can't tell the difference between the prisoners, except for height and build, then maybe, Archie had suggested, he could switch places with one of the seawallers, to try and find Kristin. Daros agreed it might be possible and said he would think about it.

At the end of the square, Archie and Daros rolled the wagon onto the ramp and pushed it up the rail track until it sat end-to-end with the empty one in the middle of the turntable. Catching his breath for a moment, Archie stepped back and listened to the distant roar of the White Waters as the waves crashed onto the rocks

313

beyond the breakwater. The taller of the seawallers started to turn the well-greased turntable clockwise to face the square, ready for the empty wagon's next trip to the tunnels.

'Not so quick,' hissed Archie, keeping a watchful eye on their Terog escort who was waiting for them on the ramp, rather than face the biting wind on the seawall. 'I want to pass on a message to Kristin.'

'Kristin? But he is here as you asked,' said the tall one, pointing to his companion.

'It's me, Archie,' said a small figure coming out from behind the wagons.

'What! But how –?'

'I sent the message, my young friend,' said Daros, also watching the guard, who had pulled something from his pocket and was now chewing it; he seemed to be in no hurry to return to the pyramid and the tunnels. 'I said that it would be better that I go, and that your friend should take my place in the tunnels. Remember, you told me that, as well as your friend, it was your mother and your father you also seek. There can only be one place you will find them and that must be in the temple.' Daros smiled as he reached out to grip Archie's hand. 'I do not believe you will succeed in doing so if you are trapped on the seawall.'

'But, Daros, the heavy stone work here –'

The old man smiled again, waving a finger in front of Archie to silence him. 'Yes, I know I am past my time for hard work. I'm old and my lungs are dying. I have been in this unholy place too long and will not see my village or family again. Now, my only wish is to end my days below an open sky, not in the bowels of the tunnels like the least of Amasia's creatures.'

Kristin had moved to stand closely beside Archie and he could sense that she was nervous. She reached for his hand and squeezed it. 'Please, Archie, don't leave me here, I don't think I can last another day hauling stones out of these freakin' wagons.'

Archie couldn't help smiling at hearing her voice again. Although she sounded anxious, she was as feisty as ever, but he realised from the grey stone dust that covered her face and hands, and the condition that her clothes were in, that her time on the seawall hadn't been any easier than his in the tunnels. 'It's OK, I'm not leaving you behind, but believe me, it's no picnic below ground, either.'

Daros nodded and said, 'It is agreed, but before you leave I must change my tunic with Kristin. The colour of the cement dust from the seawall is different to the dust in the tunnels, and might be noticed by the Terogs.'

Kristin stared at him for a moment, confirming that they were about the same size. It had been awkward, but the rough clothing she had been forced to wear had helped her to keep her identity as a girl secret, not knowing what would happen to her if the Terogs discovered her true sex. They went behind the wagon to avoid being seen by the guard. She snatched the tunic Daros held out, turned her back, and then handed her own over her shoulder to make the change. If he thought Kristin's behaviour strange, he said nothing.

Archie looked back to the Terog on the ramp, now sitting on a rock next to the rail track, protected by the seawall from the sea's biting wind. Engrossed with whatever he was chewing, he seemed to be in no hurry to return to the pyramid. He turned to Kristin, standing beside him again, and then to Daros who already looked better in the fresh air.

'OK, I understand,' said Archie, 'if you're sure that's what you want to do, but will you not be in danger here?'

'No more so than in the tunnels. Talon can depend on the Terog's loyalty and cruelty to keep the prisoners working, but it is said that he has warned them to curb their tempers and not to be so quick to kill us, as they have done in the past. The supply of slaves is dwindling and they have yet to find the golden casket ...' Daros looked out to sea for a moment, before continuing, '... and some say they never will, not before the White Waters come again to flood Copanatec.

'But there is something you must know, Archie. You have heard in the cells that the villagers are desperate for their freedom, and there has long been talk of an uprising against the Copanatecs. Rather they would die fighting than suffer without hope.'

'Why are you telling me this?'

'You asked me why the man who passed us on the track raised his hand to his cheek. It was the signal that the time has come to fight.'

Archie stared at Daros, not quite taking in what the old man meant. Did he mean an uprising would take place *now*? But before he could say anything, a sudden burst of shouting from the ramp caught Archie's attention. It was the Terog coming towards them. He had finished whatever he had been chewing, and was now cracking his whip, demanding they return with the empty wagon.

'We'd better go before he decides to come up here and discovers what we've been up to,' said Archie to Kristin, still stunned by what Daros had just told him.

*

As they trundled the wagon through the square towards the pyramid, Kristin asked Archie, 'What happens now?'

'I'm not sure, but I think I have to find a way into the temple.'

'The temple? But that sounds crazy – why?'

'Maybe so, but when we first arrived here, Talon recognised my name. He said, "*Kinross*?" as if there were another one. That *must* mean my father is here and that Talon knows him. I haven't seen him in the tunnels, so perhaps Talon has put him to work in there,' said Archie, nodding towards the temple as they passed the steps. The market traders had closed their stalls and were packing their goods into small hovervans, ready to leave the square. They paid little attention to the wagons passing by. 'I don't know, but I can't think of anything else. And if Daros is right, that the men are ready to fight, I have to move fast.'

'You could be right,' said Kristin. 'He might be in there.'

'What makes you say that?'

'I'm not sure, it was just a few days ago, Talon came to the seawall with a couple of men to inspect the work. As they passed us, I heard a name mentioned, but it wasn't yours.'

'What was it?' asked Archie.

'It was a strange name. I remember it because of the way he looked at me and it kind of freaked me out.'

'For crying out loud, Kristin, what was it?'

'All right, keep your hair on. I think it was Cosmo, or something like that. I heard Talon saying the name when he spoke to him. The third man was a prisoner, but the others on the seawall said they saw him regularly when he left the temple to check on their work.'

Archie almost brought the wagon to a halt when he heard the name: *Cosmo – it must be him*!

It was the name of the man the Lancers were seeking for the killing of one of their men. After Prince

Lotane had been killed and the Sacred Temple destroyed, Cosimo, and another man named Sandan who had held Richard in the cave, had chased them as they raced through the cavern as the mountain roared and ripped itself apart, while they made their escape through the old city. When they crossed a widening chasm, using a pillar that had fallen away from a nearby building, Sandan had grabbed at his leg, trying to pull him back, but Archie had managed to shake him loose, forcing the man to fall into the chasm to his death.

Was that why Cosimo – if it was him - was still pursuing him? That he blamed Archie, and Richard, for the man's death? But how did he come to be on Copanatec?

He had nearly succeeded in capturing Archie at Castle Amasia and if he now discovered Archie was in the tunnels, what then?

And what about his father – was he the other man that Kristin had seen on the seawall?

Chapter Forty-Three

The Builder

Richard held the pendant in the palm of his hand, trying to make sense of the mark engraved on one side of the gold disc. Although he couldn't really see the mark on his own shoulder, even with the help of a mirror, he knew it was the same. Both Archie and Chuck had described it to him and the more he thought about it, he remembered seeing it on the Transkal, and on his mother's shoulder.

But what did it mean?

He had no idea, only that in some way it was connected to Copanatec. In the past twenty-four hours since Chuck left for Zolnayta, he had tried several times to use the pendant to see Archie or his parents, but the images were broken, like the scattered pieces of a jigsaw he couldn't quite piece together. He tried again, stroking the coloured stones, allowing his mind to stay open as Shaman-Sing had taught him, ready to receive a message or image.

Quig watched him from a chair next to the cast-iron range he had lit earlier, shortly after rising from an unsettled sleep. He said nothing, but kept a careful eye on the pendant in case it attracted danger.

Last night all of them had crept in silence through the darkness looking for any sign of Terogs still in Elam and a place where they might stay for the night. After creeping through several lanes, it became obvious on closer inspection that most of the dwellings had been destroyed and the inhabitants long gone. But eventually, they had found a deserted cottage at the end of one of the many paths leading into the forest. Partly hidden by the trees, it was not easily seen from the rest of the village and, once they were certain there were no Terogs left, they had moved in.

The cottage was one of the few to escape destruction by the raiders and much of the contents were still intact. Unlike Quig, Harimon had risen after a largely undisturbed night, and by the light of an old vallonium lamp had carried out a search of the kitchen. He managed to make a breakfast from a selection of stone jars packed with pickled vegetables and some smoked meat wrapped in muslin he'd found stored in the cool cupboard.

It had been a spartan meal, but they were hungry and nothing was left on the plates. Harimon poured a glass of water scooped from the water barrel outside the kitchen door and looked thoughtfully around the room, as if someone might enter unexpectedly. He looked to Quig adding more firewood to the range.

He said, 'I think we should leave here soon, it is not safe to stay too long in this place.'

'Have you seen something?' asked Quig.

'No. I came here with three Terogs to find the pendant and now they are dead. I fear that others will soon follow when they do not return to Copanatec.'

'What do you want to do?'

'The one you call Chuck, asked us to wait for him, but I must join my friends on Copanatec. They are ready to rise against Talon.'

'I understand, but perhaps we should wait for the help that he will bring.'

'We do not know how long he will be and the people die every day on the seawall and in the tunnels. No, I must go back. We have the paraguns and I will take them there –'

'But how?' asked Quig quickly. He would not let him go alone.

Harimon smiled. 'You forget that I came with the Terogs. Their boat is in a small cove beyond the harbour.'

Quig nodded. He had forgotten.

His gaze drifted back to Richard who had said little since breakfast. The boy's eyes were closed as if asleep, his lips moving without speaking. Was the boy under a spell, he wondered.

He cursed the day he lifted the pendant from the ashes of the Man of Dust. It had been an impulse to take it and give it to Marcie as a gesture of appreciation for the kindness and care she had shown him in the days following Elisha's death. Marcie loved jewellery and often made necklaces from the shells and pieces of coloured glass she found on the seashore, for herself and her friends. But now she was angry, blaming him for bringing its evil influence to the village; for the raiders had returned to Elam to find the pendant, killing and destroying anyone and anything that stood in their way, leaving only suffering and grief in their wake.

At first, he thought he had been blessed by witnessing the passing of the Man of Dust to the next world, but now he did not know what to believe.

'No ...'

Quig glanced at Richard. He was muttering and shifting restlessly as he sat in an old carver chair below a small window by the door, his face pale in the early morning light.

'What is he saying?' asked Harimon.

Quig shrugged. He knew it was something to do with the pendant, but he didn't understand its purpose, only that it had brought nothing but trouble and suffering to his people. In Elam no one had been spared in the quest for its recovery.

Richard opened his eyes and stared at Harimon for a moment. He said, 'I saw him.'

'Who did you see?'

'The man you told me about – the one with the face of feathers, like a bird.'

'Talon,' nodded Harimon. Last night he had explained how he had been taken with the men from Elam, four years earlier to Copanatec, to work on the seawall and in the tunnels. Since then, he had watched Talon and the Terogs drive many of them, including his closest friend, into an early grave; it was why they raided the villages for more men. And now they had returned to Elam to find the pendant that the boy held in his hands. 'He asked, 'What else did you see?'

'He was with another man ...' Richard hesitated, how could he explain what he had just seen?

When Prince Lotane had tried to kill him while carrying out the Ritual Sacrifice, the mountain had exploded, destroying the Sacred Temple and killing Lotane, enabling Richard to escape a grisly fate. As he ran through the crumbling streets of the old city two men had chased him. One of them, Sandan, had been the one who held him prisoner and, along with another man called Anton, they had pursued him through the cavern. But the arrival of Archie, along with Aristo and the Lancers, had saved him from being caught. Sandan died when he fell into a crevasse, while Anton had escaped during the confusion inside the cavern. He learned later that the two men were the same two being hunted by the Lancers for the killing of one of their own.

And now he had seen Anton in Copanatec.

He said to Harimon: 'The last time I was in Amasia, a man tried to kill me. I managed to get away from him when the Lancers rescued me ... but I've just seen him with Talon.'

Harimon nodded thoughtfully. 'There is a man – an alien like you – who advises Talon on building and

322

maintaining the seawall, and the reconstruction of the pyramid and the temple. My people call him the Builder.'

'The Builder?' queried Richard. He now knew that the man he saw standing with Talon on a great stone wall by the sea was Cosimo, but he had never heard him mentioned by that name.

'Yes,' said Harimon, 'I shared a cell with him and I do not believe he is a killer, although I think he would willingly kill Talon, as would all of us who have suffered at his hands.'

'Why, what happened to him?'

'Talon took his wife to the temple and she hasn't been seen since. Talon told him she had been chosen to make the last journey, but didn't say what that meant.'

Richard had the strangest feeling he knew what had happened. His heart skipped a beat as he remembered the vision of his mother disappearing into the golden cloud above the Transkal ... *had he seen her in the temple?*

He asked, 'What does the Builder look like?'

'He is an angry man - very strong, but he has a limp and walks with a stick –'

'Dad!' gasped Richard. 'It must be him!'

Harimon frowned. 'Who?'

'My father, he must be the man you call the Builder.'

A look of surprise on his face, Harimon said, 'Your father? Is it possible? The man I know called himself Mal-Kom.'

Malcolm.

'It *is* him!' Richard leapt to his feet, pushing his chair away. Everything Harimon had just told him pointed to the Builder being his father, but what was he supposed to do now? So much had happened since his parents' disappearance from the Yucatan, posing endless questions about their fate; and Archie, taken by the slave traders, where was he? Had he ended up in the same place as their father? And his mother, had she truly disappeared in the golden cloud? With his heart still beating a little rapidly, he clutched the pendant more tightly, knowing deep down that there was only one choice. 'We can't wait, we have to go to Copanatec.'

Quig and Harimon nodded to each other; they both had their reasons to go to Copanatec and were anxious to leave as soon as possible.

'I agree,' said Quig, 'we must not waste any more time here. The Terogs may come soon to find what has happened to the others.'

'We have to leave a message for Chuck,' said Richard. 'If he comes back with help he'll need to know where we have gone.'

'Write your message and I will leave it for him at the clearing as we agreed,' said Quig. He walked over to an open wall cupboard where he saw a pen and some paper.

'Yes, tell him we have taken the Terogs' boat to Copanatec,' said Harimon to Richard. 'I will draw you a map showing a secret path that leads from the coast to a large vegetable garden behind the temple. I have friends who work in the gardens, but I do not know if they will be there.'

'Why not?' asked Richard.

'The rising against the Terogs may have started. Who knows what is happening in Copanatec now?'

They agreed that as soon as Quig had left the message for Chuck they would leave together for the cove where the Terogs had left their boat. Then set course for the hidden part of the coast on Copanatec that would lead them to the temple garden.

Chapter Forty-Four

Lieutenant Han-Sin

The three Spokestars, recently arrived from Lancer headquarters at Castle Amasia, hovered over the back courtyard waiting for clearance to land. According to Sunstone, they were the latest and most advanced of the Spokestars, Mark 8 seven seat troop carriers, armed with dual laser lances and stealth cloaks.

Chuck whistled in admiration as the first of the gleaming scarlet machines prepared to make its descent. He tilted his Stetson back from his forehead to take a closer look. He said, 'Just like a Ferrari.'

'A Ferrari?'

'Yes, back in my world there are cars called Ferraris; they are the same bright red colour, and ...' Chuck laughed, '... very expensive!'

Sunstone's eyes sparkled for a moment as he absorbed this information. 'I am familiar with the concept of cars. I have learned that many New Arrivals from your world possessed private forms of transport. It is not the same here, Amasians use public and commercial transport systems. There are exceptions, such as Dr Shah's Bonebreaker, but they require a special permit.'

They watched as the other two Spokestars followed, landing beside the first one, to form a row near the castle wall. Two of the Lancers, small figures in red and black tailored uniforms, slid back the cockpit canopy of their machine and climbed down into the courtyard to be confronted by an armed soldier in combat uniform. Other armed soldiers on the ramparts watched carefully as papers were presented to be inspected before their comrade would allow the Lancers to proceed any further.

'What is it exactly that the Lancers do?' asked Chuck. He wondered why they flew such powerful machines; what purpose did they serve? 'These guys look as if they're ready for some serious action.'

Sunstone's head swivelled forty-five degrees to look down at Chuck. They were standing on the back steps of the keep near the service quarters at the rear of the castle, waiting for the Lancers to approach them. Like his androt cousins, Brimstone and Firestone, the Castle Protectors of Amasia and Sitanga, he stood well over seven feet tall and, like them, he towered over most of the population, which was hardly surprising with the average Amasian only a few inches over five feet.

'The Lancers were originally established to seek out New Arrivals and bring them to Castle Amasia for evaluation, as well as herding wild animals into the Riverlands, but their duties have expanded far beyond that. The Lancer headquarters and depot are situated within the castle along with the New Arrivals Centre,' explained Sunstone, 'and in recent years there has been an unacceptable increase in the level of undesirables arriving in Amasia, not only in the Exploding Park, but throughout the country. Some of the arrivals have proven to be dangerous and need to be tracked down and contained. As a consequence, the Lancers' duties now encompass investigation and armed response. These particular Spokestars are the latest models from the Sitanga factory. Each one is crewed by a pilot along with seven fully armed Lancers and is capable of approaching a target under a cloak of invisibility. They have been sent to assist us during the current emergency.'

'Sounds like our special forces, the Army Rangers, back in the US, although I don't know about the cloak,' said Chuck, casting his mind back to a time when he served more than six years with a Rangers unit on highly secret special operations.

Known only to a handful of individuals, whose true identities were never revealed outside a department deep in the heart of the Pentagon, the unit's existence was denied to anyone who might voice a suspicion about its covert operations. Those dangerous, unpredictable years were the conclusion to eighteen years of flying everything from the early Stearman trainers to testing the first stealth aircraft (he wondered if the Spokestars were using a similar technology, although their sleek, rounded outlines made it seem unlikely).

And now here he was acting as a special envoy on a mission in another world to find the professor's nephew. Instead of enjoying retirement on a thirty-foot yacht he intended to buy and sail around the Caribbean, along with an old like-minded, ex-army buddy who would share the fun and the cost.

Casting his thoughts aside, he asked, 'So what about the army, how do they operate?'

'The army's remit is to protect all of Amasia against internal and external enemies of the state,' said Sunstone. 'It is why reinforcements have been sent to Zolnayta: to find those responsible for the bombing campaign.'

'Yes, we met Lieutenant Isula and his welcoming committee when we arrived on the dockside,' said Chuck, recalling the memory of the soldiers taking pot shots at the Bonebreaker.

Sunstone said nothing. His attention was drawn to the two Lancers, helmets crooked in their arms, crossing the back courtyard to meet him on the steps.

'Greetings, Sunstone, my father sends his best wishes to you,' said one of the Lancers. 'He regrets he could not come himself, but has authorised me to be attached to your command.'

'Major Hanki has my appreciation. You and your men, Lieutenant Han-Sin, are very welcome to Castle Zolnayta,' said Sunstone. He swivelled his head towards Chuck. 'This is Chuck Winters, he is on a mission to find a young man, Archie Kinross, who is missing somewhere in South Amasia.'

'Yes, I know Archie, and his brother, Richard, from their last time in Amasia. I had a meeting with Dr Shah at Mount Tengi before coming here. He briefed me on Mr Winter's mission, but I understand he ran into some trouble – '

'Excuse me, Lieutenant Han-Sin, I don't want to interrupt, but you can talk to me, if you wish?' said Chuck, smiling as he faced the Lancer. He'd just realised that the small figure with the smooth brown skin, twinkling eyes and short raven hair was a very attractive young woman. 'Maybe I can bring you up to date on what happened at Elam – that is, if you're here to help *me* find Archie?'

Han-Sin stared at the tall stranger for a moment. Before leaving Fort Temple she had collected Aristo's wife, Marjorie, a New Arrival, and taken her to the hospital before proceeding to the castle. While at Aristo's bedside she learned that he had been seriously wounded, the bolt from a crossbow narrowly missing his heart and lungs. He had lost a lot of blood and if it hadn't been for the quick thinking of this other New Arrival flying the Bonebreaker, Aristo probably would have died. It was strange, she thought, how as a Lancer, that the people she had met from the old world, including the Kinross boys, had become such an important part of her life.

She studied his face and the unusual drooping moustache which framed his mouth, a feature unknown amongst the beardless men of the Salakins, but which she found strangely attractive. His comments were bold and direct, but to his credit, he had saved Aristo's life, and Dr Shah was indebted to him for that. Permission had been granted for him to join a Spokestar allocated to the search for Archie and, because of her previous relationship with the Kinross boys, she had agreed with her father and Brimstone that she should act as the liaison officer for the mission.

'What happened at Elam?' she asked. 'Who were the people who attacked you?'

'The villager with us, Quig, said they were Terogs. They had a prisoner with them, another villager, called Harimon, who said they had come to find a golden pendant. It turns out that Quig found it four years earlier and had given it to his sister, and now Richard has it,' said Chuck. He decided not to say anything about the effect the pendant seemed to have on Richard – what had happened so far was confusing enough.

'Where are Richard and these other men now?' asked Han-Sin, 'and what about the Terogs?'

'I told Richard to wait until I returned with help. If he had to move for any reason, he was to leave a message in a special place. As for the Terogs,' said Chuck, shrugging his shoulders, 'there were three of the ugly brutes and they were dealt with, if you get my meaning,'

Han-Sin nodded. She understood what he meant, but she was mystified about where the attackers had come from. The Lancers didn't patrol the far southern territory of Amasia. With thousands of square miles covering a land mass of unexplored impenetrable jungle, high mountain ranges and hot dry desert, it was impossible for the Lancers to patrol such a vast territory.

That responsibility had been allocated by the Elders to the army but, according to her father, there was little sign of General Branvin devoting more than a few squads to that task. Branvin claimed that his duty lay in the protection of the cities and towns of Amasia, not in the sparsely populated hinterland of the south. It was only when some of his soldiers had been attacked on the coast that he had taken action, but even then, little was achieved.

She looked up to Sunstone. 'Do we have any information on the Terogs?'

'Only a few unconfirmed reports from the villages that were raided. The army are tasked to investigate such reports, but they do not confide their results to me.'

Chuck pulled the Stetson over his brow and reached for a pair of sunglasses in his breast pocket to cover his eyes against the bright sunlight. He said, 'Look, folks, I don't want to push, but if there is nothing else to be done here, I need to leave. I've been away from Richard too long .'

Han-Sin looked across to a corner of the courtyard where the Bonebreaker was parked. She said, 'You flew the Bonebreaker? You are a pilot?'

'Yes, I've done some flying in my time.'

'And you found your way back here?'

'It was no problem. I just made for the coast and followed it until I hit Port Zolnayta.' Chuck shrugged, and glanced towards the parked Spokestars. 'I didn't have much choice, I had to get Aristo to a hospital as fast as I could. But now I would like to get back to Elam.'

Han-Sin nodded. She appreciated what he had done for Aristo and that deserved recognition. And with her attachment to Archie and Richard, it was only a moment's decision that she would help him find the boys.

*

Shortly after their meeting, when Han-Sin and two of her Lancers left with Chuck for Elam, Sunstone received a call in his office. He picked up the com and listened. It was Captain Abelhorn calling about his granddaughter.

'Is there any news about Kristin and the boy?' demanded Abelhorn, his voice loud and impatient.

'Not yet. I have sent a Lancer patrol to Elam to investigate what happened there. They will report to me on what they find.'

'What about the army? Are they doing *anything* to find them?'

'They are not covering that area. All of Lieutenant Isula's men, along with the Lancers, are seeking those responsible for the bombing campaign.'

'Damn it, Sunstone, if you can't send more than one Spokestar to find my granddaughter, then I'll do it myself!'

The com connection suddenly terminated.

Sunstone's eyes glinted for a moment as he held the com and considered what Abelhorn had just said. As an androt, created by a human-like civilisation on another world – and as far as he knew, long since extinct – he was required to serve faithfully the needs of his masters, but he was not subject to their emotional reactions. Nevertheless, he had noticed he was becoming more attuned to certain behaviour patterns, especially when humans became stressed and impulsive, committing actions that would endanger themselves and others.

He decided he would need to pay close attention to whatever Captain Abelhorn intended to do next.

Chapter Forty-Five

In the Tunnels

'Keep your head low and turned away from me until we get past the tunnel guard,' said Archie. The Terog who had escorted him – along with Daros - to the seawall stayed outside, taking up a position at the pyramid entrance. They entered the pyramid, pushing the wagon a little more quickly through the cavern towards the tunnel, keeping a wary eye on the Terog as he watched their approach. 'Daros says they only pay attention to the numbers going in and out of the tunnels, regardless of who they are. With these clothes and the dirt on our faces we all look the same to them.'

'I hope you're right,' said Kristin. She kept her head low, close to the end of the wagon as they pushed it past the guard into the tunnel. 'If one of those pigheads comes anywhere near me, I swear I'll kick him where it really hurts.'

Archie suppressed a grin at the thought of Kristin kicking a Terog, but as attractive as the idea was, the consequences didn't bear thinking about. He glanced at the guard over his shoulder, but hardly any attention was paid to them as they left him behind.

He said, 'Not a good idea; those guys play rough with the whips when they get annoyed.'

She looked at him as if she couldn't care less, but he sensed a nervousness about her the deeper they descended into the tunnel. Her eyes swept around the roughly cut tunnel walls and up at the low roof only a couple of feet or so above their heads, as if the rock might close in on them at any moment. He hoped she wasn't claustrophobic.

Thick stone columns supported the huge wooden crossbeams that had been hewn from tree trunks brought to the island from the Amasian forests. As they passed one of the columns, Archie noticed, not for the first time, a creeping inch-wide fracture that had appeared in the stone under the crossbeam. Daros had pointed to similar fractures in other columns in the tunnels, saying that the colossal weight of the pyramid and the temple was threatening to bring down the whole subterranean tunnel system that now ran under both buildings.

'They can't keep digging like this,' he had warned, 'the tunnels will collapse and kill all of us.'

Ahead of them, the rail track continued as a series of U-shaped turns that descended into the lower levels where a network of branch tunnels had spread outwards like a spider's web. In each part of the web a team of diggers attacked the rock face with their drills, their helpers loading the loose rock-fill into the empty wagons to be taken to the seawall.

As they pushed the wagon down the sloping rail track towards the first of the lower levels, the light became fainter, the only illumination coming from the vallonium lamps spiked into the rock face. Besides the tunnel entrance guard, they hadn't seen anyone.

Kristin said, 'This place gives me the creeps – where is everyone?'

'The Terogs patrol each level on a random basis. They like to pop up unexpectedly and use their whips to remind us to keep working,' said Archie. He peered into the gloom ahead of the wagon, his eyes checking the crevices in the sides of the tunnel walls where a Terog might choose to conceal himself. 'But you're right, we've reached the first level and there's usually at least one of them around.'

They made the U-turn at the end of the tunnel, ready to descend to the second level, when Archie suddenly pulled a brake lever on the side of the wagon.

They stopped so unexpectedly Kristin stumbled, almost banging her head on the end of the wagon.

'What the – '

'SSShhhh ...' Archie put a finger to his mouth to quieten her. 'Sorry about that, but there's something not quite right here.'

'What do you mean?'

'It's too quiet. There are hundreds of men working in the tunnels, and there's not a sound. From this level down to the adits at the bottom there's always noise: Drilling, rocks falling, wagons rolling on the track, men yelling to each other, but here ... I don't know ... there's nothing.'

Kristin shook her head. She had no idea what he was talking about. She said, 'What are the adits?'

'They're passageways with pumps at the bottom level to take away the water that seeps into some of the tunnels. I'm not sure where the water comes from, but it's a big drainage problem down there.'

As Kristin tried to make sense of what Archie was telling her, the silence he had been complaining of was broken by the sudden and distant sound of someone screaming.

Her eyes widened. 'What the freak was that?' she asked.

Archie didn't answer. He moved slowly down the tunnel away from the U-turn and the wagon, listening intently for more sounds.

'Where are you going?' hissed Kristen.

Archie turned and drew a finger across his lips, and then beckoned to her to follow him quietly as he passed branch tunnels on his left and right. He looked carefully into both of them, noting wagons sitting on the tracks partly filled with rock fill, a few discarded tools, but no drillers or wagon pushers. He moved on down the tunnel, with Kristin following a few feet behind, until he reached the second U-turn. He held up his hand for her to stop while he crept towards the bend to look carefully into the next tunnel. Hidden by a protruding rock, he inched his head around it until he could see along the length of the track. It was empty. He stepped away from the rock to take a better look, but there was no one to be seen.

Where were all the men? Were they back in the cells? But then the next shift would be here ...

'What's happening?' asked Kristin, coming up behind him.

'I don't know. This is the cells' level as well as a work area, but there's no one here,' said Archie. 'But what's strange is that there are usually at least a couple of Terogs on patrol, so where are they?'

Kristin looked at him blankly.

'Sorry, I'm just thinking out loud. Look, there's a big cell block in the branch tunnel at the end of the next U-turn; the men are held there when they're not working. Its where I've been stuck for the past week, or longer, I'm not sure. Anyway, maybe that's where the men are.'

'But what about the Terogs?'

Archie shrugged. 'Good question. I'm beginning to wonder if the men have started something, just as Daros said -'

'Look!' Kristin interrupted him, grabbing his arm and pointing down the tunnel. 'There's someone there!'

A figure had appeared out of the cell branch tunnel but retreated into a rocky recess in the wall as soon as he saw them. He hesitated for a moment, then poked his head out to take another look. Apparently satisfied with what he saw, he stood away from the wall and waved to them with what looked very much like a crossbow.

Chapter Forty-Six

The Uprising

'It's Jona!'

'Who?' Kristin stood close by Archie, wary of the figure now approaching and waving the crossbow at them. 'What does he want?'

'Jona, he's one of the diggers on this level,' said Archie. He grabbed her hand and rushed forward down the middle of the rail track. 'Let's go, we better find out what's going on down there.'

They confronted Jona halfway along the tunnel. He was a small man, with heavy, muscular shoulders and strong, thick arms, made more so from long days working on the rock face. He displayed a thin face so peppered with red and black rock dust it was hard to tell his natural skin colour, but that was typical of all the diggers.

Archie usually saw him working with a rock drill, but now here he was handling a Terog crossbow as if he owned it. 'What are you doing with *that?*' he asked. 'And where are the Terogs?'

Jona nodded over his shoulder towards the branch tunnel behind him. 'There's one in the cell and he'll not be needing this.' He grunted, displaying a row of rotten teeth, typical of many of the villagers held captive for so long and fed an inadequate diet. 'He squealed when he felt the tip of my drill in his gut, and so will the others when we get our hands on them.'

'Daros said the men were ready to fight, but where are they –'

Before Jona could answer Archie, their attention was suddenly drawn to a group of men shouting and running towards them. Crushed together in the confined space of the tunnel, they ran as one terrifying, animal-like creature, each man brandishing some sort of mining tool as a weapon, ready to be used in their dash to freedom.

Kristin gasped, ready to turn and run, but Archie held her by her sleeve. 'Wait, it's OK, its Jona they want.'

Archie learned later, that the villagers, downtrodden and cruelly abused for so long by their captors and agitating for action against Talon and the Terogs, had finally reacted violently to another cruel act by one of the guards. That act had been triggered when one of the villagers tripped and dropped some of the rocks he had been loading into a wagon. Unfortunately, one of the guards on a random patrol chanced to arrive at the same moment and, in a flash, the razor-sharp metal tips of the Terog's whip streaked through the air to land on the villager's back. Repeated strikes tore the skin off the man's back until it hung in long bloody ribbons, enmeshed with the shredded remains of a dust encrusted tunic.

The villager's screams, which Archie and Kristin had heard earlier, had so angered Jona, that in a maddened charge from the rock face where he had been working, he knocked the Terog to the ground. Before the guard could recover, Jona had skewered him with the rock drill, almost splitting him in two, the long, hardened metal bit pinning the bloody carcass to the tunnel's red rocky earth.

Now up to twenty men were clamouring for more revenge, not only against the Terogs, but against all Copanatecs. Now they stood before Jona waiting silently for the moment, as if expecting an order or instruction that would, somehow, guide them to their freedom.

One man, a pick axe resting on his shoulder, called out, 'What do we do? Are you ready to lead us from this hellhole?'

His words suddenly spurred the men into a burst of cheers and they started to spill forward, pushing past Jona, Archie and Kristin, to make their way to the upper level.

But Jona didn't go with them. He seemed to have been taken by surprise at the idea of leading the men out of the pyramid, thought Archie. In spite of what Daros had said, there was no obvious plan of action; this was an uprising instigated by the cruel act of a Terog, now lying dead somewhere in the cell block.

The tunnellers pushed past them on their way to the cavern and the exit. Dirty and ragged, angry and seeking revenge, but poorly armed and leaderless, they were marching into a confrontation they were bound to lose.

In the muggy heat of the tunnel, Archie watched them until the last man passed by. He wiped the beads of sweat from his brow with the edge of his sleeve. 'They're crazy, they'll never make it past the guards.'

Jona, a bewildered look on his face, turned away as the last man passed him. He made no attempt to follow the men as they disappeared around the U-turn.

'We have to get out of here, before the men reach the exit,' said Archie. 'What about all the other men on the lower levels? Has anyone warned them?'

'We sent one of the wagon men down to tell them ... but he did not return –' An outbreak of loud shouting and screaming from the cavern distracted Jona from saying any more. He hurried to the U-turn and cast a look towards the next bend. There was no sign of anyone there, but he could hear a commotion and the sound of someone howling, as if in pain. He came back to them and said: 'They're trying to fight their way out of the pyramid.' But what he didn't say was obvious: that the men in the cavern had little chance of fighting their way past the guards, and any reinforcements that were called up.

'Archie, we have to get out of this place!' cried Kristin. 'I don't want to be anywhere near those pigheads if they come down here.'

'You're right, the villagers have got themselves into a fight up there that they can't win,' said Archie. 'We have to leave right now.' Whatever plan Daros thought the villagers had in place, Archie didn't like the way it was turning out. There were hundreds of them held prisoner throughout the tunnels and on the seawall, but it was plain there was no evidence of an organised uprising. He said, 'Jona, there must be another way out of here – where is it?'

The digger pointed towards the cell block branch tunnel. 'It was decided that some of the men on the lower levels would overpower the patrol guards and escape through the adits. The others would come up here and leave through the temple tunnel.' His eyes flickered as a spate of muffled cries drifted down from the cavern. 'It was not planned that we would go up there ...'

Looks like nothing was planned, thought Archie. He said, 'The temple tunnel, where is it?'

'Past the cell block,' said Jona, 'and into the old tunnels that lead to the gorge. They have not been worked for many months –'

A sudden cry made all of them turn round.

'Jona ... help me...' One of the villagers was calling out as he staggered towards them from the direction of the cavern. The man stumbled against the tunnel wall, one hand trying to clutch at the rock for support, while the other struggled to reach his back. He fell to his knees, falling slowly onto his face and chest, exposing a brightly coloured bolt protruding from the middle of his spine.

Jona ran to him. He kneeled down to turn the man's head to one side, to look more closely at the face. The eyes were wide open, unseeing. He turned as Archie came up behind him, and shook his head. 'He is dead.'

'Oh, my God! We can't waste any more time, the Terogs will be down here any moment – we have to go now,' urged Archie. He ran back to Kristin and grabbed her arm. 'C'mon, we're getting out of here.'

He had never been there, or even heard of it, but by its name, the temple tunnel had to be a passageway between the pyramid and the temple. He'd said to Kristin that he had to find a way into the temple because he believed his father to be there and now this might be the chance he was looking for. The alarm must have been sounded by now and the Terogs would soon be storming through the tunnels looking for anyone they thought to be a part of the uprising. Archie had a pretty good idea that they wouldn't be showing any mercy to anyone who resisted.

He called out, 'Jona, we have to go – you have to show us the way to the temple tunnel!'

Jona hesitated for a moment. He looked down at the body of the villager, a man he had worked beside for many years in the tunnels, a man who had hoped to return to his village one day. More sounds from above warned him that they were in danger of being trapped if they didn't move quickly. He nodded to Archie to follow him. They fled, with Jona carrying the crossbow and a belt loaded with silver bolts across his chest, in the lead, and Archie and Kristin close behind.

The next U-turn forked into two branch tunnels. The left branched down towards the lower levels and the adits, the right to the cell block where Archie and the villagers had been held when not working on the rock face. A hundred yards, or so, past the empty cell block, the tunnel ended in a network of old work areas, long disused, but one passage still wormed its way from one of the areas and through the debris of abandoned wagons and rusting tools, directly to the gorge.

'This way,' said Jona. The perpetual glow from a vallonium lamp spiked into the wall cast him in an eerie light as he entered the narrow passage that had been gouged out of the rock years earlier. He beckoned to Kristin and Archie to follow him.

'I'm not going in there ... it's weird ... how do we know what's in there?' whispered Kristin. She'd stopped dead in front of Archie, watching Jona as he disappeared into the passage.

Archie felt like pushing her into the passage. Instead, he said, 'It's OK, Jona knows his way around here.'

At least, I hope he does, or else we're in deep shit, he thought.

He took her left hand and held it for a moment, feeling the black rings on her fingers that matched the earring she habitually wore in her left ear. But he was surprised to notice that the large black hoop earring, decorated with little gold stars, was missing. Maybe it had been taken from her? It was a piercing and there was no sign of bruising or damage to the skin, if it had been taken forcibly. More likely, she had removed it, thinking it wasn't something that men wore and didn't want to draw attention to herself while with the men on the seawall.

He smiled at the thought and, for the first time he didn't feel irritated by her behaviour, her sharp tongue, or her dark moods when she was annoyed. It suddenly occurred to him how vulnerable she must feel. With her father's disappearance, possibly dead, her mother living and working in Sitanga, and only Captain

Abelhorn to look after her, when he wasn't at sea on the *Serpent*, she was pretty much on her own.

Squeezing her hand and ruffling her short, golden-reddish hair, he smiled. 'Look, Kristin, we can't hang around here for the Terogs to pick us up. We have to move on. Just hold onto me until we get to the end of the tunnel. OK?'

She returned his smile and nodded. 'I suppose you're right.'

'Good, let's go. We better catch up with Jona and see how he's going to get us out of this place.'

When they caught up with him, Jona was standing in front of a pile of rubble that lay wall to wall across the old rail track. He set the crossbow aside and kneeled down to start lifting a few small rocks away from under the crossbeam that now lay at a forty-five degree angle, one end on the tunnel floor while the other end rested on what remained of the column.

Archie was about to ask what happened, but it was a stupid question. He could see for himself. One of the stone columns and its wooden crossbar had given way and collapsed under the immense pressure bearing down on it. The massive structure of the pyramid above, along with thousands of tons of rock and soil had finally made its presence felt.

He asked, instead: 'Is there any chance of us getting through?'

Jona hauled at one of the larger rocks jammed between the wall and the crossbeam, his broad shoulders and strong arms giving him strength until it fell loose before him. He stood up and pointed to the small space he had created. 'I can see the light from one of the lamps on the other side. I think, if we are very careful when we move some of the smaller rocks, we can get through.'

Archie looked at Kristin and shrugged his shoulders, as if to say, what choice do we have?

'Well then, let's do it, before the pigheads find us!' She brushed past him impatiently, snatching at a rock below the crossbeam, setting off a stream of gravel and sandy soil that gathered around her feet. She squealed as she fell back, losing her balance.

'No!' Jona moved to catch her, and then pushed her towards Archie. 'If we are not careful we will bring down the roof. I will go first and clear a way to make room for us to get through, but we must go slowly.' He knelt in front of the crossbeam and started to work his way slowly through the rubble. To Archie, he said, 'I will pass the rock to the boy and he will pass it to you, and you will fill the hole behind us. That will stop the Terogs following us.'

'Good thinking, Jona,' said Archie, noting that Jona had said 'boy' when he referred to Kristin. He gave her a wink and encouraged her to follow Jona and take the bits of rubble he handed to her.

It took about thirty minutes to make a hole big enough for them to crawl through, with Archie hoping with every minute that passed, that the crossbeam would hold until they reached the other side. Beyond the crossbeam, about six feet in, they discovered a huge slab of rock had fallen from the roof, leaving even less room for manoeuvre. Jona clawed slowly at every rock, only removing it when he was absolutely certain it was safe to do so, passing it to Kristin who passed it back to Archie, who then packed it tightly with soil into the passage behind them, hopefully blocking any form of pursuit.

The few minutes they spent in the hole seemed as if they had created a tomb for themselves, their only light filtering through chinks in the rubble from the lamp in the tunnel ahead of them.

Finally, they were through. Each of them now covered in so much dust they had the appearance of stone statues slowly coming to life. Archie wiped some of it away from his face and took a deep breath as he faced Kristin. 'Are you OK?'

She shook her head. 'It was horrible. I never want to do that again.'

'Don't worry, I don't think we'll be coming back this way, anytime soon,' said Archie. 'C'mon, we better keep moving if we want to get out of here.'

With this section of the tunnel no longer in use, soil and stones had fallen away from the roof and walls to gather in small mounds over much of the rail track. However, unlike the pile of rubble they had just crawled through, they were able to continue without difficulty. As they approached the end of the tunnel where the rail track came to an abrupt halt, Archie saw a narrow shaft of light slowly appear on the tunnel roof.

'Where's the light coming from?' asked Archie. He hurried to join Jona who had gone ahead of them and was now stopped in front of a set of stone columns and crossbeams that were still intact, supporting the roof on the left side of the tunnel. He pushed past Jona and stepped inside. 'Where are we?'

It was a cave-like passageway leading into a chamber. Jona pointed to the far end. There was a large craggy opening where the light entered. He said, 'That is the way to the temple.'

Archie looked around the chamber with its dome-shaped ceiling. It was built with the same stone blocks as the pyramid. Fissures in the dome snaked down into the walls where some of the blocks had fallen onto the floor. Rubble on one side of the chamber covered most of a steep, marble stairway that ascended to another archway, which probably led into the pyramid itself. It was obvious that some sort of geological upheaval had taken place here a long time ago.

He felt the cool evening air on his face as he walked over to the opening. It had been much smaller, originally a doorway with pillars on either side supporting a pediment, parts of which now lay shattered on the floor. It was as if a bomb had blasted a larger opening to the outside world to reveal a bridge over a gorge that stretched to the temple on the far side.

'What was this place?' asked Archie. They walked outside onto what was left of a stepped terrace that led to the stone vaulted bridge. He turned round and looked up to see that they were standing below a side of the pyramid that seemed to reach unendingly upwards to a darkening sky. Whatever cataclysm had taken place here had destroyed a large section of the pyramid wall, with many of the great polished stone blocks lying strewn amongst the rocks in the gorge below. He looked to his left and saw that the gorge widened dramatically, wedge-shaped, as it worked its way towards the horizon from the gap between the pyramid and the temple.

Beside him, Jona shook his head. 'I do not know. It is said that the Lords came this way to worship their dead, but they have not been seen here since the golden casket was lost in the Destruction.'

'The Destruction?'

'Yes,' said Jona. He pointed towards the horizon. ' Where the land meets the sky, it is told that the Copanatecs lost a large town on the coast. The earth was torn apart and all who lived there were taken.' He spread his arms to encompass where they stood. 'The fingers of the gods also reached here and many more were also taken.'

Kristin grunted. She was tired of hearing about tales of destruction. 'OK, so the Copanatecs had a terrible time, but what about us? How are we going to get over there?' She stood with her arms crossed over her chest, trying to ward off the chilling breeze; her fear of the Terogs catching up with them was just as palpable.

She had a point, thought Archie, as he gazed across at the white walls of the temple and what was left of the bridge. As far as he could see, half of the bridge was missing.

Part Five

The Immortal Wand

Chapter Forty-Seven

The Gorge

The harbour appeared directly ahead of them as they made the turn past a rocky headland, leaving the turbulent waters behind them. Harimon pointed to the bollards above a set of stone steps as Quig brought the Terogs' boat alongside a deserted quay. Leaping onto the steps with a line in each hand, Harimon quickly tied the bow and stern lines to the bollards as Quig cut the engine and tightened the lines to the deck cleats.

'The weather's turning,' complained Quig, 'we will need something bigger than this to get back to the mainland.'

Before they left Elam, Quig had left a message for Chuck under the stone in the clearing, as they had agreed. Harimon then led them down to the cove where the Terogs' had hidden their boat. Once launched, they had made good time, in spite of Quig's worries that the White Waters would be the death of them when a heavy sea crashed over the bow, almost swamping the boat. Originally rigged for sail, she was a 30 footer with a small forward cabin. The wooden hull had taken a battering, but the vallonium engine had powered them through the worst of it.

'The Terogs probably stole this one, like everything else they take,' said Harimon. 'We will do the same if we have to, when the time comes.'

Richard listened to them for a moment, and then made his way up the steps. On the quayside he looked around the area, taking in the tumbledown stone buildings, broken glass in weathered wood frame windows, and doors hanging loose from their rusty hinges, all obviously deserted. He walked to the end of the quay, taking a closer look at the buildings. Between two of them, a weed-infested cobblestone road wound its way past a line of stone cottages, walls shattered and their roofs missing, and up a hill through a corridor of what he recognised as silver birch trees.

Just like Elam, he thought: *another abandoned community.*

'Do not wander too far away,' said Harimon, coming up beside him. 'There is no one here, but we do not know yet what is happening at the temple and the pyramid. We must take more care as we near the city.'

'What happened here?' asked Richard.

'It was a long time ago when the land was destroyed.'

'What do you mean destroyed?'

'Your father ... Malcolm ...' Harimon pronounced the name slowly, to make sure he got it right ... 'explained that such happenings are known as earthquakes. One took place near here a very long time ago. It is because of such destruction that we have suffered so much at the hands of the rulers of Copanatec in their search for the golden casket.'

'A golden casket?' queried Richard. 'What's that?'

'I do not know, but it is the reason we work in the tunnels. Talon has said that it must be found, no matter how many lives are lost, or villages destroyed. It has been so for many generations.'

Richard shook his head in confusion. 'That's crazy. If you don't know what it is, how do you know what to look for?'

Harimon nodded in agreement. 'Yes, it is a madness, and it has driven many of our people to the grave.'

'Harimon!' He turned as he heard Quig calling his name. Approaching them with his arms crossed, Quig held the two paraguns, the crossbow and the bolts belt, close to his chest. Completing the picture of a warrior-like figure was the sheath knife he had used against the Terogs, strapped to the side of his thigh. He laid the weapons on the ground.

'What is it?' asked Harimon.

Quig pointed to the weapons. 'Before we leave here, we need to know how to use these.' He withdrew his knife from its sheath and held it before him. 'When we reach the city, this will be of little use when we meet the Terogs. We need to be ready.'

Harimon sensed the hunger for revenge in Quig's voice. Ever since the killing of the Terogs in the clearing, he had talked of little else. He said, 'You are right, Quig, we need to be prepared for what lies ahead of us, but I'm afraid I know nothing about weapons.'

Richard bent over and picked up one of the stubby black paraguns. He flicked aside a slide above the pistol grip with one hand, displaying the yellow and red fire switches, and held the ridged underside grip of the barrel with the other. 'I think I know how it works. I watched when Aristo showed Chuck how to use it.'

Nodding his approval, Quig said, 'Show us.'

Looking around for a target, Richard spotted the wreck of an old boat with its mast still upright, lying in the water beyond the end of the quay. He took aim at the mast through the cylindrical target finder. A green dot appeared on the lens, identical to a green circle on the pistol grip. He guessed this was the lock-on target button; it was similar to some of the weapons on computer simulations he'd played around with at school. He locked on the mast and pressed the button, checking he was on the yellow fire position before pulling the trigger, recessed under the barrel. He felt no recoil or any reaction, beyond a little heat in his fingers where he held the barrel.

Richard dropped the paragun to his side and looked at the boat. To his astonishment, the mast was split in two, the top half lying to one side in the water.

'Look at that!' he yelled. 'A bull's eye!'

Quig and Harimon were silent. They looked in amazement at what they had just seen, but it was nothing to what they would witness next.

Richard stared at the mast. 'If that's what the yellow can do, let's see what it can do on the red position.' He felt nervous at what the weapon was capable of, but he set the red switch for another shot, held his breath and fired.

He dropped the weapon to his side again, and looked beyond the quay at the water, but there was no sign of the boat. Not a splinter of wood, only rippling circles spreading outwards in the water where the boat had been a moment earlier.

'Holy Christmas! It's gone!'

Harimon had stepped away from Richard, shaking his head, disturbed by what he had just witnessed. Quig was less concerned, his thoughts only on what they could do with the paraguns. He lifted one to examine it more closely, mystified by the power it could unleash.

*

'Do we have far to go?'

Harimon looked over his shoulder at Richard. 'Not far, but the land is difficult to travel.'

It was the second time in the past hour that Richard had asked the same question. He was tired trudging through the barren landscape, seeing nothing but field after field filled with broken rocks, fallen trees, and deep muddy fissures that made it impossible to maintain a faster pace.

They had left the harbour shortly after Richard's demonstration on how to use the paragun, and a brief discussion on how the weapons would be distributed between them. The decision was easily made when Harimon said that he was no warrior and would be reluctant to take the paragun, declaring that such a powerful weapon would be unsafe in his hands. He had opted for the crossbow and bolts belt, which pleased Quig, who had made it obvious that he was on a mission of revenge, and the more havoc he could wreak on Copanatec and the Terogs, the better.

The old harbour road had yielded to dense undergrowth as the jungle reclaimed the land, leaving them no choice but to take to the stony fields where there was less vegetation to hinder their progress. Harimon had set a steady pace in spite of the rough terrain, his stride indicating that their destination was fixed in his mind.

Another hour passed before Harimon stopped and pointed to a line of several large boulders about a hundred yards away where the land fell away before them.

He said to Richard, 'I think this may be the place your father spoke of.'

'What do you mean? What is this place?'

'It is as I told you. I believe we are near the land destroyed by what your father called an earthquake, a destruction so great that it lay waste to the town and all the people who lived there.'

'What is it to us?' asked Quig angrily. 'The fewer Copanatecs we have to deal with, it is the better for us!'

'I understand your anger, but it is not as you believe: that all Copanatecs are our enemies. It is true that some treat the villagers badly, but it is in their fear of the Lords, along with Talon and the Terogs who carry out their demands, that they do so.'

Quig looked at Harimon as if he were mad to say such things. 'How can you know this? They are Copanatecs!'

'Yes, they are, but it is also their fate to submit to those who rule them. In a sense, they are also slaves. You will see when we reach the temple gardens that there are Copanatecs who will help us. If the uprising has taken place, I only hope we are in time to help them.'

Quig shook his head, seemingly unconvinced by what Harimon said. Clutching the paragun by his side, he followed him, with Richard close behind, as they continued towards the line of boulders. They squeezed through two of the larger stones, stopping suddenly when they saw what lay ahead.

'We can't cross that!' cried Richard.

Stretching all the way to the other side, where a similar line of boulders and rocky debris lay, the land with its underlying sandy soil and soft porous rock had been weakened in ancient times by a massive earthquake. In the centuries that followed, a series of great sea storms had arrived in the aftermath, continuing the devastation of the land by flooding the old riverbed and cutting its way through the rock until the present gorge was formed. It was so wide at this point, with steep walls of razor-sharp, stony ridges rising up like dragon's teeth, it seemed impossible that anyone could cross to the other side.

'We do not have to,' said Harimon. 'It is as I have been told, that this is the place of the Destruction, which thundered its way from the coast and ended its journey between the temple and the pyramid. We will rest awhile, and then follow the same path.'

They cleared a space free of stones and sat down with their backs resting against one of the massive boulders. Harimon gazed into the gorge, contemplating a force of nature so great that it had speared its way through the land until its tip reached the temple and the pyramid; Quig, meanwhile, sat quietly with his own thoughts of destruction, and the revenge he intended to extract from those he blamed for Elisha's death.

Richard took the pendant from his pocket and held it in the palm of his hand, the golden links of the chain entwined in the other. He turned it over and studied the mark, trying once again to understand its meaning and the effect it had upon him. In spite of the cool wind blowing through the gorge, he felt the warmth of the pendant radiating through him; a sign, he realised, that in some mysterious way it was trying to make contact. He touched the coloured stones, rubbing them gently, and at the same time allowing his mind to clear, something he found he was now able to achieve with little difficulty.

Slowly, an image appeared of two men in a large room. It was the Transkal room he had seen earlier, the one where he had seen his mother disappear in a golden cloud. One of them was sitting with his head bowed, a golden chain around his neck, his hand clasped to a pendant next to his chest, but it was the other man who caught his attention, and he was someone he had no desire to meet.

Anton Cosimo.

He was one of the men with Prince Lotane in the Sacred Temple who had tried to kill him - and he was on the island!

Shocked and confused to see him, Richard couldn't understand what Cosimo was doing there, but he sensed that the man with him was using his pendant to trace what had happened to the pendant Richard now held, and he had no intention of letting that happen. If it led Cosimo to Richard, and to Archie, wherever he was,

Richard was under no illusion as to what would happen to them.

And Archie, *where was he?* Richard shook his head wearily; he was worried and exhausted by the events that seemed to be overtaking him, all of which seemed to be designed to stop him ever finding his brother and his parents.

He cleared the image from his mind, and quickly placed the pendant and its pouch back in his pocket, vowing not to use it again.

Chapter Forty-Eight

Lord Pakal

The man was tall and slender, his height accentuated by the long white robe he wore, its silken front embroidered with gold and silver thread to create the iconic emblem of the Lords of the Cloud: the Immortal Wand. A thin face, sculpted by high cheekbones and a straight nose, was dominated by a set of translucent eyes and pale skin. The image of a ghost-like figure was complete as the man seemed to glide across the marble floor of the chamber towards the Chapac Stone.

He was one of the few, at least in this world.

There had been many Lords in the beginning when they left Old Earth to travel through the portal, believing it to be their ultimate destination. The First Lord of the Copanatecs, Chapac, had claimed a vision that foretold of paradise and everlasting life. Partly true, because they had brought the golden casket with them from the pyramid on Old Earth, but in all else, it had been a false vision. Their arrival in Amasia, had been marked by the disappearance of the First Lord, and afterwards much argument had taken place on what they were to do in the new world.

In his time, Pakal had taken charge of the Lords, simply by promising them that they would rebuild the temple and the pyramid, and they believed him, and so had the small number of Copanatecs who had managed to travel through the portal to join them.

For years they wandered through the deserts and jungles of South Amasia, fighting battles and making alliances with men such as Talon, and with the Terogs, both of whom whose loyalty could be guaranteed by the promise of golden riches and long life. Eventually their journey had come to an end when they settled on the peninsula which they made their own. They had named it Copanatec after their homeland on Old Earth, but now the island they lived on was all that was left of Copanatec, after the last great onslaught by the White Waters that had separated them from the mainland.

Such was the devastation visited on the island that some of his brethren had chosen to use the Chapac Stone once again to travel to the next world, in the hope that they would find their salvation there. But he believed it to be a false and distant hope, that their only true salvation was in finding the Immortal Wand.

He sighed as he thought of the catastrophe that had befallen Copanatec when the Destruction struck the temple and the pyramid. It had taken place as the procession of Lords and Defenders carried the golden casket containing the Immortal Wand from the pyramid back to its usual location in the temple. Such an occasion was usually a joyous one, for it celebrated another great cycle, another millennium of life for the recipient. But it was not to be when the earth suddenly opened up to swallow the recipient and many of the members of the procession, along with the golden casket, into the void somewhere below the pyramid and the surrounding land. In the days that followed, more tremors and landslides followed by churning flood water had taken place, making it impossible to pinpoint the exact location of the Immortal Wand.

Since that day, Lords and Defenders alike had been unable to receive the Blessing, and like mere mortals they had turned to dust when their great cycle ended. Soon his own time would come, thought Pakal, and who then would succeed him?

He passed through the archway into the chamber. On each side, red and gold drapes hung between marble columns standing tall on golden plinths. The columns reached upwards to a stained glass dome, surrounded by a ceiling inlaid with the symbols of the multiverse. He stopped for a moment to stand between two of the columns where the drapes had been pulled back on each side to reveal a waist-high marble altar. The flat top was a solid gold base where the golden casket used to sit. It had been the location of the Immortal Wand since the completion of the temple, but now it lay empty, a shocking reminder of his mortality.

He made a silent prayer for its recovery, then made his way to the centre of the chamber, the heart of the temple complex. Directly below the dome stood the Chapac Stone, the portal that allowed those of his brethren, who chose to do so, to journey to the next world. His eyes rested on one of the glyphs, his personal emblem, engraved on the edge of the ancient stone. Would he choose to make another journey, he wondered, or would the Immortal Wand be recovered in time for his next blessing?

He dismissed the thought as he left the chamber to make his way through the courtyard and the portico to a stairwell that would take him to the upper floor, where Talon's apartment and the Defenders' quarters were situated. Many Defenders and Lords were gone, dust now, granted a final resting place in the pyramid, in the Tomb of Ossuaries. Only Talon's control of the Terog Commands enabled them to maintain their power over the Copanatec people. As he reflected on what the future held for him, Pakal knocked on Talon's door, opened it, and then entered without waiting for an answer.

Talon leapt to his feet. 'My Lord Pakal, I was not expecting you –'

'Forgive me for arriving unannounced,' said Pakal, gesturing impatiently with his hand for Talon to sit again, 'but I was anxious to meet the man you intend to propose as the next Defender.'

'Yes, my Lord. This is Anton Cosimo, the leader of the Arnaks, who fight to regain their land in Amasia.'

'Ah, I know of the Arnaks. After our departure from Amasia they sought to make use of the Chapac Stones for their own purposes, a dangerous practice when dealing with the unknown. But it is the *rebel* Arnaks you speak of,' said Pakal, nodding his head knowingly. 'And their activities on the mainland – none too successful, I believe?'

Cosimo smiled, not taking any offence at Pakal's directness; in fact, he welcomed it. It levelled the playing field, allowing him to be equally direct.

He nodded as he stood up from the bench. 'Yes, the Arnaks have experienced both failures and successes, but under *my* leadership I would lay claim to our recent ... let's say, *advances*, against the Amasian Army on your behalf.' He glanced at Talon, who seemed a little reserved in Pakal's presence. 'I think I could say that the army is worried about our bombing campaign, and the effect it is having on the Salakins. And, of course, how it benefits your own cause?'

'Talon has explained to me the nature of your strategy, and your interest in joining forces with us in our desire to return to Amasia,' said Pakal. He walked to a window overlooking the gorge and pointed to the side of the pyramid that had collapsed. He motioned to Cosimo to join him. 'That is a sign of our future destruction. Our days on Copanatec are coming to an end, but before that happens, Talon has a task to complete, and we cannot leave this island until he is successful. With your help that day may come sooner and we will reward you as he has promised.'

He turned away from the window and faced Talon. 'However, another task has to be dealt with, is that not so?'

'Yes, my Lord.'

'And your progress?'

'As you are aware, Lord Tenoch insisted on going with a Defender to Elam to see for himself how the Terogs carried out the raids on the mainland.' Talon shook his head to emphasise his disagreement with Tenoch's decision. 'This was against my advice, and unfortunately, he disappeared during the raid. Until recently, there has been no sign of Lord Tenoch or the pendant during our searches of Elam. Then we heard the rumours of a 'Man of Dust', revered by villagers on the mainland.'

'To the point, Talon, to the point. I have heard all this before,' snapped Pakal impatiently.

Talon bowed his head. 'My apologies. I do have news that the Terogs I sent to Elam have recovered an urn. I believe it may contain the remains of Lord Tenoch.'

Pakal was silent for a moment. He asked, 'And the pendant?'

'It was not found ...' Talon hesitated, unsure how to continue.

'What is it?' Speak!' demanded Pakal.

'I believe someone is in possession of the pendant ... someone with the power to use it as we do.'

'How can this be? Only the Lords of the Cloud and the Defenders who have been blessed can use the pendant!'

'I do not know, my Lord, but I believe it to be so.'

'Then you must find him!'

Cosimo listened to the exchange between Talon and Pakal with amusement. Their words were nothing but bluster, focusing only on their lost wand and attacks on the mainland to capture workers to find it. He saw them as like the dinosaurs on Old Earth destined for extinction, with no concept of what the future might hold.

Immortality and Talon's plan to return to Amasia? Yes, of course, he desired immortality – who would not? And his plans agreed with Talon's - but with one major difference.

Talon's talk of returning to Amasia to build a new empire was well and fine, for there was much to achieve in Amasia, given the manpower and the right leadership. He smiled at the thought; there was no doubt in his mind who that leader would be. He had a growing band of rebel Arnaks under his command, and if he could find a way to persuade the Terogs to follow him – and he had no doubt they would, if he satisfied their lust for battle and plunder – he would achieve all that they wanted, *but on his own terms.*

He pulled the collar up around his neck against the chill of the open window. He had discarded the sand-coloured trader's robe that he usually wore when travelling across Amasia, in favour of the knee-length, black leather coat he preferred to wear. Ignoring Talon and Pakal, he gazed down into the gorge and thought of the plan that had brought him to Copanatec.

As on Old Earth and during his time with the Mars Mining Consortium, he knew that the key to power lay with those who controlled the sources of energy. Amasia's dependence on vallonium for its energy requirements was also the key to seizing power and controlling its use, but his previous attempt to wrest the secret of the incredible mineral from the Vallonium Institute had ended in failure.

He closed his eyes for a moment as he thought of his brother, Sandan, and his betrayal. He had died when the mountain collapsed, destroying all that remained of the ancient city of Ka and the Sacred Temple. The irony of being in another temple planning another attempt, hadn't escaped Cosimo, but he swore that next time he would have the manpower to attack and occupy Fort Temple, forcing the institute to reveal its secrets.

While Cosimo pondered his plan he opened his eyes again. He said, 'What is it they are trying to do, I wonder?'

'Who are you talking about, Anton?' asked Talon.

'Them,' said Cosimo.

Talon and Pakal joined him as he pointed through the window towards the end of the gorge that separated the temple from the pyramid. Long before the earthquake struck, a stone-built, five arch bridge that connected the two massive buildings, had spanned a wide canal. During the tremors a long stretch of the middle arch had collapsed into the newly created gorge, with the remaining structure threatening to fall without warning. All that now connected the ends of the bridge was a narrow strip of ancient stone paving, in parts no more than two feet wide.

On the strip were three small figures moving very slowly, in an attempt to cross the bridge. Small pieces of rubble skittered down the sides of the arches as one of the figures lost their footing and almost fell into the gorge.

'What in thunder is happening down there?' demanded Pakal.

'Tunnellers!' snarled Talon. Although they were some distance away, he recognised the figures' dusty clothing as they continued to crawl their way across the bridge. 'They must be trying to escape. I'll have a welcome for them they won't forget when they reach this side –'

The sudden sound of heavy boots outside the room, thumping across the marble floor towards the door left open by Pakal, made him turn away from the window.

Without knocking or waiting for permission to enter, two Terogs burst into the room. Squat and short, their yellowish features beaded with sweat, both wore the traditional uniform of dark-red tunics belted over leather leggings and calf boots, but the one in front had the mark of a Terog leader, confirmed by the black skull displayed on a red headband across his forehead.

'Kanga!' cried Talon. 'What is the meaning of this interruption? How dare you storm in here while I am with Lord Pakal!'

'I am sorry, but you need to know that there is fighting outside the temple,' snorted the Terog with the headband.

Cosimo stared at him. *He could understand what the ugly brute was saying!* This was unexpected. Until now, any Terog he had come across spoke an incomprehensible, guttural language, which only Talon seemed to understand. His plan to control the Terogs, without Talon, would be virtually impossible if he couldn't communicate with them, but here was one who might be the answer to his problem.

He decided to make himself known. He asked, 'Who is fighting outside?'

'Yes, who are you talking about?' echoed Talon.

Kanga looked at the two of them, confused by the presence of a stranger asking the same question.

'It's all right, Kanga, you may answer, 'said Talon. 'He is our friend and he has come here to help us. Speak!'

The Terog bowed his head, snorted and nodded. He turned and pointed to the open door and beyond to the front of the temple. 'The slaves have broken out of the tunnels and are in the square fighting my guards.'

'Then send for the rest of your men! How many men do you need to put down unarmed slaves?'

'I have summoned the First Command from their quarters, but they have been stopped by a crowd of the people.'

'The people? You mean the Copanatecs?' cried Lord Pakal.

Kanga simply nodded and snorted again.

Talon looked to the window and thought of the tunnellers on the bridge. His voice was icy as he spoke, 'We must protect the temple and the pyramid. Summon all the commands to the square immediately. We will destroy this uprising and root out those who caused it – and those Copanatecs who support it!'

*

'Hold on, Kristin!' yelled Archie. He grabbed at the sleeve and waist of her jacket, frantically hauling her back onto the narrow stone ledge, before her weight pulled her away from his grip.

'Don't let me go!' she screamed. Her hands scrabbled for some purchase on the rough stonework as loose stones fell through her fingers.

'You're OK, I have you. Just lie still for a moment and get your breath back,' gasped Archie. He was terrified of heights and was doing his best not to look down at the rocks below. He pulled her closer to the low wall that lined the side of the bridge, away from one of the many large gaping holes that riddled the length of the road.

They were less than halfway across, Jona in the lead, Kristin in the middle, and Archie bringing up the rear, when a strong gust of wind swept through the gorge, forcing them to crouch as low as possible to avoid being blown over the edge of the hole, into the void. All that connected the arches of the bridge to the pyramid and the temple was a broken strip of stone slabs. Forming a narrow pavement, the strip ran alongside the shattered remains of the main road. But one of the slabs was loose and Kristin had lost her footing when she stepped onto its edge. Unbalanced, she had fallen, only being saved by Archie catching the tail of her jacket, before plunging into the gorge.

She sat up and stared at him. 'What the freakin' hell are we doing out here, anyway!' she screamed. It wasn't really a question, just a way of venting her fear at the thought of how close she had come to being killed.

Archie shrugged. He felt like saying if she hadn't stowed away in Captain Abelhorn's hovervan in the first place, she wouldn't be here. He didn't, instead he noticed a tear trickling down her cheek, which surprised him. For some reason, he thought she wasn't the crying type, but as he watched the tear touch her lips, he suddenly realised how vulnerable she was, and how much she had suffered. Just like him, both her parents had disappeared out of her life, and now she was in the middle of an uprising, with no idea what was going to happen to them. Not too surprising, then, she might shed a tear or two.

He smiled and squeezed her hand. 'It's going to be OK, but if we'd stayed in the tunnels, Kristin, we would have been trapped. Jona's trying to get us to safety – so we have no choice, but to follow him.'

She nodded, returning his squeeze, looking up as Jona retreated a few steps to stand over them. He said, 'We are being watched; we must get off the bridge before they come for us.'

Archie followed Jona's gaze towards the temple and beyond. They were standing over the very tip of the gorge, its walls gradually tapering into a steep rocky escarpment, to form a new barrier at the end of the square. Only a short time before, he realised, he had been pushing a wagon across the same square to the seawall.

As the wind eased, the distant sounds of people screaming and yelling reached him, as it did the watchers looking down on the bridge from a temple window.

'You're right,' said Archie, helping Kristin to her feet. 'I think your uprising is spreading, and I'm sure those guys in the temple aren't too happy about it.'

Chapter Forty-Nine

The Temple Gardens

'We are nearly there,' said Harimon. 'Soon we will see the gardens behind the temple.'

Careful not to reveal themselves, they kept to the cover of the trees as they moved through the wooded hilltop, staying close to the gorge on the other side of the hill, using it as a guideline to get them into the vicinity of the temple. They came to a halt as Harimon suggested they take a break while he checked their bearings.

Staring into the distance, across golden fields and dark green treetops, Richard let out a little gasp. Rising above the horizon was the outline of a familiar shape, one that he had last seen in the Yucatan jungle. It was the flat top of a pyramid, similar in its design to the Mayan pyramids, but different in that it supported a towering golden pillar.

'What is it you see?' asked Quig. 'Do you dream again?'

He looked at Richard suspiciously, still unsure what to make of his behaviour while in Marcie's cottage. His claim to having 'dreams' as he held the pendant – what did he mean? Since then the boy had said little more than that he sought his parents - but how did they come to be on Copanatec, and how did he expect to find them? Was the pendant, now concealed in the boy's pocket, the answer?   And of even more concern to Quig, was the thought that the mysterious disc might bring them into great danger.

'He sees the pyramid,' said Harimon. 'A mighty building, is it not, Richard?'

Richard nodded, but didn't give any hint that the pyramid was familiar to him. He saw the confusion in

Quig's eyes and knew that neither of them would understand, that not only was the pyramid similar to the one in the Yucatan, but that he had also seen it in a trance. Instead, he said, 'It is, but I was wondering where the smoke was coming from?'

At first, Harimon couldn't see what Richard was referring to, until he looked to the left of the pyramid where the gorge ended. A rocky, wooded hilltop directly ahead of them blocked any possible view of the temple, but he knew that on the other side lay the vegetable garden, their destination, and one of many that served the needs of the Copanatecs.

'Where – ?'

He had been about to ask what Richard had seen, but then he saw the smoky tendrils curling above the hilltop. A wind blowing through the gorge swept the rising tendrils together, forming an ominous black cloud that seemed to signal there was trouble ahead.

'It must be a fire at the temple!' Harimon reached for the crossbow he had laid on the ground. 'Quick! We will have to hurry and find my friend in the gardens.'

'What do you think is happening?' asked Richard.

'I don't know, but the uprising may have already started. If so, we will have to be very careful as we approach the temple – the Terogs will be out in force.'

'Let them come,' snarled Quig. He punched the air with his paragun. 'I will be waiting for them.'

*

Followed by Archie and Kristin, Jona dropped about two feet from what was left of the bridge, at a point where it used to meet an entrance to the temple, onto a set of steps that led to a wide, cobblestone path. The entrance had long been sealed by a massive iron gate, its ancient rusting lock secured with a heavy chain bolted to a side pillar. Overlooking the gorge, a perimeter wall had been constructed, running parallel with the temple.

'This way,' said Jona. He looked cautiously both ways; a glance to the right where the path would eventually lead to the temple steps fronting the square, and then a raised hand to gesture to Archie and Kristin to follow him to the left.

During the so-called Destruction, part of the temple had collapsed, leaving a large hole in the side of the building directly above them, near the window where they had seen the watchers. Large white stone blocks had fallen onto the path, creating a huge jumble, like a pile of giant sugar cubes barring their way. Luckily, they were able to squeeze through a narrow space, left between the blocks and the perimeter wall.

'Where are we heading, Jona?' asked Archie. They were hurrying now, towards a tall, wooden gate, set into a brick and stone archway, at the end of the path. 'Is it safe to go this way?'

Jona spoke as they reached the gate. 'I do not know, my friend, but if the villagers and the Terogs are fighting in the square, I think this is the best way.'

'But where will it take us?'

'I have never been here, but I have heard that behind the temple are the vegetable and fruit gardens, and beyond are the farmlands, all tended by the villagers. If we can find them, they may be able help us ...' Jona shrugged, unable to suggest what else they might do.

It wasn't much of a plan, thought Archie, but at least they were out of the tunnels and if the man Kristin had seen on the seawall *was* his father and he was held somewhere in the temple, then he had to find a way in to find him.

But what was he going to do about Kristin?

He couldn't expect her to follow him into the temple – not with Terogs, and God knows who, or what else, he might find in there – but he could hardly leave her behind, could he?

He sighed; he would have to wait and see what lay ahead of them.

The hinges squealed as Jona lifted the latch and pushed the gate open. He stepped through, stopping suddenly, forcing Archie to step to one side to avoid bumping into him.

'What's wrong?' murmured Kristin, coming up behind them. She smiled as she looked over Jona's shoulder at the rows of bright yellow sunflowers that stretched to the far end of the garden. It was her favourite flower to paint when she was in her studio at Portview Terrace. During the times when she thought about her parents, it was her way of bringing light into the dark moments. 'Did you see something?' she asked.

'I thought I saw someone over there.' Jona pointed beyond the last row of sunflowers to an area where rows of much smaller plants grew. It was bounded by a long hedge and a gravel path leading to a wooden building next to another gate.

'You're right! Get down!' Archie put a hand on Kristin's shoulder. 'There are men on the other side of the hedge, they're coming through the gate and heading towards that shed.'

Despite the sunflowers being as tall as Archie, he wasn't taking any chances on being seen. He dropped to his knees and kept watch through the gaps of the rough hairy stems and leaves.

'What did you see?' asked Jona, kneeling beside him.

'I'm not sure,' whispered Archie. 'There were two or three or of them. I could only see their heads, but I'm sure there were Terogs behind them.'

As if to corroborate what Archie had just said, a scream, and then loud shouts reached them. Three men, villagers by the look of them, dashed through the gate in the direction of the shed, pursued by a group of Terogs.

'No!' Jona shouted as he jumped to his feet. One of the Terogs had thrown a firebrand into the shed as one of the villagers ran inside. Another villager never made it, falling to his knees as a crossbow bolt pierced his side. The third villager, seeing the flaming firebrand in the doorway, turned away from the shed and raced for his life along a path that led to a rocky mound beyond the gardens.

Before Archie could stop him, Jona leapt through the sunflowers, in a mad run towards a Terog, ready to fire his own crossbow, but he was too late. The Terog spotted Jona and brought him down with a well-aimed bolt.

'What the freak is happening over there?' Kristin's voice was edgy with fear as she pushed a sunflower aside to get a better look.

Archie clamped a hand over her mouth as a sudden *woossshhhh* ripped through the air. Flames burst through the shed's roof, sending a cloud of burning wooden splinters across the sunflowers.

'My God! There must have been oil or something in that shed,' Archie pulled Kristin to her feet. 'We have to get out of here – let's go!'

'What about Jona?'

'The poor bugger's had it,' snapped Archie. 'C'mon, they might check to see if there was anyone with him.' He hauled her up onto her feet and retreated to a path between the sunflowers, a few rows further back.

He heard the grunts and shouts of the Terogs in the distance. *Had they been spotted?* He couldn't tell, but he had no time to think about it. They had to put as much space between them as possible. He peered over the tops of the sunflowers and saw a cluster of trees spread across a rocky hilltop ... *could they take cover up there?* More shouts stopped him taking a longer look, making him duck down again.

'Stay still and don't make a sound,' whispered Archie. 'I don't think they've seen us yet. They're probably searching the area to check if there was anyone with Jona.'

They lay quietly, squeezed together in amongst the leaves and thick stems of the sunflowers. Archie was stunned by what he had witnessed – the sudden shock of losing Jona just now sinking in. He could feel Kristin shivering, probably frightened by what was happening around them. As they lay there, perhaps twenty, maybe thirty minutes, he held Kristin's hand, encouraging her not to say a word. After a while, not hearing any sounds from the Terogs, he stood up and ventured a look.

A Terog was watching the flames lick up the side of the shed, sending sooty smoke swirling up into the sky, but there was no sign of the others. *Maybe the others have moved on, leaving a guard behind to watch the garden*, thought Archie. He took a look at the hill and decided they should make their way to cover of the trees. After that he would have to figure out what to do next.

'Let's go, Kristin – we'd better keep moving, while we can.'

They reached the bottom of the hill where small and large rocks were clustered together. Half-buried in the earth, they formed a natural barrier at the end of the garden. Fifty yards away to the left, above a row of very tall sunflowers, he could see the top of the perimeter wall; to the right, the hill and more rocks stretched for another hundred yards. They started climbing, clutching at thick clumps of grass between the rocks to keep their balance. It was Kristin who heard the grunts of the Terog behind them.

She screamed: 'Archie!'

Archie, just ahead of her, whirled round to see the Terog steadying himself on the rocks at the bottom of the hill, preparing to use his crossbow. He only had time to think: *Where the hell did he come from?* when a sudden streak of blinding light appeared to rush past his shoulder. For a split second, all he could see was a bright, white shimmering shape in front of him. The Terog became a hazy outline, a space filled with billions of pixel-like points of light. Archie raised a hand to protect his eyes, closing them for no more than a couple of seconds. When he opened them again, the Terog was gone. *Nothing, not an atom.* It was as if he had imagined the brute. He shook his head and looked down at the rows of sunflowers, but there was no one there.

It was someone yelling, that brought him back to his senses.

'Archie! Archie, up here – it's me!'

He looked up to see three figures standing on the brow of the hill, in front of the trees, staring down at him. To his amazement, he recognised two of the figures, each carrying some kind of weapon.

And one of them was Richard!

The other one, with a nasty looking scar running around his right eye and ear, he would know anywhere. It was Quig, Captain Abelhorn's mainliner from the *Serpent*! But the third figure, holding a crossbow, was a stranger to him.

Kristin scrambled over a rock to get to his side. 'Who are they?' she whispered.

Before Archie could answer, he was distracted by the sound of someone crashing through the trees from the far end of the hilltop, calling out a name as he ran towards Richard and his companions. It was the villager who had fled from the burning shed.

The third figure, standing beside Richard, shouted: 'Quig, don't shoot! It's my friend who works in the gardens!'

At that moment, it seemed to Archie that all hell had broken out around him. A bolt whizzed past, narrowly missing his head. Kristin screamed as it ricocheted off a nearby rock. He looked round and saw two more Terogs coming up behind him, and then the white flash of bright light appeared again. One of them vanished and the other one stopped dead, mystified by the disappearance of his comrade.

'Let's get up there before he wakes up to what's happening,' said Archie. 'You go first, I'll keep an eye on him.'

They worked their way up the rest of the hill, through a scattering of rocks and small bushes, until Richard reached out a helping hand to Kristin. Archie was next, and he immediately grabbed Richard in a bear hug, grinning and ruffling his hair.

'Am I glad to see you! But how in Heaven's name did you end up here?'

Richard pushed him away. 'I'm glad to see you, too, Archie ... but don't get so close. I hate to tell you, but your clothes are a mess, and you really stink.'

'Well, that's a fine welcome,' laughed Archie, 'but I think my clothes are the least of our worries.' He glanced at the rest of the group watching the gardens for any sign of more Terogs. 'We were in serious trouble there, but the way you guys used those weapons got us out of a tight spot.'

'Yeah, the paraguns are something else, but Quig has been using them on full power. That's when you when you want to stop a tank, leaving nothing behind.'

Quig, standing beside them, grunted and pointed his weapon towards the temple: 'I do not know what you mean, but with this I will kill many Terogs.'

'If you stop them killing us, that will be OK by me,' said Archie. He pointed to the trees behind them. 'Especially those guys!'

Harimon's friend had dropped to his knees, exhausted by his run from the shed and through the gardens, unaware that two Terogs had just burst through the trees, ready to pounce on him. Quig spotted them. With the paragun held at his waist like a wild west gunman, he let loose a lethal blast that sent one of the Terogs into the void. The other one, repelled by the shock wave, was thrown into the trees, where he picked himself up and made a dash for cover.

Archie watched the Terog run frantically through the trees towards the gardens. 'My God, Quig, if you keep using that thing, there'll be none of those guys left!'

'That is my intention,' growled Quig. 'It is a pity that one escaped, but his time will come.'

Archie noticed the glint in his eye and thought he was slightly mad, but said nothing. Instead, he turned his attention to the other man who had turned up with Richard and Quig.

'Who's your friend over there, with the villager?' asked Archie. 'And, more to the point, how the hell did you end up here?' He pointed to the paragun, Richard was holding at his side. 'And, while you're at it, how about telling me where you got that – whatever it is – from?'

'That's Harimon,' said Richard. ' And, well ... as for this ...' He handed the weapon over to Archie to examine. 'It's a paragun. I don't think I'm up to using it on anyone, so you're welcome to it, if you want it. The rest of what's happened so far is a bit complicated –'

'For Heaven's sake, Richard, I just want to know how you got here!' Archie held the weapon at his side, ignoring it for a moment as Harimon and his friend – who seemed to have recovered from his dash through the garden – joined them. 'Look we can't hang around here, waiting for more Terogs to turn up. Have you guys got a plan, or any idea on what to do next?'

'I came with Chuck to find you –'

'You came with Chuck! He's here?'

'Well, not exactly *here* ...'

'Then where the hell is he?' asked Archie.

Harimon raised a hand to interrupt them. 'May I suggest you leave this discussion for another time?' He looked directly at Archie. 'You are right that we cannot stay here. There is fighting in the temple square and my friend, Calum, has said that it has spread to the gardens and the farmlands. Many have died already, including Copanatecs who have joined the uprising alongside our people.'

'*Copanatecs?*' Quig glared at Harimon. 'I do not believe it. They are all our enemy and I will kill them as I would any Terog!'

'No, it is not so, Quig. Only a few are loyal to the Lords of the Cloud, and they are well rewarded. The rest have had their land and children taken from them in service to the temple and they have had enough. The uprising serves both the Copanatecs and the villagers in achieving their freedom.'

Quig was sceptical, but said no more.

Harimon watched him walk away, into the cover of the trees, then turned to make himself known to the others. He nodded as they each gave their names.

He said to Archie, 'Your brother has spoken of your search for your parents, and I have told him I believe it is your father I shared a cell with when he first came to Copanatec.' He raised a hand to stay Archie asking any questions. 'I understand you wish to know more, but it is not wise to stay here any longer. We must be gone before others come to find the missing Terogs.'

Some hope, thought Archie, but he said nothing, letting Harimon finish. He was desperate to hear more about his father and mother.

'Your father has been put to the task of rebuilding the temple and maintaining the seawall these many months by Talon the Slave Master, but all of this has stopped with the uprising. Lord Pakal has ordered Talon and all Terogs to show no mercy to anyone who resists and refuses to work. Calum says a stranger, an alien, is helping them with new weapons, and that the Copanatecs, as well as our people, are being slaughtered in the square and in the streets near the temple. We must take the paraguns to them as quickly as possible, it is their only hope. Calum can take us through the gardens into the temple kitchen. Once there we will leave you to find your father, and we will go to our people.'

Archie was stunned by what Harimon had just said: that his father was in the temple, only a short distance away, forced to work for Talon. And the stranger ... that must be Cosimo ... was he also a danger to his father?

He could feel the tension that had been with him since they fled the tunnels, slowly turn to anger as he realised how his father must have suffered at the hands of Talon.

And his mother: *What had happened to her?*

He looked to his brother and wondered if he had 'seen' anything. 'Richard, have you had ... you know ... any visions, anything at all, that will help us find mum and dad?'

'I'm not sure, Archie,' said Richard. He clutched the pendant in his pocket, unsure if he should mention its power in front of the others. He decided he would wait until he was alone with Archie before showing it to him. He said, 'I did 'see' something before we came to Copanatec ... It was mum ... she was on a Transkal, somewhere in a great hall .... I don't know where, then she disappeared –'

'She disappeared! You mean, in a timecrack?'

'No, it wasn't the same ... it was a different colour. More like a golden mist –'

'The golden smoke! The Man of Dust!' hissed Quig. He pointed a finger at Richard. 'He holds the pendant – he must be rid of it, before we leave here!'

Archie stared at him, not knowing what he was talking about, but before he could ask Quig what he meant, he heard yelling and a commotion in the garden of sunflowers near the temple.

Calum, standing to one side from the group, had been keeping watch over the gardens. He called to them, 'We must leave! More Terogs have arrived! They will have been told about us, by the one who escaped.'

As they turned and ran for the cover of the trees, Archie waved the paragun at Richard. 'You better show me how to use this thing; I think we're going to need it!'

Chapter Fifty

Inside the Temple

'Tell them to keep their heads down,' Calum whispered to Archie. He gestured with a hand outstretched behind him for all of them to stay below the height of the hedge. He was looking through a break where he had pushed a branch and leaves to one side. 'A line of Terogs is marching through the sunflowers towards the hill. The one who ran away must have told them about us.'

Archie nodded and passed the message to Quig, directly behind him. 'Tell the others to stay low, until they pass by.'

Quig grunted impatiently but passed the warning down the line. His finger stroked the paragun trigger, ready to use it if the Terogs came too close. Calum had brought the group down from the hilltop onto a gravel path running between the hedge and a stone wall. They were on the far side of the garden, where they crouched in single file, ready to move when Calum gave the signal.

'How do we get into the temple?' asked Archie. He kept his voice low, but he was so close to Calum he could smell the heavy farmyard odours from his clothes, mixed with the freshness of the green hedge they hid behind. He guessed that he was a couple of years older than him, maybe nineteen or twenty. It was hard to tell age on New Earth; he had the lean, tanned look that added years to someone who worked in the open air on the land.

'I work with my father on the farmlands and every week we deliver the produce into the temple kitchen. Usually, we see the cook ...' He shrugged his shoulders. 'I do not know who will be there now, but from here it is the only way for us to get into the temple. A passageway from the kitchen leads to the front and the square.'

His father, he told Archie, was a friend of Harimon and one of the leaders of the uprising. It was on their delivery today that they had hidden farm tools in the produce sacks to be used as weapons, but the Terogs had arrived unexpectedly and discovered the tools during a search of the kitchen. In the melee that followed they had become separated when his father had made a dash through the temple for the square, while Calum had fled with some of the kitchen workers into the gardens, chased by the Terogs. He was saddened by the killings at the shed, but now Harimon and his friends had arrived with powerful weapons, he had to make sure they were not caught.

Archie felt a tap on his shoulder. It was Quig, peering through a break in the hedge. 'Look, they are moving up the hill!'

Calum jumped to his feet. 'We must go before they reach the top. They may be able to see us from there.'

Hidden by the hedge, the group crept down the path to an opening in the stone wall; it was one of several in the wall between the gardens and the farmlands. They hurried through onto another path that took them past rows of green beans tied to poles, sweetcorn plants, and a seemingly endless variety of green vegetables that stretched in more rows all the way to the horizon. Calum held a hand up as they stopped to take cover by a clump of trees. Beyond the wall, they could see the upper level of the temple.

'Why do we stop?' demanded Quig.

'We have to be certain the way to the temple is clear,' said Calum.

'So what do we do when we get there?' asked Archie.

'We kill the Terogs and their masters, and anyone else who is with them,' snarled Quig.

'My father is in there!' snapped Archie. 'I have to find him!'

'If he is in the temple, your father will be in the cells,' said Harimon. He stood in the centre of the group, the crossbow slung over his shoulder, as they huddled next to the wall.

'What do you mean?' asked Richard.

Harimon turned to face him. 'We cannot waste time here, but I must explain before we enter the temple as we will probably part there. You and your brother will want to find your father, but Calum, Quig and I must take these weapons to our friends as quickly as we can.'

'I understand you need the weapons,' said Archie, 'but I need to know what you mean by my father being locked in a cell?' He was anxious to keep moving, but he needed whatever help and information Harimon could give him. 'If he is, how do we get him out?'

'He will not be locked in. Your father is not treated like the other prisoners, because he has skills which Talon needs to rebuild the temple and maintain the seawall. As a metal worker, I work with gold and silver and I have been to the temple many times to help him with repairs to the works of art that were damaged during the Destruction.'

'But the cells ...'

'The temple is built around the central chamber with a wing on each side. One wing houses a staircase leading to the rooms of the Defenders; in the opposite wing are the cells used by the priestesses.' Harimon smiled as he continued: 'Not like the cells in the tunnels, your father has been given rooms where he can work and sleep. He has freedom of movement within the temple, but you must remember that Talon and

Lord Pakal and their servants also live there; it would be wise to take extreme care.'

The sudden sound of shouts on the other side of the wall caught his attention. 'What is that?'

Calum motioned to all of them to be quiet. He crept back to the opening and took a quick look before returning to the group. 'The Terogs are leaving the hilltop, we have to move quickly.'

There was more that Archie wanted to ask Harimon, but there was no time. He kept a tight grip on the paragun and, with the others, followed Calum as he led the way to the temple.

*

Malcolm left the wall at the side of the temple where he had been working for the past three hours. Preparing the gap to replace several of the huge stone blocks that had fallen away during the Destruction was threatening to take up most of his day, but the sudden uproar outside the temple had caught his attention. One of the corner turrets prevented him from seeing the square from where he was on the wall, but the explosion, followed by screams and shouting, had forced him to set aside his tools to find out what was happening.

He made his way down the spiral stone staircase below the turret to the ground floor. His knee was stiff with the effort of trying to keep his balance on the narrow stone steps that led to the chamber and the stone he knew as a Transkal. He saw one of the temple priestesses, Leanna, standing with Talon next to the great stone. They turned to watch him when they heard the steady beat, *tap-tap-tap*, of his walking stick on the marble floor.

'You have finished your work?' asked Talon.

385

'No, of course not, I have much more to do, but I heard an explosion near the temple square –'

Talon interrupted Malcolm with a wave of his rod, directed towards the temple entrance. 'It is under control. Some of the tunnellers tried to escape to the seawall through the square, but they are being dealt with.'

'How? I heard an explosion.'

'Our new ally, Cosimo and his men, brought their weapons with them,' smiled Talon. 'They and the Terogs will soon put the prisoners back where they belong.'

'Using explosives?' said Malcolm, a hint of disapproval in his voice.

'Enough, alien!' Talon raised the rod threateningly. 'It is no concern of yours. You should be about your work and not troubling me with your questions. These disturbances must not be allowed to hinder the task of finding the Immortal Wand. It must be found at any cost. Do you understand?'

Malcolm backed away, well aware of the pain that the rod could inflict. Talon cast him a warning glance as he strode towards the front of the temple, leaving him with Leanna.

After Talon left the chamber he walked across to the Transkal. His right hand rested heavily on the walking stick, while the fingers of the other traced the outline of one of the glyphs engraved on the edge of the stone.

'You still miss her?' asked Leanna, watching him curiously. She, along with the other priestesses, attended to the care of the chamber and the great stone.

'Of course I do,' said Malcolm, angrily. 'She was my wife and she was taken from me for one your damned rituals.'

'Lord Pakal said she was ready for the next world,' said Leanna. 'And she also said she was ready, when I prepared her for the journey.'

Malcolm shook his head, not wanting to believe that Lucy would ever want to leave him.

'No. She wouldn't make such a decision without saying anything to me.'

But would she? wondered Malcolm. He had to admit he had his doubts.

It had been many months - he had no idea exactly how long - since the day they were taken and then parted by Talon, during the raid on the village where they had landed after being transported from the Transkal in the Yucatan. No contact had been allowed between them: no messages, not a word. Talon had warned repeatedly not to question him about Lucy, otherwise they would both suffer his anger.

Malcom knew it was not an empty threat, so he decided to try a different approach and offered his services as a restoration expert on old buildings, in the hope that by being in the temple he would stand a better chance of finding her. It would be better than the tunnel cell he had been held in.

Talon had accepted and Malcolm had been brought to the temple to advise on repairs to the building, only to be told later by Leanna that Lucy had voluntarily prepared herself for the ritual, months earlier.

Why would she do that? Had she seen something in one of her trances?

He swept a hand across his hair, trying to remember if she had ever said, or even hinted at doing such a thing, but nothing came to him.

He thought of his first wife, Anna, and her sudden loss to cancer, only a few short months after she entered hospital for a routine medical examination. It had been a cruel, devastating blow after such a long relationship, dating back to their childhood when they attended the same school together in Edinburgh. From there they had gone to Cambridge, both of them graduating with first-class honours, he in archaeology and Anna in history.

They spent the next few years teaching, but with Malcolm's early interest in the Maya further stimulated by his friend and mentor, the renowned archaeologist, the late Sir Archibald Transkal, he would spend more time travelling to the digs at Chichen Itza, Coba and Tulum in the Yucatan. He would come to regret these periods without Anna; although, when Archie was born six years into their marriage, they had seen it as an unexpected blessing, a fulfilment of their vows. But it was not to last, for less than a year later, Anna was dead.

Grief-stricken, he had sent Archie to one of Anna's sisters and her husband, a farming couple near Enniskillen in Northern Ireland, who had no children of their own. It was a difficult choice, but he could no longer face staying in a city with so many painful memories and when the offer of a position with a university in New Mexico was put to him, he accepted immediately. Leaving Archie behind was also painful, but he decided it was best for a baby boy to be brought up in a proper family atmosphere, which he felt he couldn't provide.

Malcolm's career in New Mexico had blossomed with his discovery of a new pyramid deep in the Yucatan jungle, but unfortunately his participation in the discovery came to a sudden halt, when working on an outside level he lost his footing and fell down the narrow steps to the base of the pyramid. He was lucky he wasn't killed, but a fractured kneecap had left him with a legacy of permanent pain, an unfortunate handicap for an archaeologist tramping through dense jungle.

It was during his recuperation that Lucy entered his life. A mature postgraduate student, she had responded to his postcard request on the university noticeboard for a temporary assistant – at least, until he was back on his feet, he had written, but it was to prove a lot longer than that.

As it happened, he was very much aware of her presence on campus. She was a tall, slender and very striking silver-blonde; and unusually, for that part of the world, she was very pale-skinned. At an informal meeting to discuss the position, she described herself as an orphan brought up by relatives in British Columbia, later working in a library in Vancouver for a number of years before applying for a postgrad course in archaeology. At the interview he arranged, she made it very clear that she had followed his work in the Yucatan and was anxious to work with him. It was really a no-brainer and he hired her on the spot.

Later, when he reflected on the frequent occasions Lucy joined him on the digs in the Yucatan, he didn't think it inevitable that working so closely together would lead to a more intimate relationship, but it was no big surprise to their friends and colleagues when it did happen. She had become indispensable, not only in dealing with travel arrangements, editing and recording his rough notes, and dealing with all the other paraphernalia associated with academia, but as the companion Anna had once been.

It was after they were married and Richard was born that Lucy's headaches started. The pain wasn't too bad, she said, and easily dealt with by a packet of extra strength Tylenol, but it was the dreams, and then the 'visions' she reported during a trance, that disturbed him. He had insisted that she see a doctor, but she refused, saying it was something she could deal with in her own way. It wasn't clear what she meant and he had learned to live with the occasions, very often lasting only a few minutes, when she seemed to retreat into a world of her own.

Things improved and he had felt able to continue his work in the Yucatan, leaving Lucy to her own studies and looking after Richard, with the help of a live-in maid. But it wasn't long before the maid contacted him to complain about Lucy's trances. They were becoming more frequent, she claimed, and they frightened her. It was not a situation she was prepared to accept.

Malcolm left the team of co-workers at the dig in the Yucatan and returned to New Mexico on the first flight out of Cancun. Knowing how difficult it would be to find another maid to replace her, he hoped an increase in pay would persuade her to stay, but by the time he got home it was too late. She had apparently left in a hurry, preferring not to face him.

History seemed to be repeating itself and, after discussing the circumstances they found themselves in, he convinced Lucy the best course of action would be to send Richard to join Archie in Ireland. It would better for all of them, he said, and in due course the boys would come out to he and Lucy when they were older. Until then they could return each year for the annual holidays, and there was the added attraction of visiting their uncle, Anna's brother, John Strawbridge, a physicist, who ran one of the US Government's research establishments in New Mexico. And so it had worked out. Time passed and Lucy seemed to improve, with the headaches and trances becoming less frequent.

Then another fateful change took place.

It was late one evening and Malcolm was on one of his rare trips home, complaining as usual about the amount of paperwork he had to deal with, when Lucy unexpectedly volunteered to set aside her own university work to join him and his team in the Yucatan. She would make herself useful and simply fit in wherever she was needed and the boys would attend the international school in Mexico whenever they visited, before eventually returning to finish their studies at Grimshaws. The boys' schooling was an unusual arrangement, but seemed to work satisfactorily, as far as their parents were concerned.

Malcolm had been hesitant, unsure if Lucy was really up to working in the jungle conditions, but he liked the idea of them being together and had eventually agreed, thinking that they would be like a real family for the first time.

Until the day he and Lucy were at the new pyramid site when the lightning storm triggered the timecrack that struck the Transkal.

He shook his head at the thought of never seeing any of them again. Trapped on this godforsaken island in another dimension, he had no idea what to do next.

He turned away from the stone and looked at Leanna. 'I think I'll go down to the kitchen and get something to eat.'

*

In the kitchen, Calum, Quig and Harimon were ready to leave with the weapons: the two paraguns and the crossbow.

'We have to get these to our people as quickly as we can,' said Harimon.

Terogs were swarming through the gardens and the farmlands, killing anyone who refused their commands to surrender. By the time Calum led them into the kitchen they had come across the bodies of several villagers lying in a ditch who hadn't escaped. It had taken forceful persuasion on Harimon's part – that they had to get the weapons to the main body of fighters in the square – to stop Quig setting off on a one-man rampage of revenge.

Calum opened the kitchen door a couple of inches and glanced out; it was the third time he had done so in the last five minutes.

'Can you see them?' asked Harimon.

Calum closed the door. 'No, they are spreading out beyond the temple. They will not think to look in here. It is only those that are running away from them they seek.'

They had arrived in the kitchen twenty minutes earlier, frightening the wits out of the poor cook, a villager from Elam, when they burst through the door. But as soon as he recognised Calum and Harimon, he'd rushed forward and hugged them both, saying he thought that the Terogs had come to take him outside and kill him.

Harimon smiled and reassured him that he was safe for the time being. 'Lord Pakal and the others in the temple will still need your food.' He pointed to Archie and Kristin, looking ravenously at plates of meat and bread on the long wooden table in the middle of the kitchen that the cook had been preparing for others in the temple. 'And so will our friends, I think.'

The cook had nodded and hurried to the table, encouraging all of them to take whatever they wanted, handing plates to each of them.

Archie grabbed a thick sandwich of spicy sausage meat between two chunks of coarse brown bread. 'Mmmm, this is good. I'd forgotten how hungry I was.'

'Yeah, me too,' mumbled Kristin, stuffing another bite into her mouth.

Richard joined them at the table. As usual, with his seemingly insatiable appetite and, although he had eaten earlier along with Harimon and Quig, he took a plate and started chewing a large piece of meat.

After a few bites he pointed to a heavy wooden door held by long metal hinges bolted to the stone of a narrow archway, halfway along one side of the kitchen. 'Calum says that door opens to a service corridor for the stores. It leads to the front of the temple and it's the way they're going to take the weapons to their friends. But what about us – what are we going to do?'

For a few moments no one answered him. Archie looked across to where Quig was sitting on a stool, Harimon standing behind him. The paragun lay across his lap and he was stroking it as if it were a pet, enjoying the texture and grip of the weapon, as well as the thought of its awesome destructive power.

Then Harimon spoke. He placed a hand on Quig's shoulder: 'We cannot waste any more time, it is time for us to leave. Quig and I agree we must get these weapons –'

Before he could finish, all of them were startled by the loud metallic clang of a latch opening a door at the top of a short flight of stone steps at the end of the kitchen. It was the door that that led to the main part of the temple.

Quig leapt to his feet. He kicked the stool aside, ready to fire the paragun at the tall figure leaning on a walking stick on the top step, staring down at them.

'NO, DON'T SHOOT!' shouted Archie. He had dropped his plate and, to everyone's amazement, dashed in front of Quig, blocking his aim, to run towards the figure now descending the steps.

Chapter Fifty-One

The Battle in Temple Square

Han-Sin kept the Spokestar on a course that would allow a closer look at the Copanatec coast which was barely visible through the low-lying mist. Behind them a huge sea was rising and falling, forming deep black troughs capped by snow-white ridges rolling across the storm-tossed White Waters towards the island.

'That's one crazy sea down there,' said Chuck. He pressed his face closer to the cockpit glass, squinting to get a better look at the forbidding coastline now coming up rapidly ahead of them. 'You still think it's OK to go in?'

'It's not a problem,' said Han-Sin, flicking a switch on the panel in front of her. 'The stealth cloak will see to that. It makes us invisible to anyone outside the cloak line; they would need to be within ten feet of the Spokestar to see us. What we face on the island is what concerns me.'

Chuck turned away from the glass and nodded. He was thinking the same thing. Earlier, when they arrived at the clearing where he had left Richard with Quig and Harimon, he had gone straight to the toadstool rock next to the road, before venturing into Elam, in case they had left a message. It was folded and pushed into a small cleft just below the flat cap of the rock. Swearing out loud when he opened it, he saw that Richard had drawn a rough map with little arrows and names, using Harimon's directions on how to reach the temple from the far coast of the island. Angry with himself for not forcing Richard to stay with him, he'd stomped back to the Spokestar and told Han-Sin to avoid Elam and head for Copanatec.

Han-Sin decided to cross the island at its tip and find the gorge on the far side, which would enable her to the follow the map's directions more accurately. She glanced at the landscape unfolding below. 'I'll follow the gorge until we see the temple or the pyramid and set down when I find the right place. The cloak doesn't work when the power unit is not engaged.' To the two Lancers sitting in the rear of the cockpit, she ordered: 'From now on, each of you keep your eyes open and report any activity you see.'

There was no problem finding the gorge. The earthquake, or the Destruction as the Copanatecs had come to know it, had created a natural harbour where successive generations of local fishermen had built their community on a flat rocky promontory near the mouth.

'There's no sign of life; the place looks deserted,' said Chuck. He pulled Richard's message from his pocket and studied the roughly drawn scribbles.

'The track seems to end beyond the harbour,' said Han-Sin. She put the Spokestar in hover-mode over the harbour, while she took a closer look at the area.

'No, it seems to be overgrown now. According to this map, the only route we can rely on to take us to the temple is to follow the gorge. It leads directly to the city, so it shouldn't be too hard to find – unless the weather breaks,' said Chuck. He glanced up through the cockpit canopy and noted the dark storm clouds gathering over the sea behind them.

'Yes, you are correct. I am picking up warning signals from Sunstone at the castle, to stay clear of White Waters airspace.'

'Why?'

'I do not know. The waters are known to be notoriously treacherous to sailors, and the area is now a designated red zone. That means it is not safe for any form of craft, even more so than it usually is around there.'

She disengaged the hover-mode and flew into the mouth of the gorge and continued flying low to enable them to see the area more clearly. As they flew further into the gorge, the sheer rock face on either side and the water below, eventually disappeared to be replaced by rocky, wooded hillsides dropping into a dry boulder-strewn gully.

A short time later, one of the Lancers sitting behind Han-Sin tapped her on the shoulder. He pointed directly ahead to the skyline where they could see the distinctive shape of the pyramid.

'I see it,' said Han-Sin.

'The map shows a square between the temple and a seawall above the harbour,' said Chuck. 'I think we need to check it out, in case we need an alternative escape route for some of the people down there.'

Han-Sin stared at him for a moment. Her priority on this mission was to find and rescue the boys, not to attempt to extricate any of the villagers on the island. The Spokestar Mark 8 was a seven-seat troop carrier, plus the pilot; with Chuck and the two Lancers on board there would only be two spare seats if they found the boys. It was impossible to consider any sort of large scale evacuation plan; that would be for others to deal with. She said nothing and kept her eyes glued to the bridge directly ahead.

The rock-strewn floor of the gorge narrowed at this point, rising to a rough spoon-shaped level below a bridge supported by five stone arches. Opposite the pyramid, the wind had cleared the clouds of smoke that had been swirling slowly around the turrets of the temple. They flew over the bridge and saw that, along with one side of the pyramid, large sections of the stonework had collapsed into the gorge.

Suddenly they were over the temple square, looking down at a nightmare scene of horrendous carnage.

'My God! What's happening down there?'

Everywhere he looked, he saw dead and injured bodies lying near burning makeshift barriers that had been erected across parts of the square. Near one of the barriers – constructed from wooden carts, market stalls, display tables, wagons dragged from the rail tracks and anything else that could be dragged into place to afford some sort of protection – a pocket of close quarter fighting was taking place. Terogs, and others he assumed to be the villagers, were attacking each other with a mishmash of weapons. Terogs with their crossbows, short swords and metal-tipped whips, were forcing their way through the barrier, while the villagers with crossbows taken from fallen Terogs, along with picks, shovels, tunnel drills, even rocks, anything they could lay their hands on, were returning the fight against a hated enemy.

Han-Sin took a position over the square. As they watched the fighting, she ensured the stealth cloak was still engaged. 'I do not know what caused the fighting, but obviously we cannot land here; we will have to find a safe place to leave the Spokestar where it cannot be seen. Once the power unit is switched off we will be visible.'

Chuck estimated there must be up to a thousand men in the square, and he wondered how many more Terogs might be held in reserve before they joined the battle. He had little time to think about it when an explosion and a cloud of smoke suddenly erupted in the middle of the square. As a light wind cleared the smoke, he saw a sickening sight he had seen on battlefields in the past and hoped never to see again. Several men lay on the ground with missing body parts scattered across a barrier, others were standing nearby staring into space, as if lost.

'Christ! Where the hell did that come from?' Chuck swore again as another explosion blew the barrier to smithereens.

'Over there.' Han-Sin pointed to the roof between the turrets of the temple fronting the square. She accelerated to a point near one of the turrets, holding the Spokestar there as they scanned the rooftop. 'Look, they are using army field weapons.'

Chuck realised she was right. Behind a low parapet at the front of the flat roof two light infantry mortars, long barrels secured to base plates supported by bipods, very similar to the type he had seen used by US army units, were being operated by three men to each mortar. Next to them, open crates of high explosive fin bombs were ready to load before being fired indiscriminately into the square below. Between the mortar teams two men lay prone firing some kind of high-powered laser rifles at anything that moved. Behind them stood a group of men, including a strange Moses-like figure waving a long staff.

'Who *is* that guy; and how did they get that weaponry? I didn't think they would have anything like it here,' said Chuck. But as soon as he uttered the words, he realised how contradictory they sounded. Here he was sitting in an invisible flying machine along with Lancers armed with plasma weapons, more advanced than anything on Old Earth. From what he had learned so far, it was a society composed of many primitive and advanced cultures – including weaponry – from his and other worlds.

Han-Sin didn't answer. They were interrupted by the roar of the mortars as more bombs were rained onto the square. She pulled the Spokestar away from the turret to a safer position. Although, they couldn't be seen, she didn't want to take the risk of being hit by a wild shot from the snipers on the rooftop.

The mortars roared again as two more bombs streaked into the sky, with no guarantee where they would land.

'Those guys are crazy! They don't seem to give a damn who they hit!' Chuck shook his head as he saw a man, missing a leg, crawling away from the debris of a barrier in the aftermath of an explosion, grabbing at the ground to try and reach somewhere safe.

Han-Sin agreed. 'This is unacceptable.' She flicked a switch illuminating a target screen on the panel between them. The screen, divided into a grid of little green squares, displayed the parapet and the men behind it on the rooftop. She turned a control showing a red circle enlarging as it settled on the target until a word appeared: FIRE. She fired. Instantly, a bright star-like flash hovered over the rooftop. When it cleared, a stretch of the parapet and a large section of the roof, along with the turret had collapsed into the square. There was no sign of the men manning the mortars, or the snipers and their rifles.

'My God!,' said Chuck, turning to look at Han-Sin as she switched off the target screen. 'I would hate to be on the wrong side of this beauty.'

She nodded, not fully understanding his words, but felt that he accepted the action she had just taken. 'We must leave here.'

'Where are we going?'

'Although we cannot be seen, we may have betrayed our presence to some of those in the temple. If so, they may also be aware that only the Lancers have the power to do what we did to their men. In that case, they will be looking for us.'

'I guess you're right, so what do you suggest we do now?'

'Our mission is to find the boys, and I believe our starting point must be the temple, so we have to find a way in without being seen. But our first task is to hide the Spokestar before the cloak is switched off.'

'And where might that be?'

'On our approach from the gorge I saw fields of corn which would be tall enough for our purpose. They are on the other side of the temple.'

'Sounds good to me, Han-Sin,' said Chuck. 'I'm ready, when you are.'

*

Nitkin and Kanga burst into the room where Cosimo had been accommodated in one of the many apartments on the upper floor of the temple.

Lord Pakal sat opposite Cosimo, astonished by the sudden interruption of their discussion on how best Cosimo would serve Copanatec. About to complain, he was silenced by the unexpected announcement by Cosimo's lieutenant.

'All of our men have been lost!' cried Nitkin.

He was a small man with an ugly, spiteful temperament and malicious tongue. Featuring a twisted nose and a foul mouth full of crooked teeth, he could claim few close friends, even amongst his own Arnak tribe. Cosimo preferred to keep him at a distance, but Nitkin was the most senior member of the rebel Arnaks, and as such, he was indispensable to Cosimo's position as the new leader of the rebels.

Shifting uneasily, an arm waving and pointing upwards, Nitkin was obviously frightened by something he had witnessed.

'Stand still, and tell me what you are raving about!' demanded Cosimo, rising to his feet.

'Up on the roof ... there was a bright light ... then an explosion. They're all gone!'

'What do you mean, they're *all* gone?'

Besides Nitkin, Cosimo had brought eight men to Copanatec: six to man the mortars and two with the laser rifles. They were weapons they had stolen from the armoury on the mainland and part of his arrangement to support Talon.

Nitkin turned to Kanga, the commander of the Terogs, standing beside him, as if for support, expecting him to confirm what he had just said. It was through their association, that Nitkin had managed to grasp a few words of the Terog tongue

'We were in the stairwell just below the roof when we heard the explosion – we also might have been killed –' said Kanga.

Cosimo held up a hand to the Terog to stop him saying any more and addressed Nitkin. 'Are you trying to tell me all our men are dead?'

Before Nitkin could answer, Lord Pakal pushed his chair away and rose quickly to confront Kanga. 'What of Talon, where is he?'

'He was on the roof with the Arnaks, my Lord. He was very angry with them because they were firing on our commands, as well as the prisoners and the people helping them.'

'But where is he?'

'He must have died with the others, my Lord.'

'No! It cannot be!' said Pakal. His voice was no more than a whisper as he looked at Kanga. 'We must go the roof and see for ourselves.'

He left the apartment and hurried down the corridor to the stairwell that would take them to the roof. Cosimo, with the others close behind, followed him.

As they stepped out onto what was left of the flat rooftop they stopped and stood in a group, unable to proceed further because of a gaping hole directly in front of them. Beyond, most of the parapet and the turret had disappeared leaving only a section of the roof around the stairwell entrance.

Such scenes were not unusual for Cosimo. He had seen such destruction before, but the question was: How did it happen?

With the unexpected horde of escaped prisoners in the square – and now with the Copanatecs helping them – he had ordered the men to use the mortars to prevent an assault on the temple. *At any cost,* no matter who or what they hit. He understood Talon's anger if he had witnessed his Terogs under fire, but he knew such weapons could not discriminate between friend and foe during close quarter combat; and if the mob entered the temple, all of them, including the temple attendants, would be at their mercy.

As he looked around at what was left of the roof, he had no doubt that any bombs that were still in the crates next to the mortars would have contributed to the massive damage he now witnessed, if they'd received a direct hit. He knew of only one force capable of carrying out such an attack at this height.

The Lancers.

Chapter Fifty-Two

Malcolm and the Boys

'I can hardly believe you boys are actually here,' said Malcolm, 'and the stories you have to tell – it's amazing!'

He stared at Archie and Richard, taking in their presence for a moment, trying to think how long it had been since he last saw them. They had changed so much, not only in height and appearance, but although he called them 'boys', there was something else about them he couldn't quite put his finger on. They were young men now, of course, but it was something else. Not only what they had already told him, but the look in their eyes that said they had seen and been through a great deal and been hardened by it.

After the shock of finding them in the kitchen with the others he'd insisted on bringing Archie and Richard, along with their friend Kristin, to the two cells that served as his living quarters and workspace. But his first act, when he realised how dirty Archie's and Kristin's tunnel clothes were – Richard's weren't so bad, as it turned out – was to rummage through an old clothing store next to the kitchen that was used by the garden workers. He managed to put together a couple of work tunics and trousers, roughly their size and held in place by leather belts, to make them more presentable.

After they left the kitchen, the noise of explosions echoing near the front of the temple, which seemed to be more frequent and getting closer, had galvanised Quig, Calum and Harimon, to make a dash through the service tunnel for the square.

Archie held his father's gaze. After so long, and two eventful journeys to Amasia, Archie was equally

403

amazed to be sitting with his brother in the same room as their father, sitting on a chair opposite. 'I know. For a while I wondered if we'd ever find you and mum.'

Archie and Richard were sitting on cushioned wooden benches, while Kristin stood at a table poring over drawings Malcolm had made of the seawall and the pyramid. The end of the room was occupied by a single bed and wardrobe, next to an open door that revealed the partial shape of a metal bathtub.

Richard had said little since leaving the kitchen, seemingly subdued by Malcolm's sudden appearance, but he perked up when Archie mentioned their mother.

He blurted out: 'What happened to her? I mean ... did you speak to her before she left? '

Sensing he might be thought guilty of not doing enough to help Lucy, Malcolm answered: 'We were separated by Talon the Slave Master, just after we landed in Elam, Richard. He brought her here to the temple, saying that she was a 'chosen one', whatever that meant. I was sent to the tunnels where I was held for God knows how long. That was where I met Harry –'

'Who's Harry?' asked Richard.

Malcolm laughed. 'That was Harimon, the man who brought you here. Harry was my name for him when we shared a cell, with about twenty other poor devils.' He stared into space for a moment. 'It was his idea that if I could persuade Talon to use me as an adviser on the restoration of the temple and the pyramid, as well as maintaining the seawall, I would have a better chance of finding Lucy ... your mother.'

'And you never found her?' said Archie.

'I never saw her again. It was the priestesses who told me she had 'passed on' to the next realm, whatever the hell that means.'

'The priestesses?'

'Yes, Archie, there are twelve of them; they attend to the rituals in the chamber. They live in the cells on the other side of the chamber.'

'I saw her,' said Richard.

Surprised by the statement, Malcolm stared at him. 'What do you mean, you 'saw' her?'

Richard felt Archie staring at him and shifted uneasily on the bench, as he pondered the question. It was not something he liked to talk about, or try to explain in a way that would make sense to anyone else – even his father or Archie. The 'sightings', 'visions', or whatever they might be called, which he saw during the trances, only gave him a partial picture of the event and usually left him confused and frustrated by what he had seen.

'It was in Marcie's cottage –'

'You were in Marcie's place?'

'Yeah, I was with Chuck and Aristo – '

'Chuck and Aristo!'

'For Heaven's sake, Archie, let him finish,' said Malcolm.

Richard hesitated, in case Archie spoke again. 'Well, anyway, we were looking for you and it was at Marcie's place we heard from Quig about the Man of Dust and the pendant –'

'The Man of Dust?'

'Archie!' warned Malcolm. 'If you keep interrupting we'll be here all night.'

'Sorry, Richard, I'll shut up.'

Richard shrugged and continued. He told them what Quig had related about the Man of Dust and the golden smoke after the raid at Elam, and that there was only dust and a golden pendant left behind when he disappeared. Quig had found the pendant and given it to Marcie, not realising that the Terogs would return to search for it. He hesitated before he told them of the trance, as if he could hardly believe what he saw: the priestesses singing around Lucy as she lay in the centre of the Transkal; and then her disappearance into the golden cloud ... He stopped, as if he were seeing it all over again.

'What is it, Richard?' asked Malcolm. He leaned forward on his walking stick, concerned about what his son had seen.

'It's just that ... she was smiling before she left the Transkal ... as if she were happy to leave.'

Malcolm shook his head at the thought she had left voluntarily; it was what Leanna had implied when she told him of the ritual.

Richard carried on with his story. He told how Aristo was injured and Chuck's decision to fly him back to Port Zolnayta in the Bonebreaker. And afterwards, how he had teamed up with Quig and Harimon to reach Copanatec.

'Once he was sure Aristo would be OK, Chuck said he would come back with help. But Quig and Harimon didn't want to waste any more time, so we left him a message to follow us here.'

They sat quietly for a moment, while Malcolm considered all that Richard had told him.

He asked: 'What about the pendant? What happened to it?'

Richard pulled the pendant from his pocket and handed it to him.

'You have it?' said Malcolm, sounding surprised. The stones glittered as he turned it over to examine the other side. He sighed as he gazed on the mark etched into the golden surface. 'As I guessed,' he said, taking a closer look.

'What is it, Dad?' asked Archie.

'It's the mark on your shoulder and on your mother's, Richard. It's the same as one of the glyphs on the Transkal, and here it is on the pendant.'

'What does it all mean?' Archie sensed that his father was trying to piece something together in his mind. 'You've always known about the mark, haven't you?'

'Yes, I first saw it on the Transkal in the Yucatan, but it was one of a dozen marks on the stone and one of several projects I'd set aside to be investigated later. We were pretty busy dealing with the pyramid and the threat of the weather turning against us *and* we were running well behind our schedule to complete the dig.'

'And you didn't think the mark was something special?'

'You've got to remember, Archie, the stone was very old and encrusted with a lot of dust and dirt, so the carvings weren't very clear when we first exposed it. The funny thing is, when I look back on it, it was your mother who really found the Transkal.'

'What do you mean?'

'She said she had a feeling, that she felt drawn to the area where there might be something important to be found. I didn't think much about it, so I told her to go ahead with a couple of mestizos and clear that part of the site.'

'But, Dad .... when you saw her mark – didn't it mean *anything*?'

'I'd never thought of it as anything significant, it was just a kind of birthmark on her shoulder, not even when Richard displayed the same mark.' Malcolm smiled as he recalled their early days together. 'I'm only now beginning to appreciate what it *might* mean, Archie. During my time here, I made it my business to learn as much as I could about the island, with the crazy hope that somehow I might find your mother and a way to escape. At first, when I was in the tunnels, I learned from Harry – our friend Harimon – about the search for a golden casket. Later, when I came to the temple, I got to know Leanna, one of the priestesses and, from her, I discovered a little more about Copanatec culture, their rituals and beliefs. And I must admit, despite the evidence of timecracks and where we have ended up, I still dismissed a great deal of it as myth and legend, including the Transkal and its rituals. Which, by the way, is known as the Chapac Stone to the Copanatecs.'

'The what ..?' asked Archie.

Malcolm waved the question aside. 'I'll explain later.' He stopped to take a sip of water from a glass sitting on a small table next to his chair, before continuing: 'But I was wrong, very wrong. I learned that the Transkals were portals created by an ancient race of twelve tribes known as the Copanatecs, enabling them to travel through the multiverse, from one dimension to another. It seems that our world and many others possess – for want of a better description – energy lines which meet at confluence points, and have done so since the beginning of time. And when such a point was discovered, that is where a Transkal would be placed by the Lords of the Cloud, the high priests of Copanatec. But only they who possess the mark – and those, like the Defenders, who have received the Blessing and the pendant – know how to use the Transkals. However, across the millennia and through each dimension, the numbers of the tribes decreased, and in each world they travelled to, they had to create a new society of Copanatecs, which they governed as they did before in their previous worlds.'

'But ... if only those with the mark, or the Blessing, can use the Transkals, how are there so many Copanatecs?' asked Archie.

'I would imagine, with their superior knowledge and powers, it was easy enough to convert less privileged societies to the Copanatec way of life, much in the same way as the Spanish did when they first arrived in the Americas. But things can go badly wrong when such societies become corrupt, as we are now witnessing on this island. And especially when they suffer a natural disaster like the Destruction, and the loss of a great treasure which led to the slave trade and the tunnels.'

Malcolm hesitated for a moment as he reflected on his time in the Yucatan, and all that had followed since. 'How little we know when we make an important archaeological discovery –'

'Like the Arnaks, when they discovered the Transkals and used them for sacrifices,' said Richard, thinking back to his own experience with Prince Lotane.

He explained briefly to Malcolm how he had been held prisoner and how he and Archie had managed to escape from a man known as Cosimo, who was intent on killing them.

'My God, how much you two have been through! You will have to tell me more, when we have time. But, the Arnaks. Yes, Leanna told me a little of their history when the tribes were dispersed throughout the multiverse. Here in this world when one of the ancient Copanatec tribes disappeared on the mainland, the only trace left behind of their existence were the stones. Later they were found by a people known as the Zahamonites, and later by the Arnaks, who discovered their unusual power, and mistakenly believed they could be used for sacrificial purposes.'

'And the mark ...' persisted Archie.

'Ah, yes, the mark ... one of twelve glyphs etched on the Transkal, as far as I can tell, it represents one of the ancient tribes of Copanatec.' Malcolm looked at his two sons. 'Lucy, *your* mother, Richard ... both of you are obviously descended from one of those tribes, as indicated by the mark on your shoulder. It looks as if over the millennia the mark evolved genetically, I suppose, just as blue eyes and fair skin can be passed on from one generation to the next. It seems to be the case that, somehow, the mark distinguishes you from the other tribes.'

'But ...' Archie was lost for words, '... how –'

'Yes, it's hard to believe. But from my work in the Yucatan, and what I've learned here, I believe the Copanatec tribes may be more than 50,000 years old; perhaps, *very much older*. Who knows what may have evolved in that time.'

'I was going to ask you about *my* mother, Dad,' said Archie, 'and why you never talk about her.'

He had listened with a growing sense of sadness and was reminded of a time when his biological mother had died when he was only one-year-old – too young to remember anything about her.

He had been sent to live with his mother's sister and her husband, on their farm in Northern Ireland and he remembered those early years as good ones. Then, as he grew older and more curious about his mother, and a father he rarely saw, he had begun to harbour a feeling that he was a castaway, dumped out of his father's life on a faraway shore. But his resentment slowly changed when Richard came to live on the farm and as he learned more about his father's work and his reputation as an internationally respected archaeologist, Archie had become quite proud, almost boastful, about his father's achievements in the Yucatan.

Later, during the school holidays when he and Richard would visit the digs their parents were working on, he had grown to know Lucy a lot better and fully accepted her as his new mother.

Reading his thoughts, Malcolm said, 'I'm sorry, Archie, I know I haven't handled our family affairs too well. I can only say that everything I did, sending you both to Ireland to your aunt and uncle, I thought was for the best at the time. But, I promise you, when we get out of this place we won't be parted again.'

Archie nodded, not sure if it was a promise that his father would keep, but before he could say anything, he was disturbed by the sound of running feet, loud voices and repeated hammering on the door.

Malcolm mumbled something under his breath as he pushed himself out of the chair with his stick. He opened the door. 'Leanna, what's wrong? What are you doing here?'

Archie, Richard and Kristin all stared at the woman in the long white robe as she entered the room. Behind her, several other women in similar robes crowded the doorway.

'They are entering the temple –' cried Leanna.

'Who is, for God's sake?'

'The people ... and the slaves ... they are fighting on the steps.'

'Fighting the Terogs?'

She nodded.

'And where is Talon?'

Leanna looked at Malcolm with fear in her eyes, as if she were hardly able to utter the words. 'He is dead.'

'Dead?' repeated Malcolm, hardly believing what he had just heard. 'But how did he die ... are you sure?'

'I do not know how he died, but word of his death has spread through the temple. Lord Pakal is with Kanga and the newcomer, Cosimo, in the chamber, I heard them say so –'

'Cosimo!'

Malcolm turned to Archie who had come to his side, uttering the name of a man Richard had mentioned earlier, someone the boys had encountered during their first venture in Amasia. 'You know the name, Archie? Could it be the same man?'

'It must be, Dad!'

'Then we better find out what is happening out there. With all this upheaval going on it may be our chance to find a way to leave this damned place.'

Chapter Fifty-Three

Hell's Pillars

As he watched another massive wave crash over the bow of the *Serpent,* Abelhorn took a chew on the plug of tobacco he had wedged in the side of his mouth. He felt the stern rise, the ship hanging above the deep green water of the trough before plunging and righting herself as she came through the other side.

He called to Daniel through the open door of the wheelhouse: 'Get in here and close that door, or you'll have us shipping water!'

'Sorry, Captain, just checking the scuppers as you asked me to.'

'Did you free the scupper plates?'

'Bleedin' heavy they were, but I managed OK.'

Abelhorn grunted, it was usually Quig and Tinkey who dealt with the scuppers in a heavy sea, but Daniel seemed to have managed on his own. If he hadn't, there was the risk that if the decks weren't cleared of a boarding sea and allowed to drain, they would begin to lose steerage and risk facing the waves broadside on. Not a prospect he relished.

He turned away from the window. 'Keep her true on this course, Orlof, until I check the chart. I want to have another look at where those rocks might be.'

He settled into a corner of the wheelhouse at the chart table and took a close look, for what seemed the hundredth time, at the only chart he had of this section of the southern coast of Central Amasia. He'd scribbled a few notes on a pad, going over what he could remember of his conversation in the kitchen back at Portview Terrace, when Archie had told him about his visit to the castle to see the old monk, Father Jamarko. Apparently, there had been an old map showing a

413

peninsula that had once existed somewhere along this part of the coast. Some believed it had disappeared a long time ago during a great cataclysm, perhaps due to the volcanic forces of nature which existed in this part of the ocean. It could well be, he thought, given the wealth of sailors' folklore he had listened to during his years at sea.

He stared through the window at the waves which had eased to a steady swell and remembered his son. Four years earlier, during a search for him, he had met with villagers near this coast who had told of Nathan and a stranger with a map. It was said that the stranger had convinced Nathan to use his boat to find a lost island somewhere in the White Waters and there they would discover a fabulous treasure.

You bloody fool, Nathan, thought Abelhorn, *you bloody fool for believing in such things.*

He took another chew on his tobacco and pored over the chart. They had been scouring this coast and sea for four days and nights, checking every rock, reef and sandbank, or any bit of surface land that was marked on the chart and some not marked, but they'd found nothing sizeable that could be described as an island. Especially one that might be populated with people who raided the coastal villages for slaves.

He shook his head; unformed thoughts were beginning to shape into an idea that the only option left to him was to sail towards a line of tall cylindrical rocks, marked on the chart as Hell's Pillars. The rocks ran through a scattering of small uninhabited islands and beyond into the White Waters, with the clear warning printed on the chart to stay clear of a designated danger zone known to be prone to violent seas.

All he knew about the zone were the usual sailors' tales of strange creatures in the deep and boats that never returned from entering the White Waters. But Archie's conviction about the existence of a land known as Copanatec came back to him and triggered the memory of an article he once read in the *Fisherman,* a quarterly journal devoted to the affairs of the trawler men and their lives at sea. The writer had posed the possibility of subduction zones; faults in the sea-floor that might explode under unknown stresses, resulting in volcanic sea eruptions, causing widespread damage to coast and property.

He knew nothing of such matters and had dismissed the article as a piece of writer's fantasy – but could this be the answer to what had happened to the peninsula? Could it be that part of it still existed ... as the island of Copanatec?

Suddenly the possibility excited him. He thumped a hand on the chart table, making the wolftan, Bran, lying beside him, look up expectantly. 'That must be it!'

Orlof held the wheel steady and looked over his shoulder. 'What is it, Captain, is something wrong?'

'Stay on this course, we're heading for the pillars.'

'Hell's Pillars! Are you sure?'

'I think the rocks there are all that are left of an ancient peninsula, but another part of it may still exist as the island we are looking for. What do you think, Orlof?'

'All I'll say, Captain, is that it's not a good place to be, but you're the skipper and it's your decision.'

Daniel looked at the two of them. He held a tray with three glasses of Sticklejuice he had poured from a bottle taken from a locker under the chart table. 'I don't suppose I have any say in this?'

Abelhorn took one of the glasses and smiled. 'Bear with me, Daniel. The sea has eased and we'll know soon enough if we are on the right course.'

*

The sky had darkened and a light rain was falling as they passed a line of tall blackish-grey rocks on the starboard side. Rising more than fifty feet out of the sea, they stretched eastwards towards the horizon, until the last one was joined by a group of smaller, partly submerged rocks, unseen but marked by crashing white waves.

'That's a scary sight, Captain, all those rocks out there,' said Daniel. 'I wonder how many poor devils have tried to make their way through this place?' He held a pair of binoculars close to his chest as he gazed in awe at the maze of rocks jutting out of the sea around the *Serpent*.

'Keep your eyes on the horizon for something larger than the rocks, Daniel,' ordered Abelhorn. 'And you, Orlof, watch the sounders and sonar. Shout if you think there is any danger as we pass through this channel.'

Abelhorn had taken the wheel, assuming responsibility for entering the danger zone and trusting in his instincts to finding a safe passage through the rocks. The *Serpent*, with its empty fish holds and fishing gear stowed away, felt different in his hands as he watched the bow dip and rise through the troughs of the White Waters.

'This ocean isn't living up its reputation,' he muttered to himself. 'Let's hope it stays that way.'

They sailed on, the time passing slowly, until a couple of hours later there were no more rocks visible to them and the pillars were lost to sight.

'We're clear, Captain,' Orlof called out, with an obvious sigh of relief.

'And you, Daniel, what do you see?'

Daniel lowered the binoculars and rubbed his eyes as he peered through the wheelhouse window. The rain had stopped and the sky had cleared. 'I'm not sure ... I think there might be something out there ... I don't know, not until we get a bit closer.'

Daniel was right. A short time later, a smudge on the horizon soon expanded into an obvious coastline directly ahead of them.

Abelhorn approached cautiously, wary of uncharted rocks, but he soon realised he was close to an island not marked on his chart. He brought the *Serpent* onto a course parallel with the coast and started a search for any sign that would give them a clue to where they were. The rocky shoreline was similar to the danger zone they had sailed through.

Was this part of the ancient peninsula?

'Daniel, shout if you see anywhere on the coast we can pick up a mooring. And Orlof, keep your eyes skinned for anything in the water we need to keep clear of.'

A prominent headland lay directly ahead. Abelhorn turned the wheel to bring the *Serpent* to a point where they would safely round the massive mound of rock and the sea crashing onto its base.

As they passed its tip he heard Daniel call out: 'You wanted a mooring, Captain? Will that do?' He grinned as he pointed towards a huge breakwater beyond the headland. Its L-shape encircled a wide harbour which fell back onto a stone jetty and a tall seawall.

They reached the end of the breakwater where a narrow entrance beckoned. Wary of the tidal stream crossing the entrance he brought the *Serpent* in slowly, avoiding a clump of rocks as he entered the harbour.

'Take the wheel, Orlof, and hold her here as best you can. I want to take a closer look at where we can tie up,' said Abelhorn.

He pulled on Daniel's sleeve to follow him as he stepped out of the wheelhouse. 'Use those glasses, scan the seawall and the boats at the jetty – tell me what you see.'

There were several boats tied up to the jetty which formed two sides of a large harbour, but one in particular had caught Abelhorn's eye. It was a strange looking vessel, longer and larger than the *Serpent*, with its wheelhouse placed well forward and the rest of the deck taken up with an enclosed structure ending at the stern. There was no deck gear or any visible sign of its purpose as a seagoing craft.

He said, pointing to it, 'What the devil is that supposed to be?'

Daniel cast the binoculars from bow to stern, taking in the barred portholes running the length of the structure. 'Looks like a bleedin' prison to me – God! Maybe that's the ship the Terogs use to bring the villagers here!'

Abelhorn nodded. 'If it is, then there's no doubt we have found Copanatec.' He turned to the wheelhouse door and shouted to Orlof: 'Bring her on in, there's plenty of room at the end of the jetty. We'll get ready to tie her up.'

As the *Serpent* drew alongside, Daniel and Abelhorn jumped onto the jetty, quickly making for the bollards to secure the bow and stern lines.

'Look!' Daniel suddenly called out. 'Who the bleedin' hell are they?'

Abelhorn looked to where Daniel was pointing. There were two men running along the jetty, one of them as he got closer was yelling and waving; another two were climbing down the steps of the seawall.

'I don't know, but we'll not take any chances,' said Abelhorn. He called to the wheelhouse: 'Orlof, get the gun! Bran, get down here!'

'A gun!' Daniel looked at Abelhorn in astonishment. 'What are you doing with a gun, Captain?'

'It's an old piece, left behind by a New Arrival I helped many years ago when he ended up in Zolnayta. I don't know if it works, I've never had cause to use it, but I always thought it might come in useful some day.'

Daniel grinned at the sight of Orlof standing outside the wheelhouse, cradling what looked like an old Wild West Winchester. 'I hope it doesn't blow up in his face if he tries to use it!'

With its incredibly sensitive six little ears, Bran heard Abelhorn's command, and was beside them in a moment as the strangers approached the *Serpent*. Nearly as tall as a young pony, the wolftan with its long narrow head, glowing green eyes, and a fearful gaping maw full of sharp yellow teeth, was a fearsome sight in any company. Sizing up the men as they came closer, Bran snarled and waited for a command.

'Stay, Bran, stay,' said Abelhorn, stroking the thick grey matted hair of the beast. 'Let's see what they want with us.'

The two men kept their distance from Bran, as one of them spoke: 'I hope you can keep that beast under control, Captain Abelhorn, we mean no harm.'

'If so, you are safe enough, but how is it you know my name?'

'Every fisherman on the Amasian coast knows the *Serpent* and its captain. And we did meet once at the auction shed in Port Zolnayta, a long time ago.'

'And you are?'

'I am Roni, a fisherman out of Elam. At least I was until the Terogs took me prisoner when they destroyed our village on their last raid.' He glanced behind him at his three companions. 'These men, with many others, were taken from their villages, long before me, and now we are ready to make our escape.'

'But ... but how did you get away from the Terogs?' asked Daniel. 'And what about all the others – what's happened to them?'

'The uprising has taken place and many have died. The fighting is still happening in the square and in the temple; who knows who has survived?' said Roni. He looked to the seawall and shook his head at the thought of what they had left behind. 'We were lucky to escape, but now we must leave quickly before the Terogs come to the harbour – '

'Not on the *Serpent*, not until I find my granddaughter, Kristin,' growled Abelhorn. 'We have to find her and her friend, Archie, and we will not leave without them.'

Roni looked at him quizzically. 'Who? ... But I know these names; I was captured with them at Elam ... both were young men I had never seen before ... not women –'

'Forget that! Kristin may have disguised herself to prevent being abused. What I need to know is where they are now!'

'But we must leave here before the Terogs come!' cried Roni.

'I do not know what has happened in this place,' said Abelhorn, 'but understand this: I will not leave until I find Kristin and Archie.'

'But – '

Before he said another word, Roni felt someone gripping his arm. It was one of the men with him: an old man, thin and wiry, his old clothes covered in stone dust.

'What is it, Daros?' said Roni.

'I know these young people.'

'What do you mean?'

'Archie worked with me in the tunnels, while Kristin worked on the seawall. He was desperate to find her, as well as his parents, but I was able to help the two of them and they are now together.'

'You helped them!' said Abelhorn excitedly. He could hardly believe his ears; this old man knew his granddaughter and Archie. 'Where are they now?'

'I do not know – much has happened since the uprising. But I told Archie that the answer to the question of finding his parents, probably lay somewhere in the temple.'

Roni pointed beyond the seawall. 'There has been much fighting and killing there – who knows where they are now. We must leave here –'

Abelhorn interrupted him: 'Listen. Help me to find them, and I will help you and your friends get back to your villages. But I need you to take me to where they might be. Will you take me to the temple?'

Roni looked to Daros, and then to the other two men who had remained silent. Before he could ask them what they thought of Abelhorn's proposal, they now raised their voices furiously, pointing to the boats in the harbour. 'We are fishermen like you,' one of them yelled at Abelhorn. 'We can take one of these boats and sail to Amasia, while we can!'

'Perhaps, but these waters are treacherous to those who do not know them. Many have ventured, but few have returned and you are likely to meet the same fate if you make the attempt. The *Serpent* is the safest and best equipped vessel out of Port Zolnayta, and the best chance you have of getting through the rocks you will find out there.'

Roni and the men stared silently at Abelhorn, confused and angry by his harsh words, but they all knew the dangers if they faced the White Waters alone, and realised they had little choice. Abelhorn nodded to them, taking their silence as a positive response to his offer.

He said impatiently: 'Let's stop wasting time and help me find my granddaughter and Archie.'

He looked to the wheelhouse and gestured to Orlof to join him.

'Yes, Captain?'

'I want you to stay on the *Serpent* while Daniel and I go with Roni. These men will stay with you until we return. Keep Bran by your side, he will see off anyone who gives you trouble.'

*

Roni was the first to reach the top of the seawall; he stood to one side as Abelhorn, and then Daniel joined him.

'My God! This is terrible ... I've never seen anything like it.' Abelhorn shook his head as he looked down onto a scene of utter devastation. 'What happened here?'

Heavy, rain-filled clouds loomed over a large square filled with the wreckage of burning carts, overturned wagons, and market stalls pushed together to form makeshift barricades. Craters filled with shattered paving slabs pockmarked the area, while bodies of men and women – dead and alive – lay like broken marionettes, their limbs sprawled in unnatural angles.

'Now you see why we must leave this place,' said Roni.

'Where is the temple?' asked Abelhorn, ignoring any suggestion that they should leave without completing the mission he had set for them.

Roni pointed to the far side of the square where a screaming mob was scrambling up the steps of a large white building fronted by tall Ionic columns. Part of the temple's pediment had collapsed onto the steps, forming a partial barrier that protected a line of Terogs armed with crossbows, firing bolts into the midst of the mob.

'I see what you mean ... that looks like a place to avoid,' said Daniel. 'I think I'd prefer to take my chances in the White Waters.'

Abelhorn ignored what Daniel said, instead he asked Roni: 'How are we going to get into the temple?'

'The gardens beside the gorge; there is an entrance there that leads into the kitchen, but I don't know if we can get through to it ...'

Abelhorn stared at the carnage that had taken place in the square. He was shocked by the death and destruction, but he felt he had no choice – he had to press on if Kristin and Archie were to be found.

He said, 'Well, we'll not find out if we stay here, will we?'

Daniels's mouth felt very dry as he followed Roni and Abelhorn along a rail track to the end of the seawall, towards a ramp that would take them down into the square.

Chapter Fifty-Four

The Temple Steps

'Richard, I want you to stay here with Kristin and Leanna until we return,' said Malcolm. 'There is a balcony at the end of the great hall that overlooks the steps and the square. It'll allow us to see what's happening –'

'But I don't want to stay here ... I want to go with you,' said Richard. He had just experienced the strangest feeling that he had to leave the room and go somewhere ... *but where*? He clasped the pendant in his pocket, feeling its sudden warmth as if it were trying to attract his attention ...

Malcolm smiled, misreading the meaning of his son's words. 'Don't worry, we won't be long, but I need you back here to warn us if any Terogs come this way.' It wasn't strictly true, but he didn't want Richard feeling he was playing second fiddle to Archie by leaving him behind with Leanna and Kristin. 'All right?'

'I suppose so.'

'Good. Once we know what we're up against, maybe we can find a way to get off this island.'

*

The noise was deafening: screams from the injured and the frenzied roar by a crowd of villagers and Copanatecs alike, enraged by the cruelty of the Terogs, came to them in waves as they made their way along the portico. To their left, through a series of archways, a large paved courtyard, flanked by another portico on the opposite side, lay host to a circular, honey-coloured, stone building. Topped by a colossal stained-glass dome and a magnificent golden spire that glowed brightly as the evening light gave way to the coming night.

Archie stopped at one of the archways. He gaped up at the golden spire, its gleaming tip signalling the mosque-like building's importance at the centre of the temple. There was something about it that seemed familiar.

'Archie!' His father was limping, but moving as quickly as he could with the aid of his walking stick. 'We mustn't stop here; if an uprising is under way and the Terogs spot us, we're done for!'

'I know, but it's like a place I may have seen somewhere.' said Archie. He pointed to the building. 'What is it, a chapel of some sort?'

'You might say that. It's the chamber where the Lords of the Cloud perform their rituals around what they call the Chapac Stone, named after the First Lord of the Copanatecs. I discovered its equivalent at a new site in the Yucatan jungle, and named it after a colleague of mine, Sir Peter Transkal; a great friend and benefactor to my work before he died.' Malcolm smiled. 'I still refer to the stones as Transkals, out of habit I suppose. As far as the rituals are concerned, Lord Pakal seems to be the only one left here to perform them. There may be other lords on the island, but I've never seen them.'

The Transkal ... the Chapac Stone ... they were the same.

It was then that Archie remembered where he had seen the golden spire: it was when Richard had been able to enter a trance and contact their mother from the stone in the quadrangle at Harmsway College. And for the first, and only time, Archie had also been able to enter a trance with him, listening as Richard spoke to her when she told of them of Copanatec. She had mentioned the stone, calling it the Transkal, but learned little else before they lost contact with her; nothing to help them understand what had happened to her and dad.

He now understood the connection between the stones: they were one and the same and were probably a means of contact for the Copanatec lords throughout the multiverse. Except for the Arnaks, who had misunderstood their purpose and used the stones for ritual sacrifice.

'Archie, we must keep going; it's too dangerous to stop here,' insisted Malcolm. The distant sounds of yelling and screaming from the square seemed to be getting closer, making him apprehensive that the fighting might spill over into the temple.

The porticos met at the end of the courtyard, bridged by a passage that met at a closed wooden door leading to the great hall. On either side of the door, wide marble stairways led to a half-landing and double return stairway to the top of the temple, but it was the exit on the landing that led to the balcony, which Malcolm wanted to reach.

As they stepped onto the balcony, Archie realised they were behind part of the remaining section of the pediment that hadn't collapsed onto the front steps of the temple. It gave them a clear view of the square, all the way to the seawall.

'My God! This is terrible!' groaned Malcolm. He gripped his walking stick, dropping onto one knee as he witnessed the people below trying to storm the temple doors. The dead and wounded lay in pools of blood amongst the craters created by Cosimo's mortars. Others sprawled over the makeshift barriers, many with bolts driven into their skulls and chests by the Terogs' crossbows.

'Dad! Look!'

Archie, standing behind him, pointed to a far corner of the square. From a collection of large stone buildings on a road leading to the farmlands, a thick, dark mass rippled and spread out as it exited the road and prepared to approach the temple.

'Oh, no!' Malcolm stood up to lean on the edge of the pediment. 'Terog Commands coming from their barracks. There must be hundreds of them! God, there will be mass slaughter here!'

The Copanatecs who had been savagely ruled by the Lords of the Cloud while they searched for the Immortal Wand, had combined forces with the villagers to make their way up the steps to try and take control of the temple. But without any obvious leadership it had become a suicidal bid for freedom as they confronted ranks of Terogs armed with metal-tipped whips and crossbows – and now they were unaware of the threat gathering behind them.

But someone did notice.

One of the villagers, a small wiry man, excited, struggling at the back of the crowd, trying to force his way up the steps, heard the heavy tread of thumping boots behind him. He turned and was shocked to see hundreds of Terogs advancing on the temple. He screamed as the man beside him fell to the ground, a bolt through his neck.

Concealed by the remaining section of the pediment, Archie watched as the people scattered from the steps in a vain attempt to escape the Terogs. As far as he could see, the commands numbered nearly a thousand of the pug-nosed brutes, snarling and grunting as they crunched through the debris and over the bleeding bodies in the square. Their front ranks were firing the crossbows indiscriminately at anyone still standing on the steps.

'It's a bloody massacre,' said Malcolm. 'The poor bastards haven't a hope of defending themselves against that lot.' The sudden flash of a bright, white light and the disappearance of one of the Terogs caught him by surprise. 'What was that – a lightning strike?'

Archie stared in amazement at the sight of some of the Terogs stumbling into each other, confused by what was happening around them. In split seconds, a series of bright flashes streaked from above his head into the square below. More Terogs disappeared, leaving only a shimmering outline of their body shapes, then nothing – not a trace of their existence left behind.

Then he remembered what had happened to the Terogs in the temple gardens.

'Quig! It must be Quig with the paragun!'

'What are you talking about?' demanded Malcolm.

Archie quickly explained that Quig along with two of the villagers, Calum and Harimon, had very powerful weapons, the two paraguns, and had gone to join the uprising, shortly after they arrived in the kitchen.

'They must be up above us somewhere ...'

'The next level leads to the turrets,' said Malcolm, shaking his head. 'From up there, it'll be like shooting fish in a barrel, but it's utter madness. No matter how many Terogs they kill, the rest will keep moving forward, using their sheer weight of numbers to overwhelm the uprising.'

Malcolm was right. The bright flashes had ceased and Archie guessed that Quig and Calum had stopped firing, afraid that they would hit their own people as the Terogs swarmed over them.

Wondering what they should do, he looked across the square to the seawall where he spotted three figures running down the ramp. One of them, with shocks of long, white hair flowing from below a flat hat, had a lumbering sailor-like gait that looked very familiar.

*

'There's nothing we can do here,' growled Abelhorn.

They passed a man lying at the bottom of the ramp, groaning and crying out for help, but there was little they could do for him; a terrible injury to his belly was obviously fatal. Daniel found a couple of discarded coats from an overturned stall and placed them over the man, mumbling a few words of comfort before they left him. With Roni in the lead, they kept their heads low behind what was left of the market stalls and makeshift barriers in the middle of the square. Picking their way through the wreckage, they stopped for a moment behind an overturned wagon where two tunnellers were sprawled across the rail track, bolts protruding from their backs.

'This is bleedin' crazy, Captain,' complained Daniel. Hidden by the wagon, he nodded in the direction of the fighting taking place in front of the temple. 'What are we supposed to do? Ask someone over there if they've seen Kristin and Archie?'

'I don't know,' said Abelhorn grimly. 'I'm hoping that Roni has the answer to that.'

'It is impossible,' said Roni, shaking his head. 'There are too many Terogs for us to pass without being seen. We must go back or we will be killed!'

Ablehorn was about to object when he felt a ripple beneath his feet and a terrifying roar as the ground was ripped apart, only a short distance away from where they stood. He managed to keep his balance by leaning on the wagon for support, but what he saw almost unnerved him, turning his determination to continue with the search into one of fear and flight. Part of the temple wall at the end of the building, on the edge of the gorge next to the gardens, had collapsed as a widening crack tore its way past the steps and across the square towards the seawall. He saw people clawing and scrambling on their hands and knees, screaming as they tried to avoid being sucked over the edges and into the gap.

He turned round and saw that Daniel was still standing nearby, but Roni, obviously frightened by what he had seen, had made a dash back to the ramp, but just as he reached it, the thundering crack hit the seawall, splitting the stones into fragments, hurling them into the air like lethal missiles. Roni fell to the ground and didn't rise.

'We have to help him, Captain!' yelled Daniel. 'We can't get through this mess without his help.'

Abelhorn nodded, but just as quickly as it had arrived, the foreshock suddenly stopped, leaving only an eerie silence, punctuated by the cries of the dying and wounded.

Chapter Fifty-Five

Cosimo's Plan

It was the distant rumble that caught Archie's attention.

At first, with darkening clouds above the island, he thought it was thunder, but the low growling sound would prove to be much worse than any storm. Deep below his feet in the bowels of New Earth, huge pressure was building as tectonic plates, one grinding against the other, began to unleash forces which would tear Copanatec apart.

The rumbling sound became an angry roar as part of the temple wall near the gorge exploded, projecting a great rent across the square, creating a cacophony of screaming and yelling as Copanatecs, villagers and Terogs were dragged into its gaping maw.

'It must be an earthquake!' cried Archie. He felt a shudder, throwing him off balance. He looked down. Shocked, he saw a spider web of cracks spreading across the floor of the balcony towards them. He shouted, 'We have to get away from here!'

Malcolm stretched his head over the top of the pediment and spotted a large cloud of dust rising above the turret near the wall he had been working on earlier

'It might be a foreshock,' said Malcolm, 'but you're right, we'd better get back to the kitchen and make sure Richard and the others are all right.'

Archie stared at the cracks. 'What's a foreshock?'

'Sometimes, before the arrival of an earthquake, a foreshock occurs. A warning of something much worse to come. There might be one, or several foreshocks before the main event, separated by minutes, or much longer. It's pretty hard to predict with any real accuracy.'

As they hurried from the balcony onto the landing, Archie became aware of someone running down the steps from the landing above. 'Dad, there's someone up there!'

It was Quig. He clutched the paragun as he tried to dash past them, but Malcolm raised his walking stick and placed it in front of him. 'Hold on there. What's happening? Where's Harimon?'

Quig grunted. 'He and Calum went to join their friends in the square. I decided the roof would be a better place to kill Terogs, but now there are too many of them, and soon they will enter the temple. We must leave here before it is too late.'

He pushed the walking stick roughly to one side and fled down the stairway towards one of the porticoes where several of the columns had collapsed, partly blocking the approach to the chamber.

'Hey, where are you going?' yelled Archie.

Quig didn't answer as he disappeared behind a pile of debris, just in time to evade a group of Terogs, led by Kanga, pouring through the great hall door into the porticoes.

Directly behind Kanga came Anton Cosimo, coming to a sudden stop as he saw Archie on the stairway. He pointed and yelled, 'It's the Kinross boy, grab him!'

Kanga stared at Cosimo for a moment to consider the order. He nodded, deciding that with Talon gone this would now be the natural continuation of command. He gave the order and several of his men grabbed Malcolm and Archie, dragging them down the steps to stand before him.

Gripping Archie by the neck, he said to Cosimo, 'Is this the one you want?'

'Leave my son alone!' said Malcolm angrily. He lurched forward, stumbling on his walking stick as he tried to pull Kanga's hand away.

He fell to his knees as Cosimo stepped forward and kicked his stick to one side. 'Listen carefully, cripple, I suggest you keep your temper under control if you and your brat wish to live a little longer. There is only one thing I need to know from you – where is the other one?'

Seething with anger, Malcolm refused to answer. Instead he tried to rise to his feet, but Cosimo struck him down.

'Stop it!' yelled Archie. Cosimo frightened him, the dark hooded eyes raking his face as if wondering how best to cause the most pain. *But why?* It seemed that no matter where he and Richard went this evil creature was determined to find them. 'Why are you after us? What have we ever done to you?'

Cosimo sneered, 'Why? Because you and your brother are responsible for *my* brother's death. At every turn you two have interfered with my plans –'

'That's not true! We never knew anything about your brother until he kidnapped Richard and took him to the Sacred Temple.'

'Enough! I have no time for this –'

Someone called to him.

Cosimo turned away from Archie as he saw Nitkin pushing through the Terogs to speak to him. He had instructed his mean-looking lieutenant to report on events in the square and how the Terogs were dealing with the uprising, while he sought Lord Pakal inside the temple. With Talon no longer available to Pakal, Cosimo saw his own position greatly strengthened and reasoned that with Kanga at his side to control the slaves, he could negotiate a deal with Pakal to find the Immortal Wand. When that was achieved, and at a time of his own choosing, he would leave Pakal and the Copanatecs to their fate, and return to the rebel Arnaks on the mainland. With possession of the wand and a force of Terogs and rebels under his command, Amasia would be his for the taking. But first, he would have to deal with the uprising and all those who supported it.

Nitkin stood before him with a villager hardly able to stand, his head gripped tightly by a Terog. 'Who is this? Why do you bring him here?'

Archie's eyes widened when he realised who it was. Harimon, his father's friend. He was barely conscious and had been badly beaten, with one eye closed and one side of his face smeared in blood and dirt.

'We managed to drive the people away from the temple, but some of the Terogs were destroyed by a very strange and powerful weapon used by two men – this is one we were able to capture,' said Nitkin.

'And the other one?' asked Cosimo.

'He and the weapon were taken with others when the earth opened.'

Cosimo nodded. The earthquake; many on both sides had been taken into its depths, but those who were left who opposed him would be no match for the number of ruthless fighters he still had at his disposal. But the weapon puzzled him; where did it come from, he wondered.

'Good, I think this earth-shattering event is to our advantage.' His sense of humour was lost on the others as his eyes narrowed, an evil smile twisting his lips as he sized up Harimon. 'As for this one: see if he can tell you where the weapon came from. He may be too far gone to tell you anything, but be rid of him and join me when you are finished. I am going to the chamber to find Lord Pakal.'

'NO!' yelled Malcolm, 'he has suffered enough!' He struggled to free himself from a Terog grip, but was knocked to the floor by a blow to the head.

'Silence! We will deal with you and your brat later,' snarled Cosimo. He turned to Kanga and ordered him to bring four of his men to watch over Archie and Malcolm. 'Leave the rest here to cover the steps to the square until we return.'

The evening light was fading as they left the portico to cross the courtyard to a porch outside the chamber, but there was enough illumination for Archie to make out the detail of the curiously decorated stonework around an archway inside the porch. He recognised one of the carvings above the archway. It was the mark, exactly the same as the one he had seen on the Transkal stone, and very much like the one on Richard's shoulder.

Cosimo ordered Kanga to open the door, its heavy iron hinges protesting against the weight of the ancient timber. The group followed Cosimo into a large room, built with the same honey-coloured stone as the exterior walls of the chamber. Much of the surface was covered with a relief depicting images and figures which seemed strangely similar to some he had seen at the site in the Yucatan. He turned to his father who nodded as he also recognised the similarity of the images to his own discoveries at the site.

Archie noticed that the noise from the square, the terrified screaming and yelling of the people fighting in the square had almost disappeared in here, an antechamber insulated by the thick stone walls.

But there was something else: a strange, haunting musical sound which seemed to emanate from behind another door at the other end of the room. A chant which seemed to rise so steeply, it was soon beyond the capacity of the human ear to hear it.

Cosimo also heard it. Archie watched him as he approached the door slowly, wary of what was happening on the other side. Kanga and the Terogs

435

waited silently, ready to take action if called upon to do so.

Archie looked to his father and nodded towards the door. Not wanting the Terogs to hear him, he mouthed: 'What's happening in there?'

Malcolm shrugged. *I don't know.*

They heard Cosimo swear angrily as he stood in the open doorway. At the same time, they heard a faint rumbling sound deep below the chamber as the floor trembled beneath their feet.

Chapter Fifty-Six

The Ossuary

After Malcolm and Archie left the cell, Richard pulled the leather pouch from his pocket and extracted the pendant. Its growing warmth disturbed him in a way he couldn't explain; even its chain seemed to have a life of its own as it coiled around his fingers like a little snake. It was as if the pendant was trying to draw him into a special place somewhere in the temple, a place he knew, that he had seen before ...

'Hey, Richard,' called Kristin. She had been watching him, curious as to why he was staring so intently at the shiny piece of jewellery he was holding. 'What is that thing? Is it valuable?'

Richard glanced at her, unsure what to say. *That he held in his hand a golden pendant that enabled him to 'see' strange scenes of places and people he knew little about?*

He ignored her as a vision began to form; a milky mist slowly dispersing to present an image of a tall, white-robed man standing over what looked like a stone box. He shook his head, trying to free himself from the image, frightened that in some crazy way it was filtering into his mind, trying to control him, in a way he had never felt before. But it was useless to resist; its influence was too strong. He stood up from the cushioned bench where he had been sitting, sensing that he had no choice but to find the man and the stone box. Holding the pendant by his side, he walked over to the cell door, ready to step outside and go where it led him.

Kristin, annoyed that he hadn't answered her, demanded to know where he thought he was going, but it was Leanna's voice that stopped him.

Leanna moved quickly across the room to his side and grasped his arm. 'You hold a golden pendant!' she cried. 'How did you come by it?'

Richard hesitated, not certain what he should tell her. That it had been taken by Quig and given to Marcie as a gift, who rejected it because of the threat it posed to her village? That it had belonged to a Lord of the Clouds who had been killed, and was known to the villagers as the Man of Dust after he disappeared in a golden cloud? As had his mother in the vision he witnessed when in Marcie's cottage?

He needn't have worried, for Leanna was well aware of the significance of the pendant.

'Lord Tenoch ... you have found his pendant!' whispered Leanna. Awestruck, her fingers reached out to touch the coloured stones in their golden setting.

'How did you know it was Tenoch's?' asked Richard, amazed that Leanna knew – or did she? 'How can you be sure?'

'There are only twelve golden pendants with the stones forming this pattern; only one is missing: Lord Tenoch's. It has to be his. The Defenders' pendants are silver and the stones describe a different pattern.' She clasped Richard's hand, her voice tense with anticipation. 'We must take it to Lord Pakal – now!'

Richard pulled his hand away, realising who Leanna must be. He should have known. *She was one of the priestesses he had seen in the vision when his mother disappeared into the golden mist.*

'You knew my mother! You were there!'

Leanna looked at him blankly, confused. 'What do you mean?'

'Your robe: it has one of the carvings from the stone on it. You were one of the priestesses when my mother was on the stone ... during some sort of ritual ...'

'Ah, I believe I understand.' Leanna smiled. 'You speak of the Chapac Stone, but *your* mother ?'

'Yes! You and the other women – dressed like you – stood around the stone, singing until she was covered in ... I don't know ... it was like a cloud of smoke.'

Leanna nodded. 'You saw her? It is strange, but you speak of Loo-see, the woman chosen by Lord Pakal to go to the next realm.'

Loo-see? *Lucy.* His mother.

'The next realm? What do you mean she went there? Where is it?'

'I cannot tell you, only Lord Pakal can answer such questions.'

'Then I have to find him. Where is he?'

Before Leanna could answer him, Kristin broke in.

'Don't mind me, but could someone tell me what the freak you two are talking about?'

Kristin was mad. Archie and his father had dumped her here without any explanation of where they were going, or when they were coming back, and now Richard and this woman seemed to be arguing about his mother. Well, she had no intention of being ignored any longer.

She marched over to Richard at the door to take a closer look at the pendant. She wanted to know what was so special about a piece of jewellery that was getting him so uptight.

Richard shrugged. How could he explain all the visions, the dreams, the sightings he had witnessed ... whatever they were, to her? *He* hardly understood what they meant, how could she?

Leanna ushered him through the door. 'I will take you to the chamber. Lord Pakal summoned all the priestesses to be there at this time.'

'Why?' asked Richard.

'I do not know; it is not our usual time, but we must attend to his command.'

Without another word, she led the way along the portico with Richard behind her. Kristin, still irritated by Richard's attitude, reckoned she had no option but to follow them. She certainly wasn't going to stay behind on her own.

They left the portico and crossed the courtyard, arriving at the porch entrance leading into the chamber. They were careful not to be seen by a group of Terogs on the steps facing the door of the great hall. The sounds of the fighting outside the temple had faded into the distance, but the Terogs were still armed with their crossbows and whips, obviously ready for any sign of trouble.

Inside the porch, Leanna leaned on the heavy wooden door, pushing it open to enter the antechamber. She moved quickly, her long white robe swishing across a marble mosaic floor, past a wall depicting Copanatec scenes and figures, to reach another door at the end of the room.

Richard and Kristin followed Leanna into the chamber. He was holding the pendant in his palm, the chain wrapped tightly around the fingers. It seemed to be getting hotter as he entered the room.

He stopped, startled by the surroundings. *The vision he had experienced in Marcie's cottage. It was the same room.*

The high walls were lined with marble columns reaching towards a ceiling inlaid with brightly coloured stars and strange symbols, broken only by a stained glass dome spreading outwards from a central golden spire. Between the columns standing on their huge gold plinths, hung richly embroidered red and gold drapes.

In the middle of the room below the dome was the Transkal ... or what was it Leanna called it? *The*

Chapac Stone. The place where he had witnessed his mother's disappearance. Around the stone stood Leanna's companions, the other eleven priestesses, as if awaiting her to join them.

Then he saw it: the stone box he had seen in the vision. It sat on a small marble plinth set to one side of the room. The pendant had cooled, no longer hot to touch, its purpose nearly achieved. Standing beside the box was the man he had also seen in the vision. Tall and lean, his crystal-clear eyes set in pale, ghostly skin above high cheekbones, narrowed as they entered the room.

The man called out, angrily: 'Leanna, you are late!'

'I am sorry, my Lord Pakal, but I bring important news.'

Pakal stared past her. 'Who are these people; why are they here?'

Leanna turned to Richard and beckoned to him to come forward. 'The pendant, my Lord; Lord Tenoch's pendant has been found!' She turned to Richard. 'See, the boy holds it before him.'

'And their names?'

She pointed to each of them. 'They are called Richard and Kristin, my Lord.'

Pakal studied the boy standing quietly next to Leanna and the young girl. *Could it be that Tenoch would finally be put to rest?* He gestured to the boy to come forward.

But Richard, overwhelmed by the surroundings of the chamber, stood his ground. He could hardly believe he was in the same room where he last saw his mother. The magnificent dome, the stained glass filtering the evening skylight onto the Transkal below, and the priestesses in their long, white robes standing in position around the great stone; all of it as he had witnessed in the vision.

441

He was aware of Lord Pakal's eyes focusing on him, seeking a pathway into his mind. Like the Vikantus who worked on the wall at Castle Brimstone, Pakal had the power to communicate without speech.

The message was clear: *Bring me the pendant.*

Nervously, Richard took a few paces forward, stretching out a hand with the pendant to give to Pakal.

Pakal took it and nodded: *Do not be afraid, you have done a great service by delivering Lord Tenoch's pendant into my hands.*

Richard spoke: 'I'm sorry, I didn't know what should be done with it – '

'It is of no matter, it can now rest with Lord Tenoch.'

Feeling a great sense of relief that the pendant, at long last, was now in his hands, Pakal studied the boy for a moment, wondering how it was that the boy was able to understand him. He searched, sensing and probing the boy's mind, until he realised what it was that disturbed him. *The boy possessed the gift of the Copanatecs.* He was of the same line as the woman brought to him by Talon and sent to the next realm. How fitting, he thought, that the boy should arrive as he prepared for his own journey.

'Leanna, you have done well, but you and the priestesses were summoned to prepare the Chapac Stone for the ritual. You must do this *now*!'

Leanna tried to question him as to who would be involved in the ritual of the passing to the next realm, but she saw a look of anger cross his face and kept quiet. Feeling a sense of shock, she realised who it would be.

Pakal turned away from her. 'Come, Richard, it will be fitting for you to see Tenoch's resting place.'

*

442

They walked over to an alcove at the side of the chamber, with Kristin trailing closely behind.

Long red and gold drapes fell generously to the floor in folds around a marble plinth supporting the stone box. It was a limestone ossuary of the type Richard had seen a couple of times when visiting his father at one of the digs. Usually, ossuaries held the bones of the deceased after their flesh had decomposed and then they were placed in a site sacred to the society they had been part of: ancient caves, crypts and catacombs. This ossuary was smaller than the ones his father had excavated and contained little more than a mound of dust. It measured, he guessed, about 20 by 10 by 10 inches, and didn't look very impressive; not sacred or important. The lid lay against the side of the plinth, its surface inscribed with a single line of marks and symbols he didn't recognise. Probably a reference to Lord Tenoch, he thought, like the name on a tombstone.

Pakal laid the pendant with its chain on the dust, then placed the lid on top to seal the ossuary while he intoned a few words which were foreign to Richard. Yet ... somehow ... they seemed familiar – like a language learnt at school; forgotten and never used.

Pakal nodded as if he knew what Richard was thinking. 'It is the language of the ancients, our forefathers, the Copanatecs. It is not the language of the people who now dare to attack the temple.' His eyes suddenly blazed with the anger of a zealot as he raised his arm and pointed to somewhere beyond the wall of the chamber. 'They are Copanatecs in name only; a conquered people to serve for the greater glory of Copanatec!'

'I don't understand,' said Richard, taking a pace back as Pakal raised his voice. 'What do you mean, they're not Copanatecs?'

'I am sorry, I did not mean to frighten you,' smiled Pakal, sadly. 'But we are coming to the end of our days here and I am afraid we have not achieved that which is necessary for our survival. The people in this land are descended from the Amasian tribes we vanquished and absorbed into our civilisation many generations ago – as were other tribes in other worlds we visited. Many sacrifices have been made by the people – and by the villagers we were forced to recruit for the tunnels.'

'You mean like my mother was sacrificed?' said Richard impatiently. He couldn't understand why what Pakal had just said had anything to do with him and his mother; only that he had seen her disappear from this chamber.

'Your mother was not sacrificed,' said Pakal. 'She journeyed to the next realm by her own choice. As a true Copanatec she had that choice, as do I – and as you do, too.'

'She wouldn't have done that and left me and my brother behind!' yelled Richard. He was angry that Pakal would suggest that his mother would no longer want him, that she would leave without leaving some sort of message.

'Calm yourself, Richard, you must know this is so. Show me your shoulder –'

'NO! Why should I?'

'Because you are one of us, like your mother before you.'

No, I don't believe it!'

'Look,' said Pakal, pulling his robe to one side over his shoulder, to expose the mark he bore.

It was the same as Richard's.

He stared at the mark on Pakal's shoulder, disbelieving, slowly accepting that everything he had seen and heard in the visions now made some sort of sense. His mother *was* different from others in a very special way. He had to accept that deep down, somewhere in his own mind, he had always known that he too, was special. But there were some things he still didn't understand.

'You said you were coming to the end of your days here – what did you mean?' asked Richard.

Pakal pulled the robe over his shoulder as he turned to the ossuary, tracing his fingers over the inscription.

'My time has come to join those who have gone before me. Tenoch is gone, but he will rest peacefully now that the pendant is with him. His life would have been eternal had he not been killed, for like all others we are not immune to violence.

'You see, we are the guardians of the Immortal Wand that has been with the Copanatecs through all of our journeys, until we reached this world. But the wand is lost and those who need to touch the wand are unable to be rewarded with a Great Cycle.'

'A Great Cycle? What's that?'

'A cycle is a period of a thousand years –'

'What!'

When both Richard and Kristin gasped at the thought of anyone living so long, he raised the palm of his hand towards them.

'Listen, for everything I tell you is true, and will always be so. Unfortunately, during the Destruction, the wand and its casket were lost in the depths below the pyramid during the Blessing of one of our lords. It had to be found, for at the end of a Great Cycle the wand must be touched to renew the cycle, or the blessed will return to dust, and I, too, will soon join them.

'That is why the Defenders were also given the Blessing: until the wand is found they are needed to control the Terogs, who in turn control the villagers and the people.'

'But the stone ... and the realm ... what does it all mean?' asked Richard, still confused.

'The stones were named after our First Lord, Chapac. They have been part of the multiverse since the beginning of time, and it was he who discovered they were pathways to new worlds.'

'But where is the realm you said my mother went to?'

'No one knows. It is the only choice we have: to be blessed at the end of a cycle or to journey to the next realm. Without the wand it is my choice to follow your mother, wherever that may be, and it is my hope that the Copanatec kingdom will be found there.'

Pakal's eyes lingered on the boy, pondering what lay before him. 'Perhaps it will also be your choice.'

Chapter Fifty-Seven

Richard's Choice

'He's crazy!'

'Huh?'

'You really believe all that stuff?' asked Kristin.

Richard looked at her quizzically. 'What do you mean?'

'That Pakal and all those people he talked about can live for thousands of years? It's crazy!'

Lord Pakal had left them standing beside the ossuary plinth to cross the floor to the Chapac Stone. He was speaking to Leanna and they could hear their raised voices above the murmuring of the priestesses in the background.

Richard didn't answer Kristin's question. Instead, he left her to hear what Pakal was saying to Leanna. He remembered that Pakal had told her earlier to prepare the stone for the ritual, but she appeared to be arguing with him, which seemed unusual.

What was the ritual? Was it to do with what Pakal had said about preparing to follow his mother to the next realm? He didn't know, but he was determined to find out.

Pakal's voice rang out for everyone to hear. 'When you have finished, Leanna, you must proceed with Lord Tenoch's ossuary and place it in the pyramid as is our custom. You and the priestesses will then be free to leave Copanatec!'

Leanna's expression was one of shock and astonishment, but she slowly bowed her head in agreement, before turning to a small, wooden table, its surface decorated with a mosaic of carved multiverse symbols, placed near the stone. She lifted an earthenware jug and poured a measure of highly

447

scented oil into its companion bowl, stirring the contents with a narrow, wooden blade as she did so. After stirring, she placed the blade to one side, nodding with satisfaction as the sharp, pungent fragrance was released into the air. She called the priestesses to be anointed and as each one stood before her, Leanna asked them to bare a shoulder while she dipped a finger in the oil and traced the outline of the mark of the Copanatecs on their skin. When she was finished, the last one did the same for her.

As the priestesses gathered in their customary positions around the Chapac Stone, the vallonium lamps set inside ornamental wall brackets began to dim around the chamber, as if in expectation of the ritual to come. Above the stone, through the dome's stained glass window, the golden spire shone with a brilliant light, like a flaming spear pointing the way to the stars in a darkening night sky.

Leanna and the priestesses began the ancient chant; their low, breathy, singing rising to a toneless chant that was as old as the first beings of the multiverse. The incantations were the sounds of the creation at the beginning of time and were the link to the realm beyond Copanatec. The high pitch of the chant ascended until it was beyond reach of the human ear, sensed rather than heard; and it was then that the Chapac Stone began to glow, with shimmering tendrils of the golden cloud beginning to appear.

Richard's mind was awhirl as he watched Lord Pakal approach the stone. He was witnessing a repeat of what he had seen his mother go through in the vision, which had left him confused and angry, and although he now knew the stone's purpose, he still felt frustrated and helpless. He could glimpse shadowy figures forming and disappearing inside the cloud as it spread out from the central trough and across the stone.

This was totally unlike a timecrack which only appeared when colossal amounts of energy were released, like the incident that had taken place at the Facility on Old Earth. And it wasn't anything like his experience on the Transkal when Prince Lotane tried to kill him during the Ritual Sacrifice inside the Sacred Temple.

So who were the figures? Was his mother among them?

As Richard continued to watch, Pakal used a wooden block placed by one of the priestesses to step up onto the stone. Unlike Richards's mother who lay down in the trough, Pakal chose to stand and gaze across the chamber to where Richard stood. The golden cloud became thicker as it spread across the stone, enveloping Pakal as he reached out a hand, beckoning Richard to join him.

Richard felt drawn to the stone ... someone from far away was calling to him. It was a warning. He didn't know who from, or what it was, but he knew he had to make a choice, or it would be too late.

*

Standing apart from Richard, Kristin was terrified by the strange cloud that had appeared out of nowhere. There was something weird and scary about it, and she had no intention of getting any closer to it. And there was Richard's behaviour, the way he was acting, that gave her the feeling that there was something mysterious happening. She only wished Archie was with her to tell her what she should do.

The stone began to glow more brightly as Pakal faded into the thickening cloud, his hand still outstretched. Then without warning, Richard dashed across the chamber to take a running leap onto the stone to join Pakal. He burst through two of the priestesses to land on the edge of the stone, throwing himself forward into the trough. The golden cloud was instantly shot through with fiery red spikes snaking around the two figures in the centre of the trough, as if they were being consumed by flames.

Kristin was transfixed by what seemed to be Richard and Pakal being burnt alive. She could hear the chanting again. It had returned as a throbbing, pulsating, ear-piercing sound that threatened to split her skull. She screamed and kept on screaming, wanting the priestesses to stop singing.

The marble floor beneath her feet trembled, throwing her off balance and onto her knees. As she tried to regain her feet the door to the antechamber flew open and she almost cried with relief when she saw Archie and his father. Instead, she gasped when she saw who they were with.

*

Archie followed Cosimo and Kanga as they stormed into the chamber towards the Chapac Stone; prodded and pushed by the Terog escort, he and Malcolm stumbled forward a few steps, but they came to an abrupt halt when they saw what was happening on the stone.

A brilliant-golden light was fading around two figures on the stone as the cloud that cloaked them began to disperse. The priestesses were still chanting the haunting music they'd heard earlier, but now they were retreating from the stone as another sound overrode their chorus. It was the horrifying roar of the floor opening up as a crack zigzagged a path past the base of one of the column plinths, sending the column crashing down in countless pieces.

Across the room, Archie spotted Kristin scrambling to get back on her feet as the dome above them shattered, raining shards of stained glass down towards the stone. Glass knives sliced into Kanga and Leanna and some of the other priestesses as they tried to escape the lethal downpour. He rushed past them, ignoring their screams as they fell bleeding to the floor, in an effort to pull Kristin out of danger as more glass fell from the dome.

'Hold onto me!' he shouted. She put an arm over his shoulders as he grabbed her by the waist and hauled her over to the alcove containing the ossuary. He pulled one of the drapes across, hoping it would give some extra protection. 'Stay here, and don't move until I come back.'

'Don't leave me!' cried Kristin.

'I have to, I have to get my father,' said Archie. 'Then we have to find Richard, and a way out of here.'

Kristin looked at him, her eyes brimming with tears. 'You won't find him – he's gone.'

'Who's gone? What do you mean we won't find him?' asked Archie.

'Richard – he's gone.' She pointed to the stone. It was deserted and there was no sign of the cloud. The ground was still again; only the bodies and the aftermath of the shock remained to remind them of what had happened. 'He and Pakal ... I don't know how ... but Pakal encouraged him, saying he was one of them, the Copanatecs, and then they both got on the stone ....'

Kristin was obviously shocked, but she told him everything she could remember about Pakal. How he had lived for thousands of years, that he and Richard had the same mark, that it was the end of Copanatec and time to leave.

Archie stared at her, suddenly realising who the two figures on the stone were. 'Are you saying Richard joined Pakal on the stone ... voluntarily?'

She nodded, not knowing what else to say.

Archie looked across to the Transkal, hardly able to believe what Kristin had told him; yet, deep down in his heart he knew it to be true. It was meant to happen, he supposed, but it was hard to take in that he might never see Richard again.

Chapter Fifty-Eight

In the Antechamber

Malcolm stood at the doorway of the antechamber glaring angrily at the Chapac Stone, hardly believing what Archie had just told him. In the midst of the shattered remains of the dome and the collapsed marble column, lay the bodies of Leanna and another priestess, along with Kanga, all struck down by flying shards from the dome's stained glass.

There was no sign of Cosimo and the Terog escort; they had retreated through the antechamber to the courtyard, obviously fearing the worst when the crack appeared, roaring and ripping the chamber floor apart, narrowly missing the stone.

Malcolm, along with Archie and Kristin, had followed them, keeping a safe distance until they reached the antechamber where the shock had stopped short. Cosimo and his men had kept on running into the courtyard.

'It's true, Dad, he's gone,' said Archie. 'Kristin heard what Lord Pakal said to Richard – and she saw him join Pakal on the stone when the cloud came.'

Malcolm stared at the deserted stone. 'I just can't believe it – first, Lucy, and now, Richard.' He had quizzed Kristin repeatedly about Richard's action, but now he had to accept the truth of the situation: Richard was gone and there was nothing he could do about it.

'Dad, we have to get out of here,' urged Archie.

He was worried that Cosimo would return to find them still in the antechamber. Cosimo had fled with his men, believing a major earthquake was taking place when the column crashed onto the heaving floor, directly below the dome as it exploded, creating a maelstrom of debris and glass across the chamber. But

453

the shock had stopped as abruptly as it had started, and Archie guessed that Cosimo wouldn't give up too easily on finding him.

Malcolm turned away from the chamber. It was obvious there was nothing to be done for the victims; it was too late for them. Their cries of pain had stopped and they now lay still, their bodies covered in pieces of marble and broken glass.

'You're right, Archie, we have to get off this island. What happened in there was another foreshock and it looks like they're becoming more frequent. I don't know, but there's a good chance the big one is on its way.'

'How are we going to do that – fly out of here?' asked Kristin sarcastically. She had recovered a little from the mayhem in the chamber, but Archie could see she was still on edge.

'There's only one way: we have to get to the harbour and find a boat. One that we can handle ourselves,' said Malcolm.

'No, I can't ... not yet,' said Kristin.

'What are you talking about? Dad's right, we have to get out of here while we can. There's no telling when another shock will hit us.'

'It's OK for you,' she snapped angrily. 'I came to find *my* father and so far I've been kidnapped, forced to work on the freaking seawall, nearly buried alive in the tunnels, and almost killed by an earthquake! And I haven't seen or heard anything about him!'

Archie hadn't the heart to tell her that if she hadn't stowed away in the hovervan, in the first place, she wouldn't be here now. Instead, he told her that they simply had no choice; if they were to have any hope of survival, they had to get off the island.

'And let's face it, Kristin, there's no way of knowing if he ever made it to Copanatec.' said Archie.

'Maybe, he's still in Amasia; maybe he had an accident and lost his memory, or something ...' he added feebly.

Her eyes blazed back at him, as if he'd insulted her intelligence and should know better. For a moment, she was like her old feisty self, but her lower lip started to quiver and she turned away, not wanting to face him, realising what he said could well be true.

Oh, no, she's not going to start crying, thought Archie. He shook his head, kicking himself for not being able to say the right thing to her. Of course, she's upset that she hasn't found her father – and it's worse in a way because she sees me with dad. And yet she doesn't appreciate how we feel that mum, and now Richard, are lost to us; but there was no point in telling her that.

'I'm sorry, Kristin, I know it's tough not knowing where your father is, but I promise you when we get out of this place, I'll help you find him,' said Archie, but as soon as he spoke, he realised he had no idea how he was going to keep his promise.

She turned to face him, wiping a tear away from her cheek, surprised by what he said. 'It's OK. I know it's not your fault ... it's just that ... well, after my parents separated, my mother went to work in a factory in Sitanga and she never came back. They'd had a big row about how my father was always dreaming of finding a secret treasure – which he never did. And now they're both gone ...'

Archie had heard part of her story from Daniel and guessed it was what made her so edgy and rude at times. He didn't know what to say, but before he could say anything, the antechamber door leading to the courtyard slammed open and someone started yelling at them.

It was Anton Cosimo and the Terogs.

'Oh, no, they're back!' Frantically, Archie grabbed Kristin by the arm and pulled her towards his father. 'We have to get out of here! Give dad a hand, he's too slow on his own.'

'Where are you going?' she screamed.

'Make your way to the kitchen and through there back into the garden. It's me Cosimo is after, so we need to split up. I'll find you there, once I lose them.'

Malcolm and Kristin both tried to protest, but Archie was already sprinting towards the Terogs who were crowded around Cosimo and Nitkin. Confused by Cosimo's shouting and anger they weren't expecting Archie to run directly at them. Before they could react he skirted around the outer ring of Terogs and headed for the antechamber door that would take him into the courtyard.

Chapter Fifty-Nine

The Corridor

Han-Sin halted when she spotted the figure running towards them. She waved a hand to Chuck to stay behind her and the two Lancers.

They had entered the side corridor that ran alongside the kitchen and the portico, past the courtyard to the front of the temple. The figure ducked in behind one of the tall, flat pillars that lined the corridor as soon as he saw the Lancers with their weapons pointed in his direction.

It was only a short time ago that Han-Sin had managed to bring the Spokestar down into a safe haven: a large barn with high double doors lying wide open in one of the fields of corn on the edge of the farmlands. The barn straddled the end of a long stony lane leading to the outer wall and gate that surrounded the temple gardens. They'd passed through the gate, wary of being exposed to curious eyes, but no one had seen or challenged their presence so far on the approach to the sprawling structure that made up the temple complex. Now they were inside, moving slowly along the corridor.

Han-Sin called out: 'Who are you? Show yourself or we will open fire!'

Before the figure could answer, the foreshock struck the chamber. The rippling effect of the tremor spread across the courtyard and into corridor, throwing all of them off their feet, including the stranger behind the pillar. It was a minor shock, and though it seemed much longer, lasted only a few seconds. None of them incurred serious injury, except, perhaps, for the stranger groaning and struggling to his feet.

Chuck stood up, sweeping a cloud of dust away from his face. In front of him, Han-Sin and the Lancers were dusting themselves down, seemingly unaffected by the tremor. As far as he could tell, except for a series of cracks in the ceiling, the only other damage was further along the corridor wall, where a gap had opened up in the middle of a supporting buttress.

Satisfied no one was hurt, Han-Sin, flanked by the Lancers, moved slowly towards the stranger, their paraguns raised, ready to fire. Chuck followed close behind, armed with a laser pistol. Supplied by Han-Sin and usually holstered across the chest, he held the weapon in his right hand, its lethal firepower belied by the lightweight feel of the grip.

As darkness fell, vallonium lamps had automatically illuminated the corridor, the light spilling through the archways onto the perimeter of the courtyard. The cloud of stone dust and dirt in the air had almost cleared and Chuck could see that each of the recesses between the pillars housed a large, decorative stone vase on a pedestal. One of them, unbalanced by the tremor, had crashed to the floor showering several sharp chunks of stone onto the stranger. Scrambling to his feet to face them, he held a hand to his head.

'My God! It's Quig!'

Chuck shouldered his way through Han-Sin and the two Lancers to reach the man he had left behind with Richard and Harimon. Quig was holding a hand over a wound on the side of his scalp that was bleeding profusely, seeping blood through his fingers.

'Here, let me have a look at that, Quig.'

He called to one of the Lancers to open the battlefield pack he carried, assuming it to contain a medical kit. 'Quickly, give me something to staunch the bleeding!'

The Lancer opened the pack and handed him a large white pad and a bandage roll. As he placed the pad over the wound and strapped it to the scalp, he asked Quig what had happened to Richard.

Quig looked at him, groggily. 'I don't know. The last time I saw him, he was with his brother and father.' He omitted to say that he had passed Archie and his father on the staircase, leaving them to their fate with the threat of the Terogs nearby.

'What, you saw *all* of them?'

But before Quig could answer him, the sudden commotion of a group of men rushing from the courtyard into the corridor distracted all of them.

'Take cover!' Han-Sin yelled the warning, ducking as something clunked the pillar behind her and fell to the floor. It was a crossbow bolt. Another flew past her head as she turned and dodged to reach the safety of the pillar. She yelled again as she saw a line of advancing Terogs preparing to fire. 'We are under attack! Return fire!'

Chuck tried to haul Quig into the recess where the remains of the vase once stood, but it was too late. Two bolts slammed into Quig's back. Chuck felt the weight of the body collapse against him, slowly slithering from his grip onto the floor, offering him some protection, before he dived into the recess behind the pedestal.

He took a quick look to assess what they faced as another bolt hit the top of the pedestal, forcing him to drop onto one knee. He grunted as he felt something amongst the rubble jar his kneecap. Thinking it was a piece of the vase he tried to brush it aside, only to discover it was a paragun. He pulled it away from the rubble, realising it must be the one he had given to Quig from the Bonebreaker, before taking Aristo to hospital.

He holstered the laser pistol and switched the paragun to the lethal mode, before venturing another look down the corridor. Dozens of Terogs had poured into the corridor from the courtyard, firing a hail of bolts at them, but they were seriously outgunned by the Lancers and their paraguns. Urged on by a tall, dark alien figure sheltering behind one of the pillars, a line of Terogs rushed fearlessly towards him – all of them instantly vaporised by the paraguns. And yet more Terogs filled their place, as if hell-bent on some sort of Kamikaze suicide mission.

Let's see what we can do about him, thought Chuck, keeping an eye on the dark figure. *If he goes, maybe these lunatics will turn tail, back to where they came from.*

He couldn't see the figure, but he placed him where he last saw him, taking cover behind a pillar near the damaged buttress at the side of the corridor.

He targeted the pillar and fired.

The Lancers were still blasting Terogs into space, but they stopped firing when the pillar disappeared and the buttress collapsed, bringing down the ceiling and part of the upper floor with it. It was as if a bomb had exploded, with pillars and archways crashing outwards into the courtyard, causing panic amongst the remaining Terogs. Some were buried under the wreckage of furnishings brought down from the floor above, while others were running for cover towards the antechamber.

Chuck stepped out of the recess and studied the pile of debris in the corridor for a moment. *That's the way to deal with the bad guys.* He looked to Han-Sin and the Lancers. 'Anyone hurt?'

'No, Chuck, we are all right.' Han-Sin smiled, nodding towards the debris. 'Thanks to you, we can now move forward, although you have a created a barrier for us to climb.'

'Sorry about that, but better that than the alternative.'

She pointed to Quig. 'What about your friend?'

'I'm afraid it's too late for him. We'll have to leave the body, cover it with some of the rubble and recover it later. He told me that the boys are here with their father, but with the Terogs on the warpath we need to find them fast before they come to harm.' said Chuck. He pointed to the collapsed archways. 'That's where we saw Quig come through, so I suggest we take a look there and work our way through this place.'

Han-Sin nodded her agreement and directed the two Lancers to lead the way over the debris, through the portico and into the courtyard. They moved cautiously, coming to a halt when they saw a trail of wreckage from the dome and golden spire lying on the portico and around the entrance to the antechamber.

To their left, a marble staircase wound its way to the first floor and a balcony; directly below, they could see that the closed doors of the great hall had been bolted on their side. Just beyond the front of the hall, was the square they had flown across earlier. There was no one to be seen in the courtyard, but they could hear the distant screams of people outside the temple drifting through the night air, creating an eerie atmosphere that had the hairs on Chuck's neck on edge.

The Lancers stepped inside the open door of the antechamber, stopping when directly ahead of them they heard loud voices coming from the chamber. Paraguns at the ready, they glanced quizzically at Han-Sin.

Standing beside her, Chuck said: 'Something is going on in there; we better check it out.'

She nodded agreement, but before she could give the order to move forward, someone came running through the chamber door, towards them.

Chapter Sixty

The Chase

Cosimo shook his head at the sight of Kanga's broken body sprawled across the chamber floor. The head and upper body had been crushed by fallen masonry; only the legs had escaped injury. He looked to the stone where he had seen the two figures disappearing into the fading, golden cloud, realising now that one of them had been Lord Pakal.

He'd heard the priestesses chanting, while Pakal journeyed to the so-called next realm, betraying the understanding that he and Talon had agreed with him. And the other one, the smaller figure? Could it have been one of the Kinross boys who had so plagued his plans at the Sacred Temple in Amasia?

Sandan, Lotane, Talon ... and now Pakal. Was he always to be thwarted by the stupidity and madness of others?

Cosimo grimaced as he looked down at Kanga's body. His plan to unite the Terogs with the rebel Arnaks, to build a mighty military force to take control of Amasia was in tatters without him.

The disgusting grunts and snorts of the Terogs were incomprehensible to him; but Kanga had taught Nitkin a little of their language, and surprisingly, he seemed to have had no difficulty with it. Nitkin was a fool, but hopefully with his help, Cosimo would be able to take command of the suicidal cretins.

Earlier, when the foreshock struck the chamber, Cosimo, with some of the Terogs in tow, had taken flight, hoping to escape what he thought was the imminent destruction of the temple. They had run into a Lancer patrol in the corridor as they tried to reach the garden. The Terogs had immediately engaged them, but crossbows and whips were no match against powerful laser weapons and he had been lucky to escape the cave-in when part of the building had collapsed. They had no choice but to retrace their path back to the courtyard, where they found Nitkin hurriedly barring the door to the great hall.

Cosimo pulled him away from the door. 'What are you doing? Where are your men and the prisoner?'

Nitkin groaned that he and his Terog escort had lost Harimon to a large band of armed slaves and villagers that had managed to take refuge in the hall, defending themselves against the Terogs on the temple steps outside, in front of the square. Looking nervously to the barred door, he said, 'Some of the slaves knew the prisoner and attacked us. I was lucky to escape with my life!'

'And you left them?'

'There is nothing but madness and death for us in there!'

As he listened to Nitkin's whingeing, Cosimo took stock of the chamber. The shattered remains of the collapsed marble column and the dome's stained glass lay scattered around the Chapac Stone. Near the opening in the floor created by the foreshock, lay the bodies of Kanga and three of the priestesses. The others had obviously managed to escape outside. A dark, all-consuming rage was slowly taking possession of him as he considered his options. He was wanted by the Lancers for killing one of their own and if they knew he was with the Terogs it was all the more reason to hunt him down. He had no idea how they came to be on the island and he had no intention of staying to find out.

The Terogs were grunting and muttering to each other, confused without Kanga to tell them what to do. As he surveyed the room around him, he spotted three figures grouped together at the other end of the chamber. One of them was the Kinross boy he'd failed to capture at Castle Zolnayta!

Cosimo, in a black rage, suddenly saw him as the bane of his existence in this new world and determined he would be rid of him, once and for all, before he made his escape from Copanatec.

He yelled and pointed: 'Look, Nitkin! All of you, grab those people and bring them to me!'

Nitkin turned to see where he was pointing, but the Terogs, not understanding what he'd said, stood their ground and continued to stare at Cosimo.

*

Archie heard Cosimo and knew there was no time to waste if they were to escape capture. He had to give his father, hindered by his bad leg, time to reach the garden before the Terogs woke up to what Cosimo was yelling at them.

Archie broke away and called over his shoulder to Kristin and his father, both still protesting, as he raced towards the antechamber: 'Just go – I'll find you in the garden!'

He guessed there were up to fifty Terogs crowded around Cosimo as he raced past them. It would be a close-run thing to reach the antechamber door before they spotted him. It was his only hope, to get outside to the portico to give his father and Kristin time to reach the garden before Cosimo and the Terogs came after him. *If* they came after him

Once they reached the garden and he met up with them, what then? His only plan at the moment, was to stay out of Cosimo's clutches, and find a way off the island.

As he dashed towards the doorway, he discovered someone there he never expected to see.

*

It was Chuck, with Han-Sin and two Lancers.

Momentarily stunned at seeing them, Archie stopped in his tracks. 'Chuck! My God, how did you get here?'

'Archie! Aaahh – !'

Chuck didn't finish. A crossbow bolt had struck the side of his right hand. More bolts flew past, another one striking the Lancer next to him. He dropped his paragun, instinctively gripping the wound with his other hand to protect it. Gritting his teeth, he dropped to his knee to reduce his exposure and looked round to see what had happened to the others. The Lancer had been hit in the shoulder; the other Lancer was helping him to cover away from the doorway. Han-Sin joined Chuck, firing her paragun at a body of Terogs rushing across the chamber in their direction.

She pulled him to his feet and hauled him back into the antechamber. She glanced at his injured hand. It was a nasty-looking flesh wound 'Are you OK?'

'I'm all right. It stings like hell, but it's just a graze. A bandage will fix it.'

Han-Sin nodded, but she was in no position to do anything for him while the Terogs tried to overwhelm them with their suicidal attack. She called to the Lancer to leave his wounded friend: 'Help me here, or we'll all be lying beside him!'

She fired into the attacking mob, atomising two of them. Ready to fire again, she spotted an odd-looking figure crouching behind a Terog. It was a rebel Arnak – as a Salakin she would recognise their kind anywhere – he was a small, ugly devil, with sallow skin and a twisted nose. Using the Terog as cover, he was close to grabbing Archie, who had just come through the door and dropped flat to the floor to avoid the volley of bolts from the crossbows.

Pinned down and wary of firing in case she hit him, she yelled: 'Archie, watch out for the Arnak!'

*

Archie, still amazed by the sudden appearance of Chuck and Han-Sin, heard her and looked to where she was pointing. He saw the Terog advancing, with an arm outstretched ready to grab him. Following him, was a little Arnak carrying a crossbow and a belt across his chest loaded with bolts, seemingly intent on doing the same thing. He guessed they were under orders to capture him for Cosimo.

A bright flash of light appeared just as the Terog pounced, he was instantly atomised by Han-Sin's paragun. The little Arnak screamed in fear as he threw himself forward to avoid the same fate. He almost landed on Archie, but Archie had scrabbled to his feet and was running as fast as he could to get out of the antechamber.

He looked over his shoulder, hoping Chuck and Han-Sin were following, but they were caught up in the battle at the doorway, trying to protect themselves and a wounded Lancer.

The Arnak had picked himself up and with another Terog, was giving chase. Archie raced out of the antechamber and across the courtyard into the portico he and his father had used earlier on the way to the balcony. He felt on the edge of panic, not knowing what he should do next; only that he should keep running and hope that he would find his father and Kristin in the gardens.

Han-Sin and the Lancers.

That was it! They must have arrived on Copanatec with Chuck in a Spokestar. Once he found dad and Kristin, that was their way to escape from the island!

Breathing heavily, Archie ran towards the portico kitchen door. It was lying open, but before he got there, he heard someone scream. He crept up to the door and peered inside. The remaining priestesses from the chamber must have fled to the kitchen during the foreshock; now they were grouped around his father and Kristin, all of them trying to get through the far door to the garden. A Terog was lashing at the priestesses with his whip, forcing them to get out of his way.

He must be after dad and Kristin!

He had to distract him. Looking over his shoulder, he saw Nitkin and another Terog at the other end of the portico.

He started yelling and waving his arms above his head: 'Hey, you pug-nosed brutes, I'm here!'

He waited until Nitkin and the Terogs spotted him to give chase, before leaving the portico to gain entry to the corridor on the far side of the kitchen. A side door led outside onto a stony path bordering the temple; beyond the path, a high wall ran its length next to the gardens. He looked up; it was dark, but a clear sky and bright starlight helped him see what lay ahead.

Archie calculated that the path would take him to the rear of the temple and the kitchen door. He was worried by what would happen to Kristin and his dad if they were caught before he could do something, *anything*, to help them.

The grey gravel stones skittered beneath his feet as he belted around a corner at the end of the path. He saw his father, hopping as best as he could with the aid of his stick, and Kristin supporting him by the arm, running with the priestesses into the gardens. The

468

Terog exited the kitchen door, pushing a priestess aside.

Archie crashed into the Terog, knocking both of them off their feet; he scrambled back up, shouting as he ran: 'Kristin, Dad! Lose yourselves in the gardens!'

He looked back to see Nitkin and his men rounding the corner. They hesitated for a moment when they saw Malcolm and Kristin veering away from the kitchen garden, leaving the priestesses behind, to take a lane leading to the farmlands.

Archie knew it was him that Cosimo wanted, so he gave them a second, before they gave chase. He glanced quickly to the lane, but there was no sign of Kristin or his father. He hoped they'd find a place to hide somewhere in the cornfields, at least until he could make it back to them. For now, there was only one way for him to go.

He ran towards the bridge and the pyramid, wondering what he was going to do when he got there. And how, he wondered, was he going to get rid of this bunch?

Chapter Sixty-One

The Man in the Tunnel

The answer came when Archie reached the pyramid.

He'd retraced his steps past the sunflower garden to reach the path that ran next to the perimeter wall on the gorge side of the temple. The brick and stone archway with its wooden gate, lay open to reveal the large, white stones which had fallen from the temple during the Destruction, blocking most of the path. As before, he'd managed to squeeze through to climb onto what was left of the bridge and cross to the terrace at the entrance to the pyramid.

The sudden sound of a deep underground rumble and the tremor that followed, threw him to one side against what was left of the rocky entrance to the pyramid. The terrace was crumbling below his feet; and this part of the pyramid, already weakened by the Destruction, was tearing itself apart, arcing great chunks of stone into the gorge. On the other side, a large section of the temple wall collapsed against the perimeter wall, pushing the stonework onto the end of the bridge.

Nitkin and the Terogs were in the middle of the bridge when the foreshock struck. Their screams seemed to linger like distant echoes as they tumbled and clawed at the air, in a vain attempt to save themselves. Horrified, Archie watched as the remaining structure of the bridge gave way, to follow the falling bodies into the yawning chasm.

All around him, the night air was filled with dust and the gaseous smell of something vile rising out of the gorge, making him put a hand over his mouth and nose. *God, that's awful*, he thought. But he had little time to think about it. Falling slabs of stonework crashing onto what was left of the terrace forced him to dive for cover inside the pyramid. As he landed on his hands and knees, with the deafening and terrifying sounds from the gorge roaring in his ears, it seemed as if the world was coming to an end.

Pulling himself to his feet, he looked across the gorge as it belched out a cloud of black smoke and a stream of red-hot lava and wondered how he was ever going to get back to find his father and Kristin.

*

Shifting another rock to one side, Archie sensed the throbbing, pulsing movement, of a tremor, deep in the heart of the pyramid – as if it were warning him that it was in the death throes of its existence.

The thought of tons of stone about to cave in on top of him, threatened to send Archie into a state of panic as he struggled to climb over the pile of rockfall in the tunnel. He tried to quell the fear of being buried alive, before it took control and killed his efforts to find a passage through the pyramid.

He was trapped. The bridge over the gorge was gone, and there was rockfall in front of him, but he was lucky in one respect: the vallonium lamps still worked. He remembered what he had been taught at the science and technology class at Harmsway College, and during school visits to the Vallonium Institute in Fort Temple: that the mineral was Amasia's most valuable energy source, and the products made with it were virtually indestructible.

A dust-covered lamp on the far side of the rockfall, shed a dull orange light on a section of tunnel he didn't recognise. As he clambered down from the pile of loose rock sliding beneath his feet, Archie realised he wasn't in the same tunnel in which he and Kristin had followed Jona, on their way to the bridge. This one had smooth, plastered walls, decorated with a series of small frescos, depicting a column of figures marching in a line from the temple to the pyramid. Unfortunately, some of the frescoes were cracked and covered in grime, but he could see that one of the figures at the head of the procession was carrying a box, held with outstretched arms, in the manner of making an offering.

He rubbed some of the grime away with the edge of his hand, and peered more closely at the box.

Was it the golden casket Daros had told him about? he wondered.

He took a step back and looked around. This must be the original passageway used by the high priests to make the journey between the temple and the pyramid, before the tunnels were dug to find the casket. The rockfall and the new opening must have been created by the recent foreshock, but as far as he could see, the passageway was clear of any debris.

The tremors had stopped, and the 'big one' his father feared, had yet to come.

*

The passageway led Archie into the subterranean world of tunnels where he had worked with Daros, pushing loaded wagons to the seawall.

He saw no one, neither villager nor Terog, as he made his way down to the lower levels of the tunnel complex. He found the cell block branch tunnel and the cell he had shared with the other prisoners. The sight of the pallets filled with bed-grass scattered around the cell, suddenly made Archie realise how tired and hungry he felt.

The temptation to lie down and rest for a while, was too great to resist. He lay down on the pallet to rest for a few minutes; he was so tired he could sleep for hours, but he knew that wasn't an option. His mind was churning with questions on how he was going to find his father and Kristin ... Where were they? ... How were they going to get off the island? ... What about Chuck and Han-Sin? ...

It was all too much, and soon he had drifted into a deep sleep, curling into a ball on the pallet, next to the cell door.

He woke up to find someone shaking his shoulder. At first, he thought he was dreaming, but the fierce grip on his shoulder was too real to be a dream.

He pushed the hand away. 'Hey, you're hurting me!'

'Who are you? What are you doing here?'

The questions were asked by a man wearing a dark navy tunic and trousers, the outfit issued to all tunnellers. His clothes, and a large, bulging goatskin tool bag, its handles slung over one shoulder, were covered in rock-dust.

Another rough shake and Archie yelled at him: 'Stop that – I'm getting up!' He rolled off the pallet onto his knees, then stood up to face the tunneller.

'You are not Salakin – or Amasian,' said the man. He asked the question as if it might be a problem for him.

Feeling a little groggy, Archie rubbed the sleep from his eyes and stared at the man. He was smaller than Archie's six feet and thickset with broad shoulders, very much like most of the diggers who worked in the tunnels. Long, sandy hair and beard stubble covered most of his face, but it was the greenish eyes which seemed familiar, although Archie was sure he had never seen him before.

'I'm not, I'm a New Arrival.'

473

'*A New Arrival?*' said the man curiously. 'Then what is your business in the tunnels?'

'It's a long story, and I don't have time to explain now,' sighed Archie. 'Look, I can see you worked in the tunnels, and so did I, but with all the fighting that's going on, we have a chance to get out of here, while we can.'

The man's eyes flickered for a moment, taking in what Archie said. Then, as if he had made a decision, he pointed a finger towards the cell door: 'There is only one way to avoid the Terogs and the fighting – the tunnel in the lower level that leads to the sea. Many of the other tunnels have collapsed and are no longer safe.'

Archie nodded. Jona had told him of the plan for the tunnellers to escape during the uprising, using the pyramid exit to reach the temple square and onto the seawall. From there they hoped to find a ship to take them to Amasia. If that failed they had planned to use the drainage adits on the lower levels to reach the coast.

'Yes, I know. That was the way I was planning to go,' said Archie.

'But you decided to sleep?' said the man, with a hint of humour.

'I'm hungry, and I was tired. I don't know how long I've been running, but I was lucky not to be caught by the Terogs,' snapped Archie, not appreciating the man's implied criticism.

The man smiled and held up a hand, as if to say he understood. He pulled the tool bag from his shoulder and placed it on the cell floor. 'There is a store in this tunnel where the Terogs keep water and food. It is why I came here before I leave, and that is how I found you. The cell door was open and I saw you inside, asleep.' He rummaged through the bag, which contained an assortment of tools and several paper-wrapped packets.

He handed one of the packets and a flask of water to Archie. 'Here, eat and drink.'

Archie opened the packet and saw that it was the tunnel food issued to the villagers: a thick sausage of reddish, spiced meat and a chunk of brown bread. He had been eating it for the past week and had no problem with it – but it was boring eating the same food all the time. He ate it ravenously and washed it down with gulps of water from the flask.

The man watched him for a few moments, then asked: 'What is your name?'

Archie finished the piece of sausage he was chewing, before answering: 'Archie – Archie Kinross, I was one of the wagon-pushers. What's yours, and what do you do here?'

'Like you, I have two names. The second is Abelhorn. I work in the tunnels, and when the machines do not work, I fix them for the diggers.'

Archie stared at him in astonishment. He realised why the man's piercing green eyes seemed so familiar. They were the same as Kristin's. And, although, her golden-reddish hair was richer and brighter, he could see the similarity in thickness and colour.

'Abelhorn! Your first name ... wouldn't be Nathan ... would it?'

Chapter Sixty-Two

The Adits

The man's eyes widened in surprise. 'We have never met. How is it you know my name?'

Where do I start? thought Archie. 'Well, it's hard to know how to explain everything that has happened to me, Mister Abelhorn –'

The man smiled and raised a hand to interrupt Archie. 'No, not Mister Abelhorn. We will be friends and you will call me Nathan. But we do not have much time here – I am afraid more tunnels will collapse and we will be trapped before we reach the coast. Tell me what you can as we leave this place.'

'OK ... Nathan ... and you can call me Archie.'

'Good, we will leave now.'

Nathan put the flask of water back into the tool bag; along with the packets of food, and tools which Archie assumed he used to repair the tunnel diggers' equipment. He slung the bag over his shoulder and beckoned Archie to follow him.

*

A horizontal wooden pipeline, about two feet in diameter, carved from the tree trunks of an ancient forest, ran the length of the tunnel. Every ten feet, or so, metal bands had been strapped around the pipeline to strengthen it and to prevent leaks. It was one of the many tasks he had been assigned, explained Nathan. Much of it was now covered by rock and dirt that had fallen from the roof and wall, shaken loose by recent foreshocks. It was a warning, thought Archie, that the same could happen to them if another foreshock struck, before they found a way out of the tunnels.

As he followed him down through the lower levels of the tunnel system to the drainage adit, Archie thought about what Daniel and Captain Abelhorn had told him about Nathan.

He had last been seen in Quig's village four years ago, accompanied by a stranger. They had spent a night there, questioning the villagers about a chart of the South Amasian Sea the stranger possessed. Someone had drawn a sketch of an island in the middle of the White Waters, but the villagers, according to Quig when told of the story, claimed there was no such island, and that Nathan was foolish to believe otherwise.

'He was a fool, a dreamer chasing lost treasure,' the captain had said of his son, to Archie. 'Ever since he was a boy, Nathan was fascinated by old maps and charts; thinking to find exotic lands and riches beyond the horizon was his dream.'

He said that Nathan had taken the stranger on his boat to the little harbour below Quig's village, tying up alongside other fishing boats next to the stone and wood jetty that jutted into the sea. They stayed up late that night, but early the next morning, the boat was gone, and Nathan and the stranger were never seen again.

As he remembered what the captain and Daniel had told him about Nathan, Archie recounted his own story on how he had arrived through a timecrack, to land on the *Serpent*.

Nathan stopped and turned to look at Archie. 'You know my father ... and the others on the *Serpent*?'

'Yes, and Kristin –'

'What! You know my daughter?'

Archie nodded. 'Yes, Captain Abelhorn let me stay at Portview Terrace, and I got to know Kristin ... in fact, she's also on the island.'

'NO! She cannot be!'

'I'm sorry, Nathan, but she is.'

'But how?'

There was too much and little time to tell, Archie realised, about all that had happened to bring him to Copanatec.

He told Nathan of his journey through the timecrack and landing on the *Serpent*; the bombings at the dockside in Port Zolnayta; the search for his parents and Richard; the journey to Elam, with Kristin hiding in the hovervan, and their capture by the Terogs; and then taken to Copanatec, with Kristin sent to the seawall, and his own time in the tunnels.

Nathan shook his head in disbelief. '*Kristin* – after all this time, she believed I was still alive?'

'Yes, although Daniel and your father said you had disappeared in some sort of treasure hunt, Kristin was determined to find out what had happened to you.'

Nathan put a hand to his forehead, as if it ached. 'No doubt, Archie, my father and others have told you of my madness in searching for treasure, sacrificing my work as a fisherman, and my family, in my endeavours to find such riches. I believe I must have been mad, especially when you tell me how Kristin has suffered.'

'What about the stranger and the chart?' asked Archie. '*Was* there treasure to be found?'

'He said his name was Cranoc, a mining engineer from Sitanga. He claimed to have information about deposits of a rare element he wished to explore on an island in the White Waters and he needed a boat to take him there. We told him we were fishermen and would not venture into such a dangerous sea and did not believe such an island existed. But he was very persistent, and so I suggested I would take him to Quig's village. That someone might know of the island and take him there.'

'But nobody did, did they?'

'No, they were not so foolish. They were frightened by the stories of demons seizing fishermen in their boats in the White Waters, and villagers taken from their homes, all of whom were never seen again. It was something they refused to discuss, in fear of such evil visiting them.'

'What did the stranger say?'

'He made me an offer. Stupidly, I listened to him, and paid for it with four years of my life in this place.'

'What happened?'

'Cranoc was a trickster. He said his true mission was to find a great treasure hidden on the island and that he would share it with me, if I would take him there. In my hunger for riches I fell into his trap. There was no treasure, it was another of his lies, simply a ploy for someone to take him to Copanatec.'

'But who was he? Was he not from Sitanga?'

Nathan snorted at the memory of how he had been tricked. 'He was one of Talon's men, who had gone missing, presumed dead, during one of their raids in Amasia. His lies were nothing more than a scheme to find a way of returning to Copanatec. The White Waters were kind to us, and Cranoc knew his way to the island. When we arrived here, he turned me over to Talon, and I never saw him again.'

He shook his head at the madness of what he had done. 'I am only thankful I did not persuade someone else to go with him.'

Archie felt sorry for him, but said nothing. Something else had caught his attention. He listened carefully, and then he heard it again: a distant rumbling sound, somewhere deep below their feet.

They looked at each other nervously.

'I hear it, too,' said Nathan. 'We must leave quickly!'

He led the way to another level. The walls were slick with dripping water, forming pools in the uneven rock floor. There was hardly any ventilation and Archie could feel the sweat trickling down his back as the heat built up inside the tunnel.

'We are still on the upper levels where the water does not drain away naturally, as it does on the lowest level,' explained Nathan. He pointed to a vertical pipe, running through a shaft in the tunnel roof. 'It is connected to a pump on the level above. There is a lot of water in the ground directly below the pyramid, and I am afraid the pumps may stop working if we are hit by another tremor. If that happens, some of the tunnels will be flooded.'

The rumbling continued, like the growling of a hungry beast in the bowels of the earth, intent on finding its prey. As Archie and Nathan ran down through the tunnels to the drainage adit, they were confronted by the sickening sight of the bloody remains of Terogs and villagers alike, lying on the rocky floor.

It was evidence that a vicious battle had taken place during the early part of the uprising, but it was also evident how the battle had been fought. Villagers lay with bolts protruding from their bodies – indicating a clean kill. But the villagers, in their thirst for revenge, had used their drills, spikes, hammers, rock chisels – anything that could be used as a weapon – to hack at the Terogs, separating flesh from bone. Now they were all entombed together.

The very sight of the bodies spurred them to keep running until they reached the main drainage adit. They ran along a raised path, next to a channel where water from the levels above rushed towards an exit below the pyramid.

'How the hell are we supposed to get out of here?' asked Archie, more to himself than Nathan. He stood by the exit as early light began to appear on the horizon from across a black sea. The water surged out of the channel, onto a steep, rocky cliff face; a waterfall pouring down onto a shingle beach, several hundred feet below.

Beside him, Nathan took a pace forward and pointed outside to a flat stone left of the exit, away from the channel. 'Look there. That is the beginning of a path that will take us to the beach.'

The spray and the roar of the water gushing out of the channel down the rockface made Archie wary of taking a step onto the slippery wet stones. He watched Nathan place the handles of the tool bag over his head to keep it from falling off his shoulder as he stepped outside. Archie followed in Nathan's footsteps, holding himself steady by gripping a series of handholds that had been carved into the rock. As the light improved, Archie could see that the rest of the path had been created by someone cutting chunks of rock out of the cliff, to form the steps of a narrow, crude weather-beaten staircase.

OK, so far, thought Archie, *but what do we do when we get down there?*

Chapter Sixty-Three

The Boatshed

The roar of another foreshock, followed by huge stone blocks tumbling down the face of the pyramid, started a rockslide above the adit exit they had just left. A cloud of dust rose above Archie and Nathan as they dashed across the shingle beach towards an arch-shaped break in a high wall of rocks near the water's edge.

'We must get through the rocks,' Nathan yelled, running close behind Archie. 'If the arch collapses, we will be trapped!'

They were in luck, the foreshock was only one of many brief tremors yet to come, each lasting no more than a few seconds. They raced through the arch to another shingle beach, untouched by the dust and rockslide behind them; but they were threatened by the sight of huge waves crashing onto the beach.

Stopping for a moment, to allow both of them to catch a breath, Nathan pointed a finger towards the cliff. 'This way. There is another path to the harbour.'

'To the seawall?' asked Archie.

'No. When we arrived in Copanatec, Cranoc brought me to a smaller harbour further along the coast, past the seawall. He told me my boat would be safe there,' grunted Nathan. 'It was – for Talon and his men. That was when he turned me over to them.'

'Do you think your boat is still there?'

Nathan smiled. 'Oh, it is, Archie. I have spent these many months preparing it for the day that I would leave this place.'

'But how could you, if the Terogs were watching you? Wouldn't they have known you were up to something?

Nathan shook his head. 'They never used my boat; it was too small for them, and so they thought to let it rot. Instead, Talon gave me use of the old boatshed to make repairs on the equipment for the tunnels, but he never thought to see what I was doing, as long as I did my job. He left that up to the Terogs and, as you know, they are an ignorant lot. As long as I kept Talon happy, they were satisfied. They never even suspected that I created the steps and a path from the adits to the harbour and the boatshed, which allowed me to take whatever I needed from the tunnel stores to use on the boat.'

Before Archie could ask any more questions, Nathan hefted the bag on his shoulder and turned away to keep moving: 'We cannot waste time here if we are to find Kristin.'

And my father, thought Archie.

*

Another half-mile along the rock-strewn beach brought them to the small natural harbour, located in a narrow L-shaped inlet.

On a flat patch of ground above a long concrete slipway, stood the boatshed, its wooden walls hinting at the blue paint that once decorated it, and a rust-covered, corrugated iron roof ready to separate its links with the walls. Next to the boatshed, a small winch house accommodated the engine and steel cable drum; the cable was already extended down the slipway and hooked to a trolley cradling Nathan's boat.

Archie was impressed. 'It looks like you are ready to go.'

'Yes, I was, until you told me about Kristin. Now I have to find her before we leave.'

'And my father,' Archie reminded him. He didn't say, but he was equally concerned about Kristin. Although she had got under his skin when they first met, she was in his thoughts a lot of the time, and not just for her safety. He missed her gutsy attitude and having her around, which he found very strange.

'Yes, you are right, I should have said so. I'm afraid that since you told me of Kristin's presence on the island, I've thought of little else.'

'That's OK, I understand, but what can we do about them?'

Nathan looked thoughtful, before answering: 'You said, that when you last saw them, they hoped to seek refuge in the cornfields. As we cannot return through the pyramid, we have no choice but to go through the temple and the gardens. Any other path would require us to find another approach from the other side of the cornfields, and that would take too long. So we must sail up the coast to the seawall, cross the square, and get through the temple without being seen by the Terogs.'

*

Archie had a look around the winch house, while Nathan checked that the cable was free to run smoothly on the slipway. Obviously well kept, the winch house was spotless and free from dirt and litter, unlike the boatshed he'd just been inside. A metal box on the wall displayed two power buttons: green 'on' and red 'off'. A sign behind a lever at the side of the cable drum showed two arrows indicating: 'reverse' and 'forward', and a neutral position. An open, sliding door gave a good view of the slipway and the boat trolley.

When Nathan returned to the winch house, Archie asked him: 'What do you call your boat?'

'She's a thirty-footer called *Fearless*. She has an open wheelhouse and she's not big, compared to the *Serpent*, but she suits me, well enough. I bought her from the family of a lost fisherman a few years ago, and they asked me to keep the name in memory of him. People thought that it was unlucky, but I had no problem with it, except that she needs a lot of maintenance.'

'Oh, is she safe ...?'

Nathan shrugged. 'Like any old wooden hull there can be quite a bit of rot, and the *Fearless* has her share of leaks ... and along with the engine, the pumps needed some work.' He smiled at the quizzical look on Archie's face. 'Don't worry, I've had plenty of time here to fix all of that, and she's safe in any sea.'

'OK, so when do we go?' asked Archie.

'With the water rising, we can leave now. Take a look here and I'll show you what you need to do. I usually manage this on my own, but it takes a lot longer. I have to guide the trolley a little further down the slipway into the water, and then you can join me when I give the signal.'

Leaving Archie to it, and with the tool bag on his shoulder, Nathan made his way down the slipway to the trolley. He climbed a short ladder he'd lashed to the boat guardrail and slung the bag over it onto the deck. Back on the slipway, he was ready to steer the trolley with a steel bar linked to the axle. He waved to Archie to start the cable drum rolling.

Archie moved the lever to the forward position, and pressed the green start button. The drum began to rotate very slowly, inching the cable down the slipway. On a couple of occasions he had to stop and restart the drum while Nathan worked the bar to manoeuvre the trolley down the last section of the slipway, as far as it would go into the water.

He waved to Archie to stop the drum, to give him some slack while he unhooked the cable, and then he gave the signal.

Archie left the winch house and hurried down the slipway, wading through thigh-deep water to reach the ladder and join him aboard *Fearless*.

'Well done,' said Nathan, lending him a hand. 'The water is rising fast and we'll be away quicker than I thought. Now, this is what I want you to do, while I attend the engine and steerage. When we are ready to float off, I'll give the word, and I want you to untie the short lines from the cleats to the trolley,'

'The what ...?' Archie looked around, unsure what he was meant to do.

Nathan pointed to a short, silver T-shaped fixture bolted to the deck, at the base of the guardrail. A line wound around it in a figure-8 was tied to one of the tall, girder-like side struts that supported the boat on the trolley.

'That's a cleat. We need to untie the lines before we can float free from the trolley. You'll need to be quick when I give you the call.'

For the next hour, or so, while they waited for the water to rise, Archie kept checking all the cleats to make certain he would be able to free the lines, without doing something stupid that would keep them tied to the trolley.

A flood of water filled the inlet more quickly than Nathan expected, urging him to get ready to leave the harbour. Archie's preparation paid off as he moved quickly around the deck to untie the lines, allowing Nathan to start the engine and take the *Fearless* into deeper water.

'That's it, Archie, we are on our way,' said Nathan, at the wheel inside the cabin, 'but I don't like the feel of the water – it's never been as rough as this in the inlet.'

Trying to keep his balance, Archie held onto a brass handle inside the door as a large wave poured over the side of the boat. 'I'm not sure, but I think there's been another tremor.'

Archie was right. A thunderous roar suddenly erupted behind him as tons of rock fell away from the cliff face onto the beach. He looked back towards the slipway as Nathan increased engine speed to take them away from the waves now pounding the shoreline. His mouth opened in astonishment when he saw the boatshed fly up into the sky: the roof, the walls, and all the stuff that Nathan had stored inside. It was like watching the scene in the movie, *The Wizard of Oz,* where the house was swept away by a cyclone.

'Oh, my God, look at that!' he cried, but Nathan was too busy to look. He was trying to keep *Fearless* stable in the rising waves as he made for the opening to take them out of the inlet and into the White Waters.

Chapter Sixty-Four

Escape From Copanatec

'Keep your head down,' warned Malcolm. He placed a hand on Kristin's shoulder, forcing her to stay on her knees beside him. 'We have to be careful, in case they are out there.'

After parting company with Archie outside the kitchen, they'd made their way up the lane into the farmlands to escape the Terogs. A narrow track through the cornfields brought them to a space where they now laid low, giving Malcolm a chance to watch the lane and anyone coming after them.

'Can you see anything?' whispered Kristin.

Malcolm held the ears of corn apart for another moment, then let them go. His leg pained him and he couldn't kneel for very long. He held his stick for support as he stretched himself slowly upright to gain a better view of the temple at the end of the lane. 'No, not a thing. The Terogs must have gone after Archie.'

Kristin stood up beside him. 'What are we going to do?'

'I don't know. Archie said he would try to find us, but what are the chances of that happening – and how long do we wait?' Malcolm sighed as he looked at the young girl staring at him, as if he had all the answers. Her face and red hair were covered in grey dust – but there was something else: a tear had slipped down her cheek to touch her lips. 'I'm sorry, Kristin, I know you haven't found your father ...' He hesitated, not able to think of the right thing to say to her.

She wiped the tear away and shook her head. 'No, it's not just that. It's Archie ... he saved my life and he's always tried to help me, so many times, and ...

well, I've never thanked him ... in fact, I've been really rude to him, and now I might never see him again.'

More tears came and she started to sob. Malcolm put an arm around her and held her close to his chest. He couldn't help smiling; he almost grinned at the absurdity of the situation he found himself in. They were in danger, lost in a strange world, and yet here he was, in the middle of a cornfield, trying to comfort a young girl who obviously had a crush on his son.

He looked across the top of the cornfield towards the lane, his eyes scanning the way they had come. He could see the temple in the distance, but there was no sign of anyone who might be following them. He turned and looked in the other direction, but it was hard to tell from their position in the cornfield where the lane might lead. Except for what looked like a barn, about a mile away, there were no other buildings. Hopefully, they would find shelter there, at least until he could figure out what they should do next.

'Kristin, it will be getting dark soon, and we need to find somewhere to rest for a while. There's a place up ahead of us that might do.'

He felt her shivering as she took a look to where he was pointing. Whether she was frightened or cold, he had no idea.

'I see it,' she said, 'but what about Archie, how will he find us?'

He pulled her closer to his side and gave her a hug. 'I don't know, Kristin, but I'll tell you this: I've lost one son, and I have no intention of losing another. Somehow, we'll meet up with Archie – I just don't know where.'

*

489

Han-Sin was leading the group away from the temple kitchen and into the lane, when they heard the dreadful roar, followed by the tremor that threw all of them to the ground.

But as quickly as the shock arrived, it stopped.

She rose slowly to her feet and looked behind to see that Chuck, who had been supporting the wounded Lancer, and the other Lancer who had taken a covering position to protect their rear, were shaken but seemed to be uninjured.

'Is everyone all right?'

Chuck checked the pad and bandage he had secured on the Lancer who had been hit in the shoulder by a crossbow bolt, during the fighting in the antechamber. He helped him onto his feet. 'We're OK.'

The other Lancer nodded the same.

'Good.' It was darker now, but as she looked back towards the temple she could see by the kitchen light and her paragun torchlight that part of the wall had collapsed. 'We have to get to the Spokestar as quickly as we can, before we run into any more trouble.'

They had fought their way out of the antechamber without further injury, with the Terogs scattering in panic when they saw their comrades atomised by the paraguns. But as they retreated from the temple, they had seen no sign of Archie, inside or outside the building.

'What are we going to do about Archie?' asked Chuck. 'We can't leave without him.'

'I understand your concern, but I'm afraid there will be more tremors that will trap us here – if not worse,' said Han-Sin. 'We must get back to the Spokestar and into the air. That way we will have a better chance of searching the island.'

Chuck realised she had to weigh her responsibility for the four of them, against the odds of finding Archie.

She was right about one thing, though: they were better in the air than on the ground, which was threating to explode under their feet at any moment.

But he was not about to give up on Archie just yet. He checked that the wounded Lancer's bandage and pad were secure, before they moved on. 'Well, there's no point in hanging around here, let's get moving.'

*

Although it was dark, the stars in this world cast a bright light, and with a only few wispy clouds overhead, Han-Sin was able to see quite clearly that one of the barn doors was partly open, wide enough to allow someone to enter. She was certain she had drawn the wooden bar across the front of the double-doors before they left. If there was someone in there, they would have been unable to secure the bar again from the inside

'What do you think?' asked Chuck.

He had spotted the open door as soon as they arrived, urging Han-Sin that they should take cover in a small copse of trees next to the lane, before approaching the barn. Their paragun torchlights were switched off and they were now deliberating what to do next when a noise from the barn caught their attention. Someone inside was pushing the open door outwards, as wide as it would go.

'Look!' whispered Han-Sin. She pointed to the other double-door, also opening wide. Two figures stepped outside to take a look back at the barn's interior.

'What are they up to?' Chuck was beginning to wonder if they were attempting to take the Spokestar, and said so to Han-Sin.

'Not unless they have the access code.'

Chuck nodded. 'Good, but I think we need to go and see what they're after, if we're going to get out of here, anyway soon. I suggest I go first and draw their attention, while you keep your eyes on the Spokestar, just in case there's someone else in there trying to break into it.'

It made sense to Han-Sin, so she agreed to let him take charge of the initial approach. She positioned the two Lancers on their rear flanks to cover them while she and Chuck advanced towards the barn. She hoped that the wounded Lancer was fit enough to engage in any skirmish they might get involved in; not knowing what they were up against, she had no choice but to use him.

Chuck studied the two figures: They didn't have the squat build of the Terogs, but in the poor light it was hard to tell who they might be. One was taller than the other, and seemed to be carrying some sort of weapon, pointed towards the ground. They both walked back inside the barn, giving Chuck and Han-Sin the opportunity to move forward unseen.

With their paraguns held ready, Han-Sin crept slowly to the open doors from the right, while Chuck took the left side. Switching on the paragun torchlights, they dashed into the barn, the Spokestar directly ahead of them, yelling at whoever was inside to drop their weapons and come forward. 'We are armed. Show yourselves, with your hands in the air.'

There was a terrified scream, and then a man's voice yelling back at them: 'We have no weapons! For God's sake, don't shoot!'

Chuck was startled by the voice. It sounded surprisingly like someone back on Old Earth. He and Han-Sin stepped aside from the open doors to avoid being easy targets. He called out again: ' Come out, *now!*'

He was even more startled when he saw the two figures appear out of the darkness behind the Spokestar into the beam of his torchlight. A man with a stocky build, about fifty years old, maybe sixty, stood before him, with one hand leaning on a stick and the other in the air. Beside him, the smaller one was much younger, perhaps fifteen, or so. They watched him nervously, eyes locked on his paragun. Both wore tunics and trousers streaked with dirt and grey dust, as if they had been living rough for a while.

Han-Sin swept her torchlight over them, demanding to know who they were: 'Who are you, and what are you doing here?'

'If you'll take that damned light out my eyes, I'll tell you,' said the man angrily.

Chuck nodded to Han-Sin: 'Let's go outside, it's a bit tight for space in here.'

The man limped out of the barn, using the stick for support, while the young one stayed close beside him. As he watched them pass by, it suddenly struck Chuck there was something different about the way the young one walked.

'It's a girl!' he said out loud.

'Good for you,' snapped the girl, turning to face him, 'but don't get any funny ideas!'

Chuck laughed. 'Well, you're a prickly one, young lady. What's your name?'

'What's it to you?'

Han-Sin interrupted their exchange, impatient to find out what their intentions were: 'Enough of this! I ask you again: Who are you, and what were you doing in there?'

Ignoring her, the man turned to Chuck. 'You're from Old Earth, aren't you? American, I would say.'

'Well, I'll be damned. I thought I recognised the accent. You're British?'

The man nodded. 'My name is Malcolm Kinross, and this young lady is Kristin. She's from Amasia –'

'Kinross!' Chuck stared at him, hardly believing his ears. 'You must be Archie's father ...'

*

Han-Sin banked the Spokestar and headed for the temple square. Once there, she would decide on a search pattern to find Archie. She felt a sense of relief to be in the air after the close quarters fighting in the temple, but she knew they were not free from danger while they stayed in Copanatec.

A few minutes earlier, she had listened to the story told by Malcolm – as he preferred to be called – of his arrival with Lucy, his wife, on Amasia, and their subsequent captivity at the hands of Talon and the Terogs. And then the disappearance of Lucy and his son, Richard; both of them supposedly to another dimension by means of the Chapac Stone. He told them of Archie's attempt to draw the Terogs away from Malcolm and Kristin at the temple, but he had no idea where Archie might be now.

He and Kristin had just discovered the barn and were opening the doors to have a better look at the Spokestar, when Chuck and Han-Sin surprised them. Malcolm had never seen anything like the scarlet flying machine, the design of which totally mystified him, although Kristin said she had seen one in the skies over Port Zolnayta.

Chuck, for his part, told him he was under orders from someone called Professor Strawbridge, to find Archie, which had amazed Malcolm, as the professor was his brother-in-law.

They had been anxious to learn much more from each other, but a sudden tremor had shaken the barn forcing them them to make a quick exit. In the air, away from the danger of more foreshocks, they felt a lot safer.

And now Han-Sin was flying them to the temple and the pyramid, in the desperate hope they might spot Archie somewhere on the ground.

A few minutes later she was hovering over the square, horrified by what she could see. There was death and carnage everywhere.

Black smoke was rising from a fissure that had opened across the square, snaking a hot lava passage from the gorge to the harbour seawall, creating hills of rock and rubble on either side of the fiery chasm. Sections of the temple building had collapsed into the square, trapping survivors between the temple and the fissure. She couldn't hear the screams of the people, but she could imagine the hell they were going through, trying to escape the inevitable destruction of the island.

Malcolm had the same thought. 'God help those people down there. How in Heaven's name can they be saved?'

'I fear it may be too late,' said Han-Sin, 'but I have sent an emergency signal with the island coordinates to Sunstone at Castle Zolnayta. I have requested help to try and evacuate the survivors.'

Chuck shook his head. 'Better late than never, I suppose, but how do you propose to do it? There are hundreds, maybe thousands, needing evacuation. Do you have bigger aircraft than this to do the job?'

'No, these are the latest and biggest Spokestars we have: Mark 8s – perhaps twelve squadrons covering Amasia.'

'How many in a squadron?'

'Twenty.'

Chuck did a quick calculation: Excluding the pilot, each one could carry seven passengers; multiplied by twelve squadrons of twenty, it would add up to over sixteen hundred – if they were all available. 'That could make a difference,' he admitted. 'I only hope there are no more earthquakes before they arrive.'

'Foreshocks,' corrected Malcolm. 'So far, what we have experienced here were foreshocks, and they were very likely warnings of something much bigger to come – like a major earthquake.'

'How many foreshocks before something like that happens?' Chuck looked down at the square, wondering how much worse it could get.

'It's impossible to say. Some of the experts I've worked with on digs around such ancient catastrophes, have suggested up to as many as twenty, or more, over as many hours.'

'And we still have to find Archie,' interrupted Kristin impatiently. She was sitting in a rear seat next to the wounded Lancer. 'How are we going to do that from up here?'

Malcolm smiled. She doesn't waste words when she wants to make a point, he thought.

Before anyone could answer her, there was an almighty roar as the temple exploded. Seconds later, something hit the underside of the Spokestar, sounding an alarm inside the cockpit as they suddenly lost height.

They dropped nearly a hundred feet before Han-Sin regained control. 'Is everyone all right?' she asked, cancelling the alarm and checking the instrument panel for problems.

Chuck looked around the cabin. They all looked a bit shocked, but otherwise they seemed OK. 'What the hell happened?' It was a question he didn't need to ask: he could see for himself what was happening as they zoomed away from the square and over the seawall out to sea.

Han-Sin banked slightly and then levelled the Spokestar, as she tried to maintain height, giving all of them a few seconds to see the island.

It was horrendous.

The 'big one' had arrived, opening a gigantic fissure across the heart of the city, crashing through the floor of the temple, spewing tons of marble and glass into the sky – a chunk of which had hit the Spokestar. Beyond the gorge, the tunnels had imploded bringing down the pyramid in a colossal cloud of smoke and dust that would spread across Copanatec. The seawall had collapsed, while in the harbour some of the boats commandeered by citizens and Terogs trying to flee the city, were engulfed in a whirlpool of boiling water.

'Oh, my God!' gasped Malcolm, as another fiery explosion lit the night. 'What are we going to do about Archie?'

The Spokestar shuddered as it suddenly lost height. Han-Sin pointed the nose away from the island as she struggled to maintain control.

Chuck stared down at a turbulent sea throwing up ridges of white water. He said, 'We're very low, are we in trouble?'

'I don't know how bad it is. Whatever hit us has damaged the vallonium drive,' said Han-Sin.

'Which means ...?

'We're losing height. Which means we have to get to Amasia as quickly as possible ... if we don't want to end up in the White Waters.'

'No! What about Archie?' Kristin screamed at Malcolm.

He didn't answer. He knew that Copanatec, and perhaps all life, was being destroyed by monumental forces beyond their power to deal with.

'I'm sorry, but I have no choice,' said Han-Sin. 'There are six of us, and I can't risk our lives for one – who may already be lost.'

*

Captain Abelhorn had known that something bad was about to happen. He still felt it in his gut as he stood by Orlof in the wheelhouse as they approached the churning waters of the open sea. Several boats still tied to the quayside were beginning to pitch while men panicked to free the lines. It was the foreshock in the square that had frightened them, and he felt that there was worse yet to come. Years at sea in the worst of conditions had honed his instincts to the point where he rarely ignored them, but he was caught between searching for Kristin and Archie and risking the *Serpent* and her crew; if he lost the *Serpent*, then none of them would escape the island.

The *Serpent* wallowing in the harbour water, straining at her moorings like a nervous thoroughbred ready to bolt out of its stall, was the early warning that made up his mind. It was a decision he felt he would regret the rest of his life.

He had ordered Roni, who had recovered from his fall near the seawall during the foreshock, and Jess, one of the other fishermen from Elam, onto the quayside to cast the lines off to make ready to leave the harbour. Yet every single moment hauling the lines and fenders on board as they left the quayside had been filled with doubt. He had been prepared to reverse his decision, given any encouragement to do so by the crew. But all of them knew that Copanatec was doomed and were only too relieved to escape the island.

Including the stowaway who had managed to slip on board without being seen.

Chapter Sixty-Five

The White Waters

The air was heavy and wet as *Fearless* slid in and out of the troughs. A gale force wind whistled across the deck as twenty-foot waves poured over the open wheelhouse cockpit and its occupants. The wind-driven rain would reach Copanatec to fall on the newly created fissure and its gases, triggering more explosions that would be heard across the White Waters.

Nathan remembered telling Archie that *Fearless* was safe in any sea, but now he was beginning to wonder as he ploughed down into another trough and then up and over a wall of green water. Ever since leaving the boatshed harbour the heavy sea had been relentless in its efforts to send them to the ocean floor, and there was no sign of it easing.

It was then that he saw something large floating in the water directly ahead of them as he crested another wave. Although the night was hardly gone, there was enough early light to see that they had no chance of avoiding a collision.

He yelled: 'Hold on tight, Archie!'

Archie instinctively reached out for the grab rail at the side of the wheelhouse as a deafening bang seemed to explode directly below him. A sudden shudder threw the boat over onto its side for several long moments as she, agonisingly, slowly righted herself, before crashing over another wave and sliding into what seemed to be a stretch of calmer water. The huge waves and gale force winds had subsided, replaced by a relatively flat sea and warm breeze.

Still holding onto the grab rail, Archie felt, and probably looked, like a half-drowned rat, but he was more worried that the boat was about to sink and that he would become a fully-drowned rat. *Fearless* was shuddering and screeching, but seemed to be making little headway. He looked to Nathan staring intently through the glass at the bow, one hand on the wheel, the other on the throttle.

'What's happened to us?' asked Archie. 'Is the storm over?'

'I'm not rightly sure what we went through was all down to a storm,' said Nathan. 'There were more explosions on the island, and I think there must have been a big one. It may have affected the weather and kept us out of the harbour.'

The sudden tremors on the island had caused the water conditions in the harbour to change dramatically. Leaving Nathan with no other choice, but to take *Fearless* out to sea for fear of being dashed to pieces on the rocks. He had hoped that conditions would improve, allowing them to make the attempt to enter Copanatec harbour later, to find Kristin and Archie's father. But it was obvious that the Destruction had returned to Copanatec, leaving little hope of finding anyone on the island.

There was more screeching and another shudder. Nathan throttled back and killed the engine.

'Stay here. I have to take a look outside.'

'What are you going to do?'

'We've hit something. I have to make sure we haven't been holed. This an old boat, propeller driven, and it sounds as if it may be caught in some sea rubbish. *Fearless* is not like the more modern boats with their vallonium drives.'

He made his way up to the bow and leaned over the side to take a look at the hull. The early dawn light made it easier to see if there was any damage, but he couldn't be sure. He returned to the cockpit to check the stern and the rest of the hull.

'Did you see anything?' asked Archie.

'We've hit another boat – or what's left of it. Take a look for yourself. We're pretty much in the middle of it and, as far as I can tell, there's an old line wrapped around our propeller.'

Archie cast his eyes over the water and saw what he took to be the wreckage of another boat floating just below the surface. A large piece of wooden decking was lying directly below the hull; a rubber boot and a jacket floated alongside with a couple of empty glass bottles; and at the stern, a tangle of boat line was swirling around in the water.

He didn't like the look of the wreckage. It gave him a tingly feeling that ran up his spine, telling him that it could easily be them floating there.

He shivered at the thought and turned to face Nathan: 'Is there anything we can do?'

Nathan pointed towards the bow. 'There's a boat hook lashed below the guardrail. Just loosen the ties and fetch it here.'

A few minutes later Nathan was standing on a narrow step at the stern outside the guardrail, prodding the water with the boat hook.

'If this doesn't work, Archie, I'm going to have to go in and do this by hand.'

The hook caught the line and he started to pull gently, coaxing it to the surface. But the propeller was out of reach under the hull and there was no way he could manoeuvre the boat hook anywhere near it. The line had snagged and wouldn't shift.

He handed the boat hook back to Archie. 'Here, take this. I'll have to go in to free the line.'

He was already wet through, but he stripped down to his trunks, before entering the water. Clutching a knife he kept near the wheel, he dived under the hull and saw the problem straight away. Part of the line was wrapped around the prop shaft and blades, but a few cuts of the razor sharp knife and the line drifted away.

Back on board, he keyed the ignition and tested the propeller, keeping an eye on the wreckage. He said: 'Keep a watch around the stern for any more rubbish. Give me a shout as soon as we're out of it.'

Once he was satisfied they were clear, he set the throttle to low and handed the wheel to Archie. 'Just watch the compass and hold her on this course until I get us some dry clothes.'

He pulled some dry gear from a cabin locker and dressed quickly, before taking over the wheel again and increasing the throttle speed. He pointed to a sweater and trousers he'd left on the cockpit seat. 'Put those on. They're old, but they'll keep the chill out.'

Archie threw his wet stuff into the cabin and donned the dry clothes. He had been shivering in the early dawn breeze and appreciated the cosy warmth of the thick sweater, even though it smelt of oil and wood dust.

As they chugged away from the wreckage, he stood beside Nathan, watching the waves rise and crash over the bow. 'It seems to be getting rough again.'

'We're in the White Waters, Archie. This is a strange and unpredictable sea that my father warned me against on many occasions. You see what we have come through: heavy seas one minute, and then calm the next. But much of it, I think, is due to the nature of the land of Copanatec, above and below the waters. As we have just seen, some have ventured here and never returned.'

Nathan was silent for a while, and Archie guessed that he was thinking of himself and Kristin.

And what about dad? he wondered.

Would he ever see either of them again? Would it be possible to go back to Copanatec to try and find them?

Or maybe they had found a way to escape from the island? He felt angry and frustrated at not being able to do something, instead of being stuck on a boat in the middle of this crazy sea.

He jumped as he felt Nathan's grip on his shoulder. 'Take the wheel, Archie, and keep holding this course.'

'What's wrong?'

'I have to go below. We may have a problem.'

Nathan disappeared into the cabin, before Archie could ask what he meant.

Archie held the wheel as *Fearless* dipped in and out of the shallow troughs of white foam pouring over the bow. What was it Nathan was worried about? What could be down below that would cause a problem?

He had his answer when Nathan came back to the wheel.

'We have a leak, Archie. There's water coming into the bilge – not much, but it will get worse if it's not fixed.'

*

Captain Abelhorn stood outside the wheelhouse door, watching Roni and his friends secure the hatches. The wolftan lay at his feet at the top of the companionway, indifferent to the activity taking place below.

'Look at them, Bran. I went to find Kristin; instead, I leave Copanatec with people I don't know. I should be grateful, I suppose, that I was able to save them from the horrors they suffered on that island, but never to see my granddaughter again ....' He shook his head at the thought and turned his gaze out to sea.

Moments earlier, even at this distance from Copanatec, he'd heard another explosion over the wind that shrieked past the wheelhouse. A deep sadness seeped through him as he thought about the fate that awaited the people left behind on the island. He wanted to turn back, but he knew he could not risk the lives of the people now on the *Serpent* in a futile attempt to save Kristin and Archie.

Roni and his friends, Daros, Jess and Luca, were securing the hatches by stretching nets over the covers, to prevent breaking waves flooding the holds. It was fortunate they were seamen and needed little encouragement to work quickly and batten down anything that might be lost to a raging sea. The others from the square he had ordered to stay below in the galley where Daniel would provide them with some food.

Abelhorn turned round when he heard Orlof calling to him.

He entered the wheelhouse. 'What is it?'

Orlof pointed to the starboard side beyond the bow, to a rolling wall of green water. 'I saw something out there, Captain. It might be another boat like ourselves, out of Copanatec.'

Abelhorn peered through the glass at the waves rolling from starboard to port. 'I can't see a thing, but keep a watch in case there are some poor souls out there.'

*

Archie did his best to keep the wheel from spinning out of control, but his fingers ached and were almost numb with cold. Thudding waves were forcing the bow deeper into the trough as he reached for the throttle, hoping that they would climb out and over the next wave. Nathan had told him to try and take the waves at an angle, to avoid burying the bow at the bottom of the oncoming waves. So far he had been fortunate to come out of each trough safely, but he was terrified that the next wave would sink them.

Nathan had the abject look of someone contemplating defeat as he climbed out of the cabin and into the cockpit. He had been below the boards in the cabin working at the bilge pump trying to get rid of the water coming in through the damaged hull.

'We're in trouble, Archie. The pump no longer works, not even when I try it manually.'

Archie gripped the wheel as they crested another wave. 'Isn't there anything you can do to fix it?'

Nathan shook his head. 'It's an automatic pump. When I switched it to manual, I thought that would work, but there is something wrong with it. It may have been damaged when we hit the wreckage; and, as far as I can tell, the leak in the hull is getting worse. I've tried to patch it, but the water pressure is too great and its likely to give way any minute.'

'What are we going to do?'

'I'm afraid we will have to abandon *Fearless*.'

Archie turned his head to stare at him. 'You can't be serious! How can we leave her in this sea?'

'There is a small inflatable raft up forward we must use,' said Nathan, pointing towards the bow. 'I'm sorry, Archie, but it is the only chance we have. The patch won't hold and when that happens the hull will split open and *Fearless* will sink. If we don't use the raft quickly, we will not survive.'

Chapter Sixty-Six

Cosimo's Revenge

There were six small cabins and a galley in the narrow passageway below the wheelhouse. One of the cabins was used to store various items of clothing, life jackets and assorted pieces of equipment, much of it piled in heaps on the two bunk beds and on the cabin floor. Some of it had been pushed roughly to one side to make space for the lone occupant now sitting on the edge of the lower bunk; his head supported by both hands as he stared at the locked door, his mind in a black rage as he contemplated all that had happened to him since arriving in this new world.

He was Anton Cosimo, the new leader of the rebel Arnaks and a fugitive on the run from the Lancers, who no doubt, would love to get their hands on him for killing one of their own. How did it come to this? he wondered. To find himself on a fishing vessel, trapped in a small cabin, hardly bigger than a broom cupboard, cowering like a cornered animal hiding from the Lancers.

After escaping from the temple, he had left the Terogs to their fate; with Talon and Kanga gone, he no longer had any use for the pig-like brutes. As for the band of rebels he had brought with him to Copanatec, they had been killed, almost certainly by the Lancers; although he was mystified by how they had tracked him to the island.

And what of Nitkin, his rebel Arnak lieutenant, whom he had ordered to capture the Kinross boy. Had he succeeded, or were they both now dead?

When he reached the temple square and saw the devastation caused by the smoking fissure and the mob of people pushing and shoving, grabbing at anyone and everyone, begging for help, he realised that the island was doomed. His only hope of escape lay in finding a boat before Copanatec and its people disappeared into the sea, into oblivion like the legendary Atlantis.

Stumbling across one of the many bodies lying in the square, he donned the man's cape and hood as a precaution against being recognised. Pulling the hood tight around his head he reached the seawall without any more difficulty. On the quayside, men and women were pleading to board the few remaining boats about to leave the harbour, including the slave vessel, but only one, the *Serpent*, had its gangway still extended to allow a few more people on board. He'd seen his chance, brutally forcing an old man and a girl to the ground as he elbowed his way past them, to join a small group on the gangway, just as it was hauled in quickly, leaving the remaining people on the quayside to find another boat.

Once out of the harbour, the captain had ordered all of them into the passageway cabins and the galley; to stay out of harm's way, while the *Serpent* tested its passage through the White Waters. However, Cosimo had his own way of doing things. He forced his way into an empty cabin, making it clear it to the others, by gripping one of the men by the throat, that he was not prepared to share it. No one objected. They were already terrified by what had happened to them on Copanatec; and this man had obviously been driven mad by the Destruction, so they said nothing.

Cosimo spent his time in the cabin, his anger rising until blood-hot, thinking of all those who had failed him. Whenever his plans to gain power and fortune suffered defeat, he never once considered that *he* might be responsible for such a failure. There was always someone else to blame. He was ruthless: capable of killing anyone who got in his way and treacherous if it suited his purpose – and yet, none of these dubious traits had brought him the success he so desperately craved.

He knew, of course, that the Kinross brothers were nothing more than an irritant, but somehow they were always involved in his recent misfortunes, and for that alone he would kill them. The very thought of the pleasure he would feel in killing them eased his black mood, if only for a few moments.

Someone yelling and then the sound of boots stomping past the cabin door interrupted his reverie. Curious, he opened the door to see a man rushing from the galley towards the open steel door leading out onto the deck.

Worried that the boat might be in danger, Cosimo threw the cape over his shoulders and followed the man outside. He saw him join another and race to a long flat box, halfway along the deck next to the hatches. They unclasped the cover and started to feed what looked like some sort of net over the side of the boat. As he watched the net drop down to the sea he was astonished to see they were approaching another boat, trying to come alongside.

*

It was Orlof who spotted the *Fearless*. He pointed to the starboard side as they ploughed through the waves of a wind-driven sea. 'I was right! There *is* a boat out there!'

'Where?' asked Abelhorn. He stepped outside to avoid looking through the salt-smeared glass of the wheelhouse. The light was better now and he could see the boat Orlof had seen minutes earlier. 'My God, I don't believe it!'

The unpredictable sea conditions of the White Waters were beginning to slacken to a swell, and he could see that the boat was sinking, its bow lower than the stern, obviously taking in water. It was a fishing boat he would know anywhere.

It was the *Fearless* and Nathan was on it, waving frantically.

He called to Orlof: 'She's foundering, try and stay with her. I'm going to call Daniel from the galley to give me a hand with the rescue net.'

Roni with his friends, Daros, Jess and Luca, had just finished securing the nets over the hatches, when he heard the captain shouting to him: 'Get some lifelines ready, now!'

Abelhorn and Daniel were at each end of the long box containing the rescue net, unrolling it while the weighted end allowed the net to drop free and flat against the hull until it entered the water.

Daniel checked to see how near they were to *Fearless*. 'She's nearly with us, Captain, but the sea's still bleedin' rough.'

Abelhorn turned as Roni handed him a lifeline with a harness attached. 'Is it secured?'

Roni pointed to a deck cleat. 'It's well secured.'

'Good man. Get another two ready. Daniel, put this one on and get yourself over the side, they're going to need a hand to reach the net. When the *Fearless* is close enough, we'll throw the other lifelines over to them.'

Daniel looked at him. 'Captain, I've never done anything like this –'

Abelhorn raised his hand before he could finish. 'Daniel, you'll be all right, but something you should know ... it's my son, Nathan, on that boat. He, and whoever is down there with him, will need all the help we can give them.'

'Nathan? But how –'

'Enough, Daniel! There's no time for questions. The stabilisers will help with the swell, but we have to work quickly before the weather turns against us.'

Abelhorn waved to Orlof to draw closer while he kept an eye on *Fearless*. Roni beside him, was ready with the lifelines, coiled to throw as soon as the distance narrowed between the two boats.

Wave after wave crashed below Daniel's feet as he held tight to the net, watching nervously as *Fearless* bobbed up and down, drawing close enough for him to see that Nathan was ready with a boat hook to grab the net. Suddenly the swell lifted the boat close enough for Daniel to get a hand on the hook and guide it onto the net until it held fast. He heard someone shouting and looked up to see Roni leaning over the side ready to throw a lifeline.

Nathan also saw him and waved that he was ready to take it. He yelled to Archie, standing next to the wheel out of Daniel's sight, to get ready to grab the harness. 'Put it on and get onto the net as quick as you can. We don't have much time left before we go under.'

No sooner had he fastened the harness, Archie felt the boat tip forward, throwing him off balance. The cockpit was filling with water as a wave slammed it against the net. He jumped, his heart thumping wildly as he sensed the emptiness of space below his feet. A moment later he felt the pull on the lifeline and Daniel's outstretched hand hauling him onto the net.

'Bleedin' hell, mate, you're the last person I expected to see!'

Archie couldn't help grinning when he saw the look of shock on Daniel's face, but before he could say anything the roar of another wave pounding the side of the *Serpent* warned they had little time left.

'Get up there, Archie, quickly! I have to get Nathan over here now – the boat's going down!'

As he climbed the net, with Roni above keeping him secure with the lifeline, Archie looked down to see that Nathan had also made it to the net. *Fearless* was almost gone; only its stern could be seen slipping under the rolling waves.

*

Some of the refugees from Copanatec watching the drama of the two men being rescued from the fishing boat, cheered as they climbed on board. Daros who had been close to the rescue net joined them. 'It would have been certain death in that sea if we hadn't found them,' he said, pointing to the sea. 'Look – their boat is gone!'

One of the villagers in the group agreed: 'It's a miracle – not many are saved from the White Waters.'

Daros pointed to a man with long, thick white hair pushed under a flat peaked cap, hugging one of the two men. 'That's Captain Abelhorn with his son who had been thought lost in these waters many years ago.' He smiled as he nodded to the other one. 'And the young man is someone who worked with me in the tunnels. I never thought I would see him again.'

Standing aside from them, Cosimo raged at what they said. Once again, the Kinross boy, *the brat*, had escaped a fate he deserved; and now here he was being welcomed like a hero!

At that moment, something snapped inside Cosimo. A swirling, black mist seemed to appear before him, and all he could see, somewhere in the middle of it, was the face and neck of Archie Kinross. His hands reached out to grip the brat.

He knew what he had to do.

Striding forward, his hood and cape billowing in the wind now whipping across the deck, Cosimo felt the strength of a dozen men inside him as he swept Daros and the villagers out of his way. He knew no one could stop him as he approached the brat and the others around him.

Daniel heard the angry shouts behind him and looked round to see what was wrong. Some of the people from Copanatec had gathered near the wheelhouse during the rescue, but one of them was lying on the deck and another on his knees holding the side of his head. In front of them was an ominous black figure, his cape flying in the wind behind him, rushing towards Daniel and Archie.

'Bleedin' heck, here comes Batman!' cried Daniel.

Archie turned from speaking to Captain Abelhorn to see what Daniel meant. 'It's him! Cosimo!'

Abelhorn looked startled. 'Who?'

'The one at Castle Zolnayta I told you about. He tried to kill me!'

They were standing between the rescue net and one of the hatches. Archie jumped up onto the net-covered hatch, but Cosimo was too quick. He was on Archie in an instant, grabbing his foot to bring him down. Daniel tried to help by grabbing Cosimo's cape and pulling him away from the hatch, but he only succeeded in ripping the cape off his shoulders.

Daniel fell back into the arms of Abelhorn and Nathan who were stunned by the suddenness of the attack. But they realised the danger to Archie and they all quickly climbed onto the hatch to help him. Roni, Jess and Luca, terrified by the devil who seemed to have appeared out of nowhere, had retreated to the safety of the next hatch, wondering how to deal with a monster that could throw men away like leaves in the wind.

Cosimo, his eyes blazing with the zeal of a madman, held Archie by the scruff of his neck, dangling him like a trophy on the end of an outstretched arm.

Abelhorn, Nathan and Daniel leapt on him at the same time, making him release Archie, but Cosimo possessed the strength of a mad bull. He threw all of them aside like rag dolls. Daniel's head struck the edge of the hatch and he fell away unconscious. Nathan was similarly stunned when he rolled over onto the deck, and with a heavy sea now breaking over the side, he was unable to gain his feet.

Cosimo grabbed Archie again, screaming that he would kill him, but he didn't see Abelhorn crawling up behind him. Using the hatch net to give his feet a firm grip, Abelhorn flung himself forward, wrapping his arms tightly around Cosimo's legs to force him off his feet. But Cosimo was too strong. Leaving Archie, he turned round and with enormous strength lifted Abelhorn above his head, threatening to throw him over the side into the sea.

*

Up in the wheelhouse, unable to leave the wheel, Orlof had watched the incredible events at the rescue net, and now he could hardly believe what he was witnessing on the hatch: the desperate attempts of Captain Abelhorn and the others to save Archie from the brutal acts of a maniac.

Where had he come from?

There was no time to think about that – he had to do something quickly – but what? Only Roni and the other seamen were near him, but they seemed to be at a loss on what to do.

The hairs on his neck stood up as he heard the dreadful, deep belly roar of an angry wolftan. Bran had

513

been lying asleep at the back of the wheelhouse, but now he stood at the top of the companionway, glaring fixedly at Cosimo; three little pointed ears, each situated in a shell of pink flesh on either side of his long narrow head, were twitching in the cold, damp air.

Orlof nodded. 'Yes, it's your master, Bran. He's in trouble.'

Bran growled as if he understood what Orlof had just said. Then in a flash he was gone. His great size and fearsome appearance would terrify the refugees below the wheelhouse as he flew over their heads, but he had no interest in them, only the dark figure holding his master.

Cosimo had only an instant to see Bran before the huge beast had him by the shoulder and chest in its gaping maw. Abelhorn fell from his hands to land beside Archie who was rubbing the bruises on his neck and still feeling a little dazed. They both looked up as Cosimo's screams pierced the air. Bran had sunk his razor-sharp, yellow fangs deep into Cosimo's flesh and was angrily shaking him from side to side as he pulled him away from the hatch.

Archie, Abelhorn, Daniel and Nathan had all, more or less, recovered, and with the others on deck they watched in horror as Bran, with one final bite and shake of the head, flung Anton Cosimo over the side of the *Serpent* into the turbulent White Waters. They stood in silence, not knowing what to say.

'God, that was awful!' said Archie, the first to speak. His neck felt raw and he was aching from head to toe, but the pain was temporarily offset by the shock of what he had just seen Bran do to Cosimo.

'Maybe so, but whoever he was, he brought the end upon himself, and I'll not blame Bran for saving us from a similar fate,' said Abelhorn, as he led them to the galley. 'I think we have all had enough excitement for one day, and I, for one, would like a little something to warm me up for the journey to Port Zolnayta.'

Chapter Sixty-Seven

Aristo's News

Two weeks later a group of people sat around the long wooden table in the kitchen at Portview Terrace. A lunch of grilled fish and steamed vegetables had been prepared by Captain Abelhorn's part time housekeeper, Mrs Flint. As plates were cleared from the table by Kristin, Abelhorn watched with a sense of deep satisfaction as Nathan poured glasses of the Sticklejuice Reserve for those who preferred something a little stronger than water to complete the meal.

In spite of all his fears that he had lost Kristin, as well as Nathan, to forces beyond his comprehension, both of them had been returned to him, safe and sound. He was neither a superstitious man, like many of his seafaring brethren, nor a religious believer, like the few in Amasia who still held true to the old ways, but in his own way he knew he had to give thanks to whatever powers did exist, and their representatives who sat at his table.

Malcolm accepted his drink and took a sip. 'Thank you, Captain, that was an excellent meal.'

'I'm glad you enjoyed it, Malcolm. I will pass on your appreciation to Mrs Flint, for I have to admit, she gets little enough thanks from me. But it is I who have to thank you for all that you did for Kristin –'

'And don't forget Archie, Papa!' Kristin was clearing the last of the dishes from the table to the sink, when she stopped for a moment in front of her grandfather. 'If it hadn't been for Archie, I wouldn't be here!'

A ripple of laughter went round the table. Kristin, as ever, was her usual outspoken self, always ready to let her opinion be known.

Smiling at Kristin, Archie was embarrassed, but it made him feel good at how she spoke up for him. 'I don't know about that. But I am glad that dad was around to get the two of you out of Copanatec.'

'I think you need to give Captain Han-Sin and the Lancers credit for that, Archie,' said Malcolm. 'Without them, who knows what would have happened to us.'

The table went quiet as they thought about the Lancers and the part they played in the evacuation of the villagers from the island. Han-Sin had sent out an emergency call to Castle Zolnayta for support and Sunstone had responded by sending every available Lancer and Spokestar to Copanatec.

The first Spokestar to arrive over the island had reported fires everywhere they looked, making it difficult to land. It was a holocaust. A volcanic fissure had appeared in the gorge, reopening like an old wound, spewing out its fiery basaltic material along the length of its sides, with more fissures spreading outwards across the island, creating ridges of flaming rock.

Hundreds of villagers were saved, but many more died along with Copanatecs and Terogs in the great abyss, as Copanatec finally yielded to the tectonic forces tearing it apart. Only the Spokestars and a few boats, including the *Serpent,* made it to Amasia. The few survivors they had managed to save were eventually returned to the villages they were taken from.

Abelhorn nodded to Malcolm. 'Yes, we must give thanks to the Lancers, and now we must help the people who have been returned to their homes and families, to rebuild their lives.

'Yes, and I have to thank you, Father, for saving us from a watery grave. I don't think Archie and I would

517

have survived very long if the *Serpent* hadn't arrived to pull us out of the White Waters,' said Nathan, pouring himself another drop of Sticklejuice.

"It was a bleedin' miracle we saw the *Fearless*, mate, and if you'd spent any more time trying to bring that bag of yours with you, we'd both be sea bait waiting for a big bite,' grumbled Daniel.

Abelhorn looked quizzically at Daniel, and then to Nathan. 'What is this bag he talks about?'

'I'm sorry, Daniel, but I had no choice. I left Zolnayta and my family on a venture to seek a lost treasure, but I was tricked by a man I trusted, and ended up in the tunnels for my foolishness.' Nathan looked to Kristin, sadness clouding his eyes. 'They were precious years I lost, unable to see my daughter or care for her, and I ask forgiveness for that. But I did find something there I could not leave behind.'

'It must have been something special to go back into a sinking boat, mate.' said Daniel.

He vividly remembered the scene. As soon as Archie had made it safely to the top of the rescue net and then hauled on board by Roni, Nathan had left the boat hook hanging free on the net to drop back into the cockpit of the *Fearless,* now rapidly filling with water. Grabbing the bag and slinging it over his head and shoulder, he had leapt onto the net to grab Daniel's outstretched hand. But at the very moment Daniel was securing Nathan's lifeline, a huge wave slammed into the side of the *Serpent*, almost taking the two of them down with the *Fearless* as it disappeared below the surface of the White Waters. But the lifelines had held and they made it to the deck, only to be confronted by the madman, Cosimo.

'What could be so special that you would risk your life again?' asked Abelhorn angrily. 'Had you not suffered enough? And we too, after waiting for four years for you to come back to us?'

Nathan stood up. 'I said I am sorry for my foolishness, Father, but I have something in my room I must show you, and perhaps all of you will understand why I took such a risk.'

Before anyone could ask him anymore questions, Nathan left the kitchen and went upstairs to his room.

*

A couple of minutes later after Nathan left, Bran growled from his place at Abelhorn's feet. His ears flickered as he padded slowly across the tiled floor to the kitchen door, waiting for someone to come through.

'What is it, Bran?' asked Abelhorn.

The door led to the hallway and the front entrance, as well as the staircase to the upper floors. The lower steps creaked loudly when stepped on, but Archie hadn't heard Nathan come down again.

The door opened. It wasn't Nathan; it was someone he hadn't expected to see in Port Zolnayta.

'Aristo!'

A young man in his early twenties, with smooth olive skin and close cropped golden hair, dressed in the uniform of the TRU – the Timecrack Research Unit – entered the kitchen. His grey eyes, touched with a hint of green, quickly scanned the room, before he spoke.

'Archie! Malcolm! It is so good to see you again. Oh, I am sorry – '

Aristo was stopped by Bran,sniffing and pushing him with its great head until his back was against the doorjamb.

'Bran! Hold there!' called Abelhorn. He stared at the intruder. 'You obviously know my guests, but who in thunder are you?'

519

Archie couldn't help grinning as Aristo, unable to move past Bran, tried to explain his presence to Abelhorn.

Malcolm, feeling sorry for Aristo, quickly cut in. 'Captain Abelhorn, this is Aristo, a friend of Archie's from the Timecrack Research Unit at Mount Tengi. We met just over a week ago, when I visited Dr Shah and his associates there, to put forward certain proposals on behalf of myself and Archie. I'm rather hoping Aristo has some news for us.'

'Captain Abelhorn, please accept my apologies for this unannounced intrusion. I did knock several times, but there was no answer,' said Aristo. He tried to slide away from the wolftan as the great beast nuzzled its nose against his chest, but he couldn't move an inch. 'I could hear voices coming from here, so I'm afraid I took the liberty of coming in.'

Abelhorn smiled at the young man's discomfort and gestured that he should join them at the table. 'Let the poor fellow go, Bran.' He grinned at Aristo. 'I'd forgotten you were the one flying that machine when Isula's men on the dockside were shooting at you.'

'Thank you, sir,' said Aristo, greatly relieved that the wolftan had returned to his place by Abelhorn.

'Here, I think you need a drink.' Abelhorn passed him a glass with a generous measure of Sticklejuice.

'No, I don't –' Aristo tried to protest that he was on official duty and couldn't drink alcoholic beverages.

Feeling a little guilty at Aristo's reception, Abelhorn wouldn't hear of it and pushed the glass across the table towards him.

'Nonsense! You're a guest in my home, so drink up and relax, and tell us your news.'

'Yes, it's good to see you in good health,' said Malcolm. 'I'm sorry we only met briefly, but before

Chuck returned to the Facility he told me you were seriously wounded in a battle with Terogs?'

'Yes, that's true, and if it had not been for Chuck, I might not be here with you today.'

After their rescue from Copanatec, Malcolm and Kristin, along with Han-Sin, the Lancers and Chuck, had flown directly to Castle Amasia to a meeting of the Elders convened by Dr Shah and Dr Krippitz. It was during the flight that Malcolm learned from Chuck all that had happened since his and Lucy's disappearance from the dig in the Yucatan: the extensive searches carried out through the jungles to find them, to no avail; Professor Strawbridge's continuing attempts to find out exactly what had happened at the dig; and in the many months following their parents' disappearance, the care for Archie and Richard which the professor had provided.

Unfortunately, on one of their school holiday visits to the Facility, a timecrack had struck the DONUT, accidentally transporting the boys and their tutor, Marjorie, and the professor, to Amasia. There was a great deal more that happened to the boys while in Timeless Valley, which Malcolm was staggered to learn when he visited Dr Shah and some of the Elders at Mount Tengi, and from Aristo who had been delegated to look after him during his visit.

In turn, the small group of Elders who supported Dr Shah's programme of exploring the benefits of inter-dimensional travel, were anxious to hear of Malcolm's experiences while on Copanatec. Somehow, they felt the knowledge he had gained about the Lords of the Cloud – of whom they knew little, except the superstitious rumours that drifted throughout the villages of the southern districts of Amasia – and the savage Terogs, whose reputation they did know. All of this, on top of the recent outbreak of terrorist outrages by rebel Arnaks, greatly concerned them.

The eastern seaboard and all the land bordered by the great Pirangas mountain range to the west was known to New Arrivals as Timeless Valley, so-called because of its citizens' reputation for longevity. The valley was also valued for its sources of vallonium ore, the backbone of Amasia's limitless energy programme. It was a land of immense promise and riches, but many of the more conservative Elders were in disagreement as to how the land should be governed.

All the Elders, representing the tribes of Amasia – known to the ancients as Hazaranet – usually convened at the Meeting House, but the more progressive members in support of Dr Shah's plans to be able to reverse the results of timecracks, by sending undesirable New Arrivals back to their points of origin, had agreed to meet at Mount Tengi.

The upshot of the meetings and the in-depth discussions which followed, covered Malcolm's decision to stay in Amasia and pursue archaeological research on New Earth. In conjunction with his work and knowledge of Old Earth societies, it was expected he would help Dr Shah and his colleagues better understand the needs of New Arrivals.

The fascinating and exciting prospect for Malcolm was that while time travel was not a practical proposition within one dimension, it was possible *between* dimensions, creating unbelievable opportunities for research by visiting the actual sites in antiquity.

But it was not the only reason for his decision to stay in Amasia.

Shortly after his meeting at Mount Tengi, he and Kristin had been flown to Port Zolnayta to an unexpected and joyous reunion with Archie and Nathan at Portview Terrace.

In the days and nights that ensued, Malcolm and Archie had discussed endlessly what they should do next. Not too surprisingly, they both came to the same decision: that by staying in Amasia, they somehow would be closer to Lucy and Richard ... and that in time, perhaps, they would find out exactly what had happened to them.

But what would Archie do with his time?

Aristo soon provided the answer.

'I have news from Dr Shah for both of you. Malcolm, it has been agreed to create a new post for you at Mount Tengi, which you can take up as soon as you wish – probably within the week, as soon as a new office has been prepared.'

'That's excellent news!' said Malcolm. 'You can tell Dr Shah, I will report as soon as he needs me.'

Aristo turned to Archie and grinned. 'As for you, Archie, it has been suggested you return to Harmsway to complete your studies –'

'What! Back to Harmsway! No –'

Archie was about to argue that he had no interest in going back to school, either on Old Earth, or here in Amasia, but Aristo forestalled him by raising the palm of his hand to him.

'Listen, Archie, it is very important that you do so, if you wish to join me and my team.'

'What do you mean – your team?'

Aristo pointed to a gold flash on the pocket of his uniform jacket. It said TIMECRACK ESCORT GROUP. 'A new division has been formed to help and protect travellers during their journeys between the dimensions. Initially, that means between New Earth and Old Earth. I'm the first head of the division and that means you will be working directly with me – but only when you complete the necessary studies to qualify.'

Archie was so surprised, he was lost for words.

'By the way, if it helps you make up your mind, your old tutor says she will help you.'

Archie stared at him for a moment, then he realised who Aristo meant: Marjorie, his tutor at Grimshaws. She had been his and Richard's escort to the USA when they went to visit Uncle John at the Facility. During a tour, they had all been on the catwalk at the centre of the DONUT when the timecrack arrived, sucking them into its vortex, before finally dumping them in the Exploding Park. They had encountered Aristo when he tried to help them save Richard, who had found himself on the back of a rampaging dinosaur.

After their arrival in Timeless Valley, Marjorie and Aristo had become friendly, and now she was his wife, and a tutor at Harmsway.

Archie felt embarrassed that he had almost forgotten her, but so much had happened since he last saw her at Mount Tengi. It was when they were preparing to make the return journey to the Facility's timecrack chamber on Old Earth, that Marjorie had announced she wouldn't be returning with them. It soon became obvious why she had made her decision to stay on at Harmsway as a tutor, when he saw her holding hands with Aristo.

'I don't know about you, mate, but I think you're being offered the best of two worlds!' said Daniel. 'If it were me, I'd jump at it!'

Archie laughed and nodded. 'I think he's right, Aristo. You can tell Marjorie, I'll probably need all the help I can get when I join your team.'

Chapter Sixty-Eight

The Legacy

With Archie's and Malcolm's decision to stay in Amasia confirmed, a party atmosphere soon developed in the kitchen with Captain Abelhorn insisting on more of the finest Sticklejuice Reserve, which he kept for special occasions such as this, be brought to the table.

Everyone had something to celebrate: the captain had been reunited with his son; Kristin had found her father; Archie was no longer under the threat of being killed by Anton Cosimo; Malcolm had lost Lucy and Richard, but had found Archie. As for Daniel and Aristo, they were simply glad to be alive.

Their stories, recounting the dangers they had faced and how lucky they were to be still in one piece, when so many had died, would be told many times in the future, but they all agreed that today was a new beginning for all of them. Only Nathan was missing, and it began to dawn on the captain he hadn't returned from his room to celebrate with them.

'What in thunder is Nathan doing up there?' he demanded. 'He said he had something to show us, so where is he?'

He poured another Sticklejuice into his glass and tried to stand up, but gravity seemed to be forcing him back into his seat. He hiccupped and sat down again, spilling some of his drink.

'Papa, stay there, I'll go upstairs and see what he's doing,' said Kristin. She rose from the table and took a paper tissue to wipe his hand and glass. 'He said earlier he was tired, so maybe he's fallen asleep.'

'I'll go with you,' offered Archie. 'Maybe he needs a hand with whatever it is he wants to show us.'

They left the kitchen leaving the others to share another drink and chat amongst themselves. The top of the staircase brought them to a landing that serviced a long hallway leading to several bedrooms and adjoining bathrooms.

Kristin entered the nearest room, which Archie had discovered when he first arrived at Portview Terrace. Musty and shadowy, the room was still filled with the same junk: the collapsed garden bench under a rusty anchor, open chests of assorted clothing, and the walls covered with old paintings and faded photographs, but there was no sign of Nathan.

On the far side of the room a heavy, maroon drape pulled to one side revealed the door leading to the suite Archie had used during his first visit to the house. Across the hallway, the room which Manuel had used, was the one he now occupied, with his father in the room next door.

'Look,' said Archie. He nudged Kristin and pointed to a glowing light emanating from the suite. 'He must be in there.'

Kristin called out: 'Father, where are you?'

There was no answer. He didn't know why, but Archie moved very slowly towards the doorway. He had the feeling all was not well, and motioned to Kristin to stay close behind him.

He stopped at the door and looked inside. Nathan was sitting on the side of his bed with the goatskin tool bag at his feet. Spread across his knees was an old brown towel, partly wrapped around an object he held at each end. He seemed to be transfixed by the bright light that radiated from its surface, casting a bluish-white, halo-like glow around his head.

'What's wrong with him?' whispered Kristin. She clutched Archie's hand as they moved a little closer to Nathan. 'And what is that thing he's holding?'

An unexpected voice behind them made them both jump: 'What's happening here?' asked Malcolm.

Kristin squealed, as she put a hand over her mouth.

Archie turned round. 'Dad! You scared the wits out of me!'

'Sorry, Archie, but the captain pressed me to come up and see if there was something wrong with Nathan.'

Malcolm stood with them for a moment, watching Nathan sitting quietly on the bed, apparently unaware of their presence. 'Has he spoken to you?'

'No. He's been like that since we came in. He seems to be hypnotised by that thing he's holding.'

'OK, let's talk to him and see what it is.'

They walked slowly across the room to the bed. Nathan turned round as they approached, smiling in the eerie glow, which gave him a strange ghostly appearance. He laid the towel with the object on the bed beside him and stood up to greet them.

'Nathan, your father was wondering if you were coming downstairs to join us for a drink?' asked Malcolm. He tried to take a closer look at the object but Nathan stood in front of him, blocking his view.

Nathan ignored the question. Instead, he said: 'It's like the softest and smoothest silk I've ever touched.'

'What are you talking about?'

Nathan stepped aside and pointed to the bed. 'Look. Isn't it magnificent?' He pulled the towel away to expose one of the most remarkable pieces of exotic objet d' art Malcolm had ever seen.

A solid gold cylinder, approximately 15 inches long and around 3 inches in diameter, with a central recess of pure white crystal, had stunned Malcolm into silence. Each end of the cylinder was capped by a gold disc engraved with some of the signs of the multiverse, the same signs he had seen many times carved into the stone walls of the temple antechamber and the

Transkal; or the Chapac Stone, as it was known to the Copanatecs.

The cylinder no longer glowed now that it was out of Nathan's hands, but Malcolm suspected he knew what it was, and its purpose.

The Immortal Wand.

He felt overwhelmed as he studied the intricate engravings. 'My God! You found it!'

The story of the wand was one he had heard many times from the lips of Talon, who loved to tell the history of the Lords of the Cloud and their immortality. But the part of the story that had truly fascinated him was how each Lord, and those who were also blessed would live a Great Cycle that would last a thousand years, once the ritual of the Blessing had been bestowed upon them.

Unfortunately, the Destruction had also bestowed a catastrophe, when much of Copanatec was destroyed, taking the wand with its golden casket into the depths of the earth below the pyramid.

Unable to renew the blessings when their cycle ended, some of the Lords had died, which had led to panic in those who were left. It was the justification needed to raid the villages of the mainland, to enslave men to work in the tunnels in the search for the golden casket and the wand it contained.

And now it lay before him, one of the greatest archaeological finds of his lifetime. The casket was gone, but the wand itself was priceless beyond measure.

Archie was bewildered by Nathan's behaviour, but he could sense his father's excitement. He stepped forward to the side of the bed to take a closer look at the object that had captured his father's interest.

'What is it, Dad?' he asked.

'I believe it's the Immortal Wand that the Lords of the Cloud were searching for in the tunnels.'

Entranced by its shimmering, golden sheen, Archie reached out to touch the wand.

'NO!' Archie felt his father's hand grip his shoulder. 'Don't touch it!'

Startled by the alarm he heard in his voice, Archie turned round to face his father. 'What's wrong?'

Malcolm nodded slightly towards Nathan. 'Just leave it for a moment, Archie. I'll explain later –'

'It's because of the cycle!' cried Kristin. Her hands clasped the sides of her head as she stared at her father in horror. 'Lord Pakal said that anyone who touched it would live for thousands of years!'

Nathan laughed as if she had told a joke. He had shaved the sandy stubble and now his skin glowed with the freshness of youth, and his green eyes were bright, twinkling as he spoke to her. 'I don't know about living so long, Kristin, but all I ever wanted was to make my fortune. It's why I left Port Zolnayta. I wanted, if nothing else, to at least leave a legacy for my family to enjoy.

'Then you found the wand, but how did you come by it?' asked Malcolm, his interest piqued by Nathan's changed appearance.

'About a year ago, I was working on the pumps to send some floodwater down to the adits to clear the tunnels. Later, when the water had cleared, I saw something glinting in one of the rock pools. I had to pick it up quickly and wrap it in one of the old towels I used and hide it along with my tools, before the Terogs spotted it.'

'What about the casket – a gold box it would have lain in?' asked Malcolm. He hoped that Nathan had also hidden it, somewhere safe from discovery by Talon's men. 'Was there no sign of it?'

'No, it was the only treasure I ever found, but it is enough, is it not?' said Nathan. He turned and lifted the wand away from the towel, cradling it in the crook of one arm, like a new-born babe. With his other hand he stroked the pure white crystal in the central recess of the gold cylinder. Slowly, it began to glow, once again emitting its bluish-white light into the room.

'No, Father, no! Put it away!' cried Kristin. She tried to rush forward to embrace him, but Malcolm held a hand out to stop her.

Archie didn't understand her panic, but Malcolm did. It was obvious to him that Nathan didn't appreciate the significance of what he had found. It was the treasure he had sought for so long, nothing more or less, and little else concerned him.

'Nathan, I realise you have spent years searching for your treasure, but you now have in your hands something of immense historical importance to Amasia and its people. And you must understand that its value will have to be assessed, before it can be decided how you will be rewarded. As an archaeologist with some experience in these matters, and as a friend, will you let me take charge of the wand until a decision is reached?'

'Please, Father, listen to Malcolm. He will look after us,' pleaded Kristin.

Nathan stood still for a moment, considering what Malcolm said. It made sense that the wand would have to be valued. He had no idea how to carry out such a task or how much he should expect to receive for such a piece, or even who he would approach. And then there was Kristin, his beloved daughter. He had pained her and sacrificed years of their life together, and as he saw her tears he knew he would do anything she asked.

He looked to Kristin and smiled as he held out the wand to Malcolm. 'I agree. I will trust you to look after our interests.'

'Excellent. There is only one thing, Nathan ...'

'What is that?'

'Would you please wrap the wand in the towel? I want to protect it from the skin acid on my hands.'

*

'Skin acid, Dad?' grinned Archie.

'I know, but I couldn't think of another excuse not to handle the wand directly. Living for a thousand years, may be quite appealing, Archie, but I want to check the downside, if there is one. There are still a lot of questions that need to be answered about Copanatec, and God knows, how long it will take to find the answers.'

Benno Kozan, sitting opposite them behind his desk on the top floor of the Vallonium Institute in Fort Temple, nodded his agreement. 'Very wise, Mr Kinross, dealing with artefacts such as the Immortal Wand can be a dangerous business. It will take all of our resources to investigate its powers.'

The next day after their talk with Nathan, Archie had suggested to Malcolm that the institute, as a foundation for scientific research, might welcome the opportunity to study the wand. It was a stab in the dark, but Archie remembered from his first journey to Amasia, how Benno Kozan, a director of the institute, had sent Archie and Richard to Naru, to meet Shaman-Sing, a holy man. It was his home village and that of the Happanot tribe, whose holy men were known for their strange, mystical powers.

With that background and as director of the institute, Archie guessed that Kozan would jump at the chance to see the wand, which he did, when they arrived earlier.

Before leaving Portview Terrace, they had carefully wrapped the wand in its towel, realising it was the white crystal, which bestowed the Blessing. Sealed into a wooden box, they brought it to the institute, and after explaining how they came to possess it, they left the wand with Kozan to await a report on his findings.

*

Archie and Malcolm left the institute and headed to one of the many coffee bars dotted around the area. They sat at a table overlooking a nearby park and ordered sandwiches and soft drinks, relaxing with their thoughts before making the return trip to Port Zolnayta.

'Well, that's that. It will be interesting to hear what Kozan comes up with,' said Malcolm.

Archie took a sip of his fruit juice, but said nothing.

'What is it Archie? Are you worried about leaving the wand with him?'

'No, it's nothing like that. It was just that I can't help thinking that the wand might be a way of finding out exactly what happened to mum and Richard.'

'Maybe so, Archie, and maybe we'll have to wait and see what the institute tells us. But you might also wonder how it has affected Nathan. Will he live a thousand years, do you think?'

'I suppose only time will tell – but we'll hardly be around to find out, will we, Dad?'

About the Author

William Long was born in Belfast on 6 June 1939.
After a long and varied career in sales and marketing, including running his own business designing and producing branded goods for a number of high profile companies, as well as smaller organisations, he retired and devoted several years to a men's hostel for the homeless.

He now explores new ideas for his books, and when not travelling, lives in Holywood, near Belfast.

Lightning Source UK Ltd.
Milton Keynes UK
UKOW04f0118170415

249819UK00002B/17/P